THE PROPHET AND THE IDIOT

THE PROPHET AND THE IDIOT

JONAS JONASSON

Translated from the Swedish by Rachel Willson-Broyles

≋ HARPERVIA

An Imprint of HarperCollins*Publishers*

Translation copyright © 2023 by Rachel Willson-Broyles.

HarperCollins books may be purchased for educational, business, or sales promotional use. For information, please email the Special Markets Department in the U.S. at SPsales@harpercollins.com or in Canada at HCOrder@harpercollins.com.

Originally published as *Profeten och idioten* in Sweden in 2022 by Bokförlaget Polaris.

FIRST HARPERVIA EDITION PUBLISHED IN 2024

Design adapted from the 4th Estate edition
Title page image © Ola Galewicz

Library of Congress Cataloging-in-Publication Data
has been applied for.

Library and Archives Canada Cataloguing in Publication
information is available upon request.

ISBN 978-0-06-337166-8
ISBN 978-1-4434-7106-0 (Canada)

24 25 26 27 28 LBC 5 4 3 2 1

THE PROPHET AND THE IDIOT

2011

When this tale begins, Barack Obama was president of the United States, Ban Ki-moon headed up the United Nations, and Angela Merkel had ten years left of what was already a six-year stint as chancellor of Germany.

Russia had a president whose name hardly anyone remembered. Yet everyone knew it was Acting Prime Minister Putin who ruled there.

The Arab Spring swept across northern Africa, led by hundreds of thousands of people who were sick of corruption and sham democracy—and who had convinced themselves change was possible.

An earthquake in the Pacific Ocean caused a wave as tall as a five-story building to crash upon the coast of Japan, destroying everything in its path, including the Fukushima nuclear power plant.

Azerbaijan won the Eurovision Song Contest in front of a few hundred million viewers. But those numbers were nothing compared to the two billion who had, only a short time earlier, tuned in for the wedding of England's Prince William to Kate Middleton. All while the United States found and shot Osama bin Laden without any viewers at all.

The age-old border dispute between Thailand and Cambodia flared up that year, and faded again temporarily. Running the show in Sweden was Prime Minister Reinfeldt, the leader of the conservative Moderate Party. He was the man who made the left's most prized issues his own and, in doing so, won two elections in a row.

In that same country, a half-stupid little brother named Johan suddenly found himself on his own when his older brother Fredrik jetted off to Rome to make a diplomat of himself. Their mother had been dead for years, while their father walked along the shores of Montevideo, hand in hand with his boyfriend.

We'll begin our tale with the half-stupid man. But it won't be long before the whole world is along for the ride. Including Obama, Ban Ki-moon, and Putin's Russia.

Bon appétit!

Jonas Jonasson

PART ONE

*In the Days Before the
End of the World*

CHAPTER 1

Summer 2011

Johan was kind. Helpful. And unevenly gifted.

There was so much he didn't understand. For instance: he did not, in fact, have the best big brother in the world.

They were only two years apart in age, but Johan looked up to Fredrik the way a son looks up to his father. Like the father neither of them had.

Although, actually, they did. A man who had deserted the family before Johan was even born. And who showed up now and then over the years. Most recently at their mother's funeral. During the post-service coffee, he gifted his sons the twelve-and-a-half-room apartment on the swankiest street in Stockholm. He told Fredrik he was proud of him and Johan that maybe it would all work out one day.

And then he was gone.

The brothers were similar in appearance and total opposites in personality. Big brother had followed in his absent father's footsteps, already on his way to a career in diplomacy with the goal of one day becoming an ambassador. Little brother, meanwhile, was failing at delivering the post.

While one was performing well in the diplomacy program at the Ministry for Foreign Affairs, the other made sure to keep the twelve and a half rooms in decent condition, since there wasn't much else he was good for.

Each evening, Fredrik would plop down in the wingback chair in the library with some important documents, ask Johan to serve him a whiskey, assess his hunger, and decide what time dinner should be served.

"Quarter past seven," he might say to his brother. "And I mean quarter past seven. Now scram, and leave me alone."

Johan felt needed. And proud to be of use. On the whole, he was content. He found flavors and aromas as exciting as thinking was complicated.

Fredrik was rarely—no, make that never—satisfied with the results. But why should he be? Johan was incompetent. And big brother was good at constructive criticism.

"Don't put so much oregano in the sauce, you idiot!"

He was also meticulous about etiquette.

"Never serve a pinot noir in a Bordeaux glass. How many times do I have to tell you?"

Once was enough. The kitchen had been Johan's domain ever since the age of twelve, when their mother had become too ill to get out of bed. Six years later, she died of something in Latin Johan could never remember.

Waiting on Fredrik began as a game. And the game continued long after they were grown.

Fredrik called it "Gentry and Servants." One of them was the gentry; the other the servants. If the poor servant boy failed to obey or forgot to say "Yes, my lord" or "No, my lord," they switched places and the game went on.

Fredrik was the best at everything, except this. He messed up every single time he was the servant and hardly ever got to be the one who served his brother. When the day of Fredrik's move abroad arrived, and everything was turned upside down,

Johan had—with very few exceptions, each lasting barely a minute—been the servant boy for fifteen years in a row.

"You're too smart for me, that's all there is to it," said Fredrik. "Now go get my two suitcases from storage. Then you can iron my shirts and pack my things. But don't forget the beef tenderloin in the oven. We said gorgonzola, right? I'm getting hungry."

"Yes, my lord. Yes, my lord. No, my lord. And yes, my lord."

And by the way—forget the beef tenderloin? Not a chance. The temperature had to be just right. Roast at 230 degrees Fahrenheit, remove when the core temperature reaches 122, rest on a platter to 130.1. That left eleven minutes to finish setting the table.

What awaited was Fredrik's first overseas post as a diplomat. Big brother had a lot to think about before the big move. With a lump in his throat, Johan braced himself to be left on his own in the luxury apartment on Strandvägen, but apparently Fredrik was too kindhearted to let that happen. He'd sold the twelve and a half rooms and used the proceeds to buy an RV for his little brother. With an extra well-equipped kitchen! Johan was also given a prepaid bank card; the PIN was 1-2-3-5. Fredrik had picked it himself "so that even you can't forget it. The bank wouldn't let me do 1-2-3-4."

"One, two, three, four," Johan repeated.

"One, two, three, five, you idiot," said Fredrik.

He had loaded the card with fifty thousand kronor and announced that from that day forward, Johan must be an adult and strike out on his own.

"Yes, my lord," said Johan, afraid of the unknown but grateful for the help he had received.

As if this weren't enough, Fredrik had taken care of selling all the furnishings that had been passed down through their father's Löwenhult line ever since anyone could remember. There was a grand piano, eight Persian rugs, just as many Renaissance paintings, china, bureaus, crystal chandeliers, cabinets, and mirrors. The auctioning firm said that, altogether, it was a "categorically stupendous" lot. Johan heard this, but had a hard time understanding difficult words. Fredrik explained that it meant the firm expected the proceeds would cover the cost of Fredrik's flight to Rome.

With that, almost everything had been taken care of. All that was left was for big brother to instruct Johan about the RV. He would need an electrical hookup to charge the batteries, otherwise he couldn't prepare meals. There were RV parks here and there around Stockholm; Fredrik had booked him a spot at one in Fisksätra. It was "expensive as shit," as Fredrik said. As thanks for his help, he demanded to be driven to the airport.

Before they'd gone anywhere the diplomat-to-be decided it was best he do the driving himself. By then, Johan had spent two minutes familiarizing himself with the steering wheel. Little brother thought the chauffeur switch was a good idea. Driving a car was just as tricky as practically everything else.

When they reached the international terminal, Fredrik said a word or two Johan didn't understand, followed by goodbye and good luck, and he took his two suitcases and disappeared.

The man who knew he was worthless was all alone in life for the first time. He decided to start by driving all the way to Fisksätra—as good a way as any to learn how the vehicle worked. It changed gears on its own; that was good. And there were only two pedals to keep track of, not three. Things would probably be fine as long as he didn't think about anything else while he drove. And he didn't expect he would need to.

But for that very reason he missed a lane change on the way toward Stockholm and took an exit he shouldn't have—only to discover he had ended up outside a shopping center.

"Oh, perfect!"

Thus the kitchen of the RV was fully stocked when Johan finally managed to find his way to the RV park southeast of the city.

"Expensive as shit," Fredrik had called it. That was surely true, but even so Johan allowed himself to admit that it looked a bit shabby. It was the size of a soccer field, more or less. More mud than grass. A few power poles here and there. A sign listing everything that was not allowed. Johan didn't have time to read it, because he had to concentrate on parking properly.

The place was deserted aside from one lone camper not far off, near a slope. People probably preferred to be out on the road in the middle of summer like this, Johan thought.

But he should not have thought at all. He already had the accelerator pedal to think of. And the one right next to it. And the steering wheel. Time to turn that so that he would stop approaching the camper. And time to brake.

But almost everything was so hard. "A stroke of bad luck found him," or however that saying went.

The lone camper happened to be parked in exactly the wrong spot. And the camper was coming closer even though it was standing still. Johan realized that this was because he himself was still moving forward.

The accelerator pedal and brake pedal looked identical. The gas was on the right, the brake on the left. But which way was right? And left?

After managing to make it all the way here from the airport, many miles away, *urgent* was suddenly the only way Johan could describe this situation.

He had to brake! He guessed wrong.

The RV leaped forward.

He guessed again. Right this time.

So it wasn't a serious crash. But still, the RV did run into the back of the only other vehicle in the whole field. But it was only a bump. And Johan had managed to stop.

The camper, however, began to roll. And it picked up speed down the slope. One yard. Two. Five. Ten, perhaps, before a lone tree stood in the way.

"That's not good," said Johan.

But, in fact, you might say that it was.

CHAPTER 2

Friday, August 26, 2011

TWELVE DAYS TO GO

The doomsday prophet secured a hook to the ceiling. She was in a grim mood, with a rope tightly looped around her neck.

Only the very last step remained: kicking the stool out from under her. After all, no one would listen to her, and there were only twelve days left before the end of the world. She might as well do without them.

She had run the calculations again and again. And yet again. She made her living as a schoolteacher, but only so she could afford food and rent while she pursued her research in astrophysics. The students who came with the job were a necessary evil. Once her doomsday calculations were complete, she'd tried to get in touch with the Royal Swedish Academy of Sciences. She had worked on the sixty-four-step equation for nine years and wanted someone to confirm her findings. Not that it was necessary, and certainly not because it would have any effect on the outcome. But she wanted some kind of acknowledgment.

The Academy had not responded to her emails. Or letters. When she contacted them by phone, her call was forwarded so many times that she eventually ended up back where she'd started. Her only remaining option had been to walk into the premises unannounced and demand a meeting with the chairman. Or the permanent secretary. Or anyone other than the security guard. In response to her demands someone called the police, who didn't have time to come. The security guard took matters into his own hands and guided her outside and down the long set of steps, where there must have been twenty university students hanging out. Some of them looked frightened as the guard came by with a firm grip on the intruder's arm. Others were surprised. What she remembered most of all was the slightly indulgent smiles. From students who all had one thing in common: they would soon be dead.

Everyone would soon be dead! Before she could share what she knew with a single soul!

So what was the point? In the end, what was the point of anything?

The prophet counted the days she had lived. Including today, the total was eleven thousand and fifty-two. Each and every one of them, as far back as she could remember, had been nothing but miserable. No one had ever understood her. No one had loved her. Had *she* ever even loved anyone, aside from Malte Magnusson in secondary school? That boy with his lovely smile and gentle manner.

A lovely smile. Essentially, that was all he had given her. And a vague sense that maybe he wanted more, but wasn't brave enough to ask.

Not much of a love story.

Then six years passed. Plus another nine of calculations that were now complete. There was no denying her conclusion. The prophet could say nearly down to the minute when the atmosphere would collapse. She didn't even bother to give notice at her job. Just stopped showing up, sure that the students didn't mind in the least.

She also didn't bother to pay the rent. Not that she needed to save money—what good would it be when everything froze to ice? It was simply pointless.

But she was evicted sooner than she'd counted on, and it

was cold to be without housing, especially at night. She had found the camper in a classified ad. Bought it as is; it would need to undergo inspection before it could be driven away from the campground where it sat.

Inspected? she thought. In light of what she knew, each detail seemed so trivial.

Her decision began to take shape. Twenty days left. Miserable day. Nineteen days left. Miserable day. Eighteen days left . . .

Why should she go on, if the rest of existence was only going to be more of the same? If, instead, she put an end to herself, wouldn't that be a tiny win? Wouldn't she be conning the world out of one last drop of absolute shit, in some way?

The idea took root and brought her peace. She purchased a hook, rope, and stool. And was seconds from stepping into eternity, twelve days ahead of everyone else.

When there was a sudden jolt.

An initial, dreadful thought ran through her head. Had her calculations been twelve days off? Surely that wasn't possible?

The hook came loose from the ceiling and skidded under the counter. The camper began to roll.

No, this was something else.

The prophet lost her balance, fell off what was meant to be the suicide stool, and landed softly on her own sofa.

The camper's journey continued for a few seconds, but soon stopped short against a tree.

She got to her feet and staggered out of the door, which was hanging askew. With the rope still around her neck.

Standing in the very spot where the camper had been until just a moment ago was a man around her own age, and behind him was an RV.

"What is going on here?" she demanded. "Can't a person hang herself in peace?"

Johan apologized. He hadn't meant to cause any trouble. It was just so difficult remembering. Which one was the brake?

After all, the pedals were right next to each other, looked identical, and were the same color.

"The same color?" said the woman outside the camper.

It had never occurred to her to notice the color of an accelerator pedal.

"Hang yourself?" Johan said once he'd absorbed what she'd just said.

The prophet announced that it was of no concern to someone who couldn't drive a car.

"You'll just have to use your RV to tow my camper back up so I can get back to what I was doing. We need a rope."

Johan hesitantly pointed at the one hanging around her neck.

"A longer rope, you idiot."

The man who couldn't drive a car wasn't bothered by being called what he'd just been called. He'd been "You Idiot" as far back as he could recall. Maybe his beloved big brother had been the first one to call him that. Or maybe it began in primary school. Or both. Fredrik was two years ahead of him. From that position he seemed to pave the way, keeping everyone informed of his baby brother's limitations. Such as an inability to find the right classroom. Or make sense of the clock.

In perfect accordance with his history, everything went wrong when Johan attempted to tow the camper of the woman with a death wish back to level ground. The towline was secured to both campers, but when you have a hard time telling the accelerator from the brake, things do tend to go as they went.

The woman stood alongside, trying to help.

"Careful now. Gas. No, wait. Slower. Take it easy, go on."

This was too much instruction in too little time. Johan stomped hard on whichever pedal it was. And a little harder on the other, to compensate.

The towline came loose. The camper had been halfway up the slope, but now it headed back down the other way. This time it wasn't hindered by the poor tree. Its journey didn't end until ninety yards on, against a rocky outcrop that, unlike its immediate surroundings, had refused to give way to an encroaching half-a-mile-thick sheet of ice fifteen thousand years previously. There the outcrop had stood, of little use, throughout the centuries. Until this moment, when it transformed an already decrepit camper into rubble.

"Ouch," said Johan.

What else was there to say?

The prophet gazed at her living quarters, or what remained of them. And then she looked at the guilty party.

"That was my home!"

Johan could still see a certain upside to what had come to pass.

"Which you were planning to hang yourself in."

"That's neither here nor there. I can do whatever I please in the privacy of my home."

The incredibly talentless man stared down the slope. What had so recently been a camper was now more reminiscent of a pile of debris.

"Shall I help you clean it up?"

He figured he could handle that.

"Are we looking at the same thing? My camper doesn't need a maid, it needs a scrap dealer. Or an undertaker!"

This last bit reminded her of what she had been about to do.

"Is there a hook in your RV I could borrow?"

Johan rarely had time to catch up with himself.

"Yes, I'm sure that's the least I could—"

Then half the penny dropped.

"Why, what do you want it for?"

"What do you think?"

The other half of the penny followed.

"Now that I think about it, I seem to recall that I've run out of hooks. Could I offer you something to drink instead?"

The prophet was resigned.

"Make it something strong."

"A Domaine Billaud-Simon Chablis Tête d'Or? Lovely vintage."

"I said strong."

* * *

While Johan might be slow of thought, he also happened to be quick to action. Before the unfamiliar woman could return to her darkest self, he had set out two camping chairs, a camping table with a red-checked tablecloth, two glasses, a bottle of Highland Park, and the plate of bacon-wrapped, goat-cheese-stuffed dates topped with roasted, salted almonds he'd whipped up for Fredrik to bring on his trip, only for his big brother to scoff at him and refuse the treat.

"The whiskey is the same age as I am," Johan said, pouring a glass for his suicidal guest.

"That's enough aging," said the woman, tossing it back before Johan even had time to serve himself.

"Whoa," he said.

"You have an interesting vocabulary."

"Do I?"

He was no better at sarcasm than he was at driving.

The prophet took hold of the bottle and gave herself a refill. This time she enjoyed it more slowly. She sipped without a word. And kept on like that as she sipped some more. She reached for the dates. For a brief moment she seemed to be content, or at least not discontent. Johan couldn't imagine why she wanted to kill herself. To be polite he'd already taken two large gulps of the Highland Park and wasn't immune to its effects. Maybe that was why he dared to ask.

The woman was a glass ahead of him. Maybe that was why she bothered to answer. Or maybe she just needed to clarify things for herself.

Whatever the reason, she sat in the camping chair in a muddy field outside of Stockholm and began to talk. A little, at first. Then a little more. She said that she'd always felt different.

"Stupid?" Johan asked.

Had he found his soulmate?

"No."

She had always done well in school, but she had no friends. Her only company was her own thoughts.

Johan thought about the fact that he'd never had any friends either, but that he'd never thought about it before. After all, he spent most of his time with his brother, and it was like Fredrik did the thinking for both of them.

The woman went on.

During secondary school, she had begun to see things more clearly. She really wasn't like everyone else. While Victoria, Malin, and Maria transformed from children into teenagers with mascara, fashion, secret cigarettes, and red wine mixed with Coke, she stayed behind in her knitted cardigan. Maybe it was that, maybe it was the laws of nature that meant she didn't develop breasts at the same rate as her friends. Or maybe they were cheating. The possibility had occurred to her, but she didn't care. The observable universe was ninety-three billion light-years in diameter, with an infinite number of billions of light-years beyond that. Looking at it from that perspective, she didn't understand the point of measuring out perfect little bags of rice to stash in a bra that you didn't even need in the first place.

"Rice?" said Johan, wondering which variety it was.

The woman's main companions at school had been her physics book, her math book, and paperbacks about hospital romance. She would have preferred physics lab romance, but she couldn't find any books about that.

"I mostly watched movies," said Johan.

During her free periods, she would sit there in her cardigan and do Victoria's and Malin's homework for them. Only to be showered with abuse as thanks.

"Aren't you done with that yet, you freak?"

The future prophet apologized for taking too long and not being sure about the answer to number twelve.

"But the first eleven should be right."

Victoria ripped the homework from her hands.

"Ugly and slow. Why do you even exist?"

This, of course, was an existential question far beyond what young Victoria could grasp. But it struck the future prophet in her very soul. Too scared to look anywhere but straight ahead, at the row of lockers, she said to herself:

"Yes, why do we exist? And who are we? Teeny, tiny dots of energy in the universe."

This was more than Victoria and Malin could handle. Or, for that matter, Maria. Or any of the rest of them.

"Come on, Vickan, let's go share a smoke before English. This freak is making me nervous."

Johan understood that he would have to keep the Highland Park flowing in order to keep the story going. Wonder what her name was, by the way. He figured he'd find out eventually.

"Would you like another date? Or a bowl of roasted peanuts?"

The woman didn't respond. She took a slightly larger gulp of whiskey than she'd meant to and kept going. There was something she really needed to get off her chest.

Everyone had a dream. Even someone who hardly ever wore anything but a cardigan, had braces but no figure, and completely lacked social skills. The woman's dream was named Malte. He was cute, sure, but above all he had a gentle manner. One time he picked up her math book when she dropped it, and handed it back with a "here you go." Then he brushed her shoulder and looked her in the eyes. And that smile.

Was it a signal of something more? The girl who had just been noticed dropped her gaze in fear, and when she dared to look up again he was gone.

He hadn't had to touch her shoulder. But he did it anyway. Could he be just as shy as she was? After all, it was the nineties by then, and girls could ask boys to the school dance just as much as the boys could. What if he wanted to go, but was afraid to ask? He wasn't one of the popular kids, because like her he did his homework. There was something between them. Mostly during class. The feeling that they were the only two present. Seated four rows away from each other, but still.

The future prophet was full of inner turmoil. She was fighting a battle between the person she wanted to be and the one she had become. In her world, there was a difference between floating free in the universe and letting yourself be mercilessly sucked into a black hole.

"That's love," said Johan, without being certain what he meant.

She bought a red jelly heart at Broman's pastry shop. It came in a small clear box with a bow on top. There was a card to go with it, hanging from a gold ribbon. On it she wrote, "Do you want to go to the dance with me?"

Then she stashed this contraption on the top shelf of her locker. There it waited for its owner to find the right moment. And her courage.

Soon enough, she saw Malte with some of his guy friends just down the hall from her. He was hanging around the edges, as though he wasn't quite part of the group. Was he darting quick glances her way when his friends weren't looking?

What would happen if the group scattered, if Malte ended up standing alone for a few seconds? And what if she acted quickly enough? Or, even better, if he did.

She was so preoccupied by the opportunity that might be about to present itself that she didn't notice Victoria coming from the other direction.

"What, are you checking those guys out? So you *can* get horny for something other than your books?"

Victoria gave a scornful laugh. And spotted the heart! She took it from the shelf. Opened the box. Fished it out—and gulped it down in two bites.

Never had there been a greater crime against humanity.

The guys disappeared around the corner. Malte lingered behind. Was he looking her way again? Or was he looking at Victoria? Victoria with the jelly heart in her mouth?

He went on his way. The moment was gone. And so, too, was the heart.

Johan wasn't sure that the strange woman needed more fuel for her tale. She seemed so sad. What if she started asking to borrow a hook again?

"Then what happened?" he asked uncertainly.

"Refill me," said the woman.

What happened was that she allowed herself to be sucked into the black hole. She immersed herself in physics, with a single break in her routine in the years that followed: she had to get a new cardigan once her figure emerged.

Her goal was a professorship, perhaps the Academy of Sciences, but her climb ended at schoolteacher. In physics, but still.

Yet the work would have been tolerable if it weren't for all the students. Students were her least favorite thing ever. They refused to listen or learn.

Johan had been a student once himself. Since he already knew he couldn't learn, he didn't bother to listen. It would have been a waste of time. Instead, he sat around inventing recipes in his head.

But he hadn't considered himself a pain to whoever was doing the teaching, despite the fact that even his homeroom teacher once managed to call him the same thing everyone else did. This had occurred when he was meant to be spelling "bicycle" on the whiteboard but it came out "m-o-p-e-d." He figured that a moped was faster than a bicycle, more functional. He truly must have misunderstood the assignment, because the teacher sighed, "Go back to your desk, you idiot."

"Now I remember," said Johan. "I was *hopeless* too. Pretty often."

Petra was too wrapped up in her own thoughts to listen or comment. Instead, she continued.

For nearly a whole decade she had devoted all her spare time and a substantial amount of her working hours to personal research. It had begun with a simple hypothesis, followed by a test of said hypothesis.

"You're using words I don't feel comfortable with," said Johan.

The prophet said that the long and short of it was that the atmosphere was about to collapse.

"Who's going to what now?"

"The atmosphere. It will fall flat to the ground and the temperature will drop to 459.67 degrees below zero. In a split second."

"Where?"

"Everywhere."

"Indoors as well?"

"What was it they used to call you again?"

Johan tried to imagine how much, or rather, how little, 459.67 degrees below zero was.

"And when is this going to happen?"

"Wednesday after next at 9:20 p.m. Give or take a minute. It's not clear yet how the proportions between aerodynamic drag and density will turn out in those last milliseconds. I scuttled that portion of the research when I realized I wouldn't have time to finish my calculations before it was too late anyway."

"Aerodynamic drag and des-nity," Johan said thoughtfully.

"Density."

CHAPTER 3

Friday, August 26, 2011

TWELVE DAYS TO GO

Darkness fell over the RV park, which was deserted aside from a single RV and the tracks of a camper that no longer was where it had been. The thirty-year-old whiskey was nearly gone. The bacon-wrapped, goat-cheese-stuffed dates had been eaten. Johan fetched two blankets from the RV, draped one over the shoulders of his new friend (that was how he wanted to think of her) and wrapped himself in the other.

"So, twelve days to go. To think I'm sitting here with a genuine doomsday prophet."

"We're probably down to eleven and a bit."

Two-thirds of the bottle's contents had gone to his guest, but the third Johan had imbibed was enough to render him philosophical.

"Eleven days, or twelve . . . but why hang yourself just for that? Shouldn't it be the other way around?"

He extended his arms in a rather Jesus-like pose.

"Isn't now the time to embrace the world? With what little time you have left."

The prophet did not share Johan's enthusiasm.

"You go ahead and embrace whatever you want. For my part, those eleven days will be just as miserable as the eleven thousand and fifty-two days before them. Tell me the point of that, if you can."

"What happened eleven thousand and fifty-two days ago?"

"I was born."

"Ouch."

The woman went on:

"I can't deal with the thought of everything ending before I had time to make something out of anything."

"Out of what?"

"Anything, I said."

"Such as?"

"I'm a *schoolteacher*! Or I was, before I quit. No one listens to me when I speak. I never became a professor. Nothing ever came of love. I didn't even get the chance to say 'I love you' to anyone. Not that it would have helped."

"You can say it to me, if you want."

"Ideally there should be some truth to it."

But then she softened.

"Although the whiskey was delicious. And the snacks. How did you manage? In an RV!"

"I like to cook. And clean."

Was that a tiny smile as she poured the last drops from the bottle?

"Great combo. Do you have a name besides You Idiot?"

"Well, of course I do!"

Now she was definitely smiling.

"Let me rephrase that: What's your name?"

"My name is Johan Valdemar Löwenhult. With emphasis on the Johan. How about you?"

"My name is Petra Rocklund. With emphasis on Petra."

"It's nice to meet you, Petra."

Johan raised his empty glass toward his guest.

"I wouldn't go that far," she said.

With that, the drunk and exhausted doomsday prophet leaned back and closed her eyes.

Was she about to fall asleep? Johan felt anxious—what

22

would he do then? He couldn't just leave Petra in the camping chair, it would be way too cold even with two blankets. And he couldn't simply shove a sleeping woman who was, let's face it, still a stranger, into his RV without her consent.

"Petra? Hello?"

Deep breathing.

"You can't . . . Petra? Want me to teach you how to make my stuffed dates?"

Didn't work.

"Petra!"

What should he do?

"Petra, I *love*—"

At that, she gave a start. Love, or the lack thereof, seemed to have an effect on her.

"Who do you love?" she mumbled without opening her eyes.

"Street corners."

Her eyelids slid open.

"Who loves street corners?"

She was back! Now he just had to keep her going.

"Maybe love is overdoing it, but I really like them. I have ever since I was a postman. Or even before. You stand there on the corner looking first in one direction, then the other. Not sure which to choose. It's almost like your life can turn on that choice, every time. There's something beautiful about it, but it's hard to explain."

His guest didn't seem thrilled to have been woken up to discuss the poetic nature of a junction.

"I'm talking about love between *people*."

Johan thought once more.

"In that case, I'd say Fredrik, my brother. He taught me everything I know."

Petra glanced at the RV.

"Like how to drive?"

23

"Well, not that particular thing. That was the driving instructor. Who turned out to be quite unpleasant in the end. I'm not just hopeless, now that I think about it—I'm also pretty bad at technology. How about you? Who is your greatest love? Is it Malte?"

When Petra was reminded of her own story from school, she grew tired again and closed her eyes once more.

"No, no, don't do that, Petra! I have a nice, comfy spare bed in the RV. Come on, you can borrow it."

When that didn't help, he added:

"I might even have an extra hook in there somewhere. Let's go see."

What had he said?! She opened her eyes again. Slowly got up. Let herself be propped up by her new acquaintance as she took the few steps to the door of the RV. She managed both the first and second stairs. Made it inside. The last thing she said before she fell asleep with her clothes on was:

"I'm too tired to hang myself right now. Let's do it tomorrow."

CHAPTER 4

Saturday, August 27, 2011

ELEVEN DAYS TO GO

The tablecloth from the previous evening had been replaced by a fresh one. On the breakfast table were freshly baked rolls with aged cheese, prinskorv sausages, scrambled eggs with garlic and herb-roasted cherry tomatoes, yogurt, granola, and raspberries.

Johan was just pouring the fresh-squeezed orange juice when Petra appeared in the doorway. Her hair tousled. Her clothes wrinkled.

"Where am I? And where is my camp—"

She caught sight of Johan.

"Oh, right."

"Good morning! Please have a seat. Coffee or cappuccino?"

The prophet managed to make it all the way to her same camping chair from the night before. She plopped into it. Took in the sight of the breakfast table.

"You're satisfied with life. You love to clean. Used to be a postman. Drive around in an RV without knowing how to drive. And prepare food like . . . well, I don't even know. Is that garlic I smell?"

"The scrambled eggs. Coffee or cappuccino?"

"Cappuccino, please."

"I've got Kalix caviar as well. Couldn't quite make it fit in with everything else, figured I'd save it for later. But if you want some . . . and if you promise not to kill yourself today."

Petra still wasn't entirely awake.

"Was I going to yesterday? Right, I was."

"Circumstances both unfortunate and fortunate got in your way. Now eat your breakfast, I'll be right back with your beverage. Then I've got news!"

The newly awakened woman was too tired and bewildered not to obey. And she was hungry as well. She ate in silence, aside from the occasional *mmm!* of pleasure at the quality of the meal. Five minutes passed before she opened her mouth for something other than food.

"News, you said? Did you find me a new camper? Or at least a hook?"

"Better! I found Malte."

Petra dropped her fork. It landed in the mud.

"Leave it there," said Johan. "I'll get you a new one."

He began to stand.

"Sit!"

He sat, like an obedient dog.

"You found Malte? How? Where is he?"

Petra looked around.

"Not here. But, you know, I used to deliver mail, I mentioned that, right? Not for long, but I took a course and we learned a lot more than I remember. Anyway, Malte's not a very common name. In combination with Magnusson, it's downright unusual. There is only one Malte Magnusson in all of Sweden who's around the age I imagine you are. He lives fifteen minutes from here. Maybe twenty, if I'm the one driving. Up to half an hour, if I take a wrong turn."

Petra lost herself in a daydream for a moment.

"Malte . . ."

Reality caught up with her.

"What could I possibly offer him?"

However, Johan didn't give up.

"In eleven days, absolutely nothing. But until then, you can declare your love for him. Or you can hang yourself. But not in my RV, and you'll have to find your own hook."

* * *

Perhaps it was the garlic-enhanced scrambled eggs. Perhaps it was the fresh-squeezed juice. Or the cappuccino. Or Petra's eternal longing for love, alongside the certainty that it was now or never. Whatever the reason, she found herself sitting beside Johan in his combination RV and fancy restaurant, on her way to the address at which her school crush Malte Magnusson was presumed to live.

The prophet tried to get the wrinkles out of her clothes and fix her hair as best she could, while Johan failed to drive smoothly. Or even straight. The vehicle lurched, jerked, and swayed.

He noticed that Petra was trying to hold on.

"Would you like to drive?"

"I don't have a license."

"You either?"

What was going on?

"Am I risking my life in a runaway RV, with an unlicensed driver behind the wheel?"

Johan hit the curb with two wheels as he made a right turn. Once he'd regained control, he reminded Petra that it wouldn't be the end of the world if he killed her with his driving, considering what she'd tried to do to herself the day before.

"Besides, I've got two hundred driving lessons under my belt. At least some of them must have stuck."

Two hundred driving lessons and no license. The lack of skill was astounding. Petra decided that whatever happened happened. At least he could cook.

"I can't cook at all," said Johan, "but I think it's fun."

Fun, Petra thought. A word that had never had a place in her life.

"What else do you think is fun?"

Maybe she could learn something.

"Cleaning," said Johan. "Or, well, it's halfway fun. That's not the thing I'm worst at. Although actually I don't know how much better Fredrik was at it. He never ended up cleaning at all."

Petra smiled again. It must have been the third time she had since her hook came loose from the roof of the camper the day before.

"So what are you worst at?"

It was hard to say. So much to choose from. Thinking, in general? Or *finding*. That was why his career as a postal worker had been so brief. He had been let go after just a day. The boss cited a sudden redundancy.

"Couldn't you find the mailboxes you were supposed to deliver to?"

Not a bad guess, but only nearly correct. For sure he had taken a wrong turn a few times. And he had found himself and his bicycle standing on some beautiful street corner for a little too long. But the right addresses were on the envelopes, and he had a map. The real problems didn't begin until he was supposed to return to the post office. That was an address he didn't have.

"You couldn't find your way back?"

"No, I did, once the sun came up again."

That was as far as they got with that conversation. He noticed that he couldn't concentrate if he was speaking at the same time. And she needed to prepare herself for what was about to happen. It was Saturday morning, and if Malte lived where he was supposed to, there was a good chance he would be home. They hadn't talked since he said "Here you go" fifteen years earlier, while handing over her math book. Petra wasn't sure that they had talked that time, either, strictly speaking. Had she even responded? She must have at least said thanks, right?

She practiced a few introductory remarks in silence. None of them sounded good. This whole idea was feeling worse and worse. At last she decided it was *too* awful.

"Turn around!" she said. "I can't do this!"

"Here we are," said Johan, and stopped the vehicle by pressing gently on the correct pedal.

Malte lived in a house. It was not large and it was pretty far out in the suburbs, but it was still a house. With a little garden around it. A Honda Civic in the driveway. Not a large car, but it was new.

Her secret teenage crush seemed to be a sporty type. As he had been back in school. Shy, smart, and athletic. Perhaps he played both golf and baseball, for part of the lawn had been mowed very short into a putting green. Next to it was a golf bag that had blown over. On the grass were a couple of iron clubs and a putter. Between the house and a nearly full-grown birch tree, Malte had strung up a net. Petra guessed he hit golf balls into it to keep from breaking his neighbors' windows. On a bench next to the house was a baseball bat, three balls, and a glove.

Johan was industrious as seldom, or never, before. While Petra took in the surroundings, he was over at the neighbor's across the street, borrowing a bouquet of flowers from their flower bed. He handed it over and nudged Petra gently toward the front door and its doorbell.

She walked slowly and uncertainly ahead. Turned to Johan when she heard a clatter.

"What are you doing?"

He had righted the golf bag and was picking up the clubs from the ground.

"I'm cleaning up. I can't help it."

"Stop it!"

Johan obeyed. One of the irons remained in his hand. He raised it to the sky in what might have been a gesture of victory.

"Hooray for love!" he said encouragingly.

But Petra just felt nervous.

"He probably has a family."

"Aw, half of all the couples in Sweden get divorced. Now go!"

"They do?"

"Don't ask me. Go! You can't spend the last eleven days of your life just standing in Malte's front garden."

Petra nodded anxiously. The chef, the cleaner, and the idiot were right.

She could hear the doorbell ringing inside. And a voice.

"Can you get that? I'm doing my nails."

A *woman's* voice! But it was too late now. The door opened.

Malte. As cute now as he was then. With the same kind, shy eyes. No smile for the moment. He looked curious.

"Yes?" he said.

"Hi, Malte. Do you recognize me?"

With those words, she had quite possibly said more to him than she ever had in their school days.

"Um, please excuse me, but . . . no? Or, hold on."

Apparently she had made some small impression.

"It's Petra, from school."

There was that smile! And Malte was placing his hand on her shoulder again! For the second time in fifteen years.

"Petra," he said warmly. "You were my first secret—"

That was as far as he got before the woman's voice drowned him out from inside the house.

"Who is it, Malte? Well, answer me!"

The woman came closer. Yanked the door open all the way, so she'd fit beside her boyfriend on the threshold. She looked at the visitor, and at the bouquet Petra held in her hand.

"What is going on? Are you hitting on my man?"

Suddenly Petra couldn't breathe. Or speak. The woman was *Victoria*! The bully. Uncultured, nasty Victoria. Malte's *girlfriend*!

THE PROPHET AND THE IDIOT

Malte looked worried, wanted to defuse the situation.

"There, there, Vickan. This is Petra Backlund from our class in school."

"Rocklund," said Petra.

Thinking: wouldn't he at least have remembered her name if she was his first secret . . . something?

Victoria's face lit up with the same old cruel smile.

"The freak? Oh, so it was Malte you were after! I could just die laughing!"

She tore the flowers from Petra's hand, dropped them on the ground, and stubbed them out just like a cigarette.

"But, Vickan—"

Malte was clearly uncomfortable. Petra didn't have time to decide how she felt before Victoria was shoving her backward, stepping out in her socks. It was going to be worth it. She would put that freak in its place once and for all.

Malte remained in the doorway, his feelings from the past creeping closer as he kept trying to calm everyone down.

"Stop that, Vickan. She hasn't done anything. She doesn't mean any harm—"

But Victoria was all wound up. Another shove. And another. And at last Petra fell over. She tried to crawl away.

In that moment, Victoria caught sight of Johan, who had been partially hidden behind the brand-new apple of her eye, the silver Honda.

"And who are you? What are you doing by my car? Don't touch it, I'm warning you!"

Johan panicked as he saw what he'd dragged Petra into. He stammered that she had just pushed his friend to the ground.

"You . . . you shoved!"

Another bark of laughter from Victoria. No kinder than the last one.

"I can do better than that, just you wait."

She kicked the defenseless Petra, who was still lying on the ground. First with her right foot, then with her left. Not *too* hard, just enough to make sure everyone knew who was in charge here.

Johan went from panicking to short-circuiting. Or both.

"Stop it!" he shouted.

And he punctuated what he'd just said by slamming Malte's seven-iron into the hood of Victoria's silver Honda.

"No!" Malte cried, but he stayed put in the doorway.

Petra lay where she was as Victoria rushed to her car to stop the stranger with the golf club. Petra should have felt totally, thoroughly degraded. But instead, something was taking root inside the prophet. *Malte's first secret what?* she thought.

Thanks to some nifty footwork, Johan managed to keep the car between him and the wild Victoria, even though he was totally out of his mind and was hitting the car with the golf club again and again. After the hood, the roof. Right rear door. The rear window. The left rear door. The right rear door again (when Victoria changed direction).

"You are dead meat!" she screamed.

While this was happening, Petra got to her knees and then her feet. She brushed grass and dirt from her shirt and pants, and realized that Johan wasn't in need of immediate aid. He was keeping the increasingly dented Honda Civic between him and Petra's former tormentor, whichever way she tried to come at him.

Petra looked away from them and turned to Malte.

"First secret what?" she said in a steady voice.

"Huh?"

He was having a hard time focusing on Petra and his raging girlfriend at the same time.

"You said I was your first secret something."

"Did I?"

He knew he ought to put a stop to the world war taking place in the driveway. But something was stopping him. Not just the fact that it had always been impossible to reason with Vickan. Maybe also a little bit that it felt remarkably good each time Petra's friend hit a new, as-yet-unscathed part of Vickan's car. Which he wasn't even allowed to borrow.

Petra felt calm amid the chaos.

"Do you enjoy your cozy evenings, you and Vickan?" she asked as Malte's girlfriend, her cheeks red, tried to climb onto the roof of her wrecked car to get to the marauder.

"Cozy?" Malte said.

It seemed to Petra that he was no better at looking out for his own interests now than he had been fifteen years earlier. To think how different everything (except for the end of the world) would have turned out if only Malte had managed to finish his "first secret" sentence back then, a long time ago, when it still would have meant something.

Petra's calm gave way to decisiveness. It was time to stop the tormentor by the car before she got her hands on Johan. The prophet headed for Malte's girlfriend; along the way she happened to pass the bench with the baseball bat. She snatched it and whacked it decently hard into the behind of the former schoolmate who had been anything but a friend.

"Ow!" said Victoria, mostly in surprise.

She slid down from the hood and turned around, only to find herself facing Petra. Was that freak looking her straight in the eye for the first time? What was going on here?

Petra let the thick end of the bat rest peacefully against her shoulder as she gripped the narrow end with both hands.

Her peacefulness went over Victoria's head. Their school years were playing like a film in the bully's mind. Three years, fast-forwarded over three seconds. Maybe they hadn't been entirely . . . how to put it . . . kind to . . . what was her name again? Petra. Was she about to get her revenge?

The former victim smiled sweetly at the former bully.

"Know what I'm thinking, Vickan?" she said.

The mood was so extraordinary that the autodidactic astrophysicist was curious about the density of the air at that particular moment. Even Johan relaxed. The right-side mirror was still intact and within arm's reach. But he refrained. For now.

"No," said Victoria uncertainly. "What are you thinking? Are you thinking about hitting me with that baseball bat again?"

On the whole, that wasn't a bad idea. It had felt awfully nice the first time.

"No, hitting people is more your thing. I'm thinking it can easily come to that, when words aren't enough. Yours ran out pretty early on, as I recall."

Mine too, Johan thought, suddenly ashamed that he had let loose on Victoria's car. He decided to leave the right-side mirror alone.

Petra's newfound strength was a direct result of Malte's unfinished sentence.

"I just learned from your boyfriend that I was his first secret something when we were in the same class. I can guess what."

The so recently enraged Victoria could not take her eyes from the baseball bat.

"And now you're thinking . . . ?"

"I'm thinking I'm going to think of you as *the backup plan* as often as I can during the next eleven days. Or the *second choice*. Haven't decided yet. What do you think, Malte?"

What Malte was thinking, as he stood there in his socks in the doorway of his and Victoria's home, was *Why eleven days?* But right now he ought to say something that might mean something.

"Crush," he said. "In response to your first question, that is. But then school ended, we drifted apart, you and I, before I could quite work my way up to—"

Victoria was still worried about the baseball bat. But she was also taken aback by what her wuss of a boyfriend was saying.

"Vickan and I hung around the same youth center that summer . . . and . . . no, it doesn't seem fair to call her a 'backup.' Or, I don't know. We had fun playing pinball. She showed interest in me, and who would be interested in me? For real, I mean."

"Me, you idiot."

The words were harsh, but the way Petra said them wasn't. Malte had wanted her, but hadn't had the courage to ask. That was how he ended up with Victoria instead, over a pinball machine. It was all so far beneath the worth Malte didn't realize he had.

The doomsday prophet was still in perfect balance. Who knew what affirmation in combination with a well-deserved whack to the butt can do. The feeling spread to Johan, on the other side of the car. He aimed a contented nod at Malte, like a greeting from one idiot to another.

Victoria tried to think. The freak in front of her didn't seem to be a freak any longer; instead she was . . . *her boyfriend's secret crush*. Malte the Wuss, who always did as she told him and was generally useful to have around. And who had just nearly agreed that Victoria had been his *second choice*! And then there was the baseball bat. Which Petra wasn't planning to use. Right?

"I think I want to go inside and finish painting my nails," Victoria said.

That was when she did her best thinking.

"You do that," said Petra, making it sound as though she'd just given Victoria permission to go. "But can't you be a dear first and thank me for doing your homework three years in a row?"

Petra was impressed by herself. When she glanced in Malte's direction, she suspected he was too.

"Thank you . . . very much," said Victoria.

The former tormentor gazed at the ground as she scurried

into the house. Her boyfriend remained in the doorway, but let her pass. Petra had control of the situation.

"Malte, I'm sorry about your choice of life partner. You and I can get married in the next life, and on another planet. Johan, I think we're done here. I see you've spared the driver's door. That was nice of you. Come on, let's go."

"And the one side mirror," said Johan.

As he and Petra strolled toward the RV, Malte managed to take a few steps into the driveway and call after her.

"It was nice to see you, Petra, after all these years. Get in touch again, if you'd like. Whenever you want. *Whenever you want!*"

It sounded like he meant it. But hastily building a romantic relationship with a man whose girlfriend was sitting in their shared home painting her nails? In eleven days, he would have time to break up with her; they could go to the movies, go to a restaurant, walk hand in hand by a lake somewhere. Followed by what she presumed would be a clumsy Malte kiss. And her clumsy response. That, and preferably a little more, in one and a half weeks.

No, it was enough to know that Malte understood now how she'd once felt. And—most importantly—that she knew how he had felt.

"Thanks, but there are a few atmospheric obstacles. I'm going to borrow your baseball bat for the time being."

Petra was still feeling satisfied.

Wait, hold on. She was *satisfied*?

Yes.

For the first time in her life.

CHAPTER 5

Saturday, August 27, 2011

ELEVEN DAYS TO GO

Johan was so bewildered by the experience that he couldn't even manage to drive poorly. The journey away from Malte's place was nice and smooth; it almost appeared legal.

He had dragged Petra along to see her Great Love in a silly attempt at making her realize that life had a purpose. And it turned out that horrible Victoria had already captured Malte and made what was bad even worse.

"I'm so sorry, Petra," he managed to say. "I couldn't have known. Forgive me! But please . . . don't kill yourself now. Don't do it."

Petra was holding the baseball bat in her lap. Johan's concern nearly made her crack up.

"Why would I do that?" she said. "Thank you, you sweetheart, for the help. Gosh, just think of all the things we've given Vickan to mull over while she finishes doing her nails. And I didn't know you were so good at golf!"

She turned on the radio and changed the channel until she found a suitable tune. She didn't know the words, but she hummed along and kept time with the baseball bat against her palm.

"Die-dee-die, hm, hm, liiiiiife!"

After a bit, Johan joined in as best he could.

"Liiiiife."

* * *

Johan felt that Petra was becoming the safe harbor he had been lacking since being separated from his brother. Once the song had faded he dared to say so.

"That's kind of you," said Petra. "How long ago were you separated?"

Johan looked at his watch. By this point he had known how to tell the time for quite a few years.

"Twenty-two hours."

Petra would have guessed longer. She said she wasn't sure she could fill the empty space left by his brother, but if she did manage it they could both rejoice that it hadn't been empty for very long. She wanted to know more about her savior and private chauffeur, but all in good time. They had eleven days left, her suicide was canceled, and she owned nothing but the wrinkled clothes on her back. Therefore, a certain amount of shopping for essentials must come at the top of the to-do list.

Johan was afraid he might say or do something wrong and thereby rekindle Petra's ebbing death wish, but he felt he needed to understand. Was her good mood going to hold?

"Sure is!" said Petra. "To the end of time—I promise."

That sounded good. Was Johan right in assuming that what Malte had said from the doorway played a part? In which case, could she please explain the connection in more detail?

The prophet nodded. Malte, Victoria, Galileo Galilei, the golf club, and the baseball bat. All of those things together. It was really her turn to ask him questions, but by all means. They did have eleven whole days.

Petra was about to say more, so Johan decided to skip asking about that middle thing, the one he didn't understand.

She started by admitting she hadn't had time yet to subject her new emotional state to a more scientific analysis. It was all so new. But undoubtedly the events in Malte's front garden had prompted her to recall her teenage years, when she got to know Galileo Galilei.

There it was again.

"Who?"

"The world's first and greatest astronomer."

"And you know him? Amazing!"

Now, it wasn't the case that she and Galilei were friends; she didn't *have* any friends and he had been dead since sometime during the Thirty Years' War. But as a youngster she had read a lot about his struggles. He spoke truths no one wanted to hear, he proved that Aristotle had been wrong, he attracted the ire of barons and counts—and he was forced to apologize to the pope for claiming that the earth wasn't the center of the universe.

Johan had no idea when the Thirty Years' War had taken place, but he could guess how long it had lasted. He skipped that question to prioritize the part about how the earth apparently wasn't the center of the universe.

"It isn't?"

"No."

The lonely thirteen-year-old Petra had been filled with a sense of affinity for the great astronomer. No one understood him. No one understood her. And so it had gone for all those years, until the minor popes of the Royal Swedish Academy of Sciences refused to listen to her, chased her out the door, and called the police.

"Times may change, but popes are forever," said Petra.

So what was there for her in this world, where no one could make any sense of her, where, after all, there was no love set aside for her?

Hence the hook in the camper. And Johan's monumental inability to drive. And everything that followed, up until they got to Malte's driveway.

It had sunk in as she lay there in the grass. What he had just said. That he was her first secret . . . something.

At long last, the church had apologized to Galileo Galilei, at which point he could have stopped feeling so alone and misunderstood, if only he hadn't already been dead for three hundred and fifty years.

But Petra was a different story! She had received her acknowledgment while she was still alive! With just eleven days left of everything, admittedly, but still! It turned out she wasn't as alone as she thought. It was her and Malte against the world! Unloved and misunderstood by everyone, except for each other!

She was his first secret crush! And he was hers. Only their mutual shyness, some unfortunate circumstances, and a pinball machine had kept them from becoming united while they were still in their teens. Nothing stood in their way anymore, except for Judgment Day.

"And that can't be rescheduled?" Johan wondered.

No—once and for all, that was not going to be a typical day. When it was over, everyone's troubles would end.

"Mm-hmm," said Johan.

If Petra was satisfied, then so was he.

But how did she plan to fill the coming days, now that acquiring a new hook was no longer on the agenda?

The prophet wasn't quite sure.

Her current sense of well-being was not solely a result of learning that she was loved. She had also managed to rewrite her entire tragic school story. The decently hard blow to Victoria's backside had played a part too. While there was only one Malte, the world was teeming with Victorias from her past.

"Maybe I should track some of them down and put even more things right," she mused.

"Good idea," said Johan. "What do you mean?"

Petra began to think out loud.

"Don't we all have past events, encounters, and relationships that deserve to be seen in a new light?"

"Yes," said Johan, thinking *Do we?*

"Unfinished business. Like what happened today. It took fifteen years, but Victoria finally thanked me for all the homework help."

What sprang to Johan's mind was the two hundred driving lessons that never resulted in a license. But did that mean he wanted to smash the driving instructor's car to pieces with a golf club ten years later? Or hit him in the butt with a baseball bat? Or even talk him into seeing reason? The instructor wasn't the one who went the wrong way at roundabouts 50 percent of the time.

"I guess I want to experience what happened today as many times as I can before it's too late," said Petra. "Go back through my life and tie up loose ends. Then I can welcome the apocalypse with open arms."

With that, she asked Johan if he wanted to come along for the ride.

He certainly did. Where did she expect to go first?

She hadn't got that far yet, of course. But with a little planning and efficiency they could fit in one encounter per day, which would add up to eleven in all.

"Plus Victoria," said Johan.

"Plus Victoria. An even dozen."

Johan was about to confess that he didn't have any unfinished business to contribute, when he caught sight of something through the windshield, ending the conversation abruptly.

"Will that do?" he asked, pointing at a large ad with an arrow pointing right. "Ninety shops under one roof."

Ninety shops was plenty and then some. Petra needed clothes and a toothbrush. Johan figured he could take the opportunity to stock the RV's fridge and food cupboard; after all, the number of household members had doubled in one day.

Since he was incapable of parking the RV in any sensible

way, and because Petra knew this, she asked him to park diagonally across the main entrance. When they returned they had received parking fines worth nine hundred kronor, with fourteen days to pay. Petra crumpled up the ticket.

"Good luck with that," she said in the direction of the parking company.

* * *

One ingenious feature of Sweden is Everyman's Right. Anyone can pause to rest for a while or two, as long as it's not in someone else's garden or cow pasture. Since there's water just about everywhere in and around Stockholm, the prophet and the man who considered himself useless didn't have to go far to find a spot that was considerably more pleasant than the RV park in Fisksätra.

Now they were sitting outside the RV again, this time with a view of the dark waters of Lake Mälaren under a late-afternoon sun. After a tarte flambé with cold-smoked salmon, pickled red onion, and lemon crème fraîche, Johan selected two further hors d'oeuvres from the sea. He tried never to get caught in a rut of tradition. Following the king scallops topped with the Kalix caviar he'd saved came the most well-balanced lobster bisque he'd ever managed to produce. Fredrik might have been nearly satisfied. Or not.

They washed the food down with three shades of white. The first course was accompanied by champagne. After that, a German Riesling and a white Bourgogne.

Petra showered praise over each course.

"You are outstanding! And you made all of this in an *RV*! What other talents do you have that we might put to good use? And don't say cleaning!"

Johan got the sense that they were a "we" in a way he hadn't experienced since his brother moved abroad. Or was this perhaps even better? It amazed him that she wanted *him* to come on her trip and help set things right.

But what could he do that she couldn't? His career at the post office was nothing to brag about. Nor was anything else he'd done. Might as well tell the truth.

"I'm sure you've already suspected it, but here it is: the thing is, I'm stupid. Or an idiot. Or hopeless. A little of all of those."

Before Petra could formulate any words of comfort, Johan realized something:

"I know! I can recite eighty American movies by heart."

The prophet wondered if she'd misheard.

"What? That's impossible."

The self-identified idiot decided to prove it:

"You talking to me? Well, who the hell else are you talking to? Are you talking to me? Well, I'm the only one here."

Followed by a dramatic pause. Followed by:

"*Taxi Driver.*"

Petra laughed until the wine nearly sloshed out of the glass in her hand. Johan pointed at it and pretended it was something else.

"That's a pretty fucking good milkshake. I don't know if it's worth five dollars, but it's pretty fucking good."

Petra jumped in to say *Pulp Fiction* before admitting that she was starting to believe him. But Johan wasn't finished:

"'Frankly, my dear, I don't give a damn.' A little before our time, but *Gone with the Wind* is still *Gone with the Wind.*"

"We shall all soon find our paths leading that way," said Petra.

The difference between her new acquaintance and a hopeless idiot was clear. He couldn't drive a car despite having taken more lessons than should even be possible. And he didn't know that the earth revolves around the sun. But when it came to cooking, few could beat him.

How was it possible to be so unevenly gifted?

"May I ask what sort of grades you got in school?" said Petra.

"Yes, you may."

"What sort of grades did you get in school?"

"As in English, Fs in everything else. Except woodwork, they didn't let me take that."

Petra was about to ask why but was too curious about the movies. It no longer seemed so absurd that Johan might know all eighty by heart. What *was* absurd was the reason.

"I didn't have much else to do after school."

"No friends?"

Johan hesitated. He'd had classmates, of course. Who hardly ever wanted to play the same games he did.

"What did they want to play?"

"The egg-throwing game."

"How do you play that?"

"Everyone brings an egg from home, except me. Then they throw them at me."

Petra thought this sounded more like bullying than a game.

"You think so?" said Johan.

His childhood didn't seem much different from her own. Had he also lived in a cramped one-bedroom apartment on the outskirts of town with an alcoholic father and an anxious mother?

No, he and his big brother had grown up on Strandvägen in the city.

"*The* Strandvägen? The most expensive street in Sweden?"

Could a street be expensive? Johan knew nothing about that, but a brief stint delivering post had taught him that there was only one street with that name in the capital city. Perhaps there were more out in the suburbs.

"And your place had more than two rooms, I imagine?"

"Twelve and a half."

Now Petra was truly astounded. Who lived in twelve and a half rooms on Strandvägen in Stockholm?

"Me," said Johan. "The half room was mine. Mom and Fredrik liked to spread out more. Up until she couldn't get out of bed, that is."

"What about your father?"

"He was hardly ever home. Except for when Mom got buried, and she only did that once."

Petra didn't know where to start prying. Who was his father, and why was he never home?

Johan said he'd been something called an "ambassador." Those have to travel a lot and often end up living abroad. Now he was retired, and lived somewhere in . . . well, somewhere. In any case, he had given the apartment to his sons when their mother died.

"Did she die early?"

"No, late afternoon. I had come home from school and had time to clean and make dinner first."

Petra reflected that it was important to choose your words carefully when speaking with Johan. That left the question of how twelve and a half rooms on Strandvägen could turn into one RV. And as recently as the day before, as well.

"Lots of people would probably consider that a downgrade."

"How so?" said Johan. "Fredrik moved to Rome. What would I do with twelve and a half rooms all to myself? After all, he can't come home all the way from Spain each night, just to sleep."

Petra said that Rome was in Italy, but agreed that it was far away.

She thought about the twelve and a half rooms. Had Fredrik sold them and given his little brother an RV for the money? In that case, *forty* RVs would have been more appropriate. But they still had a week and a half left, she didn't need to know everything at once. So she amiably allowed Johan to change the subject. He wanted to respond to her indirect question about whether he had any unfinished business to contribute, since he'd had time to consider it now.

Petra's curiosity was piqued. Did he?

"No."

But he wanted her to know that he had taken her question seriously. Gone back through his whole life, including all his encounters along the way. Beloved Fredrik, of course. His driving instructor. His boss at the post office, the one who fired him.

Petra imagined that his dismissal from the post office wasn't worth digging into, given that the employee hadn't been able to find his way to his workplace. The driving instructor probably hadn't had it so easy, either.

"What's your favorite thing about Fredrik?" she said insidiously.

Johan couldn't really say. Maybe how he knew everything, took care of everything.

"Like selling the twelve rooms?"

"Yes, and the half one."

"How did you split the money?"

"What do you mean?"

Petra stopped there. Fredrik appeared to be Johan's greatest hero, and it wasn't her place to destroy that image, not when there were only eleven days to go. In other circumstances, a clarifying conversation between the brothers wouldn't have hurt. Preferably with Petra alongside, the baseball bat peaceably parked on her shoulder. It had worked before.

Johan didn't notice her silence. He asked who Petra had next in line. Someone like Victoria? Or that pope who had been mean to her friend?

Yes, who would she pull from the heap? In just over thirty years of life, Petra had alternately made herself small and been rendered invisible by others anyway, even those few times she'd tried to claim the space she was entitled to. Not a single day had begun or ended better than the day before, and the day before had been just as pathetic as the day before that, and so on and so forth all the way back to her father's alcohol-soaked breath as he explained to his six-year-old daughter how it came to be that he left her costume on the bus, the one she was supposed to wear at preschool the next day. And how, instead, he smeared her face with used motor oil, put her in a dirty black T-shirt that came down to her ankles, and sent her to school dressed as a chimney sweep instead of a princess.

She told Johan about her father.

"Are we starting with him?"

"Sadly, no. The drink got him ages ago. He's as dead as Galileo's pope."

She ventured on through her life. Her school days offered a number of options, not just Victoria, but it didn't quite feel like the right thread to pull at. The worst of them might as well stand in for them all.

Perhaps her highest-priority candidate came from her time at teacher training college. These many years later, she bristled at the thought of how the chancellor had treated her, and how she hadn't resisted in the least. With the best of intentions, and out of concern for her fellow students, Petra had posted warnings about the risk that Asteroid 2002 NT7 might collide with the earth. College chancellor Carlshamre had subsequently called her into his office to chew her out.

"Because you put up a sign?"

"Eighty signs. When you have an important message to share, you have to spread it far and wide."

"There's an asteroid heading for earth?"

Johan sounded worried. Petra told him that it wouldn't happen until 2019.

"And the world can't end more than once in a single decade."

Johan imagined that the world probably couldn't end more than once no matter the decade, but he wasn't sure.

"What did the chancellor say while he was chewing you out?"

"He said the risk was "negligible.""

"Is it?"

"One in five million. But the way he said it! And the way he forced me to take down all my signs."

Some time after this incident, Carlshamre had also come close to expelling Petra for using his letterhead to invite Neil Armstrong to the college Christmas party.

"Neil who?"

"Armstrong. Famous astronaut."

"Like Galileo?"

"He was an astronomer."

Petra used a lot of tricky words, just like Fredrik. Fredrik's most recent one had been outside the airport when Johan couldn't get his door open.

"What does 'imbecile' mean?" Johan asked now.

"Idiot," said Petra. "Why do you ask?"

"No reason. Let's get back to Carlshamre, please. Did he kick you out of college?"

No, Petra made it through thanks to the fact that the chancellor changed jobs right around the same time. Snob that he was, he accepted a position as marshal of the court for the king.

Astronauts, astronomers, marshals of the court . . . it was like the words never stopped coming.

Petra had more to say on Carlshamre, but Johan excused himself. The kitchen called. Now that the three courses of appetizers had sunk in, it was time to shift into fifth gear.

"Dinner in two hours. Aperitif in one hour forty," he said, vanishing into the RV.

* * *

Petra was left alone with her thoughts. The chancellor's crime was, first and foremost, that he had railed on while Petra just sat there taking it in silence. Maybe it would do if *she* was the one who spoke next time they met. Perhaps something along these lines?

"Hello there, Carlshamre. I see you haven't lost any weight since we last met. Or grown any taller. I'm here to tell you that I only took down seventy-nine of the signs that time, years ago. The eightieth one, in the women's bathroom, stayed put."

That might prompt him to stammer something about not quite being able to place Petra or the incident, at which point she would have to cut him off before he got the upper hand.

"Incidentally, the risk of that asteroid strike is no longer even negligible. In just over a week you will freeze solid along with everyone else. Put on a warm coat if you think it will help. And that's all the time I've got for you, tell the king hi."

Too much schadenfreude? Or just the right level of unpleasant and patronizing? She would have to think it over. Of course, she also had the baseball bat to rest against her shoulder should circumstances dictate.

But, above all: a *monologue*! Just like last time, but in the other direction.

The prophet was extremely pleased with how everything was turning out. Her wounds from school had healed. All the wounds from four years of general discontent at the teaching college were about to follow suit. What's more, Johan had returned with the promised aperitif.

"Whiskey sour. The balance isn't bad, if you ask me, but you probably won't."

He handed one glass to Petra, who thought it looked more like a work of art than a drink.

"Thanks. I've stratified all the layers, not quite sure why. Sometimes things just happen the way they happen when I'm in the kitchen. What shall we drink to?"

"To Marshal of the Court Carlshamre," said Petra, raising her glass.

It sounded to Johan as though Petra had found her candidate. If they could track him down, that is. But she didn't think it would be a problem. Marshals of the court were usually wherever the king was.

"And where's the king?" Johan asked.

"The palace wouldn't be a bad guess."

The planned destination reminded Petra of how humiliated she had been in her encounter at the Royal Academy of Sciences. After Carlshamre, maybe they should look there. Just imagine if she could direct some carefully chosen words at any of the senior Academy members, and hand over her painstaking calculations showing the day and time when everything would end, along with an admonishment to "Read this and shut your face!"

"I'm afraid that security guard will get in the way, though," she said. "Wide as a barn door and impossible to reason with. The question is, can he even spell 'doomsday'?"

"One *m* or two?" said Johan.

"Forget it. I'm thinking about how it's the *Royal* Academy of Sciences. We're on our way to see the king, aren't we?"

Of course, it wasn't His Majesty himself who had refused to answer her emails. He wasn't the one who had called the police and chased her off when she came to the Academy to try to explain.

"But he does let them use his name, he's got the backs of all those reactionaries. You know, just like the barons and counts in Galileo's time."

Petra wondered if perhaps the topmost patron of the Academy didn't also deserve a sentence or two flung back at him, if he happened to be nearby when they found Carlshamre. One weak point of that plan was that Petra and the king had no unfinished business between them to take care of.

"Well, you could always slap him, couldn't you?" said Johan. "That'll teach him."

Petra looked at Johan in surprise.

"Why? And what would that teach him?"

Johan was suddenly unsure. But that was what Fredrik had done sometimes. Not hard, just a whack of his open palm against his little brother's ear. Johan had never really got the point of it, but then again, he was so stupid. The king was probably a faster learner, didn't Petra think?

Had the world's best big brother regularly slapped Johan during their upbringing? Petra thought they should dig into that a little more when they had the chance. Right now, she settled for saying that she didn't wish to get into fisticuffs with her head of state, and that upon closer reflection she thought they should stick to the marshal of the court. His Majesty was surely a good man and she felt plenty sorry for him already given that his kingdom would soon freeze to ice.

"We shouldn't take on too much," she said. "Shall we head out now?"

But Johan drew the line at that. He had prepared sole Walewska in the RV, to be served with potatoes tourné, an airy champagne sauce, and fluted mushrooms.

Petra could taste it already.

"We'll leave first thing in the morning. Or, hold on. What's for breakfast?"

CHAPTER 6

Sunday, August 28, 2011

TEN DAYS TO GO

According to the criminal code of 1864, assault of a royal was tantamount to lèse-majesté. The punishment was execution or life in prison. It was up to the king himself to decide.

This law was rewritten in 1948. The term "lèse-majesté" vanished, but that didn't make the action any more lawful. Accordingly, *not* laying a hand on Carl XVI Gustaf was a smart decision. That didn't stop Johan and Petra from setting off for Drottningholm Palace, though. They imagined that this was where the corpulent former chancellor Carlshamre would be found.

One good thing about the building of roads and their resulting traffic jams is that even the most eager of motorists must stop, and, at best, reflect. This is precisely what happened just before they reached Brommaplan on their way to the king's residence.

With no one moving, gears began to turn in Johan's head. After a few moments' silence, he said:

"I've been thinking about something."

"I'll be damned."

"If the *atmos-fear* falls down in ten days, it will be so cold that you die."

"And you too."

"That's just it. So, we're all going to die?"

"Did that just occur to you?"

"Maybe."

Johan didn't say anything for a moment. Petra didn't either; she waited for whatever was coming.

"What do you think would happen if you did the math again?"

Petra felt a warm fuzzy rush inside. There was something truly sympathetic about the man who had been called an idiot all through his childhood and consequently didn't understand that people who threw eggs at him didn't have good intentions.

"I'm glad we met, Johan. I'm glad that I'm glad for the first time in my life, that's all thanks to you. At the same time, I'm sad that it's all going to end just over a week from now. There's nothing you or I or even the king and his damned Academy of Sciences can do about it. I don't know about you, but I take comfort in the knowledge that for the first time ever, everyone on earth will be treated equally. At exactly the same time."

This was an advanced line of reasoning for Johan. And what's more, the traffic jam was opening up. The cars were moving again.

"I'm thinking about my brother," he said.

"What about him?"

"That he struggled for so long in something called the diplomacy program at something else called the Ministry for Foreign Affairs, so one day he could become a third thing called ambassador, just like our dad. Without knowing that there was no point."

"Is that why he's in Rome? He works at the embassy?"

Johan nodded. Embassy, that's what it was called.

* * *

The Swedish king and his queen had got tired of living right in the middle of the capital city. Not that the palace there had been particularly cramped. Six hundred rooms got you pretty far even if you did have two kids and a third on the way.

It was nature that tempted them. After all, both adults and children need green space. And there was plenty of it on the island of Drottningholm, and proximity to the water as well. At the same time, it didn't take very long at all to get back to the city center in case a foreign dignitary or Nobel banquet should demand the royal couple's attention.

Construction on Drottningholm Palace had begun in the sixteenth century and was finished a few hundred years later. The palace, the surrounding buildings, the Baroque Garden, and the English-style park have been shaped by the country's regents ever since. In 1991, the palace—parks and all—landed on UNESCO's list of World Heritage Sites. No wonder seven hundred thousand people come to see it each year.

But the king and queen don't have to invite them all in for coffee. They've arranged a private corner of about an acre in the southern portion of the palace. With their own private garden and pier.

Security around the palace is as thorough as it is discreet. Surveillance cameras both obvious and hidden. Visible guards and invisible security service officers. Plus the extremely visible royal guard in a blue uniform and beret. With extremely good posture and a firearm. The traditional police are never more than minutes away.

* * *

It was a late-summer Sunday morning, a beautiful day. The seven hundred thousand annual visitors were not all there at once, but there were enough of them that Johan and Petra would have had to park the RV quite far away if they had any reason to care about parking tickets.

"Pull in here," said Petra. "You can stop now. Stop, I said!"

It was that whole thing where the accelerator and brake looked the same.

The stopping happened in fits, and drew the attention of those nearby. A few yards away stood a young royal guard outside a booth. Even he turned his head. His job was otherwise to stare straight ahead and look solemn.

Johan wondered if they should bring the baseball bat just in case, but was informed this would be very ill-advised. Violence was just about the last thing they should engage in on royal grounds.

Little did Petra suspect that this very violence was no more than three minutes away.

They climbed out, caught sight of the guard, and started there.

"Good day, young man," said Petra.

Johan wanted to be included.

"Beautiful weather today."

The royal guard was a kid from Sollefteå stationed here as part of his compulsory service. His name was Jesper, and he had strict instructions never to respond with anything but "yes" or "no" to questions from tourists. This largely meant saying "yes" to the question of whether photography was allowed.

"Yes," said Jesper.

"Young man, do you have any idea where we can find First Marshal of the Court Carlshamre?" Petra asked.

"And Last Marshal, as far as I understand," said Johan, "assuming they're not going to change marshals in the next ten days. It's not like we want to beat him up or anything. We just want to talk. We left the baseball bat in the car."

Jesper wished he were back home in Sollefteå.

"No," he said.

Petra felt that the royal guard was being unnecessarily reticent.

"Then do you know who might know?"

Jesper did know. His commanding officer, for instance. Unfortunately, he gave an honest answer.

"Yes."

"Well, who's that?"

Oh hell! What was he supposed to say now? Another "yes" would be the only thing stupider than the alternative.

"No," said Jesper.

Johan glanced at Petra.

"Do you think there's something wrong with him?"

"There must be. But he might also be following instructions. He looks really nervous, don't you think?"

"Yes," said Johan.

"Yes," said Jesper.

The illegally parked RV and the couple bothering a lone royal guard had just transformed this sleepy Sunday into something halfway intriguing for Security Service Officer A, who was dressed as a tourist with a camera dangling against his belly. He radioed his equally plain-clothed colleagues B, C, and D to say that he intended to approach a situation that had the potential to develop into an incident. According to procedure, the channel would remain open from now until this event had played out.

A "spontaneously" walked up to the royal guard and asked if photography was allowed. Jesper knew who A was, hence his response:

"Yes, please."

Sollefteå was three hundred miles away. Felt like three thousand.

Johan and Petra were still standing very close by.

"Would you please move away? I want to take a picture."

"Of course," said Johan.

"But we're not done talking to the guard," said Petra.

"Of course not, I meant," said Johan. "We're looking for First Marshal of the Court Carlshamre. First and last. It's about an urgent matter."

A could tell that something strange was going on. For one thing, the marshal of the court spent his time at the royal palace in central Stockholm. For another, it was Sunday. Now he needed to keep the conversation going.

"Oh, I'm sorry. I'll wait my turn then. Have you booked an appointment with the marshal? That's exciting. And is that your vehicle, by the way? Nice."

"Thanks!" said Johan.

But Petra had grown suspicious. This tourist was asking too many questions. And was too ingratiating.

"Who are you? And what do you want?" she asked.

Security Service Officer A committed them to memory: Woman, five foot seven, around thirty, Swedish, ash-blond hair, blue eyes. Man, five foot nine, around thirty, Swedish, ash-blond hair, gray eyes. Neither of them obviously armed.

Petra made note of his intense gaze. Something really wasn't right here. Whatever this man wanted, it wasn't good. It was one thing if they couldn't get hold of Carlshamre for that monologue. That didn't mean they had time for any police interrogations about nothing.

At the same time, Johan was performing his own situational analysis. He thought the tourist looked worried. Maybe it would be best to reassure him.

"Like we already told the young guard here, we don't want anyone to think we wish First and Last Marshal of the Court Carlshamre any ill. And we're definitely not going to slap the king around the face. We can't imagine what that would teach him."

Police interrogations, thought Petra. *And maybe jail, if Johan keeps talking.*

Security Service Officer A thought it was time to introduce himself. He took his badge from his inner pocket, held it up, and said that he had a few questions for them, just for informational purposes.

Petra *refused* to waste the last few measly days of her existence locked up in a police station. If the jailers did their job, it wouldn't even be possible to hang herself there. She launched into rapid and spontaneous action, spiced with a dash of panic.

Security Service Officer A had many years of experience. He had skillfully defused threatening situations before. But he was totally unprepared for the woman in front of him to butt her head into his chest full-force. Embarrassingly enough, A fell backward and landed on his behind.

"No!" said Jesper, and had no idea what else to do.

"Come on!" said Petra to Johan.

A was quickly back on his feet. But Petra was faster. She dashed for the RV with Johan just a step behind. They were already pulling away by the time Officers B, C, and D had arrived to provide backup to A.

"What happened?" said B.

A preferred not to answer. He gazed at the retreating RV and saw it turn left onto Ekerövägen.

"MLB490," he said. "Swedish couple. Around thirty. Both with ash-blond hair. She's five seven, he's five nine."

"I'll check the registration," said B.

"I'll send a patrol car after them," said C.

"To think that those idiots turned left," said D.

"Why did you turn left?" said Petra.

"Did I?" said Johan. "Was I being stupid again, just now?"

CHAPTER 7

Sunday, August 28, 2011

TEN DAYS TO GO

If you find yourself in Stockholm and want to visit the wonderful Drottningholm Palace and environs, you must first travel about six miles in the direction of Bromma. You can be there in twenty minutes, if the traffic isn't too bad.

Once you get to Bromma, head left off a roundabout and continue along Drottningholmsvägen for another two and a half miles. After one bridge you're on Kärsön, and after another you're on Lovön. The palace will be on your left, you can't miss it.

Let's say you do miss it, though, and you keep going straight. A branch in the road leads to either Färingsö or Ekerö.

These are some pretty big islands in Lake Mälaren. It's possible you might get lost if you can't find your way. But here's a crucial fact: your only option to leave is to take the car ferry to the mainland, south of the capital city.

Or to turn around.

And head back to Drottningholm.

Security Service Officers A, B, C, and D immediately worked out that the pair of suspects were caught on one of the Mälaren islands. All the officers had to do was surveil the car ferry from Ekerö and beyond that, wait at Drottningholm to spot a white RV with the license plate MLB490, preferably with a thirty-year-old man behind the wheel and a thirty-year-old woman by his side. In order to keep from waiting longer than necessary, though, they decided to send out a few cars, one in the direction of Ekerö, the other to Färingsö. If these patrols found what they were after, they would simply need to call for backup.

The list of suspected crimes began with illegal parking, continued with assault of a government official (mild assault, but still), and had just expanded into vehicle theft. It wasn't clear whether the suspected offenders had, on top of everything else, threatened to slap His Majesty the King around the face. The RV turned out to belong to a Swedish diplomat at the embassy in Rome. He was *not* under suspicion of being in Sweden and Italy at the same time.

* * *

Petra understood the situation she'd landed in just as Officers A, B, C, and D did. She explained it to Johan, and told him that the car ferry was the only possible route of escape and that she imagined hardly any police officer would fail to come to the same conclusion. It would only take a phone call to make sure the ferry stood still until the police got there.

Johan wondered if they could hijack the ferry. Petra said this wasn't the best idea he'd ever had.

Johan was disappointed in himself. And sick of how everything always went wrong, no matter what he did. Petra was just about to say something kind when he saw flashing blue lights in the rearview mirror. Things, which were already bad, had just got worse.

"Take a left here," said Petra, pointing in the direction she meant to be on the safe side.

With that maneuver, they left the main road while the patrol car didn't have them in sight. Petra didn't know exactly where they were headed, but for now the most important thing was to shake the immediate threat.

"Right here. Left. Straight."

Johan was looking backward as much as forward. He was feeling increasingly stressed out. After all, he already had as much trouble telling right from left as accelerator from brake.

And so, what happened happened.

"Left, I said!" Petra cried as the RV nearly bounced down a gravel road to the right, and found itself on an out-of-the-way waterside property.

Johan was about to ram a boathouse, so in a panic and by mistake he hit what he thought was the accelerator, at which point the RV stopped about a foot in front of the door.

"Good braking," Petra said in admiration.

Sometimes, things go so wrong they're right.

CHAPTER 8

The Old Lady with Violet Hair

Agnes was sitting in front of her laptop in her cottage. Her fingers moved nimbly over the keyboard; she was comfortable with the internet. She wore her seventy-five years with dignity. Her waist was as trim as ever. Her once-blond hair now had a hint of violet. The color was elegantly enhanced by the dress she wore, no matter the dress.

She was working on the daily update of her account on this new invention called Instagram when she heard a noise from the yard. Was there someone there? She never had visitors.

From the window you could see across the yard and all the way to the boathouse, if you leaned over the kitchen table and moved the geraniums.

An RV?

* * *

Fifty-seven years earlier, Agnes was uniquely beautiful and sparklingly radiant. In another era, "Parisian fashion model" would have been the least of her accomplishments. If circumstances had allowed it.

The year: 1954. The setting: a parish in the southern-Swedish province of Småland, a settlement so small that God probably would have forgotten it if not for its double churches.

There was Dödersjö New Church, from 1790. And Dödersjö Old Church, from the thirteenth century.

The population had reached a few hundred people, spread over a hundred acres. The houses were widely scattered, except for in town. By "in town," people basically meant the not-yet-shuttered Konsum grocery store. Those who came to call at Grankvist's general store next door could purchase a can of gas, while supplies lasted. This was the closest Dödersjö ever got to having a gas station.

Agnes lived with her parents in a fiber-cement house not far from the cemetery. She was of an age to marry, and this all took place in a time when parents still had a certain amount of influence over their children. Or at least over their daughters.

The fact was, clog manufacturer Eklund courted Agnes with flowers *and* new clogs. Her parents couldn't stop raving about him. A manufacturer! Which would make Agnes a manufacturess! Eklund had four employees and a practically new maroon Saab 92. It would be crowded in the tiny apartment above the factory, but Eklund's frugality was really nothing but a virtue. Agnes couldn't expect a better catch.

"Not on your life!" she said, before the spark inside her was smothered.

The wedding took place a year later. The manufacturer chose the *new* church, the one from 1794. It had to be fancy.

They never had any children. First because neither the manufacturer nor the manufacturess knew what to do. Once they figured it out, the manufacturess knew she never wanted to do that again. Not with the manufacturer, anyway. And there was no one else available.

For in truth, Eklund was as wooden as his clogs. And as stingy as his reputation said. He didn't get a TV until well into the sixties. He didn't trade in his Saab until 1975 (for another Saab, not quite as used). When times got tough, he fired two of his four employees and replaced them with his wife. Agnes, who hadn't had anything to do during twenty-five years of marriage, now toiled twelve hours a day, six days a week. This lasted into the early eighties, when Eklund stepped on a nail, got blood poisoning and waited too long to travel all the way to the clinic in Växjö, because it took seven liters of gas to get there and back. Those general-store jerry cans weren't free.

The funeral service was held in the *old* church, because it was up to the widow.

Agnes was suddenly both a manufacturess and a manufacturer. She was in control. She dialed down the production of clogs to a minimum and increased the production of wooden boats. She had good business sense and was soon the boss of twenty employees and no longer stood on the factory floor herself.

She was well over sixty by this point, and had lived almost all of her life within the bounds of Dödersjö parish, with the occasional jaunt to the Lenhovda dairy and a total of two journeys all the way to Växjö. Both times had been before she was married and learned that a journey of twenty-two miles was not something they should waste money on. For what did Växjö have that Dödersjö didn't? *Life*, Agnes thought, but fell in line anyway.

As a widow, she noticed that there was still something left of her youthful self. From the days when she had been radiant. And she wanted to see what was possible. That gene of hers discovered that there was something new out there in the world, a place where you could travel without moving an inch. It was called *internet*.

Around the turn of the century, she expanded the company. The boatbuilding arm was basically taking care of itself. Agnes bought Dödersjö's only pastry shop for three pairs of clogs and one rowboat. She tossed out all the pastries that no one ever bought anyway and turned the place into an *internet café*. One lovely Sunday in May, she stood on the church steps and explained to the churchgoers what they could do there.

"Discover the world, dear citizens of Dödersjö! From right here in Dödersjö! One hour of internet, a cup of coffee, and a bun for the introductory price of ten kronor. An unforgettable experience!"

All seventeen of them listened. None of them showed up at the café the next day. Or the days that followed.

There sat Agnes with her three computers and her 56k modem. Taking comfort in the buns, which would have otherwise gone stale. Infinitely tired of the citizens of Dödersjö. Almost as tired of the boat factory.

It was called *surfing*. You started on AltaVista. A *search engine*. From there, you could go wherever you wanted.

Agnes wanted to go to Paris. London. Milan. Not so much New York. She was no coward, but flying all the way across the Atlantic?

But the internet was different in every way. Fear of flying was irrelevant in the virtual world. And what's more, a trip to America, Japan, or Australia cost less than a round trip to Växjö in her deceased husband's stinky Saab.

Agnes had had enough of the old ways. She broke up with life as she knew it. She quit clogs. She quit boats. She quit Dödersjö and its half-dead citizenry. She sold the factory with its living quarters, furnishings and all. She junked the Saab. She kept the truck—after all, she needed something to make her getaway in.

For the money she bought a red cottage by the water outside the capital. To go inside it she bought a bed, a chair, a desk, a computer, and geraniums for the window. The woman who had hardly ever left her home parish now took the bus and metro into and out of Stockholm every day. The truck was best kept in the boathouse, which she turned into a garage. She didn't want anything to do with boats anymore, anyway.

She was sixty-five years old and had wasted almost her entire life. But only almost. In Stockholm, she went to the cinema. She went window-shopping. She bought fruit and vegetables at Hötorget. She bought a pair of expensive sunglasses and had a glass of wine on a patio on Stureplan in the evening sun. She browsed Sweden's daily paper, *Dagens Nyheter*. She saw teenagers with their noses buried in their Nokia phones. They were *surfing*! On their phones!

She smiled inwardly.

Her spark was returning.

"Now I'm going to learn the damned internet!"

CHAPTER 9

Sunday, August 28, 2011

TEN DAYS TO GO

Agnes was spry for her age. She stepped lightly down the stairs and into the yard, following the gravel path to the boathouse and the white RV. There she caught sight of a man and a woman.

She had lived where she lived for over a decade now and still made regular trips into Stockholm and back. At first, she'd done so for pleasure and to attend a course that taught retirees how to use the internet. In time, she went for pleasure and the even greater pleasure of increasingly advanced courses in programming, web design, marketing, and positioning.

But someone born and raised in the backwater that is Dödersjö is not used to socializing and making new acquaintances. The only person you could have more than one-syllable conversations with back home had been old man Björklund. He was the gravedigger at the cemetery. His greatest merit, in Agnes's eyes, was that he had once buried the manufacturer. The citizens of Dödersjö didn't dare to refer to him as what he was. They thought it would bring them closer to the grave. Instead, they called him Blooming Björklund for his green fingers. Agnes assumed his ability to hold a decent conversation was down to the fact that he regularly talked to the flowers he grew. Practice makes perfect, after all.

But Björklund died and would have had to dig his own grave, if only that were possible. Since then, Agnes hadn't practiced conversation apart from those she had at her internet classes.

Now here she was, faced with two uninvited guests in an RV.

"Welcome to Sjölyckan," she said.

Johan thought the lady looked nice. Sjölyckan must have been the name of the house.

"The baseball bat stays in the car here too, right?" he said to Petra.

"Thanks," said Petra, waving off Johan's inquiry.

"May I ask what business you have here? Or . . . never mind. Perhaps you would like a cup of coffee?"

Petra studied her. Stylish. Friendly smile. Definitely not a target for the baseball bat! What the doomsday prophet really needed was a cup of Johan's cappuccino, but a simple cup of drip coffee didn't sound bad. If it weren't for the current complications.

"That would be great," said Petra. "May I ask . . . this garage, does it by any chance belong to you, ma'am? And do you suppose our RV would fit inside?"

Agnes said that it was a boathouse, not a garage. Which, in truth, she had turned into a garage because she was tired of boats. The RV probably would fit, as long as Agnes first moved the truck that was already inside.

"And I'd be happy to do that."

Five minutes later, the truck and the RV had switched places, without a single question from Agnes about the reason for this arrangement. But on higher ground, further inland, was a residential neighborhood. A police car was circling around up there with its lights on. Searching for something, or someone? Agnes noticed her guests' wary glances.

"Should we go ahead and close the garage door, perhaps?"

Apparently she had read Petra's mind.

"That's a good idea," said Petra. "We wouldn't want it to slam and bang if the wind picks up."

* * *

The coffee couldn't match Johan's cappuccino for quality, but it held its own. Plus, cinnamon buns were included. And refills. And seconds on buns.

After an hour and a half of true conversation in the spirit of gravedigger Björklund, Agnes, Johan, and Petra not only knew one another's names but had also exchanged the short versions of their life stories.

"So the world will be ending in ten days?" said Agnes.

Her doubt was almost palpable.

"And we're all toast, every one of us," Johan confirmed. "Not just people without enough clothes on or who happen to be outside."

"Johan gets it," Petra nodded. "My calculations are exact and confirmed beyond all reasonable doubt."

"Am I still allowed to allow myself a reasonable portion of doubt?" their violet-haired host wondered.

Petra said that she was, but also that there wasn't really much point. What was about to happen was not something you could *wish* away.

"Haven't there been a number of doomsday prophets throughout the centuries?" said Agnes.

"Please don't compare me to the many bumblers of history."

"But, your plan to confront the marshal of the court—how prudent was that?"

Petra said that there was no problem with the measure in and of itself. It was meant to be nothing more than a quiet conversation. But she did confess that she hadn't given enough thought to the whereabouts of His Majesty the King and what that might mean for the level of security.

"And now you've painted yourselves into a corner."

"We have?" said Johan.

"She means that we're stuck on an island and can't get off it without being locked up."

In the past hour, Agnes had realized how lonely she had been all these years without reflecting on it directly. Now she was loath to let her new friends go, no matter how strange, chaotic, and unlawful they seemed to be. Or maybe that was exactly why. Johan and Petra seemed to live more in a whole day than the entire community of Dödersjö had done in the past five hundred years. What's more, the metaphor of being painted into a corner had given her an idea.

"I used to be a boatbuilder, you know," she said.

"Do you have a boat we can escape in?" Petra asked.

"That's not what I'm saying. But there's been a bunch of junk in the back of my truck for over a decade."

"And?" said Petra.

Agnes was happy to prolong this. It was so nice to have company.

"A ladder, if I recall."

"And?" said Petra.

"A rusty scythe. My dead husband thought it was a good idea to keep it. He got it for cheap. And then the Grim Reaper got him."

"And?" said Petra.

She could tell Agnes knew where she was heading.

"A lot of painting equipment. Rollers and so forth. And probably twenty-five liters of bright-blue marine paint. A decade old, like I said. But I never scrimped on quality."

"You're saying . . ."

Yes, that was what Agnes was saying.

"What is she saying?" Johan wondered.

* * *

As the late summer evening fell, the white RV turned blue. On Agnes's suggestion, they also let the RV and the truck switch license plates with one another. The paint would dry overnight. Agnes proposed that the guests check in, allow themselves to be served chicken casserole and boxed wine, and try to get some sleep on the sofa and in the easy chair. That was as luxurious as things got at her hotel.

Johan said that chicken casserole sounded good, especially with some lemon thyme, fried apples, and a dash of calvados, but suggested he visit the RV to fetch an alternative to the wine. A 2006 La Mateo, for instance.

"What was his name again?" asked Agnes.

During dinner, Johan's inner pocket rang.

"Fredrik!" he exclaimed with delight before he'd managed to take the phone out.

"How do you know?" Petra asked.

"I don't know anyone else. Except you, of course, but why would you be calling? You're sitting right here. Do you even have my number? Hello, dear brother!"

But the diplomat was not in a brotherly love sort of mood. He spoke so loudly that everyone around the table could hear him. The first thing he wanted to know was whether Johan and the RV were at the RV park Fredrik had booked.

"No, I—"

"Good! Everything else has gone to hell, but that's good."

Johan tried to say something, to ask how his dear brother was doing. But Fredrik had not called to listen; he had called to tell Johan what was what. He said he was angrier and more annoyed than ever at his imbecilic brother.

"Imbecile means idiot," said Johan.

"Yeah, it sure does!"

Creating a scandal outside the king's palace—how stupid could you get?

"How did you know we were there?"

"Because the police called me in the middle of a meeting with the ambassador and seventeen other people. I knew instantly that you had made a fool of yourself again, and I had to sit there and lie. Do you hear me? Lie! 'My RV outside Drottningholm Palace? I'll be damned! It's supposed to be at an RV park in Fisksätra. If it's not, then someone must have stolen it.'"

Following the lie, he'd been stuck in the meeting for another four torturous hours, and a banquet after that. He hadn't had a chance to call until now.

"For Christ's sake, don't go back to the RV park, they'll arrest you."

"There's no risk of that. We're stuck on an island some-how. We—"

Fredrik cut him off again.

"Listen carefully. There is only one thing I am going to say: I. Don't. Want. To. Know!"

"But I made a new friend, and—"

"Did I not just say I don't want to know?"

"Yes, you did. Did you forget already?"

Fredrik remembered who he was talking to.

"One more thing."

"That will be two things, altogether."

"Shut up and listen to me. If the police do get hold of you, you have to tell them you stole the RV from me and I had no idea."

"But you gave it to me. How can I steal what's mine?"

"It's registered in my name. You don't have to understand, just do as I say."

"Are we playing Gentry and Servants again?"

"No!"

"Okay then. How are things in Spain?"

"And this conversation never happened. Are we in agreement on that as well?"

Johan thought so hard he nearly got a headache.

"You mean that if someone asks, I should pretend we never talked?"

"Exactly."

"Just this time? Or ever?"

"Just this time. This conversation. We still grew up together, and you're proud that I'm a diplomat. In *Italy* for fuck's sake."

Italy, thought Johan. The country was called Italy. The city was called Rome. Spain was something different.

"But, dear Fredrik, you have to tell me how things are—"

The third secretary hung up without saying goodbye.

"Nice guy," said Agnes. "Wasn't he behaving like himself?"

No, Johan thought he rather was.

"What was that about 'Gentry and Servants'?" Petra asked.

Johan giggled. He would tell her. It was their favorite game! He and Fredrik had played it since they were small until just the other day, when his big brother moved to . . . Italy. The idea was that they divided up into gentry and servants. Whoever was gentry bossed around the other, who had to obey every order and say, "Yes, my lord." If you didn't, you lost.

"Did you draw straws to see who would be who?"

Johan couldn't recall how it had started, but it turned out that Fredrik lost all the time and so had to sit there being gentry. Not that he was upset when Johan won, but it must have been a bit annoying that Fredrik could never catch his brother out.

"Once in a while I would forget the 'Yes, my lord' part, but he never realized."

Agnes and Petra exchanged glances. The prophet wondered what sort of tasks the gentry might give his servant.

"Oh, anything you can imagine!" said Johan.

There was vacuuming, cooking, running errands, fetching a blanket if the gentry's feet got cold while he was sitting in the wingback chair, serving whiskey and cigars—there was always something.

"But didn't Fredrik do the cooking?"

Johan laughed.

"Him? Cook? Are you nuts?"

"Well, who taught you how to make food, then? You said Fredrik taught you everything you know."

"He did! When Mom got sick, we decided the kitchen would be part of the game."

"You both decided that."

"Well, he decided it, let's say. I made food, he was rude; I made more, he was even ruder. But he was so good at being rude that I learned. A little, anyway. I think. Or not. But still."

"Did he take the same tone as during that call just now?"

"What do you mean?"

All at once, Agnes and Petra understood two things. One: Fredrik had spent all these years exploiting his little brother, and two: Johan had no idea. This prompted Petra to recall something else:

"When you sold the twelve-and-a-half-room place on Strandvägen, how much did you get for it?"

"How should I know? Fredrik took care of all that. He had a heck of a time selling. There were all the agent fees, moving costs, and weird taxes. Yet there was still money left over for the RV."

"And maybe a little besides?"

"You'd have to ask Fredrik. All I know is that it's really expensive to live in Spain or Italy and he hardly gets paid any salary at all."

"Because he told you that?"

"Yes."

* * *

While Johan answered the call of nature in the bathroom, Agnes and Petra got a few minutes alone. The violet-haired woman had already figured out that Johan's aptitude was of a mixed variety, not least because he'd just admitted as much as he told his life story. But now it seemed that Fredrik had not only *exploited* his brother throughout their whole upbringing, but had, in addition, committed actual fraud.

Petra complicated matters by bringing Judgment Day into the mix. Johan had looked up to his older brother for more than three decades—could it really be right to destroy that image with only ten days left of everything?

"If your calculations are correct," said Agnes.

"Don't start that again."

They were at a standstill, until Agnes realized that Petra herself had started a brand-new relationship with her own life with only eleven days of it left, according to her calendar. Didn't Johan deserve the same chance? Or did she feel that he ought to be frozen solid in the middle of a lifelong lie?

The argument hit home. The prophet and the violet-haired woman shook on it: they might as well rip off the Band-Aid right away.

* * *

They began by sowing doubt in Johan's mind. What was the deal, really, with this gentry-and-servant game? And the dividing up of rooms? And big brother's tone of voice? And the slapping of his ears?

But it wasn't until they got to the presumed price tag on the apartment that little brother fully understood what big brother had done to him over those many years. The RV would have cost around seven hundred thousand kronor (Agnes looked it up

online). The apartment must have gone for fifty to sixty million—
or more. So rather than an RV with a custom kitchen, Johan
should have received about thirty million kronor from his brother.

He began to cry. He cried as quietly as he could, because he
was ashamed.

"I *am* an idiot," he said.

"Don't say that," said Petra. "No idiot in the world can
cook like you do. You're a master chef, a genius!"

Who can't tell the difference between Spain and Italy, left
and right, accelerator and brake. She didn't say.

Agnes got out a bottle of aquavit, imagining it might be of
help given the circumstances. The self-appointed idiot reacted
better than she and Petra might have hoped.

"Not aquavit," he said, sniffling. "I'll be right back."

Accompanied by two bottles of the 1996 Paolo Berta Grappa
Invecchiata, Agnes and Petra did their best to comfort the
not-so-easily-comforted. They praised his talent in the kitchen
and his perfect movie-English some more, but nothing worked.
Fredrik must have oppressed his brother too much, for too
long. Johan played scenes from the past in his head. Old scenes,
in a new light. Like the reason Johan was always the one who
dealt with the trash.

"*Is it even possible to be allergic to taking out the trash?*" he
said to his brother.

He gazed out the window as he spoke, as though Fredrik
were somewhere outside.

Agnes tried to reach him. She addressed both of them.

"Shouldn't you track down Fredrik just like you did with
that Victoria? And have a word with him? Or a whole lecture,
perhaps."

Johan wasn't listening. He spoke to the darkness outside:

"*It wasn't because you cared about my dental health that
you ate all the Saturday sweets.*"

Petra made a try as well.

"What do you think of Agnes's idea, Johan? Maybe we could even get out the baseball bat."

But he was lost in his own world:

"The half room was mine. The other twelve were yours. Just think how much I cleaned for you. And did you ever even thank me?"

Petra's heart swelled with sympathy for Johan, that sympathetic character. Agnes was right! It was high time that Fredrik heard the truth about everything, including himself. While Johan continued to stare out at nothing, the prophet got herself all fired up. They would find Johan's big brother just as they'd found Malte (and got Victoria into the bargain).

"Let's do it, dammit!" she said loudly.

It's funny what a fifteen-year-old grappa from heaven can do for the mind and soul.

CHAPTER 10

The deepest sleeper that night was Johan in the easy chair, thanks to the copious amounts of grappa he'd found reason to cap off the evening with. Next-deepest was Petra, on the sofa, mostly because it had been a long day with a lot going on.

All while Agnes lay wide awake upstairs in her bed.

The first time she'd lived it up since her teenage years was when her husband the manufacturer stepped on a nail, followed by the blood poisoning and burial courtesy of Blooming Björklund. The second time was when she uprooted herself and left Dödersjö, never to return. What followed—life in Stockholm, internet courses, and her online activities—was not a kick so much as the welcome feeling that life had some sort of purpose after all. That it was chugging along.

Until Johan, Petra, and the RV showed up unexpectedly. A doomsday prophet and a swindled little brother. With the cops on their tail. Agnes experienced the third and perhaps final kick in her seventy-five-year-old life. And now they were about to leave her. It made her feel . . . well, what? Empty?

The violet-haired host served fried eggs and toast for breakfast. It wasn't Johan-quality, but neither the eggs nor the bread were what concerned the doomsday prophet as she drank her coffee.

Had she really decided, the night before, that their next stop would be Rome? Over the head of Johan, who had sat there staring at nothing?

How many roadblocks would they face along the way? The first one was only a few miles away.

Of course, the white RV was now blue. And the license plate—which undoubtedly would have been caught on camera during those few minutes outside the palace—had been exchanged for another. But Johan was still Johan, and Petra was Petra. They ought to have a different driver when they passed through the police checkpoint that was sure to await them, while they themselves hid in the back.

Worry number two concerned Johan specifically. He'd already managed to drive over a pavement, turn left when he meant to go right, hit the accelerator when he should have braked, and, above all, nudged a camper down a slope to certain death. And through all of that—in contrast to right now—he'd been sober. Even if they managed to get past the checkpoint at Drottningholm—how far would they make it with unlicensed driver Johan at the wheel?

Damned grappa! It was beyond delicious. And it had thoroughly muddled her mind.

Then again, that might be the solution! After all, Johan had downed at least twice as much as she had. If she was lucky, he wouldn't remember a word of Petra's declaration from the night before.

"Would you like tea or coffee, Johan?" asked Agnes, arranger of breakfast.

"How far is it to Rome?" Johan asked. "When do we leave?"

There was no going back, then. But: one problem at a time. What if Agnes could lend a hand with the most pressing issue? Petra asked if she knew how to drive an RV.

* * *

"No," said Agnes. "I've never tried. But I've driven a truck all my life. How hard can it be?"

Question two was whether she might consider sitting at the wheel when they passed through the police checkpoint they expected to encounter at Drottningholm. Partly because Petra and Johan didn't want to be spotted when their vehicle passed through. Partly because you could never be sure when Johan might mix up the pedals again. If it happened at the wrong moment, all their efforts would be for naught. And Johan's brother would get away without the telling-off he so deserved. Petra said she would understand if Agnes didn't want to subject herself to any of this.

Was this about to turn into the happiest moment of Agnes's life? Well, she wasn't there yet.

"I can get you through the police checkpoint at Drottningholm," she said. "On one condition."

Was she going to demand money?

"That I get to stay behind the wheel."

"What do you mean? All the way to Italy?"

"I've never been abroad. I renew my passport every five years, but that's as far as I've got."

Petra could hardly believe her ears. But suddenly she was seeing the possibilities again, not just the threats. She was sure that anyone who could drive a truck would do an astronomically better job piloting the RV through Europe than someone who couldn't drive at all.

Johan was on his fourth glass of juice. Was starting to perk up. Wanted to contribute to the conversation, speaking of how Agnes had just admitted she had never been abroad.

"I've been to Sundsvall," he said.

Agnes and Petra responded with silence. Johan interpreted it correctly.

"That's in Sweden, isn't it?"

*   *   *

The RV was the wrong color and bore the wrong license plate. Behind the wheel sat a person of the wrong age and wrong sex, with the wrong-colored hair. She was also the wrong number of people in comparison to what the police were looking for. And she blended into her environment. It was summer, after all, with a considerable number of RVs on the road.

The upshot of all this was that Agnes never even came close to being waved onto the shoulder for further scrutiny outside of Drottningholm. The trio slipped right through the police net. All that remained were the fifteen hundred miles to the Swedish embassy in Rome, for the purpose of restoring Johan's honor vis-à-vis his brother. Or, rather: bringing him the honor he had never actually received.

Petra found having a real driver at the wheel a joy. She no longer felt as though each minute between now and the end of her life, just over a week in the future, put her in danger of a traffic-related early death.

Once Johan sobered up, he, too, had the good sense to appreciate this arrangement. While Agnes and Petra sat up front, he puttered around the kitchen farther back. He didn't know that, according to the law, he ought to be belted in for the journey. Petra saw no reason to inform him, either, especially not once the aromas of whatever he was creating wafted into the front seat. Agnes didn't have any opinions in that direction either. She had been raised long before the era of seat belts.

*   *   *

The distance between the RV and the Swedish capital increased. After a few hours' journey southward, Petra felt that the long arm of the Stockholm law was not long enough to reach them. This allowed her space to do a certain amount of reflection.

Three days ago she'd tried to hang herself. Two days ago she had defined a meaning for her thus-far-meaningless life. The next day that meaning was redefined, in a fit of drunkenness. As a result, they were now on their way abroad, to a place where Petra had nothing left undone or unsaid with a single person.

This meant that Carlshamre, the minor popes of the Academy of Sciences, and her old neighbor with the dog would be spared. She and he certainly had a few things to discuss. Or not. It was really the wire-haired dachshund with the personality disorder she should have had a talk with, but how did you talk to one of those?

Agnes noticed that the prophet in the roomy passenger seat was mulling something over.

"What's on your mind?" she said.

Maybe nothing. It had all just happened so fast. They were about to leave behind everyone she'd planned to talk some sense into.

"Can't you talk some sense into *me*?" the driver asked. "In the absence of anyone else, I mean."

The prophet shook her head. It would have to be about her mistrust of Petra's calculations, if anything. But there was no point in getting upset about general ignorance among non-astronomers, because then all you'd ever do was walk around being upset.

Might as well shake it off. It was really quite simple. Johan had helped Petra to find Malte, which changed her life. Now it was her turn to help Johan find Fredrik. Last night's grappa had been right.

But they'd better make sure to get hold of big brother in time. It was a long trip, and their remaining days were dwindling. They mustn't dillydally along the way.

* * *

Johan had only himself to blame really. After the totally ordinary breakfast at Agnes's house on Ekerö (a breakfast of which
he was innocent!), he threw together a snack and served it to
the driver and prophet on the road. With that, he had established a routine he was fundamentally opposed to. Food should
be treated with love and respect; a meal deserved a nicely set
table at the very least.

The snack was very simple, spelt muffins with sunflower
seeds, feta, and sun-dried tomatoes. Oven-baked and served
piping hot. Petra fed bites to Agnes, enjoying her own portion
between times—as well as the fact that the group was saving
time by not stopping.

When it came time for lunch, as they approached Ödeshög
along European Highway 4, Petra suggested they reprise the
muffin setup. Johan said he should have realized he was giving
her a pinkie finger and now she wanted the whole hand. Her
argument—that doomsday was coming nigh with such speed
that each minute could be crucial—led to a compromise. Their
lunch of ravioli with creamy ricotta, spinach, and roasted ha-
zelnuts could be served in a bento box and eaten with just a
fork, but on two conditions. One: both driver and passenger
would enjoy the meal with Johan's hand-picked and already-
aerated Italian red with a hint of dark cherries, plum, vanilla,
and roasted coffee beans. And two: this evening's dinner would
be eaten in the traditional manner, with a parked vehicle,
set-up table, and the five courses Johan was planning and had
already begun to prepare. This would be followed by collective
sleep all through the night. Johan was sure they would arrive
in time, whether Rome was in Italy or Spain.

Petra accepted the chef's conditions, with the proviso that
Agnes probably shouldn't guzzle wine while driving.

But their violet-haired chauffeur came to Johan's defense.

For one thing, who said anything about guzzling? A little alcohol never killed anyone. She herself was seventy-five years old and had no patience for all the nitpicky little rules established in Swedish law. If they were stopped at a police checkpoint, this would all be over anyway. Just consider the minor detail that the license plate belonged to a different vehicle and the fact that while Agnes undoubtedly was a hell of a driver, she had never seen the point in getting a driver's license.

Three people without licenses in a vehicle heading through Europe. Petra gave in—one glass of wine behind the wheel couldn't make things any worse than they already were. But she felt that she must, for the sake of accuracy, point out that alcohol certainly had killed a few people here and there over the years. And that wasn't always a bad thing.

* * *

North of Jönköping, the group made a pit stop to fill up the tank.

"Do we have time to stretch our legs as well?" Johan asked.

"No. Just nine days left," said Petra.

"Or not," said Agnes. "I'll go inside to pay."

Back on their continued route southward, Petra turned the conversation to finances. They could afford fuel, food, drink, and whatever else might come up on this trip, right? She herself didn't have all that many thousand-krona bills to wave around. The only reason she had a charge card and her passport in her possession at all was because they happened to be in the back pocket of her jeans just as she failed to hang herself.

Johan was decently flush with cash, but no more than that.

"My formerly beloved brother gave me fifty thousand kronor to live on. Aside from the RV, that is. There might be about half of it left now, along with a well-stocked wine fridge and a liquor cabinet that can hold its own. I suppose I'll have to start making more budget-friendly choices in the kitchen."

"No!" Petra blurted.

O, horrid thought!

"I've got enough to get us through," said Agnes.

With both hands on the wheel and eyes forward, the seventy-five-year-old began to tell them about her financial situation. She had got a lot of money for the boat factory, much less for the clogs, and almost nothing for the apartment in Dödersjö. Altogether, it had been enough to purchase the house and boathouse in Ekerö with a little to spare. After some time with her internet hobby, she discovered the new phenomenon called Instagram. For fun, she created an account called "Traveling Eklund," scanned in a portrait from the day she turned nineteen, touched it up in her photo-editing program, and stole body parts from all over the place until she had recreated herself as young and unmarred by life.

"I'm not sure I follow," said Johan.

"Forget that," Petra said impatiently. "Go on, Agnes!"

Traveling Eklund headed out on her first journey, while Agnes never had to leave the kitchen of her red cottage in Ekerö. The first experience was an obvious choice: the Eiffel Tower.

"London," said Johan.

After Paris, nineteen-year-old Agnes moved on to Berlin. Then Moscow, Milan, Budapest . . . once in the swing of things, she took on the rest of the world. Hollywood, Hawaii, Tokyo, Seoul, Hong Kong. From there she went to New Zealand and Australia, up to China, and back down to Indonesia. In Africa she mostly stuck to the cities—the wildlife there felt dangerous even in Photoshop. From Nairobi to Johannesburg, from there to Cairo. At least one update a week, sometimes several in a day. But she never let her fantasy travel lose touch with reality. You can't be in South Africa in the morning and posing in front of the pyramids of Egypt later that same day.

Agnes really got swept up in her luxurious life of travel. She always flew business class and dressed fashionably (and sometimes quite provocatively). If she was going to Photoshop a watch onto her left wrist, she saw no reason to make it a cheap one.

She was really quite satisfied with everything as it was. Flattered to have apparently gained thousands of followers from all over the world. She wrote her brief captions in English. Or, "English." The captions were just as linguistically limited as you might expect them to be when composed by a retired clog-factory owner from the parish of Dödersjö, Sweden.

"I can help you," Johan said, in English. "I'm not so bad at cooking, I'm starting to realize. Or at cleaning. Beyond that there's nothing else I'm good for, except that I've watched so many movies I almost know more words in English than Swedish."

Petra noticed that Johan's faith in himself was growing. It wasn't unlike the new self-confidence that had so recently filled her, thanks to Malte and a baseball bat.

"Thank you kindly," said Agnes. "But it all worked out in the end."

Among her followers was an American called something she could no longer remember. Anyway, he wrote kind things about Traveling Eklund on something called a "blog," which he was apparently a world leader in (he was otherwise known for hardly ever writing nice things). The kind and (more commonly) mean articles he wrote drew in eight million visitors—per day. This gave Agnes an idea. Besides Instagram, she got

Traveling Eklund accounts on both Twitter and Facebook—and she linked them all to a blog of her own. If the American could do it, why couldn't she?

Instagram, Twitter, Facebook, blog. These were not words that had appeared in *Gone with the Wind*. Maybe Johan didn't speak English as fluently as he thought. That left cleaning. And the prophet's many words of praise regarding the flavors of his food. They clashed with Fredrik's comments, but which should he listen to?

He decided to go with Petra's.

On her blog, Agnes could really live it up. Under Traveling Eklund's name she grew ever more exhaustive in the captions for each picture. She told her followers where she'd bought the dress she was wearing. And about the agonizing decision of navy blue over pink when she picked out her luxury watch. She gave tips on earrings, travel destinations, meals, purses, and just about everything else. Always in lousy but charming English.

"Instagram, you say?" said Petra.

She'd heard of that.

"That's where it started. But it was the blog where things really took off."

"Did lots of people find you?"

"Not as many as the American whose name I've forgotten. But more than when I tried to lure people in from the church steps in Dödersjö."

"How many?"

"Outside the church? Seventeen, I think."

"Out in the world."

"Four million per day."

"Wow! Do they pay?" Johan wondered.

"They don't need to," said Agnes.

Because suddenly brands began to get in touch. Not the very

biggest names, but the ones who wanted to claw their way out of obscurity. First up had been a competitor of Gucci.

"They said they'd be happy to send me a watch if I promised to put it on."

"They sent you a watch? Was it expensive?"

"What was I going to do with that? I asked them to send fifty thousand big ones instead. I got the watches for free online."

"How much have you brought in so far?" Petra wondered.

Agnes smiled and elected to give an indirect answer.

"Johan, you've got an unlimited budget for food and drink over the next nine days. After the end of the world, we'll renegotiate."

"We will not," Petra said acidly.

"Good!" said Johan. "Then can we stop at a well-stocked supermarket? And preferably also the liquor store? I'm feeling inspired."

The evening's five-course meal deserved fine company.

* * *

Afternoon came, and early evening. The RV was approaching Öresund and the nine-mile bridge and tunnel that had linked Sweden and Denmark since the turn of the century.

For the first time, the seventy-five-year-old was about to leave her motherland, which might give her online alias Traveling Eklund a good laugh.

In their final miles on Swedish soil, Johan offered details of his childhood with big brother Fredrik and mother Kerstin before she got sick and eventually passed away. He was suddenly seeing certain incidents with fresh eyes. One hundred times out of one hundred, little brother had had to collect Mom's prescriptions from the pharmacy—no matter the weather—because people in white coats gave Fredrik panic attacks.

So he said.

* * *

What neither Johan nor Fredrik could account for was how their mother and father became a couple, the reason their father was never at home, and—most importantly!—their mother's secret!

CHAPTER 11

The Löwenhult Family Secrets

The marriage between Bengt and Kerstin Löwenhult was not a happy one. At least one of them could have predicted that this would be the case. In the couple's defense, it must be stated that the pursuit of happiness was not a central aspect of the arrangement. She came from an ennobled family while he had a bank account full of Daddy's money and also found himself at the threshold of what would become an outstanding career as a diplomat. To put it bluntly, Bengt and Kerstin were useful to one another.

In bed, though, not so much. They succeeded in consummating the marriage, but otherwise there wasn't a great deal of sex happening. None at all, in fact! Kerstin sensed that something was fishy even before she got pregnant with Fredrik.

Still, it wasn't until she returned from a shopping trip with her girlfriends one afternoon that her suspicions were confirmed. The group had caught an earlier train home than they'd planned, and as a result Kerstin found her husband in their marital bed along with his secretary.

"It's not what you think, darling," said Bengt.

"Nice to meet you, Mrs. Löwenhult," said Gunnar the secretary.

Both Bengt and Gunnar were naked and sported erections.

Which meant it was exactly what Kerstin thought, and had for a long time.

"Would you please both get dressed," she said. "Preferably before I throw up."

Negotiations ensued, beginning with the assumption that it would be counterproductive to separate. He had the money and the career. She had her noble origins and reputation to consider.

Once all the puzzle pieces were arranged, what remained for Bengt was a difficult conversation with his head of ministry. Might as well tell it like it was: he would never get used to the idea of being with a woman. Or any man that wasn't Gunnar, for that matter. His love for his secretary was eternal!

"Homosexual. I've suspected as much for a long time," said the minister for foreign affairs. "Glad you told me."

It was a simple matter for the pragmatic head of the ministry. He certainly didn't want to lose one of his most talented diplomats. Nor did he need to, since Bengt had chosen to come out. All they had to do was spread the news through every diplomatic corridor Löwenhult moved in. In so doing, foreign powers would understand that it was pointless to try to recruit him. Blackmail only works when there's a secret worth revealing.

Simply put, Bengt was brilliant, capable of making connections like no other. Even before he was promoted to ambassador, he had managed to spend a whole evening reciting Shakespeare with Richard Nixon and drinking vodka from a lady's shoe with Leonid Brezhnev.

And then his career took off. Young Löwenhult was constantly given new assignments all over the world. Always accompanied by his secretary. Never by his wife.

Even so, it was a delicate situation for the Ministry for Foreign Affairs. It was not among the duties of the government to encourage the splitting up of a marriage. The solution was to regularly invite Mrs. Löwenhult to various diplomatic banquets in Stockholm while her husband and his secretary were somewhere on the other side of the world. The arrangement was, by nature, a diplomatic one. Mrs. Löwenhult would be assigned a seat at a not-too-fancy table and served international luxury adjusted to domestic taste. In return, she never demanded to follow her husband on his posts, not even when he was assigned to Paris.

Dismissing Bengt Löwenhult was not an option. When he told Russia's first president, the eternally merry Boris Yeltsin, about that time with Brezhnev and the lady's shoe, the president bought a shoe off his assistant for a hundred rubles and got Bengt to do it again. This second episode of footwear diplomacy led, in the long run, to a bilateral agreement between Sweden and Russia that was worth four hundred million dollars. All while the Russian assistant limped home to the suburbs with only one shoe.

During his years in the service of the Kingdom of Sweden, Bengt Löwenhult worked in no fewer than eighteen countries and had four different ambassador assignments. No task was too difficult nor too small. Whatever he was asked to do, he tackled it with the same enthusiasm. And always, always with his loving secretary very close at hand.

The diplomatic genius was rarely, or never, at home. When Fredrik was born in Stockholm, Bengt was in Egypt, busy monitoring the reopening of the Suez Canal eight years after the Six-Day War. Perhaps the canal would have opened anyway, but among other things diplomacy was based on being where things happen when they happen. Politically, that is. In comparison, a private birth seemed boring.

When Kerstin got pregnant with Johan two years later, father-to-be Bengt and secretary had long been in Buenos Aires, working on the hopeless task of setting the military junta to any sort of rights. Eleven months after that, when the diplomat had a rare errand to Sweden for a conference, son number two had already been born. Both Mr. and Mrs. Löwenhult avoided getting into any details, such as the difficulty of impregnating someone in Sweden while you yourself were in Argentina. Bengt acknowledged paternity and took off again.

That things turned out the way they did was down to the fact that Kerstin was only human. When her thirst for intimacy was not extinguished after almost two years, she happened to get caught up with a young diplomat from a far-off country during a banquet at the Ministry for Foreign Affairs. He had pale skin, dark eyes, and white teeth. It wasn't like he was excessively charming, but he spoke English with a French accent and that was all it took for Kerstin, given the circumstances. After three hours they went to the hotel bar for one last drink. Followed by an elevator ride up to the diplomat's room to take in the lovely view. Neither of them noticed that the room faced the courtyard.

Bengt never asked who the other father was. In any case, Johan resembled his half brother; the post-banquet adventure didn't leave any obvious traces. Even when her sons were old enough to have understood, Kerstin decided it was best to leave out the detail about who was whose father.

And Bengt had already forgotten all about it. After an exemplary career he took early retirement and moved to Uruguay for the sake of warm weather, the tango, and love. Two men can walk hand in hand along Playa Carrasco in Montevideo without having rocks *or* slurs hurled at them.

The young diplomat was the only one who knew. Kerstin found his business card in her purse, and wrote to tell him that the result of their night in the hotel room was a little boy, that his name was Johan, that he didn't look a thing like his father, and that the diplomat was not to engage in this matter any further.

And he didn't—he had his own life to worry about. But when he read the letter, he nodded contentedly at the knowledge that his machinery worked—and burned the evidence.

Thus the children grew up with neither father nor fathers. Their mother Kerstin raised them to the best of her ability. Speaking of which, she discovered early on that big brother had a great deal more of that commodity than the one who existed as the consequence of her rendezvous with a young diplomat who had dark eyes, white teeth, and English with a French accent. While the twelve-year-old memorized as many decimals of pi as he could, his ten-year-old half brother tried to figure out how the toilet seat worked. Big brother's record was eighty-five decimal places. After some time, little brother did indeed solve the mystery of the toilet seat.

But in their mother's world, there was something special about Johan. There was an awkward thoughtfulness about him that she loved. To think that he could be so sweet and so clueless all at once. Fredrik didn't need Kerstin in the same way. He was a self-starter and had his eye set on his future. Big brother was his father's son. From that perspective, Kerstin sometimes thought it was too bad Bengt was never there for him.

And then she got sick. And even sicker. Johan sat at her bedside all the while, anytime he wasn't at school or in the kitchen. He never understood why she had to die. Fredrik said she had come down with pancreatic adenocarcinoma. That didn't make little brother any the wiser.

Their father Bengt came home for the funeral. He tousled Fredrik's hair and said that sometimes life seemed both difficult and unfair, and that his son shouldn't hesitate to get in touch if he needed help in the future. The ministry knew where to find him.

"Take care of yourself, kiddo," he said.

Johan wondered if he should take care of himself as well. "Yeah, you probably should," said Bengt.

* * *

Bengt Löwenhult was a deeply inadequate father. He needed the affirmation he got from his diplomatic brilliance. And he needed his Gunnar.

He actually needed his son Fredrik as well, but it all just went to hell from the start. And it went even more to hell when little brother showed up. Johan, that was it. Bengt simply couldn't find it in himself to engage with that one.

What could he even do for Fredrik, from such a distance? Bengt pulled the right strings, of course, and got him into the diplomacy program. And he was proud and delighted when he received the report that the pupil who'd slipped in the side door with his father's help was delivering results as good or better than those who had earned their spots in the program.

After that, he had second thoughts. By this point, of course, his son would have heard the hallway gossip about Bengt's sexual orientation. And that probably would have been the end of it, if it weren't for that Johan kid, who had, in an intellectual sense, turned out to be a mixture of Bengt's wife and God-knows-what. What if Fredrik had begun to wonder?

The star diplomat felt that he had no right to cause a rift between the brothers. So he decided to leave his son to his fate. The alternative was more than he could manage: to give equal amounts of support to diplomat-material Fredrik and good-for-nothing Johan.

* * *

What Bengt and Kerstin had created together was a boy and, soon enough, a young man who desperately needed to prove himself to his mother and later, his father. At which point his mother died and his father continued to keep his distance. What they left behind was an ass of a little brother, if his father was even involved in that? Whatever. Under no circumstances would Fredrik let Johan stand in his way. Johan or anyone else.

Trampling over others to get what he wanted? Sure. If necessary. Trampling over Johan? Yes please!

CHAPTER 12

Monday, August 29, 2011

NINE DAYS TO GO

The parking area along the E47 highway to Rødby was dreary, with nothing to suggest the Danish traffic planners had further ambitions for it.

On this particular evening, six artics and a manure tanker had stopped for the night. The latter still had its engine running. The advantage to this was that the odor of diesel overpowered most of the stench from the two filthy bathrooms right next to it. The neglect was so thorough that the drivers preferred to perform their nightly toilet in the yellowish-brown, half-dead grass nearby.

The gray asphalt was blackened with motor oil here and there. Litter had drifted into small trash banks on either side, while the cigarette butts remained glued in place.

Petra thought they should find a nicer place to spend the night, but Johan called from the kitchen that dinner was almost ready. So it was what it was. He apologized for the fact that dining al fresco was their one option no matter the weather. The part of the RV that had been meant as a dining area was taken up by a wine fridge, deep-fryer, extra stovetop, and a plate warmer.

"Fredrik said that this renovation cost fifty thousand kronor and that *I* should have financed it."

"You could have used the thirty million he never gave you," said Petra.

* * *

After a long day behind the wheel, Agnes was sitting in a camp chair outside the RV with her tablet in her lap. She couldn't quite figure out how to compose the next update for her blog. Traveling Eklund, that nut, had gone to Svalbard. What could she do there?

"So you don't feel that you have a certain amount of responsibility for her destinations?" asked Petra.

"You just don't get it," said Agnes.

"Can't you have her go to a nightclub? Have some fun?"

"Two thousand citizens, one thousand polar bears, no nightclubs."

Petra wondered whether the polar bears might live a fraction of a second longer than the human citizens of Svalbard when the temperature dropped to 459.67 degrees below zero, but she decided it didn't matter. Instead she carried on setting the table with china and glasses according to Johan's instructions, finishing up just as he came out with his hands full and asked them to take a seat.

"We'll begin with a crispy shrimp cone filled with egg and lumpfish roe. Accompanied by a Gustave Lorentz Riesling Reserve."

The wine happened to be the same color as what the Danish manure tanker driver was eliminating into the grass about ten meters away.

"*Velbekomme,*" he said, greeting them in Danish as he stuffed his wiener back into his pants before he was all the way finished.

Agnes made a face and Petra considered getting out the baseball bat, although she wasn't really clear on what she would do with it.

"Would you like to join us?" Johan said. "There's enough for you as well."

* * *

His name was Preben and he didn't wash his hands before grabbing the first of the crispy shrimp cones.

"This is the best damn thing I've ever eaten!" said Preben. But in Danish.

"What did he say?" Johan asked.

"He was wondering if you have anything he can use to wash his hands," said Agnes.

Johan was quickly on his feet and just as quickly back with a damp towel and a few drops of soap.

"I've got some wet wipes too, if you'd like."

To be on the safe side, Preben switched from Danish to Swedish. He told them he'd lived in Landskrona, in southern Sweden, for the better part of his adult life. There, until recently, he'd had a Swedish girlfriend called Kajsa, and a daughter who was only maybe his. She showed up right around the time Preben and Kajsa met. The paternity didn't matter so much, Kajsa thought it was someone else, but Preben could see the similarities between him and his daughter, who had flown the nest by now. In any case, they were equally ugly.

The Swedes thought the Dane was refreshingly forthright, and now that everyone's hands were clean the appetizer and main course flew by without incident. Inspired by Preben, Johan, Agnes, and Petra briefly shared their own stories before dessert. Preben kept up a running commentary. He told Johan he didn't have much to say about wavering brotherly love except that he hadn't seen his own older brother in ages and it was just as well. Traveling Eklund's world trips was another topic of conversation that didn't suit Preben's tastes. The internet was good for some porn now and then, and it was practical to receive shipping notices and stuff by email. Much less paper to keep track of today than just a decade ago.

But this bit where the end of the world was imminent—he thought that sounded exciting.

"Just nine days to go? Then what happens?"

"Once the atmosphere collapses? Absolutely nothing," said Petra.

Preben Lykkegaard was mostly Danish, but also a little Swedish. Born and raised in Helsingør, he had moved to Landskrona in the name of love and commuted to his homeland each day for the sake of his job, until his partner suddenly threw him out after twenty years. Kajsa said he smelled horrid and she was finally fed up with it.

The ousted Dane was aware he was an entrepreneur in the field of cow manure and it was all too easy to bring home certain odors from work. But Preben suspected there was something more going on. He was back in Helsingør now, and not showering as frequently (because what was the point), but took the occasional trip over the sound to spy on his former home in Sweden. He felt he had to know.

On his third spying mission his suspicions were confirmed. Another man had taken his place. Judging by the license plate on the car, he was German.

It's not easy to hide a Danish manure tanker in a Swedish residential neighborhood. Kajsa spotted Preben as he was taking a picture of the German's black Audi. She blew up, accused him of spying, and told him to scram—or stay until her boyfriend got back from his jog, because there would be no mercy for Preben then! She bellowed that it was *fate* that had brought her and Dietmar together. She was winter, he was summer, and they had met for the first time in the spring, when the first lilies of the valley were blooming. They would be married in the autumn.

"I didn't quite get all that," said Johan. "Although it's not the first time."

"Me neither, at first," said Preben. "But then I was informed that lilies of the valley smell like the exact opposite of me."

"But I'm sure you don't smell?" Petra said politely.

"Anyway," said Agnes.

Preben didn't wait for the jogger. He took his manure tanker and went back to Denmark with a broken heart and a lingering need to know more. You could say a lot of things about Preben, according to Preben, but not that he was stupid. With the help of the Audi's license plate, and the information Kajsa had given him, he soon knew everything worth knowing about the man who had taken his place. Kajsa's last name was Vinter—Swedish for "winter." So Dietmar must have the surname Sommar, and that's a name you can have in Germany, with a minor linguistic adjustment. The car was registered to an industrial packaging company in Bielefeld. They happened to employ a sales manager for Scandinavia by the name of Dietmar Sommer. Further investigation turned up that Herr Sommer had a wife and two kids. Which meant Preben's beloved Kajsa was nothing more than a plaything for a German salesman with false intentions.

"Lilies of the valley, my ass!" said Preben, who was now on his way to Bielefeld to track down the German and give him a solid punch to the face. Or two.

He had it all planned out. He would start with a straight right. Followed by a left hook, although it sort of depended on whether Dietmar was still standing up or had already fallen down.

"What do you imagine that will teach him?" Petra wondered. "Other than that it hurts to get beaten up."

Johan answered for the Dane. He said he couldn't even count all the times Fredrik had hit him over the years, even as he learned nothing about anything. Except for how to cook, and he didn't think that had anything to do with being slapped. Incidentally, he'd received a heck of a lot of praise for his cooking

over the past few days. Master chef! Genius! Plus whatever
Preben had said in Danish that was impossible to understand.

"Soon I might start believing you all," he said.

"As well you should," said Petra.

But now they were getting off topic. Petra confessed that it
hadn't felt entirely wrong to whack Victoria in the butt with a
baseball bat, but it was the words that flowed out after this
that had really done the trick. The former bully was probably
still painting her nails out of sheer terror.

Preben scoffed at Petra's objection. So typical of people on
the other side of the sound! If it were possible to convene and
reason oneself to death, there wouldn't be a single Swede left.
The manure entrepreneur called his fists "Danish dynamite";
he rubbed them together and said it would be a pleasure to
clobber the German.

Johan asked if he was scared Dietmar would hit back.

"Scared?"

You could say a lot of things about Preben, according to
Preben. But not that he was dumb, and not that he was scared.
In his younger days, he'd often spent Saturday nights practicing punches—both giving and receiving. Mostly giving. Each
time, without too much chitchat beforehand.

Agnes listened, enjoying herself. Who knew that a chance encounter in a Danish parking area could be so much more interesting than all the encounters between the people of Dödersjö
in the past five hundred years. To keep the discussion from
dying out too soon, she added a little fuel.

"Wonder what kind of sentence assault carries with it in
Germany?"

"What do you mean?" asked Preben.

What she meant was that Germans were pretty good at
locking up troublemakers, weren't they? Preben's tanker was

surely good for a lot of things, but as a getaway car she imagined it wasn't optimal.

Preben hadn't thought that far. He had four manure-spreading appointments scheduled in Jylland later that week, and more all across Denmark in the weeks following. It wouldn't do to be arrested by the German police. But would he really end up with more than a fine?

Agnes was quick with the search engine on her tablet. She found a site about the kinds of punishment for assault in the federal republic.

"Best-case scenario: heavy fines, depending on how hard you hit. Six months in the clink if you give it a little more juice, up to ten years if there's as much dynamite in your fists as you say. Maybe you should settle for just the first whack, or the second?"

God, how the Swedes liked to complicate things! Couldn't they just help him out somehow? In the name of humanity.

"Help you how?" said Petra. "By holding Dietmar while you hit him?"

No, the Dane didn't dare hope for that much. He realized he needed an escape plan that could be put into action immediately following the punch to the face. You could say a lot of things about Preben, according to Preben. But not that he was stupid. And not that he was scared. And not that he was good at escape plans. Up to now, this whole vision ended with his marching into Dietmar Sommer's place of work, asking to see him, and as soon as he showed up, *bang*!

In front of a whole lot of witnesses, of course. And with the tanker right outside the door. He was realizing now.

Petra told the Dane to stop dreaming of help. She and her friends were on their way to Rome on an important errand, and time was short, as Preben ought to have understood by now. For the same reason, it wasn't that big a deal if he got locked up, was it? Would he even have time to appear in front of a judge before Judgment Day judged them all? And dealt out the same punishment to everyone, no matter how many fists had been in play immediately beforehand.

Agnes, of course, wasn't convinced that Petra's doomsday calculations were accurate, and she wanted to have as much fun as possible along the way.

"Then again, Bielefeld wouldn't be that big a detour for us," she said.

At which point she had an infernal idea. She turned to Petra:

"Maybe you would get the chance to talk to Dietmar about his reprehensible way of life before Preben follows up with his Danish dynamite. And then we'll help him get away. I feel like in that case you will have got yours, Preben will have got his, and Dietmar his as well."

"And then I can treat everyone to a meal," said Johan.

"Maybe not Dietmar," said Agnes.

Petra saw a way she might expand upon the Meaning of Life in the pitiful shred of time they had left. Now that things had been cleared up between her and Malte, and now that Victoria had received her telling-off, it was time for Johan's brother Fredrik to be given his. But the journey to Rome was long, and what a bonus it would be if, along the way, they could put yet another wrong to right in the eleventh hour of life on earth. They would probably have to stay there overnight, though, since Johan refused to let them eat dinner on the road. Exiting the highway, tracking down a German sales manager, and delivering certain truths about right and wrong likely wouldn't take more than an extra hour. If, into the deal, they could help the Danish manure-spreader avoid meeting his maker in a German jail cell, wasn't that a deed as good as any?

"Time for dessert!" Johan said, hurrying into the RV.

Good, thought Petra. That would give her some time to think.

* * *

The meticulously designed dessert, served in parfait glasses, was sadly ill-suited to accompany Preben's lecture on the criteria for top-quality, organic Danish cow manure. He took a massive spoonful from the glass, which was filled with chocolate mousse layered with seaberry marmalade and blackberries, noting aloud that the dessert and the more solid portions of the manure had certain visual similarities. Everyone demurred when he offered to fetch a sample to demonstrate.

When coffee and cognac were served, Preben held up his snifter and studied the liquid swirling inside. Agnes guessed what was coming.

"Dearest Preben, may I kindly request that you don't compare the cognac to anything I suspect you might be about to compare it to?"

Preben was affronted. He said that people didn't understand how important cow dung was to the ecological cycle. But by all means—they might as well talk about doomsday instead, why not. Was Petra sure it would afflict Bielefeld to a sufficient extent? Because that was a comforting thought.

Petra was tired of people's failure to grasp that the atmosphere cannot collapse just a tiny bit, and only here or there. Just think of Preben's reaction when he heard that in a tenth of a second the world would be 459.67 degrees below zero: his main concern had been that the manure in the tanker would freeze, along with the brake shoes on his truck.

"If you'd just enjoy your food in silence for five minutes, Preben, and let me explain one more time the implications of a collapsed atmosphere, I promise we'll help you in Bielefeld tomorrow. I think I have a plan already."

CHAPTER 13

Tuesday, August 30, 2011

EIGHT DAYS TO GO

The Dane performed his morning toilet in a bush on the other side of the parking area, quite a way from the breakfast table that had been set outside the RV, because he understood that the Swedes would appreciate this gesture. He drew attention to his consideration by asking Johan for a wet wipe afterward and making sure everyone heard the request.

After they'd slept on it, and eaten eggs Benedict and salmon with dill-and-mustard sauce for breakfast, the agreement was to continue southward in a caravan. Between Preben's manure-tanker pace and the ferry from Rødby to Puttgarden, they wouldn't reach Bielefeld until evening. Their meeting with Dietmar would have to be postponed until the next morning.

"First dinner, then wallop," said Johan. "With or without a telling-off between. It's a bad idea to fight on an empty stomach. It's best not to do anything on an empty stomach. Any particular requests, menu-wise?"

"Hamburgers?" said Preben.

"Or not," said Johan. "I'll think of something."

* * *

Agnes was behind the wheel, still feeling annoyed with her online alias. In certain respects, Svalbard was an experience, but once everyone else had long since dozed off, the violet-haired scammer sat up for a long time, trying to manipulate photos into something that had a decent chance of corresponding with reality. An average temperature of thirty-seven degrees Fahrenheit in August. Would there be snow? How much? Plus, all the polar bears sneaking around. That was flat-out lethal. No way to make money on product placement, either.

She shared her concerns with the prophet.

Petra didn't want to start anything, but had Agnes just described Svalbard as an "experience" without ever having been there except for in her imagination? Was she sure she knew the difference between real life and fantasy?

Agnes replied that this particular comment would perhaps be more impactful coming from someone who wasn't a doomsday prophet.

With that, the atmosphere at the front of the RV remained a bit tense until the aromas from the kitchen reached them. Petra just had to ask what awaited them. Johan said they could expect potato pancakes as an appetizer, that's what was currently in production. The main course would be of a similarly rustic nature. After all, Preben's hamburger suggestion indicated he felt that simplicity was to be preferred.

"What is a simple main course, to your extraordinary mind?" Petra wondered.

"Pizza," said Johan.

"Well, imagine that!"

"With Russian sturgeon caviar."

*   *   *

It's tricky enough to park an RV overnight in countries other than Sweden, where you can put down temporary roots wherever you please. If you're also in the company of a full-size manure tanker, it takes even more planning.

So that's what Petra did. She ordered Preben and Agnes to drive the whole crew to KIPA Industrie-Verpackungs GmbH at Friedrich-Hagemann-Strasse 7, where she found exactly what she was looking for: an industrial park that was closed for the day, with plenty of space for both vehicles and dinner table.

Between starter and main course, Petra pulled the Dane aside to explain her planned course of action. This was possible now that she had been able to study their surroundings in detail.

"We'll park the RV and tanker here, aimed that way. I'll go into the lobby to ask for Dietmar Sommer, and he'll come out to meet me. He'll follow me outside to see someone who wants to talk to him."

"But I don't want to talk to him."

"Don't talk to me either, please. Not right now. Just listen."

Petra intended to toss Preben's ex-girlfriend into the drama. She would tell the German she had a message from Kajsa in Sweden, if Herr Sommer would be so kind as to follow her outside. Logic dictated that this should prompt both anxiety and curiosity in the unfaithful family man. Petra would lead him around the corner of the industrial building, a walk of sixty-five or seventy-five yards. If their pace was slow enough, that would give her a few minutes. She planned to use this time to explain the importance of keeping one's family together, being a role model to one's children, and living up to the promises one has made. If these words fell upon receptive ears and were absorbed as she hoped, Dietmar could freeze solid as a slightly better person one week from now. Perhaps the German would even have time to thank her before they rounded the corner.

"Then, when we do come around the corner, you'll be there waiting. Without any witnesses. As I understand it, it's just going to be 'BAM!' with no chitchat first. Followed by fifteen seconds' mad dash to the vehicles."

Preben smiled. Now he understood! He said that he was actually planning to talk to Dietmar while he was beating him up. Along with the straight right he would say, "This is from Kajsa." And, with the left hook, "And that one's from me."

Johan ordered the crew to the table. It was pizza time.

"Some might say champagne on a Tuesday is overdoing it, but I want to do the caviar justice. A 1996 Dom Pérignon Oenothèque. A long, cool year with great acidity."

"Pizza!" Preben chuckled. "Delicious!"

The detailed planning could wait until morning.

"Is it okay if I pick off this black goo? You don't happen to have any beer, do you?"

* * *

Darkness fell over the industrial park. Coffee and digestifs were drunk, plans for the next morning finalized.

Time to say goodnight. Everything felt right.

At which point nothing went as planned. It rarely does.

CHAPTER 14

Son of a Sugar Beet Farmer

While three Swedes and a Dane were eating pizza with Russian caviar at an industrial park in central Germany, a Russian named Aleksandr Kovalchuk was pouring himself a tumbler full of vodka in another part of the world. He did this on occasion, after a long day.

Soon enough, fate would cause him to collide with Agnes, Johan, and Petra, but it would not do Aleksandr (or anyone else) any good to know this as he sat on the vast terrace of the palace under a starry sky, with a cool breeze blowing in from the sea. He told the servants to go to bed. He preferred to enjoy these quiet nighttime moments on his own.

Aleksandr had been born fifty-five years earlier into very different circumstances. His father and mother toiled as sugar beet farmers in a poor and remote part of the Soviet countryside. The years after the Great Patriotic War had not been kind to anyone. If it wasn't raining too much, it was raining too little. The soil cracked, the wells ran dry. It was impossible to reach the levels of productivity set by the Soviet Council of Ministers' State Planning Committee from their offices seven hundred fifty miles away. The fact that Stalin had two of the seven members of the Council of Ministers executed in order to light a fire under the remaining members resulted in nothing more than those members' terror-stricken decree, in their next five-year plan, that the weather would be 60 percent better.

Aleksandr hadn't even been born yet when his parents abandoned their life in the countryside. They moved to the metropolis of Sevastopol, where their immediate survival wouldn't be decided by better or worse weather.

With their move came a change of luck. Aleksandr's father started hanging out with young men who were courageous enough to speak ill of Stalin behind closed doors. One of them was a childhood friend from his years in Privolnoye. His name was Mikhail Sergeyevich, although no one ever called him anything but Misha, and he had been popular in the village because he owned an old tire they could play with.

Mikhail Sergeyevich helped himself like no other. He joined the Communist Party. He made a career for himself in the youth association. He took up a position in the reasonably corrupt world of Sevastopol politics. He led secret conversation groups in various basements with no witnesses aside from the many rats who had, until that point, got to keep the underworld to themselves.

Before he continued his career in Moscow, he organized a job for Aleksandr's father, putting him in charge of keeping all of Sevastopol clean. Childhood friends had to stick together. Aleksandr's father thanked him by handing over a brand-new car tire tied with a big red bow, saying that now Misha would have something to play with during the many lonely nights to come, in the capital city.

Future president Aleksandr Kovalchuk learned to walk, matured, changed from teenager to adult. All while his father kept Sevastopol as clean as he could around that portion of its inhabitants he could make use of. He went from stooping over a hopeless field of sugar beets to looming large as a powerhouse in Sevastopol. And he wanted nothing more than for his firstborn son to take another step in the same direction. Accordingly, he forced upon his son philosophy tracts and political pamphlets in French. The general consensus in the basement conversation circles was that it was only a matter of time before the French communists took over central Europe, and then they would need bridge-builders between Stalin in Moscow and the new leadership in Paris. Aleksandr's father thought his son should find a place for himself in all of this.

Aleksandr read, paged through a turn-of-the-century dictionary, understood at best half of what he was reading, read a little more, understood more—and came to the conclusion that the French Stalinists were as bonkers as Stalin himself. But French was lovely, in contrast to the slurring English he also practiced. Why create a whole language around the fundamental idea of never pronouncing the letter *r* properly?

His father's childhood friend Misha, meanwhile, joined the ranks of the anti-Stalinists even above ground, without rats. This was made possible now that Stalin had had the good sense to die.

Mikhail Sergeyevich's family name was Gorbachev, and he made such an impression in the corridors of power that chairman Khrushchev named him party secretary in charge of agricultural matters and thus launched him fully into the Politburo, the youngest ever of his kind.

Future president Kovalchuk was, at this point, just twenty-some years old, but his father gave him a genuine university diploma in economics for his birthday (it wasn't cheap; the dean of the school was a greedy bastard). With his freshly purchased education and links to his father's childhood friend, Aleksandr took the bus all the way to Moscow and joined Mikhail Sergeyevich's team as an advisor. He was in charge of imports and exports since he was the only one on staff who knew any language other than Russian.

Apart from what he'd learned from his DIY language studies, Aleksandr's image of how the world worked was totally colored by his father's stories of his days as a sugar beet farmer in Privolnoye, the village whose collected assets when the family moved away had comprised eight sugar beet hoes, twelve chickens, three horse-drawn carts minus the horses, and an old car tire.

His father had raised his son according to the best of his communist knowledge. He took for granted that the ideology he'd grown up with would be around forever. This included the fact that the trash-collecting general could use his political muscle to keep the poorly organized local gangsters pretty well under control, the people whose fortune depended on shortages of most things in the Soviet model society.

The advice he gave his son was to keep the mafia at arm's length. Perhaps things would have gone better for Aleksandr in Moscow if he had listened a little less to his father on that particular point.

For the mafia was on the offensive.

CHAPTER 15

Wednesday, August 31, 2011

SEVEN DAYS TO GO

It all looked so promising at the start. Preben found Dietmar's Audi in the staff parking lot. He recognized the model, color, and license plate. So the adulterer was on the premises.

The RV and the escape vehicle were in position. Preben went to stand around the corner. Petra strode through the packaging company's door and informed the receptionist that she had an important message for Herr Sommer, was he by any chance in the building?

He was—but who should the receptionist say was asking for him?

Petra hadn't thought that far.

"Tell him it's me. I am a very important person from Sweden. Business secrets. Rather hush-hush, if you get my drift?"

The receptionist reluctantly went along with this. And apparently it was enough to pique Herr Sommer's curiosity, because he said he was on his way.

When the elevator doors opened, all the fun ended before it could even start. Dietmar Sommer turned out to be over six foot seven and looked more like a shot-putter than a sales manager for Scandinavia. Two hundred eighty pounds would probably be a low estimate. And it all looked like muscle.

"What is this in regard to?" he said.

He had a deep voice, on top of everything else.

Well, this was in regard to how he was about to be taught a lesson in good manners followed by a round of thrashing. But surely this *giant* standing before Petra would barely notice if Preben whacked him in the head with Malte's baseball bat, if he'd even had it at hand.

Sure, she could fulfill her task of leading the shot-putter around the corner, but what would *that* lead to other than Petra's becoming party to manslaughter? And the most likely victim of said manslaughter would be the Dane. And possibly Petra herself.

"Yes, what *is* this in regard to?" she said, thinking fast.

"Well?" said Dietmar in his rumbly voice.

"She says she's from Sweden," said the receptionist, ashamed of what she'd allowed to happen.

Perhaps Dietmar Sommer made the connection between this strange visit and his adventures with Kajsa in Landskrona, because he looked troubled when Sweden came up.

"Sweden," said Petra, worried that the massive human before her would in fact make the correct association.

So she added:

"Denmark. Germany. The Netherlands. Australia. Vietnam. We're all citizens of the world first and foremost, are we not?"

This wasn't going well.

"Are you lost?" Dietmar Sommer wondered.

What a great idea!

"Yes, I sure am! I don't think I've ever been as lost as I am right now. I wonder if I didn't mix up Bielefeld and Białystok."

While the gigantic Dietmar Sommer wondered how one could mix up a city in western Germany with one in eastern Poland, Petra apologized.

"I won't be any more trouble. Farewell, Herr Sommer. And hallelujah!"

Where did that come from?

Petra backed out the door and hurried to find the waiting Preben. The shot-putter was far too astonished to follow the odd woman.

Petra took a right and, sixty-five yards on, another right, rounding the building to rendezvous with Preben.

"You're alone? Wasn't he there?"

Petra countered with a question:

"Do you want to die, Preben?"

He didn't. Not for a while, anyway.

"But what do you mean?"

"I'll explain later. Come on, let's get out of here."

* * *

Once Preben was given a rundown on Dietmar Sommer's anatomy, he said that you could say a lot of things about Preben, but not that he was stupid. Had he said so before? Beating up someone who wouldn't notice he was being beaten up before he hit back? No, that's where Preben drew the line. He thanked Petra for her resourcefulness. She had truly saved his life!

"By all means," said Petra, thinking that it was time for the Dane and the Swedes to say farewell to one another.

Agnes, though, was hoping for a bit more time. She had looked up Dietmar Sommer's home address. Since the shot-putter was clearly at work, couldn't they think up some mischief for him to discover when he got home?

But Petra was back to her usual self. She, Agnes, and Johan had business to see to in Rome, and time was short. She wished the Dane good luck in love, but now it was time to go their separate ways.

Preben looked dejected. Agnes comforted him by saying she could help him create a message from Kajsa for Preben to stick in the shot-putter's family mailbox. That ought to mess things up for him, wouldn't Preben agree?

* * *

And so it was that the sales manager came home after work, about the same time as the RV was leaving Germany on its journey south and the manure tanker was crossing the border into Denmark. Sure enough, Preben had dropped Kajsa's greeting as composed by Agnes in the Sommer family's mailbox. But he didn't stop there. No one appeared to be home at the excessively fancy villa, which sparked in the Dane the idea that he might help the family fill their nearly finished swimming pool.

With manure.

Dietmar's wife Christiane was waiting for her husband in the driveway.

"I found this in the mailbox," she said, holding up a letter. "Someone named Kajsa in Sweden sends her warmest greetings."

Dietmar went cold. It didn't help his grasp of the baffling situation that there was a horrible smell coming from somewhere nearby.

"What did she say?" he asked, fearing the worst.

"She writes that she misses her darling teddy bear."

Shit!

"Teddy bear?" he said.

Christiane was not stupid.

"The teddy bear is you."

Dietmar Sommer could come up with no better response than:

"What stinks so bad?"

And she had a quick retort:

"That's you too, Dietmar."

CHAPTER 16

Wednesday, August 31, 2011

SEVEN DAYS TO GO

The friends in the RV never learned of Preben's manure attack on the shot-putter, but Agnes told them about the contents of the letter she'd composed for the Dane. It had taken a little extra time for Johan to understand it all. How could Kajsa send her greetings if Agnes was the one writing?

Petra understood at once. And she was slightly ashamed of the schadenfreude she felt over Dietmar's presumed fate. The meaning of what remained of life was to put things right, not sow discord.

* * *

Their violet-haired pilot studied the map and declared that there would be at least one, and more likely two, overnight stops before they reached Rome. That would leave them four or five days before the sky would (in all likelihood not) collapse upon them. Petra wasn't quite of sound mind, but aside from that Agnes had few complaints. Their adventure with the Dane had been a delight. Besides, Traveling Eklund had finally found a flight out of Svalbard. She was in Oslo now, blowing all her cash at Tiffany's. Thirty thousand in the bank from a Tiffany-wannabe, which was actually terrible.

Speaking of money, it was really starting to pile up. And in a Swedish account. It would be preferable if they could find a different solution.

"I had an idea," Agnes said.

"What's that?" said Petra.

Johan piped up from the far reaches of the vehicle.

"We're out of garlic, can we make a pit stop or do I need to rethink the menu?"

Agnes went on:

"Wouldn't it be exciting to see yet another country while we're out and about?"

"Depends on the country."

"Switzerland. It's just next door."

"Is anyone listening up there? Garlic!"

"We'll get you some, Johan," said Agnes.

"Why Switzerland?" Petra asked.

"Zurich. I've got a few million in the bank back home, and I was thinking it'd be best for it to disappear somewhere where it can't be found. Before it can be discovered by, for instance, the Tax Authority."

"And you think that's likely to happen in the seven days we've got left?"

Agnes didn't want to start a fresh round of bickering. A white lie was vastly preferable.

"If we're really unlucky, they'll make their move tomorrow morning and then we'll be sitting here with a bulb of garlic and not much else."

"Did someone say garlic?" said Johan.

Zurich wasn't a huge detour. Yet it was far enough away to make it a good place to stop for the night. Petra agreed to the proposal. She didn't like the idea of living her last week of life without Johan's unlimited budget for food and drink.

There was no risk the Tax Authority might come marching in the next day to seize Agnes's assets at the Bromma branch of

Handelsbanken, that's not how it worked. But there was no reason for Petra to know this. The white lie was just a creative way to avoid calling the prophet's doomsday calculations into question yet again. Questioning them in silence was good enough for Agnes. If Agnes was right, there would be plenty of time to point out Petra's error after the fact. If she was wrong, none of them would even notice until it was all over.

So far, Traveling Eklund hadn't reported a single krona she'd earned; hadn't paid a single one in tax. This would not do, in the long term. It was risky to let the money keep pouring into a Swedish account that followed Swedish banking rules. Agnes wanted to minimize that risk.

Hence, Switzerland.

* * *

Johan got his garlic. Now he could finish preparing the evening's three-course meal plan: a mild smoked salmon sashimi with pickled white onion and trout caviar, steak Provençale, and lemon mousse à la Parisienne. The Parisienne part he had come up with all on his own; he thought it sounded like it tasted.

These many delights would be enjoyed in camp chairs pulled up to a camping table in an IKEA parking lot in Dietlikon, a stone's throw from Zurich.

"They probably have a lot of kitchen utensils in there if there's anything you're missing," said Petra. "And they don't close for a bit."

"Thanks but no thanks," said Johan.

He didn't trust a spatula that cost nine kronor.

CHAPTER 17

Thursday, September 1, 2011

SIX DAYS TO GO

Herbert von Toll had been waiting forty years to take over the bank from his father. But the old man was still sitting in the president's chair in his president's office.

There were no statistically relevant reasons to explain why he wasn't long since dead and buried. He was ninety-six years old, smoked cigars, and took his first whiskey of the day at nine in the morning. He poured the second at ten. He said it kept his blood and his mind moving, and, to his seventy-six-year-old son's despair, he wasn't wrong. The old geezer wasn't even senile.

When a stylish lady with violet hair stepped into the small bank's offices, ninety-six-year-old Konrad immediately claimed her. But only until such time as he realized that she represented no more than five million Swedish kronor.

"Herbert!" called the old man. "Stop emptying the trash and doing other important things right this minute, I have a client for you."

The son was going to have a client! This had almost never happened before.

The lady introduced herself as Agnes Eklund from Sweden. She had a minor fortune held by the Bromma branch of Svenska Handelsbanken, outside Stockholm, and she wanted the money to vanish immediately from that account, in order to instead pop up where no Swedish authority might find it.

Herbert von Toll wasn't much more impressed than his father at the sum Mrs. Eklund represented, but he was still taken with her. The bank was so rarely brightened by female beauty. Banks and the financial sector were still the domain of men. And ninety-six-year-old geezers.

What's more, Mrs. Eklund had a warmth that was hard to resist, and apparently antennae as well.

"That man in there, the one who looks like a raisin, is that by any chance your father?"

"Uh, yes, how could you have known that, Mrs. Eklund?"

"*Widow* Eklund," said Agnes. "My husband had the good sense to pass away ages ago."

"Many congratulations, Widow Eklund," Herbert let slip. "I've long suspected that Father is immortal."

"Let's hope not," said Agnes, finding herself on the verge of offering comfort to the pleasant Herbert von Toll by sharing her unconfirmed intel that the old man would kick it in just six days. "My name is Agnes, by the way. We're not quite so formal in Sweden."

Oh my, she had dropped titles after only a few minutes.

"Herbert," said Herbert. "Very, very lovely to meet you, Widow Agnes."

"Just Agnes, please."

Herbert and Agnes were already on casual terms. He thought it was great that she was a customer of Handelsbanken, because step one was to move the whole sum from her local bank outside Stockholm to the same group's Zurich branch. Herbert intended to speak with the manager of the Swedish offices and inform them of Agnes's foreign loan commitments, assuming that his colleague in Sweden would have no reason to make a fuss.

"Except I'm not aware of any loan commitments," said Agnes.

Herbert looked sheepish. He said that the truth was relative and that the ends justified the means. For the money to end up in Zurich, the two of them could take a walk to Svenska Handelsbanken on Löwenstrasse. It wasn't far—they would just have to watch out for the treacherous trams.

"I promise to protect you."

All the pieces were in place by the end of the lunch hour. A numbered Swiss account, a shell company in the Condors, and a mutual agreement between Herbert and Agnes to meet again.

"Perhaps you could invite me to your father's funeral?" she suggested.

"I hope we don't have to wait that long," said Herbert, kissing her hand in farewell.

*　*　*

"Did it go okay?" Petra asked.

"It was great," said Agnes. "The money has disappeared from Sweden. I've even got a company now, in a country whose name I forget."

"Your own company? Why?"

"Don't ask me."

Johan was extra pleased that the group's finances were now secure, because he was planning a tasting menu extraordinaire for their arrival in Rome, and had accordingly scoured Zurich for suitable ingredients.

"They talk weird in this country. And they have a flag that looks like a hospital. But there's nothing wrong with their groceries."

CHAPTER 18

Son of a Sugar Beet Farmer

When Mikhail Gorbachev had spent enough time failing at agricultural policy, he was considered ready to do the same thing with the whole country. For in fact, no one had failed as little as him. Plus, he had some luck on his side. After Khrushchev came Brezhnev, and after he died, of course, Andropov and Chernenko did the same in turn.

The Soviet Union couldn't keep changing leaders the way most people changed shirts or underpants. Gorbachev was young, healthy, and cautious with alcohol. He was unanimously selected as the new general secretary before Chernenko's body was even stiff.

And, as always, by Gorbachev's side: future president Aleksandr Kovalchuk. Now promoted to chief advisor.

As such, he printed business cards with his real name but with eighteen different specialties. He could be anything from an expert in the oxygenation of inland seas to a doctor of metallurgy. In this way he made sure to be invited to a number of different seminars, banquets, and diplomatic events around Western Europe, without having to pay for them himself. Aleksandr thirsted for knowledge now that he must single-handedly build the new Soviet Union (with some help from his father's childhood friend).

With all due respect to Helsinki, Stockholm, Berlin,

Brussels, and Dublin, it was Paris where he learned the most and which made the greatest impression on him. It became clear to him even before he left the airport that things had gone well for the French, even though communism had never quite taken hold. There were piles of consumer goods of all sorts. That had been Stalin's weak point, in Aleksandr's opinion, that or the five million victims of his leadership. Or ten million.

During his days in the French capital, he was dazzled by toasters, pocket calculators, bread-making machines, cigarettes that didn't taste like crap, wine that didn't taste like cat piss, and cars that may have been dented here and there on account of how the French apparently liked to bump into one another in traffic, but started when they were meant to and turned off on command. There was food on the shop shelves and meat in the butcher counters. Plus, the sun was shining.

Still, the most remarkable part was that Aleksandr was at one point shown to a window table at a fancy restaurant on the Champs-Élysées without first being encouraged to tuck any bills into the maître-d's breast pocket.

In short: if it weren't for the fact that everything smelled like garlic, Aleksandr would have classified Paris a communist's dream. All this and more he shared with his general secretary upon his return to Moscow.

Gorbachev nodded thoughtfully. He too had done some traveling abroad, and had had time to reflect on one thing and the next. But was young Kovalchuk telling the truth? Had he really been given a window table at a restaurant without anyone trying to lure some dough out of him in return?

Yes, as he lived and breathed, it was true.

"On the other hand, they served snails in garlic. Do you suppose, Mr. General Secretary, that this might have been my punishment for failing to offer a bribe?"

Gorbachev didn't think so. But it was becoming ever clearer

to him that Stalin had been beyond wrong all along, on every level! He'd put all the focus into heavy, industrial production, so that each citizen who desired a toaster or even just the bread to put in it had to stand in lines miles long—or turn to the black market. Which flourished.

Aleksandr suggested that the Soviet Union simply adopt the French constitution as is, minus the dented cars, garlic, and snails.

Gorbachev put a lot of trust in his chief advisor and had done so ever since his agricultural advice resulted in the nation's reaching 38 percent of the production targets, in contrast to his predecessor's 19. But turning the Soviet Union into France overnight—wouldn't that be going too far? Wouldn't most of the Politburo have a fit at such a transformation?

The general secretary hesitated. Could they consider a stealthy transition, with just the right amount of socialism blended with other stuff?

Aleksandr was worried that his boss would chicken out before they even got going. He clearly needed a nudge in the right direction. The chief advisor said he'd noticed something during his travels, in France for instance. There you were allowed to say whatever you wanted, even in a group, even while carrying signs where you'd written rude things about someone or something you didn't like. This was called "demonstrating."

Gorbachev nodded again. Unlike his chief advisor, he was well acquainted with that tradition. But what was the advisor getting at?

Well, what if they were to go ahead and create a new sort of openness in Soviet society? Shouldn't that lead to people doing similar things to the French—walking the streets in crowds, with or without signs?

Aleksandr's boss wondered what the point would be.

The chief advisor smiled. Mr. General Secretary was surely

underestimating his people's love for him. These demonstrations would, of course, be to his advantage. Aleksandr pictured endless processions where the masses chanted "Gor-ba-chev, Gor-ba-chev" in support of the bold reforms suggested by their leader.

"That, if anything, ought to soften up the old goats in the Politburo, right?" he said.

It was taking a chance to call them that, but it hit home.

The general secretary had no choice but to pursue the image young Kovalchuk had painted for him. Thus the final Soviet Communist leader loudly taught everyone the word "glasnost." Loosely translated it meant that from that moment on, you could say whatever you wanted without being executed or even locked up.

It was the next-to-last nail in the Soviet coffin, because people took their leader at his word.

Poor Gorbachev was attacked from two directions: those who thought he'd gone too far, and those who thought he'd done too little, and that too slowly. The endless processions proclaiming that the middle of the road was the best way never materialized. All as the Vory—the ever-crafty mafia—closely studied the developing situation and maneuvered into position.

The final nail in the coffin was dubbed "perestroika": "reconstruction" or "renewal." They certainly couldn't call it "privatization," which was perhaps the dirtiest word in the Russian language. This renewal involved, among other things, making sure that Soviet civil servants at all levels were given more latitude to make their own decisions.

"Thank you kindly," said the Vory.

The result of Aleksandr Kovalchuk's politics in Gorbachev's name was that the Soviet Union split from one end to the other.

One consequence of this dissolution was that the Soviet mafia, which had thus far been largely provincial, would soon blossom and transform into internationally oriented commercial enterprises that in many respects kept their hands clean. The only thing that stayed the same as ever was the complete lack of respect for what the law actually stipulated.

CHAPTER 19

Thursday, September 1, 2011
SIX DAYS TO GO

After almost a whole day spent on finances, it was out of the question that the RV would make it to Rome before evening.

After many short tunnels and one very long one, Agnes, Petra, and Johan emerged on the other side of the Alps.

Agnes deeply regretted her actions afterward, and Petra could not understand how she'd let it happen. But in the vicinity of Bellinzona, north of Lugano, and with at least an hour left before it was time to stop for the night, Agnes's eyelids began to close again and again. The road was wide and it was mostly downhill all the way to the Italian border (whatever that had to do with it). In any case, Johan offered to take the wheel for a while, if Agnes needed to rest. And she did.

Thus the very worst person was steering the craft when the trio began to search for a good spot to spend the night on the outskirts of Como. Johan, of course, made a mess of things. First a little, then a little more. Petra attempted to guide him with her "left here, no, *that* way" and "right here, no, *right*, I said." But the journey ended with Johan running into a cyclist. Not at high speed, and not very hard, but still; it was like another nudge to the back of a caravan next to a slope.

Anyway, he managed to stop the RV after that. Petra hurried to see if they had a case of manslaughter on their hands. The recently slumbering Agnes was now wide awake.

The cyclist had hit his head and was totally shaken up. Not to mention confused.

"What happened?" he asked in perfect English.

"That's exactly what they said in one of the scenes in *The Hunt for Red October*," Johan said. "If I'm not getting my movies mixed up. Sometimes I do get them mixed up."

"I'm so glad he speaks a language you understand," Petra said angrily. "That way you can explain to him why you elected to almost kill him with your driving."

Johan hadn't elected to do any such thing. It just happened. The apparent Englishman was lying flat on his back on the pavement; he repeated his question.

"You just got run over," said Johan.

"I did? By who?"

Petra thought fast. The man clearly didn't know what had happened.

"By a black Audi with German plates," she said.

And then she turned to the astonished Johan. And said in Swedish:

"And you—zip it, starting now."

The Englishman went from lying to sitting to trying to stand up. He was wobbly, but it worked. Then he caught sight of his bicycle. The front wheel was all bent.

"My Bianchi," he said in a tone that suggested the wreck at his feet was a deceased relative.

"Terrible," said Petra. "I can't believe the way the Germans drive. Do you need to go to the hospital? Can we help you get there?"

"I'll drive, in that case," said Agnes.

No, the hospital would be overdoing it. But he would love a ride. The Englishman said he lived a few miles away, he was feeling strange, and walking the whole way seemed like it would be difficult. With his wrecked bicycle and all.

"You didn't happen to catch the license plate of that German's car?" said the black-and-blue man.

"I'm sorry," said Petra.

"I think I'm catching on to what you're thinking," Johan said in Swedish. "Should we call Preben? Maybe he still knows the license."

If Petra hadn't known Johan by this point, she wouldn't have believed her ears.

"You know *you're* the one who hit the cyclist, right? Not Dietmar, in his Audi. It's still in Bielefeld."

"Oh, yes, I know. But was just thinking . . ."

Johan fell silent for a moment before speaking again.

"Or maybe I wasn't. I think I'll go back to being quiet."

The Englishman turned out to be a Welshman, but that was close enough. His name was Gordon, he was a lawyer and had some well-to-do English-speaking types among his clientele. He was most proud of George and Amal Clooney. Then Gordon realized that this was something he probably shouldn't have shared. Discretion was a point of honor, after all.

"I wonder if I don't have concussion."

"I'm sure you do," said Agnes. "It can make anyone over-share. But please do tell us more."

She was eager for information about the high life around Lake Como. Traveling Eklund had been there a few times already, but this was the first for Agnes.

"*That* George Clooney?" said Petra.

"'Congratulations, you're a dead man,'" said Johan.

"Huh?" said Welshman Gordon.

"*Ocean's Eleven*. I know a bunch of movies by heart. And I can cook. And mess things up."

* * *

The three Swedes helped the Welshman through the door to his five-room place with its terrace and lake views. Johan took over the kitchen while the others settled in on the terrace. He fetched some ingredients from the RV.

"You're all very thoughtful," said Gordon as he was served an appetizing whiskey. "Kindhearted, even. Not like that German who ran me over. Hope he sleeps like crap tonight."

There was no way for the others to know, but the truth was that Dietmar Sommer was doing just that in the hotel he'd been banished to by his wife. Who had, incidentally, already talked to Kajsa on the phone.

Johan had to run back and forth between the cupboard and fridge in the RV and what little Gordon already had in his kitchen. But the three-course meal would have been a lifelong memory for Gordon if it weren't for the fact that he hardly remembered anything the next morning.

What had *happened*? Wasn't he run over by an RV? Which they said was an Audi? And then they drove him home in the Audi, or RV. How did he end up eating a meal after that? Wasn't it the man in the Audi that looked like an RV who cooked it? In Gordon's kitchen? Where he had hardly anything but some canned goods? How could it have been so delicious? Had any of this even happened?

Gordon decided it must have been a dream. He went out on the terrace to have a cigarette and calm down.

There stood his beloved Bianchi. With its mangled front wheel.

CHAPTER 20

Friday, September 2, 2011

FIVE DAYS TO GO

As the Welsh lawyer stubbed out his cigarette, canceled that morning's meeting with George Clooney, and went back to sleep, Agnes, Petra, and Johan were already many miles away, headed for Rome.

"Nice guy," said Petra. "And he had so many exciting stories to tell. To think that the Clooneys have a nonprofit foundation to fight corruption all over the world. That's really inspiring. Not that they'll have time to get much done in the five days that are left, but still."

Agnes noted that the countries the not-yet-established Clooney Foundation for Justice planned to focus on were South Sudan, Congo, the Central African Republic—and the Condors.

"Wonder if that isn't where all my money is," she said.

"As long as your credit card works, it can be wherever it wants," was Petra's opinion.

"Gordon mentioned Eastern Europe too," Johan recalled. "Where's that?"

"Just east of Western Europe," said Petra.

Johan refrained from asking the obvious follow-up question.

* * *

They still had over 370 miles to go to their final destination. Agnes had planned to wrap up the previous evening by Googling a good place to park an RV in Rome. But when the last thing she heard from the prophet was that they should get an extra early start the next morning, since they would soon only have five days left, it was as though she got sick of that sort of talk once and for all. Life was smiling upon her after all these years—couldn't they just let her enjoy it in peace and quiet? What all doomsday prophets had in common, since the dawn of time, was, of course, that their predictions were wrong.

The violet-haired skeptic had lived too long to believe all the nonsense around her. She couldn't have been more than thirty when her husband lamented Sweden's switch to driving on the right. He argued that Dödersjö, of all places, ought to be exempted. The principal reason—according to him—was that otherwise he and his Saab might risk a head-on crash with Farmer Fagerlund's tractor when they met on the only real street in the parish. Because who could believe the farmer would switch sides of the road from one day to the next? Did he even own a radio that could tell him what was going on?

In reality, the manufacturer had listened too well to the rumors that significant life changes resulted in an increased risk of stress-related cancer. He didn't want to switch from left-hand to right-hand driving because it might make him sick. At which point he stepped on a nail and died instead.

Her memories of the past prompted Agnes to read up on Petra's pet topic. She memorized the most crucial bits and wrote down the rest on a Post-it note.

With many long hours to go before they reached the Italian capital, Agnes figured she might as well share what was on her mind. When it had been quiet in the front seat for long enough, she said, as if out of the blue:

"The end of the world? Seriously, Petra. I can't find a single person online who says it's going to happen on September 7, 2011, at nine twenty p.m."

The prophet sat up straighter. It was as though she had been waiting for the discussion that ensued.

"Plus or minus a minute or so," she said. "Why would anyone be saying so? Were you expecting me to take out an ad?"

"No, I was thinking that maybe other people had been sitting around doing the same calculations, but if they were, none of them came to your same conclusion."

Petra was getting Academy of Sciences vibes. People were so stupid. Well, at least Agnes was *talking* to her, she had to give their driver that.

"My dear Agnes," she said. "The atmosphere is not an easy thing to understand. Closest to the earth's surface we have the troposphere, then the stratosphere, and after that the mesosphere and even further up, the thermosphere."

"And?"

"These spheres are at different altitudes. Partially in relation to one another, but it also varies based on which part of the world you find yourself."

"I find myself in the vicinity of Bologna, as do you. What's it like here?"

"I haven't studied Bologna specifically, but to give a rough estimate, the troposphere likely extends about seven miles over our heads. It's a little different at the poles. When I said that the whole world would end simultaneously, that was only partially true. But the difference should be no greater than a few tenths of a second from place to place. Probably more like a few hundredths."

"Can't we head to where the earth will survive the longest?" said Johan, who had overheard the conversation from the kitchen.

"You're saying you'd prefer an extra hundredth of a second?"

"Preferably several of them."

"Do you know how much a hundredth is?"

Johan thought a hundredth sounded like a lot, but he sensed from Petra's tone that it was really quite small instead. He said he was busy folding napkins.

Petra continued.

"In any case, the troposphere isn't the problem here."

"That's good to hear," said Agnes.

"It's the thermosphere. The sun's ultraviolet rays cause ionization there. The word 'thermosphere' comes from the Greek *thermos*, which means heat."

"Weren't you talking about cold?" said Johan. "Heat sounds better."

"Three thousand, six hundred degrees?"

Petra sighed. Talking to Agnes and Johan was like talking to a glass of milk and a paper plate.

"Forget the technical stuff," said Agnes. "What I keep coming back to is that you're not the first to discover that everything is simply going to end one day. Humanity has made it through quite a few last-day-of-everythings, and yet here we sit, breathing and talking."

"I'm standing," said Johan.

"You may sit, if you like."

Petra wondered which ones Agnes had in mind, more specifically.

"There are any number of examples."

"Then pick one."

Agnes was holding her Post-it note discreetly between thumb and index finger of her left hand, which was resting on the RV's steering wheel.

"Well, according to a Spanish monk, the end of the world was going to happen on April 6 in the year 793. It kind of didn't."

"Are you comparing my scientific knowledge with that of an

THE PROPHET AND THE IDIOT

eighth-century Spanish monk? I'd be willing to bet he brought Jesus into the mix, right?"

Agnes had to admit he did. The Messiah was supposed to reappear that day, and turn back at the door, taking the whole world with him. But how about Christopher Columbus, then? He claimed that Judgment Day would happen sometime in 1656.

"You mean the guy who couldn't tell America from India?"

Agnes wouldn't give in. And her memory was solid. Plus she had the Post-it.

"Jacob Bernoulli!"

"Who?"

"A prominent man of science! No religion this time. No 'I-can-just-feel-it.' Pure analysis!"

"And what did that analysis say?"

"That it would be sayonara in April, 1719. A comet was supposed to strike the earth. 'Poof!'"

"Comets are tricky to predict. A near miss doesn't put dinner on the table. When earth's gravitational pull begins to affect whatever's heading our way, we have to recalculate. And before we have time to do that, the comet has whizzed on by. It's smart to warn folks about comets, but only an *idiot* would carve anything in stone."

"Did someone call for me?" Johan said.

"No. What's for dinner tonight?"

"It's a secret."

Agnes had more to read from her Post-it note.

"Jeane Dixon, 1962. Notable astronomer, if my understanding is correct."

"No—notably bonkers astrologer," said Petra. "What else? Hit me with everything you've got."

Agnes thought of all the poor Jehovah's Witnesses who had to come to terms with at least twenty ends of the world in the past century. She didn't know if it was Jehovah himself whispering in the Witnesses' ears, but just imagine being so wrong twenty times in a row.

She knew Petra would dismiss them for religious reasons, so there was no point in bringing it up. But maybe Harold Camping, the famous numerologist, would do.

"He's been wrong three times out of four, so far. The fourth time is in October this year."

"Then I expect he'll be seriously bummed on September 7, if he has time," said Petra. "You're not planning to bring up the Maya and 2012, are you?"

Agnes had considered it, but now she refrained. Instead, she reminded Petra of the Russian named Kuznetsov who had convinced a few dozen poor souls to lock themselves in a cave to escape the end of the world in May of 2008. They brought six months' worth of food. Agnes didn't understand what they planned to do after that.

"What kind of food was it?" Johan asked.

She didn't know.

"Shall I explain what will happen to the electrical charge of air molecules in the thermosphere under a given condition, at a point in time I have personally scientifically determined, and what it will lead to in the long term?" Petra asked.

"No thanks," said Agnes. "I'm sure everything will be fine."

CHAPTER 21

Friday, September 2, 2011

FIVE DAYS TO GO

The driver decided it was best just to accept the bad with the good. Petra was allowing all of existence to rest on a sixty-four-step equation that no sensible person could comprehend. And Johan—well, who knew a person could be so talented and talentless at the same time.

Still, together they had provided Agnes with a life that crackled with excitement. What was it the kids said these days? Chillax?

With an hour and a half left to the Italian capital, the violet-haired chauffeur wanted to stretch her legs. Besides, it was time to stop for gas.

She turned off at a gas station near Orvieto, filled the tank, and parked. She was feeling hungry.

"Do you have a sandwich, Johan? Or anything, really."

"How about pine-needle-smoked celeriac, grilled whole, with foie gras and apple? A Värmland specialty. Where is Värmland?"

Speaking of talented and talentless at the same time, Agnes thought.

"Värmland isn't far from Dalsland, which isn't far from Bohuslän, which isn't far from Gothenburg. A simple sandwich would have sufficed."

Meanwhile, Petra was standing outside the RV, doing some gymnastic exercises with the aid of the baseball bat. It was easy to get stiff, with all that sitting.

An Italian motorist in a Porsche honked at her, feeling that she was hindering his free passage. Then he made the mistake of rolling down the window and saying something fresh. Not that the prophet understood what he was saying, but there was no mistaking his tone of voice.

Petra was filled with that same old new urge to set things right. She approached the motorist, apologized profusely for standing in his way, and asked if there was anything he felt he had to get off his chest. By the way, did he speak English? If not, he could disregard this whole conversation.

The Porsche man's knowledge of foreign languages was limited, but not nonexistent. He was in dental prosthetics sales, in Great Britain among other places. Accordingly, he knew such English phrases as "complete dentures," "fixed bridge," and "implant consultation." He had a harder time with many other words. Worse still was his mood. He had just argued with his wife. Or, she had argued with him. For the thousandth time. Most of all he would have liked to smash in her teeth, if only he had dared and if only he wasn't aware of how expensive it would be in the long run.

"Couldn't you exercise somewhere else?" he said gruffly. "I'm in a hurry."

Petra laid the fat end of the baseball bat against her shoulder and smiled.

"I apologize for my cluelessness," she said. "Obviously I should have chosen to work out on the other side of the RV. But how do you view your own aggression? And how would you have handled this situation if you knew you only had a few days left to live?"

The prophet was standing beside the driver's window, but the irascible Porsche man's seat placed him much lower behind the wheel. This put him at a disadvantage he wasn't comfortable with. Add to this the fact that he thought the woman with the baseball bat over her shoulder had just threatened his life. *How* long had she just said he had to live?

In all situations aside from those involving his wife, the dental prosthetics salesman had lived by the motto that a good offense was the best defense. Accordingly, he said "*Cazzo!*" and flung open his door with such force that it knocked the woman and her baseball bat to the ground. A second later, he found himself outside the car, bent over the eliminated threat. To be safe, he confiscated her weapon.

While he was searching for the right English words to say to the presumably lethal but disarmed woman, he took a frying pan to the head. Johan had been busily working on his pine-needle-smoked celeriac when he spotted a strange man through the RV window. The stranger was bent over his prostrate friend and life companion, with a baseball bat in his hand. A few instants later, the Italian was the prostrate one, while Petra had got to her feet.

"Thanks," she said. "Nice frying pan."

"Cast iron," said Johan. "From Ronneby Bruk. Good quality isn't cheap."

Agnes came out and discovered the mayhem. She felt that this particular moment was life at its most exciting. Given that their vehicle had falsified plates, and that she had no driver's license, she was less interested in what Stooge 1 and Stooge 2 had done than she was in getting out of there.

"Boarding is *this instant*!" she said. "We will depart in ten seconds."

* * *

Petra was relieved that she had time to see, in the rearview mirror, that the Italian was able to get to his feet with support from his Porsche. Admittedly, he would kick the bucket along with everyone else in just a few days, but there was no reason she and Johan should have sped up the process.

Traveling Eklund had already experienced the Italian capital three times, but this would be Agnes's premier visit. Now she was behind the wheel, her eyes darting anxiously toward the rearview mirror to check for Italian police. She listened with only half an ear to Petra's description of what had happened; something about how she was having a friendly chat with a man who had interrupted her workout session, at which point the man had attacked her out of the blue.

Instead, Agnes was summarizing the past week from her point of view. Petra's and Johan's peace tour of Europe had thus far resulted in one wrecked vehicle, one head-butted security service officer, one run-over Welsh legal advisor, and one knocked-out Italian in a parking lot. And they hadn't even reached the man they really should be talking sense into. Agnes said that if necessary she could go along with the idea that the world would end in a few days, and if so good for it. But did they really have to dismantle it ahead of time?

Petra said she had forgotten about Dietmar in Bielefeld. Hadn't they solved that issue in the most calm way imaginable? Johan said nothing; he was busy seasoning his cast-iron frying pan from Ronneby Bruk, apologizing to it as he did.

When enough time had passed without the Italian police popping up in Agnes's rearview mirror, she calmed down. She said she appreciated that none of the days had been at all uneventful since she met Petra and Johan, but that anyone who was able to formulate sixty-four-step equations would perhaps also be capable of finding the right word in the right order during their next encounter with any representative member of humanity, so that they wouldn't all be thrown in jail before they reached their destination.

Petra still considered herself innocent of the incident at the parking lot. But what Agnes had just said sounded quite exciting. A foolproof equation, but with words instead of numbers.

"I think I'll try to put together a flowchart of some sort," she said. "To make sure the words definitely end up in the right places. Something like that would also be helpful to Johan when he meets his brother. None of us wants there to be frying pans flying around outside the Swedish embassy, am I right?"

Agnes didn't know if she'd made things better or worse. But since there was nothing to suggest the Italian police were on their heels, she elected to keep "chillaxing." Even more so, given the activity she suspected was taking place in the back of the RV. Apparently Johan had forgotten the recent drama and was completely absorbed in what he had planned for the evening.

*　*　*

Petra steered from the passenger seat as Agnes used her tablet to search for a good spot to park the RV in Rome. She found a relatively centrally located campground.

The campground had a space for the RV, but it was cramped and tight. Petra promised not to argue with the neighbors, at least not before her flowchart was finished.

"What do you think of always beginning with: 'My dear sir?' Alternatively, 'My dear madam?' Then again, that doesn't sound as good. I'll keep thinking."

Johan was taking his time in the kitchen. He said that tomorrow was the Big Day and that deserved a little extra something on the table.

Petra thought that "a little extra something" was what she'd been served for every single meal since she and Johan met, but she understood things had reached a whole new level now. She wasn't sure if she'd ever seen so many utensils on one table setting.

"No point in doing things halfway," said Johan, passing his friends a handwritten menu. "You'll have to share this one, because it took me fifteen minutes to write."

RESTAURANT RV THIS EVENING

*Cold-pressed rapeseed-oil ice cream with Russian caviar
and fresh walnuts*

*Crisp pear straws with pickled kohlrabi
and horseradish*

*Crunchy potato cones filled with smoked halibut
and lumpfish roe*

*Drink: 1995 Charles Heidsieck
Blanc des Millénaires*

*

*Confit of rabbit with sautéed foie gras, lemon thyme,
and toasted fennel seeds*

*Consommé of baked and fermented tomato, fermented aji
amarillo chilis, and cold-pressed rapeseed oil*

*Vegetable ragu with baked tomato, pickled onion, cucumber,
green peas, and almonds, topped with herbs
and tomato tuiles*

*Drink: 2008 Würzburger Stein Silvaner Erste Lage
Juliusspital*

*

*Raw-fried lobster tails with carrot beurre blanc and fennel
crudités, topped with fresh-picked dill*

Drink: 2001 Domaine Langlois-Château,
Saumur Blanc Vieilles Vignes

*

Marrow-smoked fillet of pike perch with poached white
turnip and watercress sabayon, topped with caviar

Drink: 2004 Joseph Drouhin Chassagne-Montrachet

*

Roasted whole pigeon with a blood-orange glaze
and a toasted fennel- and coriander-seed rub

Yellow endive salad baked in apple juice,
honey, and lemon, with a ramp filling

Lightly caramelized crème of red apples

Sauce of roasted garlic with blood orange,
bay leaves, and chicken

Red endive and ramp salad

Drink: 1998 Brunello di Montalcino Pianrosso,
Ciacci Piccolomini

*

Herb sorbet with lemon meringue and
preserved peach, flavored with champagne
and lemon verbena

Drink: 2002 Château Suduiraut

The self-taught chef apologized once more that Agnes and Petra didn't each get a copy of the menu, but he still had a few things to see to before it was time to come to the table.

"A few things to see to?" said Petra. "When did you start on this? A week ago?"

Johan said that anyone who took a closer look at the courses would likely find a shortcut here or there. And, to be frank, some cheating. There was one thing he was prepared to admit up front:

"After all, the dill can't be *that* freshly picked, given that it's been two days since I bought it."

On the whole, though, he didn't think he had too much to be ashamed of. When he got the chance, he would be happy to develop a few ideas around long-term planning in the kitchen, but at the moment the kitchen in question was calling his name.

"I'll be back in fifteen. Don't put away too much wine while I'm gone."

* * *

The trio didn't get further than the rabbit confit before Petra had to say it again.

"I don't understand how you do it. How do you come up with these flavors? How do you make it all go together so perfectly?"

Agnes nodded and chimed in.

"I was proud of my chicken casserole all those years, but this—this is otherworldly."

"It is?" Johan blurted, before he realized that this was the same praise as before, just in different words.

Now he supposed he had to accept that they weren't saying it just to say it. They really thought it!

"Master chef and genius. That's me," he said proudly, raising his glass of Würzburger.

"Oh my," said Agnes, when she tasted the wine.

"Fruity, with certain floral hints," said Johan. "If you try, you'll taste yellow pear and honeydew and a few other things too. The rabbit would have been proud to be in this company, if only . . . well. It weren't dead."

Belittled by his brother from the day he learned to walk, so thoroughly convinced that he was incapable of learning anything that he didn't even try. Instead he became obsessed with flavors and aromas, on their own and in combination with others.

But since he met Petra, he hadn't been called an idiot, an imbecile, or stupid even once. Except for when Fredrik called while they were sitting around Agnes's kitchen table. Johan's self-confidence was growing day by day.

Even as the gaps in his knowledge remained.

Around the time Johan was serving the herb sorbet with lemon meringue, the friends got to talking about their strategy for the next day—their meeting with Fredrik, the very reason for all that had developed over the last week. It had to take place at the Swedish embassy, because no one had any way of knowing where he lived. Little brother would give big brother what for to his heart's content. But how?

"There's so much I want to say now that I've started to understand, a little bit, anyway. I think I want to start with our Saturday sweets. Gummy rats and raspberry boats every Saturday for as long as Mom was alive. Fredrik took it all. I still don't know what a gummy rat tastes like, but I did find a raspberry boat on the floor once while I was vacuuming."

"You ate it?" Agnes said.

Johan nodded.

"Too much corn syrup."

Johan's point was that he, a man who was otherwise clueless, knew that children were supposed to like both gummy rats and raspberry boats. And that Fredrik had fooled him by letting him think he was doing Johan's teeth a favor by eating them all up for him.

But then the bamboozled little brother realized he would never win a raspberry-boat debate against Fredrik. His big brother was too slick for that. After all, he was the one who knew all the words.

As Johan talked about Saturday sweets, Agnes and Petra tried the final course.

"Sweet baby Jesus!" said Petra.

"Well put," said Agnes. "And I agree."

"The background flavors are champagne and lemon verbena," said Johan.

"You're nuts!" said Agnes.

Johan gazed at her sadly. Petra jumped in to explain what Agnes meant. That what he had created was crazy good. Not that it meant Johan himself was crazy. More like . . . well, a master chef and genius.

Johan was smiling now. A new, confident smile.

Back to the problem at hand. Petra wondered what would happen if they skipped all the historical details and bet on the genius part? If Johan had been an "idiot" in Fredrik's eyes all his life, couldn't little brother just walk up and slay him with a complicated recipe?

Agnes said she understood what Petra was getting at.

"Not me," said Johan.

Petra sank her own idea by thinking it through a little more. Shoving a menu in Fredrik's face wouldn't help. Wouldn't it take the whole camp table full of courses, anyway? And what made them think such a thing would cause Fredrik to capitulate, no matter how divine it tasted and smelled? After all, he'd been fed fancy food all these years, and his response had been to complain and deal out cuffs to the ear.

They were at a standstill.

Petra felt it was her responsibility to make the meeting between Johan and Fredrik a success. The definition of which was that big brother learn a thing or two. But after hearing how Fredrik dealt with "the idiot" over the phone, while the crew was still stuck on an island outside Stockholm, it didn't seem likely that their next conversation would go any better. And Johan insisted that it was up to him and no one else to clean up his own past. Thus a smirking Petra half a step behind him, with a baseball bat over her shoulder, was out of the question.

She had almost come to regret riding in on her high horse in the case of manure-entrepreneur Preben. He wanted to punch that stupid Dietmar in the face, and she wanted to talk sense into him. None of that would work now that they were faced with reality. But Fredrik wasn't a shot-putter. And it seemed unlikely Johan could knock him off his pedestal with words.

It turned out Agnes's thoughts were on the same track. She said that, on the one hand, Johan hadn't learned anything from all those slapped ears over the years. This lent support to Petra's theory that people ought to use their words rather than their fists.

On the other hand, she was happy to use her deceased spouse as an example. He was beyond stingy and kept Agnes unhappy for decades. It had been impossible to talk him into living and not just striving.

"I truly tried, but I didn't get anywhere."

"Do you regret not slapping him in retrospect? Or what are you trying to say right now?"

Petra was surprised at her own question.

Agnes took in this thought with a grin:

"Well, you might say he slapped himself, in a sense, when he stepped on a nail that went straight through his foot. Not that he learned his lesson in that moment, but I clearly recall that once he was delirious with fever he regretted saving those three liters of gas by refusing to drive to Växjö Clinic."

This last bit wasn't true. The manufacturer took his stinginess to the grave, but all's fair in love and war, and this was all about getting results. For Agnes had realized what she wanted to gain from this ongoing discussion. In the name of getting results, it was okay to stretch the truth. Or even pretend to believe the prophet's prophecy.

Agnes continued her line of reasoning:

"Thanks to your scientifically proven doomsday calculations, Petra, we know for sure that Fredrik will avoid up to six years in prison—that is, what he should get for aggravated theft of Johan's millions from the sale of their apartment. Doesn't that give us a certain amount of latitude à la Preben?"

Petra thanked her violet-haired ally for her constructive input. And she was extra appreciative of Agnes's indirect acceptance of the incontrovertible truth about the imminent end of the world. She was inclined to agree with Agnes's assessment, given the circumstances. But first she wanted to hear the protagonist's take on the matter.

Johan had sat quietly while being reminded of Fredrik's many slaps to his face.

"Two or three a week for fifteen or twenty years," he said. "How many is that?"

He turned to the prophet, who said that the input values Johan had provided did not allow her to give an exact answer. But it seemed Fredrik had assaulted his brother somewhere in the region of two thousand times.

"What are you trying to get at with this, friend? Aside from pointing out how terrible it is, of course."

Both Agnes and Petra were hoping for something; neither of them knew quite what.

Johan said he had practiced slapping Fredrik's ears right back in his imagination, but it never really worked, not even in his mind. The blows from Fredrik came from slightly above, since he was a good few inches taller. The same maneuver from the opposite direction would probably land on his chin.

"So you don't think hitting back will work?"

Petra could hear the disappointment in her own voice.

"I didn't say that. I heard what you were saying about nails through a foot, but where can we get hold of a nail and how would I get him to stand on it? What would you say if I made a fist instead and punched him in the nose?"

CHAPTER 22

Son of a Sugar Beet Farmer

In time, Aleksandr Kovalchuk abandoned Gorbachev, quickly got better at tolerating larger quantities of vodka, and charmed his way in with Boris Yeltsin, the first president of the new Russia.

Yeltsin was so impressed by young Kovalchuk's drinking talents that he gave him even greater responsibility for the new ways than Gorbachev had dared. One day, alongside his morning vodka, Aleksandr was tasked with plugging as many loopholes as he could in the fragile and hastily cooked-up Russian constitution. A free-market economy in combination with laws and rules that were not set up for any such thing meant it was nearly impossible for someone with a sufficiently skilled lawyer to do anything illegal. And if he did, there was always bribery. More and more fancy Western cars were turning up on Russian streets. A considerable number of them were owned by higher-ups in the justice ministry. Most of those higher-ups took home salaries that wouldn't cover more than a tank of gas for the car in question, and not very often at that.

By comparison, the American Wild West was a bastion of law and order.

While the state, in its eagerness to privatize, sold off hundreds of thousands of institutions by way of a complicated voucher system that only the very most gifted and cunning understood, Aleksandr set about reforming the Russian taxation system. He patched and mended, but there were so many numbers to weigh against one another. For the first time, he had reason to regret that his university degree in economics was nothing more than a sham.

As a result, things went so poorly that anyone who followed the new rules to the letter would have to pay 118 percent tax on their earnings, once all the exemptions and additions in Aleksandr's attempts at reform were taken into account.

Of course, no one was that stupid. Thus the very rich didn't bother to pay taxes at all. Instead they bought new lawyers for the money. To the extent that they themselves weren't members of the mafia, they made sure to keep the Vory and others in a good mood in order to protect their own good health.

Mother Russia was languishing more and more. These days you could buy anything, just like in Paris, and yet not. In 1992, the price of consumer goods and services rose twenty-five-fold. Anyone who sadly had trouble staying afloat before that found himself twenty-five times sadder in just ten months.

Those at the top within the Vory realized they were about to take over vast parts of the country, but they needed the local mafia leaders on their side—and those leaders complained vociferously. How much could you demand to protect a regular old barbershop when the price of a trim was doubling every two weeks? And could you even demand *anything* when people couldn't afford a haircut?

The top dogs of the mafia held a strategy meeting. This couldn't go on.

After some mature consideration, they decided *not* to defy Yeltsin. The state may have been half falling apart, but the Vory knew that even a wounded wolf could tear out your throat. The old communists had years of experience in keeping the mafia under tight control. Should they be underestimated now, just because they were bleeding? No, that would be stupid.

But Yeltsin's damned advisor! The one with his 118 percent taxation. The one who had shaken things up to such an extent that corruption would soon no longer be profitable. The one who refused an audience with the Vory, no matter what they called themselves.

Such a stupid bastard, he didn't know who he was dealing with.

And for that very reason: he would soon be as dead as he was stupid.

The decision was unanimous.

You might think the Vory's aversion to Yeltsin's chief advisor wasn't actually well motivated. After all, it was that very advisor's cheerful perestroika advice that had led to 80 percent of the new, capitalist Russia landing in the hands of the Vory and their collaborators. After glasnost and perestroika, it was time for the world to learn the term "oligarch."

But the death warrant had been issued, and that was that. In 999 cases out of a thousand.

Aleksandr Kovalchuk happened to be the thousandth.

Which is why, years later, things turned out as they did for Agnes, Johan, and Petra.

CHAPTER 23

Saturday, September 3, 2011

FOUR DAYS TO GO

Johan was about to back off the idea of taking a fist to Fredrik's nose. For he had just remembered what Agnes had said about the punishment that might await Preben if he resorted to similar measures in Bielefeld.

The violet-haired schemer had already been stretching the truth when she said her stingy manufacturer had learned something from that rusty nail as he lay on his deathbed. Now she thought it was in everyone's best interest if she stretched it even more.

Johan certainly knew his way around food (and American movies). Petra knew all about mathematics and physics. Agnes herself understood a great deal about the power of the internet. Just take the nonchalant way in which she glanced through the Swedish criminal code and convinced Johan and Petra that a punch in the nose, given that it resulted in nothing more than a nosebleed and minor fracture, in this particular case and given this particular context, would be considered *self-defense.*

"It's crystal clear, according to chapter twenty-four, paragraph one," she lied.

"Self-defense?" said Johan.

Self-delusion, thought Petra, but she nodded in agreement.

"That means that if you're backed into a corner and have

no choice but to fight your way out, it's not illegal even if someone else should happen to get a nosebleed along the way."

Johan's eyes sparkled.

"Self-defense," he said. "A massive self-defense, right in the nose, blood and everything. That's what we'll do!"

*   *   *

Sweden's embassy in Rome was located in a quiet neighborhood of grand buildings, east of the most central parts of the capital. They had no problem finding a parking spot for the RV, with a view of the entrance.

The embassy building was four stories high and had an orange plaster facade. Unfortunately, the whole thing was surrounded by an iron fence that was both sharp and tall. Climbing over it to sneak up on Fredrik was not an option.

The iron gate in the middle of the fence would be just as difficult to penetrate. Unclear whether it was locked. Presumably it was, because Petra discovered an intercom on one of the brick pillars the iron gate was attached to.

It would probably be possible to talk their way in, but that would mean Johan's encounter with Fredrik would take place indoors. After the unanimously agreed-upon and necessary punch in the nose, it might be tricky to get away. The same logistical problem as with Dietmar Sommer, that is. Before the discovery that he was a shot-putter.

"Can't I just claim myself according to paragraph twenty-four of the defense code?" Johan said.

"Chapter twenty-four, paragraph one," said Agnes, "of the criminal code. You'll have to practice saying that. Preferably in Italian as well. I think it would be better if we escaped first and gave our reasons later. Best of all would be to meet him out on the street. Near the getaway vehicle."

"Wonder where he lives?" said Johan.

"Not in an RV, I'm sure," said Petra. "Sixty million kronor will get you more than that, even in Rome."

It was eleven in the morning. There wasn't much traffic through the gate. None at all, in fact. Suddenly, Petra was struck by a horrible realization. Followed by an even more horrible one.

"Dammit, it's Saturday," she said.

"How's that?" said Johan.

He wasn't used to hearing Petra swear.

"And tomorrow is Sunday!"

Agnes clarified:

"She means that the embassy is probably closed. Not just today, but also tomorrow."

So, it seemed, they would not be able to confront Fredrik until Monday at the earliest. With two days left of absolutely everything, the margin of error was getting to be too narrow for Petra's liking. She considered whether they might drive around Rome looking for Fredrik, but she quickly cast that idea aside. Two and a half million citizens, and only God and the pope knew how many tourists besides.

Their only option, and it was a tremendously awful one, was to spend the rest of Saturday and all of Sunday outside the embassy if necessary. *Someone* would have to come or go over the weekend, and that someone ought to know who Fredrik Löwenhult was—and where they could find him.

As it approached seven in the evening, Johan raised the question of where they stood in the hunt for Fredrik's nose in relation to the absolutely essential dinner he had already planned. Agnes elected not to interfere. Petra would have been happy to stick around a while longer, but after all: Johan's fist, Johan's decision.

"Okay, we'll drop this for today. But how about we rise before dawn tomorrow?"

Johan returned to the kitchen at the rear of the RV. Agnes began to steer them back home to the campground. And noted Petra's obvious disappointment.

Saturday evening, late summer, vacation season. It was clear to see among their nearest camp neighbors that a party was in the works. Even the night before, Petra had muttered that one or two of them could use a corrective conversation. And this time she was in a bad mood as well. Agnes feared another Porsche-type incident. Which was more than she was willing to take part in.

"You're not planning to start any fights, are you?" she said to Petra.

"I never fight. Besides, my flowchart is ready. Shall I read it to you?"

"Absolutely not."

On their way back from the embassy they had taken the opportunity to get provisions. They blew a not-insignificant portion of Agnes's assets on lightweight clothes for the heat, food and drink, even more food and drink, as well as a proper grill for outdoor use. They could always leave it behind after their task was finished. Or donate it to a rowdy neighbor.

The fourth-to-last night of everything's existence was a late one. It was rounded off with grilled food and anesthetics galore to counteract Petra's frustrations. Or, as Johan called it:

"La Rioja Alta, Gran Reserva 904."

CHAPTER 24

Sunday, September 4, 2011

THREE DAYS TO GO

The average Italian is in the habit of having later nights than a Swede. The fact that it was also Sunday explained why the RV, with Agnes behind the wheel, was nearly alone on the ring road around Rome at five minutes to six in the morning. The trio reached the embassy at quarter past. It seemed highly unlikely that Fredrik or anyone else would have arrived before them.

Quarter past six became quarter past seven with no signs of life. And quarter past eight. Petra was getting increasingly difficult to deal with—until the truly sensational moment when an employee actually tumbled in around eight thirty. And soon, another. And two more.

"On a Sunday?" Petra said, as surprised as she was filled with a certain amount of hope.

Agnes wondered if they shouldn't stop one of them and ask about Fredrik, but Petra advised against it. If four had appeared, there would probably be more coming. Otherwise they could ring the bell and take it from there.

From the RV they had a good view of the iron gate just ahead and across the street. But only Johan recognized the right person.

"There!" he suddenly said, at 8:56.

"Where?"

"Coming down the pavement, by the red car."

Fredrik was a hundred yards away. Ninety. Eighty-five.

"What do we do now?" said his little brother.

Petra realized they could have discussed the details the night before, instead of competing to see who could drink the most wine. Incidentally, she was fairly sure that she had won.

Fifty yards left. Soon big brother would vanish through the gate and create new problems for the trio. Petra took command and made a snap decision.

"You get out there! Get out there and give him a good belt. Right in the nose. Hurry! And hurry back too."

Johan stumbled out of the RV and across the street. He reached the iron gate to the embassy at the same time as his brother.

"Hi, Fredrik," he said.

Big brother was astounded!

"Idiot? What on earth are you doing here?"

Johan lost a bit of his determination. The very fact of Fredrik calling him what he'd always called him transported them both back to the days of old.

"Are you here to ask for money, or something? How did you even find your way here? Last I knew you couldn't find Germany on a map of Central Europe."

"I know where Bielefeld is," Johan said, "and that Western Europe is west of Eastern Europe."

He balled his right hand into a fist. Was he supposed to punch first and explain later? Or explain first and punch later? Or punch twice with no explanation? What would Petra have done?

None of the above happened. The brothers were interrupted by a third person.

"Good morning, Fredrik. Who's this you're talking to, if I may ask?"

Fredrik lost his ability to speak . . .

"Aren't you going to introduce us?"

. . . but had no choice but to recover it.

"Certainly . . . This is my brother . . . Johan. All the way from Sweden. And this is Ambassador Ronny Guldén, my boss."

"Nice to meet you, Johan," said the upbeat and popular ambassador, extending his hand in greeting. "What brings you to Rome? Brotherly love alone, or will you have some time left over for sightseeing?"

Johan told him the truth. After all, it was best not to lie.

"I'm here to punch my brother in the nose. Once or twice—I was just pondering which it would be when you came by, Mr. Ambassador."

"What?" said Fredrik.

Ambassador Guldén was delighted.

"Brotherly love! You're too much. I myself have a beloved little brother. But I've never called him anything but 'you little shit.'"

Ronny Guldén chuckled at his own tale. And then he thought of something:

"Fredrik and I have a planning meeting with some tired old ladies and gentlemen at the embassy now, at nine. It's a special day today. But, Johan: couldn't you come back this afternoon at four? It so happens we're holding our annual ambassador social mixer then. I know, it's Sunday, but this is what tradition dictates. There'll be hors d'oeuvres, champagne, and boring diplomat talk half the night, or, if we're really unlucky, the whole night. Won't you join us? If you'd like to be a little bored, that is?"

The ambassador chuckled at himself again.

"No, I'm sure he won't want to join," Fredrik began as he felt the panic creeping in.

Was one of the dumbest people in Sweden going to be allowed to mingle with his boss and the entire diplomatic corps of Rome? That could be a threat to Fredrik's entire career.

"Yes, I'd love to," said Johan, so seriously that it sounded like a joke. "I can always break his nose during the hors d'oeuvres. You don't happen to have the recipe, do you, Mr. Ambassador?"

"You're hilarious," said Ambassador Guldén. "It was nice to meet you, we'll talk more this evening. Come back at four. I'll add you to the guest list. Let me guess—you have the same last name as your brother? Dress code jacket. Come along, dear third secretary, I've got a planning meeting to lead and you have a photocopier to operate."

* * *

"What happened?" said Petra. "Who was that man who showed up and ruined everything?"

"What's a third secretary?" asked Johan.

"Oh, probably a diplomatic title."

"And what does 'dress code jacket' mean?"

"That you're supposed to wear a jacket. Or rather, a suit. Why do you ask?"

CHAPTER 25

Sunday, September 4, 2011

THREE DAYS TO GO

Petra decided Agnes should decide.

They ended up with a dark-gray Canali suit, a patterned silver tie, and calf-leather Branchini shoes, a cheeky design with navy blue at the toe, shifting through light blue, gray, purple, red, black, and bright yellow closest to the ankle.

"Stripy shoes?" said Johan.

"You don't understand all this," said Agnes.

She had just dressed him up in brands she could have made money on if Traveling Eklund were a man. Agnes considered whether she should give her alias a brother but quickly dropped the idea. There was enough to deal with as it was.

Petra was feeling increasingly troubled. The days were flying by. Then again, they now had access to the embassy. Johan's primary task for the evening should be getting Fredrik to tell him where he lived. For just like Preben, they would prefer not to meet their maker in a jail cell. It would be much safer to beat big brother's nose bloody outside his own front door.

"Can you tell me again that you understand?" she said to Johan.

"What?"

"That the self-defense excuse isn't valid inside the embassy."

Johan nodded.

*   *   *

This time they parked the RV a bit farther away. Fancy folks had already started flowing in from various directions. None of the guests had to fight with the intercom. The gate was wide open and the guests were welcomed by a representative of the embassy. Petra took a closer look through the new binoculars they'd bought for the occasion.

"Third secretary, you said? He looks more like a doorman."

Johan wanted to handle this on his own, without the presence of Agnes, Petra, or the baseball bat. Not that he wasn't feeling nervous about what awaited.

"Just be yourself," said Agnes.

"Let's not get carried away," said Petra. "Lie low—that's better advice."

"Will you be waiting here?"

"All night, if that's what it takes."

The question was whether any Swedish embassy worker had ever looked unhappier than Fredrik as Johan approached.

"Hello, brother," he said.

Doorman, he thought. Little brother's confidence swelled.

"You damn well better not make a scene," Fredrik hissed. "Do not talk to anyone. Do not do anything. Just leave after ten minutes. Got it?"

He had no time for further instructions, because the ambassador from New Zealand walked up arm in arm with his wife. There was no need for a limousine; the New Zealand embassy was right around the corner, next door to Lesotho and Estonia.

Fredrik took his assignment as doorman seriously. He had studied photographs of each ambassador who might show up. It was also important to have a handle on their titles.

"Dr. Matheson, Mrs. Matheson. A hearty welcome."

The ambassador couple nodded formally and made their entrance. And Fredrik discovered that Johan had already followed their example.

"God help me," he muttered to himself as the first secretary from Lesotho approached.

"Mrs. Mable Malimabe, welcome to Sweden."

CHAPTER 26

Obama, Ban Ki-moon, and Portions of the World's Collected Misery

On occasion, Ban Ki-moon wondered what he'd got himself into.

Born in the middle of the Korean Peninsula while the Japanese still occupied the country. Fled up to the mountains with his family as a small boy, where they remained hidden throughout the Korean War.

When North and South entrenched themselves on either side of the thirty-eighth parallel, his mother and father dared to return to Chungju. Their nine-year-old son could finally attend a real school.

He made the most of the opportunity and became a star student. Won a scholarship to the United States. Bachelor's degree in Seoul. Master's from Harvard. Political career. Became foreign minister. And—rather unexpectedly—secretary-general of the whole UN.

Now he was sitting at the American embassy in Rome along with Ambassador Thorne and President Obama himself. It might have been a Sunday, but presidents and secretaries-general didn't have time for weekends.

Once, as a young student in the United States, Ban Ki-moon had got to shake hands with John F. Kennedy. Now he was hanging out with Kennedy's successor's successor, eight or nine times removed. As an equal. And with the American ambassador Thorne acting as server and refiller of coffee. Or, even better, tea.

As was so often the case when the president and the secretary-general chatted, the conversation revolved around corruption, that global movement and constant threat to economic development, democracy, and the environment. On this topic, Obama and Ban Ki-moon were in total agreement.

The American president had come straight from a session with Angela Merkel and would be headed to Warsaw the very next day to meet with Prime Minister Donald Tusk. Poland held the EU chairperson's gavel this autumn. According to Obama, both Merkel and Tusk were members of the shrinking group of politicians whose main goal was to bring about positive change. But that didn't mean they were always in agreement.

Ban Ki-moon, for his part, had the chaos in Syria to deal with. It had started up early that year. Or sometime in the seventh century, if you wanted to get philosophical about it. Or maybe it was the iron grip colonial French powers had on the country starting in the 1920s that had sown a crucial seed. Or perhaps it was the Soviet Union's support of Hafiz al-Assad, the man who had steered the nation with that Soviet-backed hand until the day he died and his son took over.

That son, Bashar al-Assad, thought that human rights were no human right at all. He spat on the United States and spewed on Israel. He gave the Islamists the finger and—worst of all, according to many—he marketed the idea that women were people too. Alongside this, it turned out his homegrown version of Soviet socialism was not functional. Unlike the corruption.

Now he was under attack from all directions, all at once. Which was fair enough, the secretary-general allowed himself to think. That shouldn't stop the UN from stepping in. For far beneath every political, religious, or geographical struggle for power there were always thousands, hundreds of thousands, or millions of regular people whose basic philosophy was as simple as feeling that it would be nice to be able to have breakfast on the table in the morning when you woke up after doing an honest day's work the day before. And also that you wouldn't be showered with grenades at lunch.

In oversimplified terms, you might say that the strife in Syria was between an irreligious man who didn't think anyone had the right to anything and a group of Islamists who thought man had the right to everything. Neither of them cared about what the average citizen really wanted.

As October turned to November, Obama and Ban Ki-moon would be feeling ambitions to make a real difference during the November G20 meeting in Cannes. The most important G20 meeting in years! The war in Syria would likely blow over soon, it wasn't even a topic of discussion. But they had other reasons to roll up their sleeves. Both knew that you won't get anyone to agree that it's necessary to reform the global system of currency if you don't show up fifteen minutes early to the meeting. As little as you could, in that case, push through stricter rules for financial transactions or open new paths to battling corruption. Hence the series of preparatory meetings.

Between this Sunday and the approaching G20 meeting, there would also be an extra session for the constituents of the African Union. Obama and Ban Ki-moon had been invited to attend as observers and guests of honor.

Corruption in Africa was so widespread that it would soon catch up to Russia's levels. But that didn't make it a top priority for the session. It wasn't on the agenda at all, in fact. On the schedule instead were the global financial crises (which hit the least responsible continent the hardest); unrest, especially that in Libya (whose leader had taken greed and self-absorption a few steps too far); and the environment (because the member states knew that this topic was popular with the American and the South Korean).

Barack Obama and Ban Ki-moon's afternoon conversation was sensationally frank when it came to which country's leaders could and should take on greater responsibility, and which ones they both would have wished nothing but ill for, if only such wishes weren't so very improper.

"A movement to sway public opinion, then," said Ban Ki-moon. "Against all the world's tax havens."

Obama nodded.

It was in these tax havens that the majority of the world's collections of corrupt money landed. Thence it could finance terrorism, in the worst case. In the best case, the corrupt fat cat in charge could just buy something fun with the money, such as an entire football team. All while the nation the money had come from became impoverished. Soon, the only way for each hardworking citizen to survive was to do what everyone else was doing and snatch up as much as possible.

Obama and Ban Ki-moon couldn't avoid veering onto the topic of the appalling Aleko, president of the lilliputian Condor Islands in the Indian Ocean. There was a great risk that they would run into that asshole during the upcoming extra session of the AU.

While the OECD, the WTO, the EU, and others battled the tax havens and tried to stymie their reach, Aleko was doing his best to make the Condors the worst of the worst. The only rule the country seemed to want to stick to, when it came to international financial transactions, was that rules were bad.

*   *   *

Aleko was disliked by an entire continent even before the Condors set out to become a tax haven. This was on account of how, for seven years in a row, all he had done was sabotage everything each time the member states of the African Union met. It was not possible to close him out of the sessions, because the unfortunate fact was that his group of islands formally belonged to Africa. And according to the union's bylaws, the head of state or head of government of each African country was a voting member.

The African Union sets policy for all of Africa: which measures should be prioritized in peacekeeping, security, economy, and the environment. The resolutions are often comprehensive, and historically members had endeavored to make them unanimous.

This last bit hadn't occurred since 2004, when the Condors went from one president to another in the span of one day.

At first, the other members tried to coax the newbie into cooperation.

"But please, Aleko, what is your objection to the formulation 'We shall not spare any effort in the work of eradicating HIV and AIDS?'"

"I'm not telling."

As if he were a nine-year-old in a huff.

After a few sessions, the new chairman of the union changed tack.

"Then all that's left is the declaration itself. President Aleko, how would *you* suggest we put it?"

"That the fishing industry is underrated."

"But right now we're discussing a continental pact of non-aggression."

"If everyone ate fish, there would be less fighting."

"Please, Aleko . . ."

"*President* Aleko, if you please."

The assembly that had, for decades preceding Aleko's arrival, grown used to coming up with unifying formulations was soon united in what the up-and-comer from the Condors ought to be called. *President*, of course. Officially. But unofficially, they needed something more vivid and less polite. The leaders of fifty-four countries declared that their colleague from the fifty-fifth was:

An asshole.

*   *   *

Ban Ki-moon and Obama had thoroughly prepared themselves during their respective long-haul flights, coming from opposite directions to the Italian capital (the fact that they were meeting in Rome specifically was because the secretary-general had, a year previously, accepted an invitation to morning tea with Pope Benedict to take place the next day). This was part of the reason the Sunday meeting at the embassy was a quick one; both already knew what they wanted and for all intents and purposes they wanted the same thing.

Agreed. Handshake. And it wasn't even four in the afternoon yet.

"An early dinner together, perhaps?" said Ban Ki-moon.

"Sounds nice," said Barack Obama.

"Or we could crash the Swedish embassy," suggested Ambassador Thorne. "They're having their annual ambassador mixer today, it's starting soon. I'm invited, and I imagine I can get the two of you in as well."

The president and the secretary-general smiled. An ambassador mixer sounded lovely.

"Seven minutes by car," said Ambassador Thorne.

The Secret Service had no reason to object.

CHAPTER 27

Sunday, September 4, 2011

THREE DAYS TO GO

Ambassador Guldén's mood had not changed since he and Johan met out on the street that morning.

"Oh, you came, delightful. You have to tell me about your brotherly love, isn't it the best thing?"

That was as far as the conversation between Guldén and Johan got. An assistant whispered in the ambassador's ear.

"Ban Ki-moon? Obama? *Dammit!*"

Johan was clueless about what might be happening, but he wasn't concerned. He'd caught sight of a server holding a tray of hors d'oeuvres.

"Excuse me, but what is this?" he said.

"Salmon canapés."

"I can see that. But what is *that*?"

Johan pointed at something nearly hidden beneath the salmon on one of the canapés.

"I wonder if you haven't mixed wasabi into this fresh cheese? Am I right?"

The server looked unhappy.

"I don't know, I'm not the one who makes them, I'm just a server. But I can certainly ask the chef . . ."

"It's not a bad idea. But if I were to say 'Dijon, apple, walnut, horseradish' . . . what would you say?"

"I'll get the chef."

* * *

Fox, the Canadian ambassador, had no sooner caught sight of his American colleague Thorne before he commandeered him.

"Dave! Come here. Get a load of this."

Ban Ki-moon immediately found himself involuntarily linking arms with the Belarusian-ambassador-slash-unofficial-former-lover to the Belarusian president.

"Madam Ambassador. So lovely to see you here," lied the secretary-general.

Meanwhile, Barack Obama wasn't being accosted by anyone. He walked straight to the nearest tray of hors d'oeuvres. People left him alone because no one was quite sure whose company he was in. The Swedish ambassador thought feverishly. His American colleague had vanished in one direction; Ban Ki-moon in another. What should he do now?

Wait and see, he decided. Don't rush into anything.

"Here you go, Mr. President," said the chef of the Swedish embassy, who had ventured into the crowd to chat salmon canapé recipes with one of the guests.

"Wasabi," said Johan to Barack Obama.

"Obama," said President Obama.

"No, the canapés contain wasabi. I contain wasabi too, now that I think of it. I've got four canapés inside me. My name is Johan."

Barack Obama was already enjoying his present company. The chef quickly retreated; it was not his place to mingle with the guests more than necessary. Especially not when one of them was the president of the United States.

"Not bad, wasabi. I'm more of a Dijon guy myself."

"You too? But Dijon mustard can be tricky. Just a tiny bit too much and you've ruined everything."

"Dijon mustard and pickled apples," said Obama.

"And cress," Johan added (surprising himself at what funny words he knew in English).

* * *

Across the room, in a corner, stood the embassy's third secretary, feeling ill. His prize idiot of a brother—of all the people in the place—was having a lively conversation with the president of the United States of America.

Fredrik had his reasons for lurking in a corner. He wanted to avoid ending up in a social conversation with anyone, because he needed to keep a careful eye on what the idiot was up to.

The strategy didn't work. Finland's second secretary misread the situation and thought that his Swedish colleague was feeling lonely so decided on a rescue mission. The Swede was Swedish, of course, and the Finn Finnish, so they could always talk ice hockey.

Johan guided the conversation from salmon to one of his favorite recipes for beef carpaccio and was surprised to learn that the person before him had never heard of Västerbotten cheese. Who even was he? It would be impolite not to ask. Although he might as well start by introducing himself.

"I'm Johan, like I said. Löwenhult. Master chef and genius, I've been given to understand. Brother of one of the employees here at the embassy. Came here to punch him in the nose, but then I ended up among the hors d'oeuvres instead. And now, the Västerbotten cheese."

Obama had the same laugh as the Swedish ambassador.

"But what is it that you do?" Johan continued.

The American president immediately became serious. He interpreted the question philosophically.

"Well, you know, Johan. I ask myself that every day."

"You don't know?"

"It seemed so much simpler before. 'Yes, we can' and all that. I definitely still have the drive, it's not that. But it's just as you say. *What do I do?*"

He seemed pleasant, this—*Obrama*, was it? Well-versed in food. But not knowing what you did? That was strange.

Obama lowered his voice. Not that it was necessary. No one dared to approach him and Johan, and the room was pretty noisy.

"Just take the AU, for instance."

Johan had just learned what the EU was. Petra had given a lecture about it as they drove into and then out of Switzerland. Either Switzerland was EU and the countries around it weren't, or the other way around. It was important to seize the rare opportunity to appear knowledgeable whenever he could.

"The European Union," he said.

"No, African. That continent is facing enormous challenges. And the secretary-general and I spent half the day sighing over a little troll who obstructs every last measure the union tries to take. To think we have to treat presidents as though they were children. Indeed: *What am I doing?*"

"Who's the child?" Johan asked.

"Aleko."

Johan wondered if he should know who Aleko was. Or, for that matter, the secretary-general. But you couldn't know what you didn't know. He might as well start with the first one.

"Who's Aleko?"

"Right, you see? You don't even know who he is. Hardly anyone knows who he is, yet he's holding half the world and all of Africa hostage. He's the president of the Condors. Two hundred sixty-two thousand citizens against a billion other Africans. He's widely known as 'the asshole.' A well-deserved nickname, if you ask me."

President Obama felt that perhaps this was a bit too forthright, but he had clocked out for the day, so to speak, and it was a Sunday, and this new acquaintance, the chef and genius in front of him, appeared so laid-back. It was only fair to return the favor.

Twenty yards away, the Swedish third secretary was trying to peer over the shoulder of the overweening Finnish second secretary who was standing before him and talking ice hockey. Apparently the Finns were world champions. Fredrik couldn't care less. But what was going on over there?

It couldn't get any worse, and yet it did. The secretary-general of the United Nations, Ban Ki-moon, joined in with the president of the United States of America and Fredrik's brainless brother. Goodbye, career in diplomacy. Might as well throw in the towel. Might as well talk hockey.

"Yes, the world championships were very exciting this year. Especially your first game, I was on tenterhooks."

"Against Denmark? We won that 5–1."

"Did I say the *first* game? I meant the last one."

"6–1, us. Against you."

"Secretary-General! Let me introduce my new friend, Johan. Master chef, genius—and, I dare say, philosopher."

"Nice to meet you, Johan. I'm Ban Ki-moon."

Was he the one Obrama had just mentioned? The secretary-general? Wonder if he knew Fredrik. Maybe secretaries stick together.

While Johan mused over this, Ban Ki-moon told Obama he'd just had a chat with the ambassador from Belarus.

"I'm sorry. What did she have to say?"

"The message wasn't entirely clear, but I think the idea was I could have a dacha by the Dnieper if her former lover and his country were awarded a spot on the UN Security Council. Or else I would have seven years of bad luck."

Barack Obama sighed.

"How many Alekos are out there?"

A name Johan recognized.

"The asshole!" he said.

Ban Ki-moon smiled. He personally didn't use language like this, but the epithet wasn't entirely uncalled for. President Aleko had been trying for a number of years to do the impossible and *battle* his way into important positions within the African Union. An ambition as tasteless as it was futile.

"I'm not the one who came up with it," Johan confessed. "It was this guy here who doesn't know what it is he does who said it first."

Ban Ki-moon seemed to expect more of an explanation. Barack Obama clarified:

"Our friend Johan here is a frank and forthright sort. In point of fact, he's right. I don't always know what it is I do, but I do know one thing: the world does not need troublemakers like Aleko."

There was something about the master chef and the breath of fresh Swedish air that made Obama feel at home. This ambassador mixer had been a good idea.

A server swept by with a silver tray and supplied the trio with champagne. Johan noticed from the corner of his eye that Fredrik was standing quite a way away and glaring at him. He probably didn't like to see his little brother making new friends. It would have felt good to punch him in the face in front of everyone, but Petra had forbidden it. Of course, taunting him was still on the table.

Johan demonstratively raised his glass toward Obrama and . . . the other guy:

"Cheers, my dear friends. Cheers to Aleko. Or rather, *against* him, eh?"

Barack Obama and Ban Ki-moon grinned and raised their glasses too.

At this point, Obama was reminded of his responsibilities as president of the United States.

"I'd love to stay and exchange more ideas with you, Johan, but I should do the rounds, represent my country a little bit."

Wonder what country that could be? Johan thought.

"Just one more thing," Obama remembered. "And this might be going too far, we hardly know each other."

"Tell me," said Johan.

Was he about to make yet another friend? That would make three in a week. Four, if you counted Preben.

"This Västerbotten cheese."

"What about it?"

"Do you think you could send me some?"

* * *

At long last Fredrik managed to extricate himself from the conversation with the Finn and hurried over to Johan just as Barack Obama and Ban Ki-moon walked off.

"I told you not to talk to anyone. And you were supposed to leave after ten minutes. What kind of mess have you made this time? What were you three talking about?"

Johan was very close to falling into old habits. To saying, "Yes, my Lord," "I'm sorry, my Lord," and following Fredrik's orders.

Then he remembered who big brother truly was and had always been. Above all, he saw fear in Fredrik's eyes. Fredrik was *scared*! Of his little brother! Johan was filled with a measure of self-confidence he'd never felt before.

"We were talking about what a dive this place is. Mediocre canapés. Crappy champagne."

"For Christ's sake," said Fredrik.

Scared!

"And also we were discussing Africa. The problems in . . . the American union risk becoming the downfall of the whole incontinence."

"Oh my god!"

Perhaps he hadn't quite got the right words that time, but that only made it better. Fredrik was in acute distress.

* * *

Ambassador Guldén joined them.

"Great to see you've made yourself at home, Johan. Wonderful to see the president of the United States enjoying Swedish company like this."

"Who?" said Johan.

It just came out; the ambassador must be referring to Obrama.

"But Fredrik, what were you thinking? Hiding in a corner? And prioritizing ice hockey talk with a Finnish secretary who is nearly as insignificant as you are? Yes, I heard you. Besides, they outplayed us in the world championship final, what were you thinking?"

Fredrik was beyond dismayed, but he couldn't produce a word. If the ambassador had arrived a second earlier, he would have heard Johan mixing up Africa and America, and continent with incontinence. And he must have noticed just now that the blockhead didn't even know who he'd just been talking to. Didn't he *see*? Didn't he *hear*?

"I remember your father well. I had the honor of serving under him in Istanbul. What an amazing man! The way he took full advantage of every situation! Everyone still talks about the time he sat up all night long, reciting Shakespeare with Nixon. Absolutely invaluable at a time when the world was going up in flames. What did you and Obama talk about, Johan? Does he know his Shakespeare as well?"

179

Johan didn't know what Shakespeare was.

"We mostly talked about salmon canapés, with and without wasabi. Before we got on the topic of that asshole Aleko."

"Well done! Foodways, forthright language, and international responsibility. Quite the opposite of standing around with a loser and talking about how bad we are at hockey. You've got much to learn from your big brother, Fredrik."

This whole thing was only getting more surreal.

"He's my little brother," Fredrik said pitifully.

"Well, there you go," said the ambassador, and he clapped Johan on the shoulder and put his empty champagne glass in Fredrik's hand.

"You can help out with the cleanup around here later. Then we all will have done some good for our nation before the day is out."

With that, he walked off.

Fredrik and Johan were left behind.

"Obrama is president of the country of America, eh?" said little brother.

CHAPTER 28

Son of a Sugar Beet Farmer

PART 4 OF 5

While Gorbachev was still party secretary in charge of agricultural matters, his advisor had reason to visit Berlin. There had been a handful of trips to the capital city of the German Democratic Republic. On one of them, Aleksandr met the dynamic Günther, a man of around his own age with an eye to the future who knew enough Russian for them to understand each other well. After a few enjoyable evenings together they began to exchange visions. Günther in particular had an enormous need to be able to speak frankly to someone. He couldn't do so with a fellow East German. Aside from the ninety thousand employees of the Ministry for State Security, there were several hundred thousand registered informants who were encouraged to spy on friends, coworkers and neighbors.

With Aleksandr—Sasha—it was different. He was Russian.

Günther said he worked for a state-owned logistics company and had the ability to organize various databases within the Stasi in such a way that he could gain advantage by reporting citizens who were not only innocent but dead. For the fact was, death certificates were located in a different database, which was also under Günther's control.

Thus the Stasi found itself, following tips from Günther, looking for at least thirty suspected enemies of the state without finding any of them. They were all buried already, every last one.

"Upside for me, downside for no one," said Günther. "Cheers, my friend!"

This worked for several years, not least because Günther had made sure that those he'd identified as enemies of the state had no family for the Stasi to interrogate. But then, one day, he was in too much of a rush to get to the pub where his buddy Sasha was waiting with beers already poured. Günther mixed up a few documents and happened to turn in the wrong woman in Dresden, an extra bad seed according to Günther's report. It was possible she had moved to Leipzig to support herself as a madam at a brothel, but the informant wasn't sure.

Someone was sure, however, and that was the top boss and director of the Stasi who had just buried his wife, his heart full of sorrow. Now he sat with Günther's report before him, the report that claimed that his beloved, snow-white Heidrunn had risen from the dead on the third day and traveled to Leipzig to start a brothel.

The hunt for the thirty people no one could find was immediately canceled. Instead, everyone began to look for Günther. Who survived by smuggling himself all the way to Moscow in Sasha's car trunk.

Once safely in the Soviet capital, he started his own business. That is to say, he sold fake ration cards out of the back seat of a taxi. Or, rather, seventy taxis, when the organization was at its zenith, right before the Soviet Union fell to pieces. Günther was a survivor and his became a respected name within the Vory, for he had the good sense to share the wealth. And not to say a word about who, in the inner circles of the Kremlin, was his best friend.

* * *

So it came to be that no more than twenty minutes passed after the death warrant of Yeltsin's chief advisor had been signed before Günther caught wind of the plans. One minute later Aleksandr knew as well, and in all haste he packed his two largest suitcases, filling them to the brim with three pairs of underwear, some letters he was eager to keep, a toothbrush but no toothpaste, and—taking up the rest of the space—tightly packed bundles of hundred-dollar bills. Unreported and untaxed, of course. Why should he do the right thing when no one else did? To be safe, he took his best friend with him when he fled as well.

Until that day, the son of the former sugar beet farmer had been called Aleksandr Kovalchuk. The first thing he did, when he arrived in the country he was sure the Russian mafia would never find, was change his name. It cost him one hundred dollars. For another hundred, "Aleko" with no first name could also become a Condorian citizen. "Ale" from Aleksandr. "Ko" from Kovalchuk.

A new name and new citizenship, in a new country. With two suitcases full of money and vast amounts of knowledge about how to stake out a position for oneself in society, no matter the society. Aleko began a new climb to the top. This time, he intended to go all the way.

CHAPTER 29

Sunday, September 4, 2011

THREE DAYS TO GO

Johan was back with Agnes and Petra. Everything had gone well at the embassy, even if he did feel most at home in the RV.

The others, of course, wanted all the dirt. First and foremost, they wanted to know whether they were in a hurry to leave.

"No, no rush."

"So you didn't deal out any blows?"

"No. Or, yes. I guess I did. Could I digest all of this in peace and quiet?"

* * *

The three friends spent the evening outside the RV at the campground. Johan was still in his Canali suit and his handmade, rainbow calf-skin shoes. He looked so out of place in his surroundings that children from nearby tents came to ask for his autograph.

After a while, Petra ran out of patience. She canceled the autographing, chased the children off with the threat that they would otherwise be subjected to her communication flowchart, and demanded Johan tell them what had happened inside the embassy.

He said that there had been lots of people at the mixer, but he had hardly spoken with any of them. Just with someone called Obrama and his secretary, Ban Ki-something.

"Obama and Ban Ki-moon?" said Petra.

"That sounds right."

"Are you messing with me?"

Johan took a business card from his breast pocket and handed it to her.

"What does it say?" Agnes wondered.

"I'm not positive," said Petra, "but I believe that what I am looking at right here is the private cell phone number of the president of the United States."

Johan confirmed that Obrama likely was the president of the USA.

*　*　*

They had to spend a whole half hour listening to his scattered impressions of the event before Agnes and Petra could make any sense of the situation. Johan had, it seemed, managed to befriend Barack Obama on account of some salmon canapés and also became acquainted with UN secretary-general, Ban Ki-moon. Without having any idea who either of them was.

"Can you explain that UN stuff again?" Johan requested.

He had also severely assaulted his brother without even touching him.

"I didn't need my fists, a baseball bat, or a frying pan from Ronneby Bruk. All it took was Obrama."

"Obama," said Petra.

"Yes, but there's an *r*."

"No, no *r*."

"Is too," said Johan, taking out the president's card again. "No, dangit, you're right! Obrama without an *r*. See for yourself!"

Agnes was eager to change the subject.

"What do we do now?" she said.

"I don't know," said Petra.

"I do," said the master chef.

Johan decided that the next morning they should get in the RV and head for a country called the Condors. There they would give someone called Aleko a good talking to. They could put a checkmark next to Fredrik; he'd got what he deserved even though it hadn't gone according to their original plan. But that meant they had some punches in the nose left over for future use.

"I'll echo the words of Obrama without an *r*, Aleko is an asshole."

He had to explain further. He told them that the Condorian president kept blocking important decisions from being made in the American Union.

"The African Union," said Petra.

"That too?"

"Only that one."

Anyway. It seemed that the UN's secretary was in agreement.

"Secretary-general," said Petra.

Agnes realized that the Condors was the same country where that delightful Herbert von Toll had got her a shell company and that George Clooney wanted to clean up. It would be difficult to get there in the RV.

"The Condors are an island in the Indian Ocean."

It looked like Johan wanted to say something.

"No, there's no bridge there. And it's far away. But it does sound fun. Doesn't it, Petra?"

The prophet was enjoying life more than ever. Too bad it would soon be over.

"When do we leave?"

CHAPTER 30

Monday, September 5, 2011

TWO DAYS TO GO

Agnes searched for airline tickets while Petra and Johan slept in their opposite corners in the back of the vehicle. Over breakfast, she shared doubly bad news.

The flight to the Condors didn't leave until just before midnight, later that day. Two stopovers. First in Addis Ababa, then Dar es Salaam. They wouldn't arrive until the afternoon of the next day.

"And by then there'll only be one day left," said Petra.

Were they aiming too high? Would they even manage to reach the Condorian president before everything turned to ice?

"Maybe there are other assholes, closer by?" Agnes mused. "I mean, the tickets are booked and paid for, but we can take the loss."

Petra thought about it and settled on a decision: "No." She had so much to thank Johan for.

"It's true that time is short, but we said we were going to the Condors and to the Condors we shall go."

"Good," said Agnes. "And who knows—maybe the atmosphere will change its mind."

"Atmospheres have no will of their own."

Agnes didn't want to argue. She said she had a different problem to deal with.

Johan, who had only been listening thus far, thought this sounded dire.

"Something worse than the end of the world?"

"Not yet."

The thing was, her much younger alias was in a scrape. After her visits to commercially ice-cold Svalbard and Oslo, Traveling Eklund had moved on to Paris, her favorite city. Perhaps it was the stress caused by manure tankers, shot-putters, bank visits, et cetera, in her parallel reality that caused Agnes to make a miscalculation. She, who had always been meticulous about travel logistics, made a fool of herself in the name of Traveling Eklund by landing in Seoul almost before she'd even managed to take off from Paris.

When it should have been the other way around. In addition to the day the journey itself took, another half day was eaten up by the fact that the earth is round.

"We all make mistakes," said Johan, who knew what he was talking about.

Sure, but the internet was full of nitpickers. Within twenty minutes, a storm had begun to rage on Traveling Eklund's blog and Instagram. A number of people promptly took a closer look at all the pictures she'd posted since she started blogging over a year earlier. In the beginning, before Agnes was well-versed in her photo-editing software, she'd been a little sloppy. Not hugely so, but if you knew what you were looking for, you could find mistakes.

The examiners turned their fault-finding into a competition. When magnified at 800 percent, it was clear that Traveling Eklund's first luxury watch had been pasted in. The same went for her whole arm, in fact. And furthermore, how could the shadow be falling to the southwest at one edge of this picture from London, and to the southeast on the other? Why was a juniper bush missing behind the Leaning Tower of Pisa? And this lovely picture from Tokyo, with Japan's tallest mountain in the distance: how much snow was there on Mount Fuji in July? This picture looked more like March. Or April, at the very latest.

As night passed at the campground in Rome, more and more evidence piled up that Traveling Eklund was a fraud through and through, that she never went anywhere except in a virtual sense. Then came the conclusions that internationally renowned luxury brands were behind the account. One of them in particular.

* * *

The first two letters in LVMH stand for Louis Vuitton. The final two stand for Moët Hennessy. A few months before the Traveling Eklund scandal hit, LVMH had bought a controlling interest in Bvlgari and in so doing cemented its position as one of the world's leading companies in the luxury-goods sector.

Secretly sponsoring an internet phenomenon with the aim of increasing sales would be a grotesque idea for a group that took itself very seriously. Thus it was not LVMH that had filled Agnes Eklund's bank account with money. Rather, the money had come from a whole slew of striving brands, the imitators who wanted more than anything to attain the same success as the original.

In time, Agnes had learned how best to package the message that brought her the big bucks. One of her most frequent tricks was the "Look what I just found!" followed by showing off something tasteful but not especially well known. The striver brands had no problem sending this anonymous internet phenomenon thirty, fifty, or a hundred thousand kronor to thank her for her assistance, even as LVMH spent thirty, fifty, or a hundred million euro on its own brand development.

At the same time, Agnes couldn't allow Traveling Eklund to seem cheap. Most of her posts were indirect homages to the best of the best, such as Versace, Gucci, Rolex, and—Agnes's very favorite—Bvlgari.

There was something irresistible about Bvlgari in particular. It didn't matter whether it was a watch, a piece of jewelry, glasses, or a handbag—it was all so tasteful that it gave Agnes a warm fuzzy feeling. She was so far gone that she could almost smell the luscious scent with just a glance at a perfume bottle, as long as it said BVLGARI on it.

Traveling Eklund shared all of this with the world. And overnight, as the court of public opinion pored over image after image, caption after caption, what began as a vague suspicion was elevated to the highest of truths: Traveling Eklund was actually a fictitious persona created by . . . Bvlgari.

The first hashtag, #boycottbvlgari, popped up before Agnes was even awake. As she drank her morning coffee, it multiplied hundreds of thousands of times over.

Now she was sitting at Johan's incomparable breakfast table and looking at her tablet. While the innocent Bvlgari was dragged ever deeper through the mud, DMs began to pour in from the striver brands. Was Traveling Eklund *made up*? Kindly refund all payments! Remove the images in which you display our products! We want nothing to do with you!

Hundreds of thousands of girls and young women followed Traveling Eklund's carefree, spendthrift travels throughout the world. As well as the occasional man. The younger alias of the violet-haired Swede was a role model. A dream.

And now, too, a phony.

Petra could see that Agnes was gravely concerned about the situation, and she tried to find the best way to offer solace. She said it was too bad Traveling Eklund's travels were apparently over, and that no new money would be pouring in. But they must not forget they only had two days left of everything. With almost five million kronor in Agnes's account, they could spend two and a half million per day.

Agnes thanked her for her kind words. Indeed, the fictional Eklund would have to stay in Seoul. Nice city. Lucky for her she wasn't still stuck in Svalbard when it happened. Two and a half million per day sounded reasonably fantastic, as long as doomsday didn't turn out to be as fictional as the character who had now retreated from the limelight in Korea.

"Oh, dear Agnes, don't worry about that," said Petra.

"What do you think of the mango bread?" Johan asked. "It's my own recipe, with walnuts, ginger, and a couple of other ingredients you'll never guess."

He thought the other two were talking too much. Even the breakfast table deserved respect.

CHAPTER 31

Tuesday, September 6, 2011

ONE DAY TO GO

It ended up being a long wait at Aeroporto Leonardo da Vinci. Ethiopian Airlines flight 703, bound for Addis Ababa, didn't take off until five minutes past midnight after a twenty-five-minute delay. Agnes was exhausted from the long afternoon and evening spent at the international terminal. Fresh revelations and new accusations continued to stream in. Above all, more and more people were demanding the top brass at Bvlgari step forward and admit to everything they had no reason to admit to.

Meanwhile, she'd had to keep a watchful eye on Petra, who wanted to walk around with her completed flowchart to practice on anyone she met. The prophet said all it needed was initiating conversation, which in the best-case scenario would lead to a conflict, much like her encounter with the angry Italian in the Porsche three days earlier. Only with a more peaceful resolution, of course. That was the whole point.

Agnes pointed out that there were few places worse for starting fights than an airport. Even an animated discussion might lead to their being denied boarding.

In line for passport control, she was forced to give Petra a direct order.

"I don't care if he looks unhappy. Let him look at your passport and let you in. Do not say a word about how he should think about reexamining his life."

Petra listened and obeyed. With a vague sense that perhaps Agnes wasn't entirely wrong.

At the same time, the prophet had her own issues to deal with. As boarding time drew near, she had to spend quite a while looking for Johan before she found him in the kitchen of the Star Alliance lounge, trying to show the staff how to roll wraps in his role as master chef and genius. Astoundingly enough, the kitchen staff wanted to keep him.

"Thanks, I'd love to," said Johan.

Petra explained that it was impossible for him to get on a flight and stay on the ground all at once. He had to choose one or the other. Preferably the option he, she, and Agnes had already agreed upon.

"Of course," said Johan, once he'd thought it through.

Petra was causing trouble for Agnes; Johan was causing trouble for Petra. And the internet was causing trouble for them all. The escalating rhetoric online felt ominous. All the better, then, that they were about to change continents. The way things were going, hanging around for too long in Bvlgari's hometown couldn't possibly end well.

But at last they were all onboard. The seventy-five-year-old fell asleep in her seat before the meal was served and didn't wake up until breakfast over Sudan about an hour before landing.

The next flight, the one for Dar es Salaam, took off at quarter to ten. There, they had only fifty uneventful minutes until the long journey's final and fairly short leg, bound for Monrovi and the Condors.

Departure: 1:25 p.m.

One twenty-five p.m.

Eleven twenty-five a.m., in Italy.

CHAPTER 32

Tuesday, September 6, 2011

ONE DAY TO GO

The International Criminal Police Organization, better known as INTERPOL, is headquartered in the French city of Lyon. In September of 2011, this intergovernmental organization boasted an impressive one hundred eighty-seven member countries. Another three were in the pipeline: Curaçao, Sint Maarten, and South Sudan.

INTERPOL specializes in the type of crime that doesn't observe national borders. But each nation is sovereign; there are no super-police to send out from Lyon to arrest rotten eggs wherever they might appear in the world.

Let's say one of these should happen to pop up in Rome. The alarm would be sounded in Lyon to alert the special unit within the Italian police, which functions as the long arm of INTERPOL. This unit is called the NCB, or National Central Bureau. Code red means "Arrest the person in question if you can." Code yellow is "Find the person in question." Code blue: "Find out what's going on." Code green: "This rascal might be headed your way to cause trouble." Code orange: "Heads up for bombs, grenades, and other items intended to cause destruction and harm." And finally, code black: "This criminal is already dead, but we want to know more about them. What do you know?"

Now, on occasion it turns out to be a bafflingly small world. The vice president of Moët Hennessy—Louis Vuitton SA

(LVMH) in Paris was not only originally from Lyon, he was also a former member of the same tennis club as the secretary-general of INTERPOL's right-hand man. In hopes of minimizing the harm to the Bvlgari brand, it would be necessary to find whoever was behind that fake Traveling Eklund account and bring her to justice. Tennis buddy #1 put the pressure on Tennis buddy #2, who was in a good position to issue a three-color alert (blue, yellow, red). This meant "Find out what happened, find this jackass, and arrest her."

Sometimes it turns out to be an even more bafflingly small world. The CFO of Bvlgari in the Italian capital also happened to be the chairman of the leading membership organization for fly-fishers in the southern metropolitan region. In third place on the waiting list for the exclusive membership was special agent Sergio Conte with the long arm of INTERPOL, NCB, in Rome.

As these coincidences added up, Conte found himself faced with a three-hued (what he considered to be) piece-of-shit task that couldn't be ignored. The special agent was facing pressure from two directions: one tennis player in Lyon, and one fly-fisher with the power to let him in or forever banish him from the club he wanted to join more than anything.

As the clock struck eleven, the special agent launched into a lecture for his insufferable boss and a small group of colleagues at the NCB. The topic was one Agnes Eklund, born in 1936, Swedish citizen. An Instagram account, indirectly linked to Mrs. Eklund by way of its ties to a bank account at Svenska Handelsbanken in Sweden, suggested she was currently in Rome. At least, she had been twenty-seven hours ago, which was the time stamp of the most recent login to the account in question (INTERPOL in Lyon and the NCB had coordinated resources; they knew who was where as long as the object of their interest was incautious enough to turn on their laptop or tablet).

Special Agent Conte admitted to his boss that this matter might seem to be of low priority. He said a little about the pressure from Lyon and nothing at all about his own interests with regard to the fly-fishing club he longed to join. Instead he argued on a theoretical level. Instagram was a new phenomenon. Basically the whole internet itself was half new. The NCB could expect a series of similar matters to emerge as time went on, matters that crossed borders—that was the whole point of the internet. Its lifeblood, even.

"In light of what I've just reported, my recommendation is that we listen to Lyon and devote resources to this matter. Levels: blue, yellow, red."

Sergio Conte's boss lowered his glasses to the tip of his nose. He regarded him over the frames.

"I'm surprised at you, Special Agent Conte," he said. "But by all means. If you have such a burning desire to track down this Swedish fraudster, you're welcome to do so. But the only resource we will provide is the special agent himself. The rest of us will toil forth with our unimportant little matters such as trafficking, global terrorism, threats against democracy, and billion-dollar currency scams."

Conte felt stupid.

"Thank you," he said. "I'll get started right away, Boss, if you'll allow me to. I'm guessing that the suspect will be captured before the day is out."

The matter was raised, discussed, and decided in twenty minutes. One minute later, the group went their separate ways. Four minutes after that, Conte started up his fancy search engines.

This was at 11:25. By 11:26, it was clear that the suspect had left Rome for a final destination of Monrovi by way of Addis Ababa and Dar es Salaam.

The sham democracy known as the Condors, in the Indian Ocean, was one of INTERPOL's 187 member countries, but only on paper. Mrs. Eklund must therefore be arrested in Dar es Salaam at the latest.

Special Agent Conte established this two minutes after flight 856 took off from Julius Nyerere International Airport, bound for the extremely inaccessible Condors.

"Damn you, Julius Nyerere," he said.

Now things were going to get tricky.

CHAPTER 33

Tuesday, September 6, 2011

ONE DAY TO GO

Aéroport Aleko International (recently renamed after the country's president, by the very president in question) consisted of a single runway. The surface was made of hard, red, iron-rich dirt, not asphalt.

Not only did flight 856 from Dar es Salaam land on time, it landed on time down to the minute. Good order and organization were otherwise not traits their destination was known for.

The plane parked outside terminal A. This was its designation, despite the lack of any terminal B, C, or D. The passengers were led down the steps for a short walk to the terminal building itself. On the way, they were subjected to salespeople of all sorts. Not too many of them, for only those who had stuffed enough Condorian francs into the right pockets were allowed to stand on the wrong side of the security checkpoint that did not live up to its name.

Outside the ramshackle airport, Johan looked around for the RV for a moment before he realized it was history. But his, Agnes's, and Petra's very light baggage was waiting on a cart, guarded by a guard who knew all the potential bag thieves by name and could therefore tell them from other people in his sleep.

"What do we do now?" said Petra. "We've got about thirty-one hours."

"I miss my kitchen," said Johan.

"I thought you wanted to flatten the nose of President Aleko?" said Agnes.

"Not on an empty stomach. Where can we find him?"

"Kings live in castles, presidents typically live in presidential palaces," said Petra. "Why don't we search for a hotel near there and start by checking in?"

"What does the kitchen look like at this hotel?" Johan wondered.

"I'll answer that when I know where we're going to stay," said Agnes, typing on her tablet.

All while Special Agent Conte in Rome, via his search engines, observed that the old lady had apparently arrived at her destination.

* * *

The Hôtel du Palais was not as palatial as its name suggested. The view from their three single rooms was nothing Traveling Eklund would have written home about, even if she hadn't already retired in Seoul.

Agnes had a backyard beneath her window, one that might have belonged to a tire company. In any case, there were stacks of used car tires, half sheltered by corrugated metal.

Petra's room was one floor up, and she could see past the tire company, which seemed to be more tire than company. On the other side of the narrow street was a three-story building whose roof seemed to have blown off without anyone doing anything about it. Apparently it was possible to live there even so.

Johan didn't care about their surroundings; he was roaming about the hallways looking for the hotel kitchen. He tried to make himself understood in the lobby, but the older man behind the desk only knew passable French and a language Johan didn't know existed.

"Excuse me."

Someone behind Johan was making their presence known— in English! At least twelve of the movies Johan knew by heart contained this very phrase. He turned around and automatically selected a quote from the pile available to him in response:

"'Excuse me, excuse me. Excuse you for what?' *It's a Wonderful Life*, 1946."

He was standing eye to eye with a middle-aged man in a uniform. Who found himself temporarily tongue-tied on account of this rapid-fire answer. Thus Johan managed to be the first to continue their conversation.

"You speak English, that's great. Could you tell me where I'll find the hotel kitchen? I was going to pop by and see if they need any help."

The man in uniform made a quick recovery.

"No. But instead could you tell me where I might find Agnes Eklund?"

Johan lit up.

"Of course! Do you know each other?"

"Not at all. I'm just planning to arrest her."

* * *

The Condorian chief of police was President Aleko's best and only friend.

When someone who called himself a "special agent" had got on the horn from Rome to rant about a woman who ought to be found and returned to Dar es Salaam, he called the president to let him know.

"NCB?" said Aleko.

"Like, INTERPOL," said Günther.

"Oh, that's not so bad. Ignore them. But find that old lady and figure out what she's doing here."

* * *

This was a development Agent Conte had expected. That is to say: no help from the Condors. It was now formally Lyon's job to delegate the search for this woman to the member country in the Indian Ocean. Italy was off the hook. But if that happened, in all certainty nothing would come of it. Not on the arresting front, nor with the waiting list to Conte's beloved fly-fishing club.

Since the Condors were no larger than a small Italian region, there was reason to believe Agnes Eklund planned to stay there for the rest of her life. True, she was seventy-five years old, but if she remained in good health she would surely return to civilization sooner or later. Conte saw to it to have surveillance in Maputo, Dar es Salaam, and Nairobi. There were no other alternatives unless she wanted to *sail* to the mainland—just as little as there was any system in use at Aéroport Aleko International that could send out an advance alert about where she was heading once she was on her way.

With Johan's help, the chief of police captured not only Agnes but Petra and the informer himself. Until further notice they were considered guests of honor and their jail accommodations were assigned accordingly. Three real cots—they wouldn't have to stand or lie on the floor. The toilet bucket was separated from the rest of the room by a curtain. A sink in one corner. Brown with rust, but still.

"Don't drink the tap water," said the chief of police. "I don't want any stomach bugs around me. I'll ask my assistant to bring a carafe."

"For the fourth time," said Petra. "What. Is. Happening?"

"We're going to figure that out. But not today—I don't have time. It's my daughter's birthday and we're having a party."

"What do you mean 'not today'? We don't have time to stay

here, we've got important things to do and we're in a hurry! Let us out of here, for God's sake!"

She was far more upset on Johan's behalf than Johan himself was.

"All in good time," said the chief of police. "I'll be back tomorrow when I wake up. It shouldn't be that late. Unless Ibrahim shows up at the celebration, he's dangerous. Never stops partying."

While Petra did her best to handle her frustration, Agnes tried to figure out how Bvlgari and her spurned sponsors had managed to make this happen.

And Johan was being Johan.

"What's your daughter's name?" he asked. "How old is she?"

The chief of police smiled.

"Angelika, the apple of my eye," he said. "She's turning six today. Can you imagine?"

"Lovely name. And what is your name, Mr. Chief of Police, if I may ask?"

"Forget it, Johan," said Petra.

"Forget it," said Agnes.

Fraternizing with the man who was about to ruin everything?

"Günther," said Günther.

* * *

It was now 11:20 p.m. Condorian time, and the friends sat where they sat, on their respective cots in the finest cell the jail had to offer. Now the countdown had begun for real. Petra took a whole minute to consider this privately, and then she said:

"Twenty-three hours and fifty-nine minutes to go. We won't be able to reach the president, that much is clear. Should we settle for breaking the nose of his chief of police instead?"

Johan thought this was a bad idea.

"Angelika's dad?"

Petra was annoyed. Was she the only one who understood the situation they were in?

"She won't have time to notice her dad's crooked nose before they are reunited on the other side, why can't you get that into your head?"

"If your calculations are correct," said Agnes.

"Idiot," said Petra.

"Her, or me?" said Johan.

Agh. That was a word she should avoid.

The atmosphere was tense. But there was more sorrow and resignation in the air than anger.

*   *   *

Angelika's sixth birthday party turned out better than she ever could have imagined. It was held in Uncle Aleko's garden on a point surrounded on three sides by the green ocean waters.

The palace was fit for a president. Eight buildings, an outdoor theater, a horse-jumping arena, a swimming pool, and a lawn the size of four football fields, cozily planted with palms and miombo trees.

A hundred and ten invited guests, and one who wasn't—the wild Ibrahim who saw to it to arrange a karaoke competition on the theater stage at two in the morning. President Aleko won with his rendition of "The Winner Takes It All." By then little Angelika was long since asleep, her head full of lovely dreams of the pony she'd just received. She had named it Pocahontas.

Aleko celebrated his victory by sharing some Russian vodka with his friend Günther.

"What was up with that old lady INTERPOL wanted to get their hands on?"

"I don't know yet. I locked her and her companions up and

went to pick up the pony. According to the man in Rome, the one who called, it's fraud of some sort."

Aleko smiled.

"Seems like she's a firecracker. Bring her here tomorrow and we'll interrogate her together."

"If you like. What about the others?"

"They might be good to have around. But don't come too early, I need to sleep in after tonight. Who invited crazy Ibrahim?"

"He just showed up."

President Aleko sighed. His deceased wife's many cousins sure liked to take liberties.

CHAPTER 34

Son of a Sugar Beet Farmer

It's better to have friends than enemies. If you absolutely must become enemies with someone, the Russian mafia is just about the worst one you could choose. They never forget, never forgive, and never give up.

The contract out on the 118 percent man could not be fulfilled. That very same day, President Yeltsin's damn chief advisor stopped showing up at his job at the Kremlin. The next day, the president voiced suspicions that organized crime lay behind his disappearance. Only the Vory knew that the president was thinking along the right lines but was wrong even so. And now came the wrench in the works. Before Yeltsin got too drunk each morning, he ordered a series of crackdowns on the mafia's various core operations. And each afternoon, when he was drunk as a skunk, he became even bolder. He reckoned that those who had most to lose when taxation exceeded available assets were people whose assets far exceeded those of everyone else. For instance, the gas and oil industry oligarch who had bought his enterprise from the state for the equivalent of 180 million dollars and found himself sitting, three weeks later, on the equivalent of 6.5 billion in the same currency.

This successful businessman was arrested for speeding and charged with violent resist of arrest followed by contempt of court and, unexpectedly, possession of narcotics. It was beyond imagining, not least for the oligarch himself, how a pound of pure heroin could have ended up under his pillow in his jail cell. Instead of his traditional summer vacation in Saint-Tropez, he now had sixteen years in prison to look forward to.

With that, Yeltsin was content while the mafia was enraged. With the president, sure. But mostly with Aleksandr Kovalchuk, who had vanished without a trace.

* * *

The Russian word *vor* means "thief." In a rather narrower sense of the word, a *vor* is a member of the Russian organized crime syndicate. In the plural it is *vory*, "the thieves." Or, if you prefer, Vory—the Russian mob.

Crowding all instances of organized crime in Russia under the Vory umbrella would be a gross oversimplification of history. Over the previous century, various criminal networks developed in different parts of the country, often loosely connected and without the strict organization and hierarchy that characterizes their Italian counterpart. Still, one exciting aspect of the Vory is that they long considered themselves too good to mix with communist commissars and government employees, but this changed as time went on. After all, Stalin had criminal and political renegades sent to the same labor camps. Spending seven years in a row breaking rocks side by side will encourage the formation of certain bonds. Long story short, thief and communist got to know one another in those camps and came to understand each other's needs.

Then, when Stalin died in early 1953, his feared secret police chief Lavrentiy Beria found himself too alone in life for his own liking. He tried to make new friends by granting amnesty to over a million thieves from the gulags. New friends notwithstanding, Khrushchev soon saw to it that Beria was executed, accused of three hundred rapes and quite a bit more besides. Some of it was made up. Most of it was absolutely true.

But the now-released thieves couldn't be re-imprisoned. They all tipped their hats and set about building new, strong, eternal bonds between themselves and Soviet Communist leaders and officials on all levels.

A new type of Soviet corruption was established during Khrushchev's reign, a type where the powers that be and the thieves walked hand in hand. It matured under Brezhnev. When Andropov took over, he had no sooner launched a vain attempt to fight corruption than he was taken out by kidney failure. The Soviet higher-ups felt at that point that it was Chernenko's turn; he was a seventy-three-year-old plagued by nearly every illness there was, including advanced cirrhosis. When he, in turn, kicked the bucket a year later, it was Gorbachev's turn. At his side, Aleksandr Kovalchuk. With a terrible lack of understanding about what the Vory was and—above all—what the Vory was turning into.

Vexingly enough for the mafia, the insufferable Kovalchuk did not go down with Gorbachev; instead, he bounced right into his next job.

As chief advisor to Yeltsin, he had invented tax rates that should not have existed and toyed with the mafia without even being aware of it. He was tipped off about the Vory's wrath just in the nick of time and left the country instead of life on earth. He landed, so to speak, in a secret location and under a secret name. His new career took off, not least thanks to his two suitcases full of dollars. In just a few years, the man formerly known as Aleksandr took on the role as chief advisor to yet another president—this time in a country where it was much, much easier to shove your boss aside when the opportunity arose.

With that, he could have lived happily ever after.

If not for the fact that the Vory never forgot, never forgave, and never gave up.

CHAPTER 35

Wednesday, September 7, 2011

NO DAYS TO GO

The chief of police, who went by the not-at-all-Condorian-sounding name Günther, coasted in past the ten-foot-high wall that surrounded the presidential palace on the point.

In the back seat of his jeep sat the fugitive Agnes and her entourage. All three were in handcuffs since the police-chief-slash-former-German-Russian-Stasi-informant and quasi-mobster did not have eyes in the back of his head.

Once they arrived, Günther led them into the library and sat each of them down on a chair. It was a large room, with a thirty-foot ceiling. Yet the bookcases were empty because President Aleko's predecessor had decided that all the country's literature should be burned, partly because he himself couldn't read, and partly as a show of strength when he was new in the job. He started with the books in his own library to set a good example. There were so many that it took fourteen days.

Up to that point, Aleko had managed to remain close to the center of power for several years. But when the book-burner took over, he got a little too close for his own good. He was not only vice president and minister of foreign affairs but chief of executive protection as well. This meant his own career would end alongside the president's unless he made sure to act rather than be acted upon.

So that's what he did. In his capacity as chief of executive protection, he drafted a presidential order stipulating that all the guards should be replaced by ones who would show unfailing loyalty to their top commander. Since the president couldn't read, he signed the order, believing instead that he was purchasing a piano for his wife's fiftieth birthday.

Thereafter Aleko was able to stage his coup in peace and quiet. Not a hair was hurt on any head, but the book-burner was put in a fishing boat and sent to an island twenty-five miles offshore. He was well cared for but forbidden to leave. No books other than the president's own ever had time to be burned. And the ex-president's wife got her piano.

* * *

President Aleko entered the bookless library flanked by two armed cousins of his wife. He nodded at Chief of Police Günther and looked at the trio, all in a row.

"Are they in handcuffs? Remove those at once. They're not animals!"

The chief of police obeyed.

Aleko came closer. He studied Agnes, Petra, and Johan one by one. Was handed their passports. He opened the first:

"Agnes Eklund," he said.

Agnes didn't respond. Petra responded on her behalf. Angrily.

"Why did you arrest us? We haven't done anything!"

"Not yet, anyway," said Johan.

President Aleko told numbers two and three in the line to shut their traps—he was dealing with number one at the moment.

The asshole was barely a meter away from Agnes. Johan was aware that Petra was next, and then it would be his turn. That punch in the nose was going to happen after all. There was no telling what would go on after that, but if he could just borrow a telephone he could call Obrama and tell him the news.

"Agnes Eklund," Aleko repeated. "Wanted by INTERPOL. Suspected of fraud. Excuse my curiosity, but what kind of fraud are we talking about here?"

Agnes replied that she was wondering the same thing. All she'd done was post personal updates on something called Instagram and on a blog, at which point companies right and left had begun sending her money.

"Which you gratefully accepted?"

"Not only that, Mr. President. I moved it here to the Condors. To be perfectly honest, I don't quite understand how it happened, my banker in Zurich is the one who handles that sort of thing."

Aleko was immediately enchanted by this woman.

"Very clever of you," he said. "Very clever. We'll dig deeper into your enterprises in a moment, but first I'd like to get to know your friends."

The president opened the next passport.

"Petra Rocklund," he said.

While the president and the woman with the violet hair had been chatting about finances, Petra had been thinking about what action would be best for the group. Johan's comment just now had given her to understand that he intended to follow through on his plan even though the chances of escape afterward were almost nonexistent. Because he wasn't sitting there thinking, *Self-defense*, was he?

Since this very day was all that was left of anything, she felt that the best plan was for her to take one for the team. That would mean Johan remained blameless. They'd probably ship Agnes off to INTERPOL, and Petra to prison—but the master chef should have time to get word to the American president about what Petra had just done in Johan's name. After all, it was what Johan wanted more than anything.

"Petra Rocklund," Aleko said again. "Answer me when I address you."

The prophet answered, and then some. She jumped up and gave him a right hook, followed by a left hook. The president ended up on the library floor with Petra looming over him.

"His nose, Petra!" Johan called. "His nose!"

She didn't make it that far, having already been neutralized by the president's chief of police and the two guards. Günther locked her arms behind her while one of the president's wife's two cousins aimed a pistol at her head.

Although there couldn't be more than eight hours left of everything, Petra stopped struggling. Somehow, getting shot in the head seemed extra unpleasant. A collapsing atmosphere was vastly preferable. Besides, she'd got two good blows in, even if she had missed his nose. That on its own felt quite nice.

The president stayed surprisingly calm. He got up, rubbing his cheeks.

"That was a violation of Condorian law, Petra Rocklund, but perhaps you were aware?"

"I don't know the laws of this country, but sure, I imagine I just broke one or two of them. Did it hurt?"

The president had to admit that it had and still did. But since he prided himself on being civilized, he wasn't going to repay her in kind. Mrs. or Miss Rocklund would be brought to trial and judged according to the laws of the constitutional state. The fact was, the president himself was in charge of adjudicating this sort of matter. He would do so this very moment, in fact. Did Petra Rocklund have anything to say in her defense?

The prophet thought about how best to protect Johan. She had already taken one for the team, but the more she stepped up, the more it would look like she was acting on her own rather than as part of this group. Okay then.

"In my defense, Mr. President, I would like to say that your tie is horrifically ugly. The only thing it could possibly match, in my estimation, is your face."

"Duly noted," said President Aleko. "Seven years."

"Seven years of what?" said Petra.

"Internment."

Petra laughed. Not as part of her act, but for real. Seven minutes would have stung, but seven years truly made no difference.

CHAPTER 36

Wednesday, September 7, 2011

NO DAYS TO GO

The president had not been expecting Petra to laugh at the sentence he'd just handed down. But he turned away from her and back to the last of the three people who'd so recently been sitting in a row.

Johan was moved by what had just happened. He viewed Petra's unleashing the attack on his behalf as an act of love. It wasn't the end of the world that she'd missed the nose. But it had been traumatic to see that pistol pressed to her temple. He would have to tell Obrama.

The president opened Johan's passport.

"Johan Valdemar Löwenhult," he said.

"That's me. Emphasis on Johan. Master chef and genius. Could I borrow a phone by any chance?"

The president found each member of this trio more confounding than the last. He responded with a question of his own:

"Is Löwenhult a common name in your country?"

Johan considered this. None of the people whose mail he'd delivered had been named Löwenhult, he would remember that. On the other hand, he hadn't had time to do much delivering before he was fired.

"I don't know. It's really common in our family, but maybe that doesn't count?"

"Born in Stockholm," the president stated.

"Yes," Johan confirmed.

"Thirty years ago."

President Aleko suddenly looked thoughtful.

"Is your mother *Kerstin* Löwenhult?" he said.

"*Was*," said Johan. "She's dead. That's one Löwenhult less, if you're trying to count us."

"My condolences," said President Aleko. "Truly, my condolences."

Petra got loose from the chief of police after demonstrating, with her hands, that she was done fighting. Her palms open, she approached the president.

"Listen here," she said.

"Not quite the way to address a president," said Aleko. "But by all means, what's on your mind? Further opinions about my tie? My face?"

"How did you know his mother's first name? That's not in his passport."

Aleko had somehow suspected this revelation might come up. Perhaps he hadn't expected it to come from that ferocious woman, but it made no difference.

He braced himself.

"Because I have just realized that . . . the master chef and genius here . . . Johan Valdemar . . . is my son."

CHAPTER 37

Wednesday, September 7, 2011

NO DAYS TO GO

Following Kerstin Löwenhult's night with the young diplomat from a faraway land, and what it led to vis-à-vis an unwanted pregnancy, she had written a number of letters to Johan's father in Moscow over the years. Aleksandr burned the first one but saved the rest. He didn't know quite why. Years later, under a new name in the Condors, he wondered if, in some psychological sense, it had to do with needing to be reminded of the quality of his sperm. He and his Condorian wife never had children. She thought it was because of him. He didn't want to tell her he was sure the opposite was true.

His wife followed Kerstin's example before her fifty-fifth birthday. She had been sickly for a long time. There were only four doctors in the Condors: an ear specialist, two general practitioners, and a Tanzanian fax-machine repairman who realized one day that he would get further in life if he faxed himself a fake medical license.

Unfortunately, it was the last of these who had treated Aleko's wife. His secret was revealed a little too late, and he was sentenced to twelve years as prison doctor at the only prison facility in the Condors. He was still a fraud, but Aleko imagined he must have learned something about medicine over the years, and of course it didn't matter as much with the prisoners as it had with his wife. The fake doctor had eight years of his sentence left to serve.

The president took out the letters from Kerstin and launched into a recitation. As a result, Johan both understood and believed what he'd been told: his father Aleko, in his capacity as advisor to Gorbachev, had traveled around Europe to attend various events and had accordingly landed in Stockholm at a conference and diplomatic banquet. And what had happened happened.

Johan also understood, from his mother's letters, that the man he'd thought was his real father, Bengt Löwenhult, was gay and devoted himself full-time to diplomacy and his boyfriend the secretary until he retired someplace.

Johan was pleased. Bengt had left his son Fredrik to fend for himself, but he hadn't deserted Johan, not in the same way. Because if you weren't someone's dad, then that was that.

The person who understood least and last was the president's East German sidekick. Aleko had never told him about this little youthful indiscretion of his, and why would he? There was no way he could have guessed it would catch up with him this way. After thirty years!

Still, he sensed that an apology might be in order.

"I'm sorry, Günther," he said. "But now that I've got a son . . . would you consider becoming my brother? For real, that is. I can make that happen."

Günther smiled. He gave his newfound brother a hug and said this was an administrative matter they could skip. He and Aleko had been "brothers" ever since those wild nights in Berlin years ago.

Then Günther turned to Johan.

"I'd like to welcome you to the family."

"Thanks, you too," said Johan.

"Not that it matters," said Petra, "and I'm mostly asking out of curiosity: Am I still facing seven years in prison?"

"A sentence is a sentence," said Aleko. "It can't be undone. But in my capacity as president, I do have the right to refer cases to the Supreme Court for pardoning. It is about to convene this very minute. And now, convene it has. You're pardoned."

Petra was glad. This way, she could meet her maker in peace and quiet. And what's more, their task had been completed; that asshole Aleko had got what he deserved. She'd missed his nose, but given recent developments she didn't want to punish him more. In fact, she would have preferred to take it back, if only that had been possible.

Agnes sat where she sat, truly astounded at the fast pace of her life these days.

"I don't mean to make this all about me," she said to the president. "But am I correct in my assumption that INTERPOL still hasn't found me?"

"INTERPOL doesn't find anything in this country without asking me first," said Aleko.

"Or me," said Chief of Police Günther. "I suppose I should start pretending to look for you tomorrow. There's a special agent in Rome who keeps calling to ask how it's going."

With that, most everything was settled. For all but one of them.

"Dad?" said Johan.

"Yes, my son?"

"Where's the kitchen?"

CHAPTER 38

Wednesday, September 7, 2011

FIVE HOURS TO GO

Agnes, Petra, and Johan were each assigned an elegant suite on the second floor of the east wing of the presidential palace. The doomsday prophet was absolutely horrified by the wallpaper in her room. It was floral. And leafy. Full of little birds, red berries, yellow fruits. A monkey. A giraffe's head. The pattern repeated across all four walls. Even the door was wallpapered. Who could sleep here?

Well, it didn't really matter. At 11:20 p.m. local time, plus or minus a minute or two, everything was going to end. Less than five hours to go.

Petra's stomach was rumbling. When the group gathered on the terrace for a papaya-based welcome drink, she asked the president about his eating habits. Aleko told her that dinner was served at eight o'clock each evening, and followed by sandwiches of the more elegant sort toward midnight.

"We'll miss the sandwiches," said Petra, "but I'm looking forward to dinner. What might be on the menu?"

The president didn't know, but Johan did. He had just returned from the kitchen, where he'd had a challenging conversation with the palace's executive chef.

"Fish," he said.

"What kind of fish?" Aleko wondered.

"I don't know, because the chef only speaks something called French, that's a language they speak in France. But it looked more or less like my shoes."

The president looked at his newfound son's calf-leather Branchini shoes. Navy blue at the toe, followed by pale blue, gray, purple, red, black and bright yellow.

"Triggerfish," he said. "*Baliste* in French. Which is spoken in the Condors as well. And here and there around the world, for that matter."

Johan nodded. *Baliste* might have been the word the chef had kept repeating each time Johan asked for salmon. He still had to find out what Västerbotten cheese might be called in French.

"*Fromage de Västerbotten*," Agnes guessed.

Johan thanked her for her help and wondered where Papa Aleko kept his wine cellar. Now that the master chef thought about it, he did know quite a bit of French after all.

"Bordeaux," he said. "Bourgogne. Champagne. Loire. Gérard Depardieu. 'You don't like me, do you?' 'We don't have to like each other, we just have to be married.'"

President Aleko didn't follow.

"Your son knows every movie in existence by heart," said Petra. "Gérard Depardieu triggered something for him. That last bit must have been from *Green Card*."

"Nineteen ninety," said Johan. "Maybe ninety-one. So, about that wine cellar?"

Aleko said there wasn't one, but that he had plenty of vodka.

"What's the point of being president if you don't have a wine cellar?"

The president said he'd had no way of knowing that he was about to gain a son-slash-master-chef, or else he certainly would have been better prepared. He snapped his fingers, at which point an otherwise invisible assistant showed up. Aleko ordered her to fetch the best wine the finest hotel had in stock.

"White or red?" asked the assistant.

"All the colors you can get your hands on. As many bottles as possible. Tell them I'll stop by to pay for it when I get the chance, if I remember to."

CHAPTER 39

Wednesday, September 7, 2011

FOUR HOURS TO GO

As they waited for dinner to be served, the president thought the general mood demanded a little extra something in their papaya juice. Or rather a lot extra something. They had to celebrate that Aleko had become a father at the age of fifty-five.

"Papaya vodka sours all around," he said to the nearest waitress. "Without too much papaya or sour in relation to the rest."

Petra glanced at the clock and saw no reason to meet her maker with a frown on her face. When the server returned with a tray full of drinks, she grabbed one and thrust it in the air.

"Cheers," she said. "Cheers for all that has ever been!"

"And all that is still to come," Aleko added.

It looked like Petra wanted to explain a thing or two to him, but Agnes whispered at her to skip it.

"Let the president be happy to the end," she suggested. "Now that he's a dad and everything."

What she didn't say, but did think, was that they could explain Petra's crazy ideas to Aleko the next morning. What she additionally forbade herself to think was, what if the doomsday prophet was right? If she was, it would be more disappointing than ever.

* * *

After a few rounds of drinks that weren't too weak for anyone but Aleko, the assistant returned with 280 bottles of wine and champagne. The hotel director had meekly asked to be reimbursed with seven hundred fifty thousand Condorian francs. And perhaps a little extra, given that he now had nothing but Coca-Cola and water to serve his guests.

"Fine, fine," said Aleko.

Johan was already browsing through the many boxes and striking gold in several of them.

"Here's what we'll have with the starter," he said. "And this one's for the fish I forgot the name of. And we'll have this one right now."

He pointed at a box containing twelve bottles of 2002 Chablis Grand Cru Les Clos.

"Fruity and fresh, with a hint of yellow apples," said Johan.

"Apples?" said his father, who had for all intents and purposes been raised on tea and vodka.

CHAPTER 40

Wednesday, September 7, 2011

THREE HOURS TO GO

The fish course was given a reluctant seal of approval by the master chef, despite the lack of Västerbotten cheese in the pesto. But *ice cream with hot fudge sauce* for dessert? Unacceptable.

"What is the chef's name, Dad?"

"Malik, I think. Why?"

"I need to talk to him."

"Should I fire him? Just say the word."

"We'll deal with that tomorrow. Mostly I need to understand what he's saying, and to make him understand me. Aside from everything to do with wine, I only know two words in French. One is Gérard. The other is Depardieu. How do we solve this?"

"It's called an interpreter," said Aleko.

After their spiked papaya beverages, the Chablis, the fish, an accompanying chardonnay, and the grotesquely rudimentary dessert, the guests spontaneously spread out on the large veranda. Agnes had her tablet. Johan was nearby, analyzing the flavor differences of a number of chocolate pralines. And Petra was in a comfortable deck chair, with both hands behind her neck and a smile on her face.

The prophet was counting on remaining conscious for a sufficiently long fraction of a second to have time to enjoy receiving confirmation that her equation consisting of sixty-four complicated steps was quite accurate. In that fraction, she and no one else in the world would understand what was happening. Except for maybe Agnes. Johan? Hardly.

President Aleko was holding the glass of sweet Tokaji Eszencia his son had put in his hand, marveling at the revelation that something other than vodka could make him feel so good. In the company of a day like this, it filled him with affection for humanity.

He decided to wander among the guests, and began with Petra in her lounge chair.

"You look happy," said Aleko, trying to smile back at the woman who had so recently punched him in the face twice.

"I *am* happy," said Petra. "For the first time ever, we're all about to be treated equally. And by all, I mean *all*."

What was she on about?

"Are you a communist?" asked the former chief advisor to the last leader of the Soviet Union.

The prophet smiled even wider.

"Nah. I'm the last realist on earth. Agnes has asked me to lie low, so I won't say more. We could have continued this conversation over breakfast tomorrow morning if only things weren't the way they are."

All Aleko took from this was that Petra must have a screw loose. To think she had jumped up and punched the president of the Condors in the face, only to enjoy expensive wines on that same president's garden terrace as punishment. Petra Rocklund must have been closer to being locked up for seven years than anyone in all of the history of confinement.

*   *   *

224

The president wandered on to the next guest. He sat down beside Agnes with his Hungarian dessert wine in hand. He wanted to make sure she was having a good time too.

Like Petra, the violet-haired visitor was truly satisfied. But for different reasons. She was enjoying the way her life, which had been at a standstill for so long, was suddenly doing one-eighties every day. She was also enjoying the fact that for the moment it was standing still again, so she could recover. After all, she wasn't a youngster anymore.

Günther had let her borrow his tablet. He'd learned quite a bit about police work since he became chief of police, and he suspected that the special agent in Rome knew his stuff. Günther then clapped Agnes on the shoulder and said it would be wise to keep her own tablet turned off so he couldn't use it to track her down. Günther, that is. The special agent had no business coming to the Condors, the chief of police would see to that.

While Günther slipped off to see to Angelika and Pocahontas, Agnes turned on the tablet. She began by reading about the country she and her many millions now found themselves in. It wasn't a cheerful read. And now, the man in charge was standing in front of her and asking how things were going.

"Thanks for asking, Mr. President. The wine is delicious, the evening breeze is warm, and here I sit reading all about your country. It seems you rule over absolutely everything here, Mr. President—I get the sense I've dumped my entire fortune right in the presidential lap."

"Stop 'Mr. President'-ing me this minute, please. I'm called Aleko . . . these days."

"Did you change your name? What was it before?"

"Long story. I'll tell you another time."

"Then let's talk about my money instead. Why did my advisor in Zurich want me to move it here? A lovely man, by the way."

Aleko took another sip of his Tokaji. Then he wiped his lips and told Agnes that congratulations were in order. Her fortune couldn't be in a safer lap. *Curiosity* was not part of the Condorian national spirit; no one would ask where her money had come from or where it might go. If another country, organization, or authority came around asking questions, they would receive no answer. The People's Republic of the Condors did not cooperate with anybody, or capitulate to them either. In return for this simple, honorable principle, the nation took only a tiny percentage in fees. It was likely this low fee that had prompted Agnes's Swiss advisor to recommend Banque Condorienne, where Aleko himself just so happened to be chairman. Or maybe it was CEO. Something like that. Anyway, he was in charge.

Thanks to her now-retired alias, the violet-haired pensioner was more widely traveled than most people. Thus she recognized a shithole country when she saw one. Surely her money was secure, but the Condors didn't have much else to brag about.

"I was just reading that half the adults in your country can neither read nor write," she said.

Perhaps she sounded more accusatory than she'd intended, because the president's tone shifted.

"Isn't that just as well? People write so much nonsense everywhere. What would be the point of people reading it?"

Agnes went on:

"And the child mortality rate is absolutely horrific."

Now the president was truly annoyed.

"Well, shouldn't that make you happy? After all, that way not as many of them will grow up to be illiterate."

This was possibly the stupidest thing Agnes had ever heard, and she had been born and raised in Dödersjö. But this was the evening father and son had found each other. Who was she to get Johan's dad all worked up without an obvious reason?

Given that attitude, a presidential tiff could have been avoided if only Johan hadn't butted in. He was sitting near enough, with his chocolate pralines, to realize that a certain chill had arisen between Agnes and Aleko.

"What are you talking about?" he asked.

"Oh, nothing," said the president. "It's just that your friend Agnes here can't quite understand how complicated it is to build up a country that's had to endure the tyranny of imperialism for centuries."

What kind of nonsense is this? thought Agnes. Well, if he wanted to keep bickering, she wasn't going to stop him.

"But weren't Ethiopia, Liberia, and the Condors the only African countries that were never colonized?" she said, sending up silent thanks to Günther for the tablet.

Aleko was well aware of this, even though he'd essentially slipped on a banana skin and landed in the banana republic he now controlled. But how did this old hag know it?

"Exactly!" he said. "I was just getting to that. Only three nations resisted when the brutal wave of colonialism took over Africa. 'Don't mess with the Condors,' I always say. All my people say so, in fact."

"Or maybe it was because Ethiopia and Liberia demonstrated stability and economic viability while not a single soul wanted to bother with a tiny island in the middle of the ocean?"

Aleko realized that the violet-haired rabble-rouser was far too worthy a debate opponent to deserve a debate. Best to chastise her now.

"Why ask questions if you already know the answers?"

Johan didn't follow, but now he was positive Dad and Agnes weren't getting along.

"Are you arguing? What about?"

"Turns out Madam Agnes here is an expert in running a country," said Aleko. "And now she wants to teach me how."

Johan, who was terminally bad at sarcasm, was impressed.

"You *are*, Agnes? I thought your specialty was building wooden boats? Or was it clogs?"

The retired manufacturess fortified herself with a sip from yet another glass of the American chardonnay that had elevated the fish course rather well.

"No, I just happen to have been reading up on this stuff. Your father is the leader of one of the poorest countries in the world, where the average life expectancy is eighteen years, child mortality is high, and 50 percent of the population is illiterate. The principal industry on the island used to be forestry, until all the forest was cut down without anyone thinking to plant more trees. Since then, fishing and farming have kept people afloat, but the soil is eroding without any trees to keep it in place, waterways are becoming clogged with silt, and the coral reefs are being destroyed. I think any old boatbuilder or clog manufacturer could have done a better job. With the possible exception of my husband—but luckily he stepped on a nail and was too stingy to go to the doctor."

Harsh words. Aleko didn't know where to start.

"What does 'eroding' mean?' asked Johan.

Chief of Police Günther was back among the others after putting Angelika to bed and leading Pocahontas into her stall. He noticed the tense atmosphere at once.

"What happened?" he said. "I thought this was a party."

"Nothing," Aleko said sullenly. "Except that this old lady here, who is so very skilled at making clogs, wants to take over my country and run it."

Günther knew his friend and brother in spirit well.

"Excellent," he said. "I've been wondering for ages when we'd get an attempted coup on our hands. After all, it's been seven years since the last one, and that was the time you and I took over, if I recall correctly? If you stop fooling around with wine, dear brother, and go back to vodka, you'll soon be back to your cheerful self."

Just think—this drew out a presidential smile. And the vodka *was* on the table, so why not?

"You're right, Günther, as always."

Aleko poured a glass and raised it toward Agnes.

"This is a night to be joyous. Cheers to that, my dear clog manufacturer."

Agnes didn't hold a grudge when she didn't have to.

"Cheers right back atcha, my dear dictator."

* * *

Petra left the table and the company early, and took a seat in an even comfier lounge chair in the garden below the terrace, with a glass of red wine in hand (variety is the spice of life). And that eternal smile on her lips. There she sat now, counting the stars in the sky. Three hours to go became two hours and forty-five minutes. Soon merely two and a half. A server came by and asked if she would like a refill. Petra accepted and said she would like one each time her glass got low.

"From now until the end of time."

The server nodded and pretended to understand.

CHAPTER 41

Wednesday, September 7, 2011

TWO HOURS TO GO

Malik, the chef who had served ice cream with hot fudge sauce for dessert, did at least venture out to the terrace to serve coffee and copious amounts of *avec*. This reminded Johan that, in addition to Gérard and Depardieu, he also knew the French word "cognac."

Everyone around the table was getting on again, while Petra was still in her spot a bit farther off, humming "What a Wonderful World." A server stood nearby, keeping watch with a bottle of wine in hand.

The president didn't want to start any new fights, but he did feel the urge to offset Agnes's poorly disguised criticism of his leadership. It might be possible, if he treaded carefully.

"Shall I tell you all how I've managed to stay in power for seven whole years?" he said. "It's not a violent story."

"You make sure to surround yourself with friends?" Agnes suggested, nodding in Günther's direction.

"That's part of it."

It was true that his now-deceased Condorian wife's siblings and whole and half cousins held all the country's most important positions (except for that of chief of police; Aleko had given that one to Günther, who had always wanted to wear a uniform). It was also true that Aleko had rewritten portions of the country's constitution. These days it stipulated that any president who'd held that seat for five years was automatically given an extension, as long as the Supreme Court didn't rule otherwise.

"And the Supreme Court is made up of . . . ?" said Agnes.

"Me. Why?"

"Very practical. A clog manufacturer remains in their position until they can no longer sell any clogs. Or until they step on a nail. Or both."

For the sake of peace and quiet, Aleko elected not to comment on this clog lecture. He said the most salient reason he was still securely in his post after seven years was that he was *popular*.

"You think people love high child mortality, illiteracy, and nonexistent healthcare?"

Aleko ignored the violet-haired quibbler. He was done sulking, once and for all.

"My people love me because I stand up to the outside world—that is to say, all the pigs in the African Union."

"Pigs?" said Johan.

"Figuratively, Johan," said Agnes.

"Turn on the TV anytime. You'll see story after story about the union's attempts to bring the continent's smallest nation to its knees, and about the president standing strong in the name of the proud Condorian people."

"Fantastic!" said Johan. "Is *that* why they call you an asshole?"

"How many channels are there on this island?" Agnes asked.

"One," said Aleko. "I know what you're thinking."

This lady was no dummy. The manager of the TV channel, Fariba, was the twin sister of the president's deceased wife. Her leadership skills were undisputed. On her first day on the job, she had fired the first three people she encountered, just to have fired someone. Those who remained became unwaveringly loyal from one second to the next.

"They say I'm *modern* as well," said Aleko.

His most recent initiative had been to establish his nation as a haven for people all over the world who saw no point in paying tax in their own nations. Like Agnes. And for all the people who had incomes it wasn't possible to pay taxes on even if they wanted to. The disadvantage of dirty money was that it was dirty. Everything had been so much simpler before, when a plastic bag full of cash was a good thing to have, rather than a liability.

For the first time, Agnes had no biting comment ready to go.

"Long story short, people's lives are better under my leadership," said Aleko. "Not much, but a little. And there's so much pride! We were in the running to host the World Cup three years from now."

"Did you win?"

"No, Brazil did. I don't think there is any organization more corrupt than FIFA."

"Do you even have any arenas?"

"I think it's about time for some karaoke," said Günther.

CHAPTER 42

Wednesday, September 7, 2011

THE FINAL HOUR OF
ABSOLUTELY EVERYTHING

Despite two papaya drinks, two glasses of champagne, many glasses of chardonnay, and three cups of cognac, Agnes was keeping an eye on the clock as it neared 11:20 and the potential consequences it had for the rest of the night. Johan, in contrast, was absorbed in the fun of the singing contest and wanted his loveliest friend Petra to join in. She'd been sitting there for a few hours now, just gazing up at the sky.

"Isn't it about time you get moving?" he said lovingly as he tugged at her arm.

Petra allowed herself to be brought to the presidential palace's outdoor stage. She held the bottomless wineglass in one hand and now there was a microphone in the other. The ground was swaying back and forth. Were they at sea? Maybe another sip would help stabilize her.

She waved off Günther's suggestion of "Hotel California" and refused to browse through the hundreds of other available songs. Her time under the starry sky had been far too serious for that.

"Allow me to offer some poetry," she said. "Emily Dickinson."

There were perhaps fifteen minutes left of all of existence. Petra would recite her favorite poem. Nothing could be a more fitting farewell. But goodness, how everything was rocking. Wait, how did the poem go again?

It was gone.

Petra took another sip. Which didn't help. And another. Still nothing. And silence onstage.

Everyone was waiting for Dickinson; she couldn't simply switch to "Hotel California" now. So, this would have to do:

TWINKLE, TWINKLE, LITTLE STAR.
HOW I WONDER WHAT YOU ARE.
UP ABOVE THE WORLD SO HIGH,
LIKE A DIAMOND IN THE SKY.

Agnes was the only one who knew Emily Dickinson was innocent of what the prophet was reciting. Johan applauded with enthusiasm. He liked Petra so very much, and he hoped, for her sake, that she would be right about the end of the world, whenever it was supposed to happen. The first thing he would do, when it did, was give her a big hug.

Günther realized that Petra was having some serious trouble standing on her two feet. Her declamation of that beautiful Emily Dickinson poem seemed to have taken a toll.

Aleko's deceased wife's wheelchair had spent the last four years in a corner of the stage as a reminder of her continued spiritual presence. Günther looked at his brother in spirit and received a nod in response. Aleko's wife had sat in that chair for the last three weeks of her life, while the fax-machine repairman treated her for vitamin deficiency instead of cancer. Now it was clearly needed once again.

At 11:15, Petra was rolled into her room. Still with a wineglass in one hand and the microphone in the other. It had long since dropped its connection to the amplifier onstage, but that didn't stop the prophet from changing her mind about Günther's original suggestion.

WELCOME TO THE HOTEL CALIFORNIA.
SUCH A LOVELY PLACE. SUCH A LOVELY PLACE.

By 11:17, Agnes had more or less managed to get the doomsday prophet undressed and into bed. By 11:17:30, Petra was fast asleep. By 11:19, Agnes was back outside with everyone else. She was still keeping an eye on the time, and she took Johan aside and said softly:

"It's 11:20, plus or minus a minute or two."

"Is it?" said Johan. "I'm crossing my fingers for Petra."

"Sometimes I just don't understand you," said Agnes.

"Me neither," said Johan.

PART TWO

*The Time After the End
of the World*

CHAPTER 43

Thursday, September 8, 2011

Petra woke up. Her head was buzzing. Could it be the wallpaper? That floral pattern. All the leaves. The tiny birds. The red berries, the yellow fruits, the monkey. And the giraffe head.

Maybe it wasn't the wallpaper's fault. The buzzing might have come from all the drinking instead. After all, so much had happened in such a short time. They were arrested, thrown into jail, taken to the palace, put in front of the president.

And she'd landed two massive blows.

"Well done, Petra," she said to herself.

And on top of that . . . They were father and son! She had decked *Johan's father*! Not so good after all.

Festivities and fraternization. A glass of wine in her hand. A bottomless one. Was there karaoke after that, or had someone only suggested it?

Couldn't remember.

A worthy end, in any case, to the nanosecond of eternity that they had known as "humanity."

Soon it would all be over.

"Farewell, everything," she said, and closed her eyes once more to keep from taking that psychedelic wallpaper with her into the great beyond.

But . . . wait a sec.

What time was it?

Petra opened her eyes again.

It was *light* out.

The truth crept over her. She closed her eyes. What if . . . it couldn't be . . .

Her eyes were still closed. She didn't want to open them. Ever again.

She opened them again.

The wallpaper. The light. The chirping birds that came not from the wallpaper but from the garden outside.

The world still existed.

Petra's calculations had been wrong.

* * *

When Johan arrived in the reception room for breakfast, Papa Aleko and Agnes were already there.

"Good morning, my son," said the president. "Agnes and I are sitting here talking politics. She was just saying that the Condors ought to have a program for the elderly. Just think how little she knows about our country. No one grows old here. Most people croak not long after they hit fifty."

"What about decent healthcare, then?" said Agnes. "That way people will live longer, and there will be a use for those retirement homes I was talking about."

"Sounds expensive," said Aleko.

Johan wasn't listening. If he understood correctly, the time last night had come to be both 9:20 and 11:20 plus or minus a minute or two. There had been a lot of karaoke and wheelchairs toward the end there. And Agnes saying it was time, even though it wasn't. Eventually he'd collapsed into the bed he'd been assigned with his rainbow shoes on. By that point, he wasn't thinking at all.

But now.

He had to know.

"Where are we?"

"Same place as yesterday. At the presidential palace. Why do you ask?"

"The world didn't end?"

"What are you talking about?" said Aleko.

"I can explain," said Agnes. "No, Johan. The world is in just as good and awful shape as it was yesterday and likely will be tomorrow. Petra is a wonderful person, but her calculations were wrong. To be honest, I had an inkling that might be the case."

"Poor Petra," said Johan. "She must be absolutely devastated."

Just then, the devastated group member appeared.

In a fantastic mood.

"Good morning, dear friends," she said.

"Nice weather today," said Agnes. "*Any* weather is more than some of us were counting on."

"I miscalculated," said Petra.

"You don't say."

"Go ahead and tease! I had a few rough minutes when I woke up, but I've already figured out where I went wrong in my calculations. *More or less* where I went wrong."

"So when will the world end next time? Might be nice to know, for planning purposes."

"I'll ask that we circle back to that later. When you change one parameter, all the other ones get pulled along in a complicated chain reaction. A bit much for you to take in, I think."

"Can someone explain to me what is going on?" said Aleko. "I'm the president, dammit!"

The doomsday prophet clarified. When she was finished, Aleko wondered if this was why she'd merely laughed at him when he sentenced her to seven years' internment.

Petra nodded and smiled.

Aleko felt duped and asked what would happen to that smile on her face if he decided to take back her pardon. But Petra couldn't accept such a thing. The president himself had expressly said "a sentence is a sentence."

CHAPTER 44

Thursday, September 8, 2011

A sense of calm settled over the presidential palace. Petra and Agnes were sitting in deck chairs under an umbrella near one end of the pool. The doomsday prophet had paper and pen. She calculated, crossed out, underlined and calculated some more.

"It's fascinating in all its complexity," she said to the skeptic next to her. "Everything is connected to everything else."

"Really?"

"Look here. If I assign this parameter a value of seven . . . the world will end in . . . let's see here . . . 212 years."

"Good. Then we all will have ended first, with plenty of time to spare."

"But if I assign it the value of six instead . . . the world will end . . . last spring."

"Let's go with six so we don't have to have this conversation."

"I can't just choose parameters and values willy-nilly. How dumb can you get?"

Aleko was dangling his feet in the water at the other end of the pool. His newfound son was doing the same thing, right next to him. Aleko felt that at his side was a potential successor in some distant quasi-democratic election. Might as well start the work of initiating the boy into the way it all worked.

He began by explaining that domestic and international politics went hand in hand in the Condors. The best way to last a long time at his post was to enjoy popular support.

"You mean making sure the Condorians have food on their table?"

"Hell, no. We don't want them to get used to that. It'll only make them want more. What the people need above all are pride and self-esteem."

Johan was not in possession of these particular traits, although he had made some progress in the past week. But he wanted to know more.

The Condors were the smallest country in Africa. A quarter of a million inhabitants, depending on how many had perished since the last time anyone counted.

"Compare that with Nigeria's 180 million. Or the hundred million in Ethiopia, Egypt, or Congo. Or all the rest: Tanzania, South Africa, and Kenya must have fifty million each. That shithole Sudan is nothing but sand, and yet forty million people live there."

Johan did and did not understand. Mostly not. What did the population have to do with anything?

Aleko said this was the way the countries' relative importance was calculated. As a result, the Condors were never even considered when the African Union filled important positions in the organization.

"Like, for example?"

"Commissioners, chief investigators, special envoys . . ."

"What does a com . . . mishner do?"

That was hard to pronounce.

"It varies. He might be in charge of peace and security or economic affairs or infrastructure and energy . . ."

That was a lot of tricky words at once. Johan decided to grin and bear it.

"Which one would you be best at?"

The president hadn't thought that far. Peace and security might mean being forced to visit war zones, and that sounded neither peaceful nor secure. Aleko certainly did have considerable experience in economics, but none suited for the current state of reality. On Gorbachev's behalf he had tried to develop a bilateral business relationship with North Korea. He had fifty thousand Soviet fur caps sent to Pyongyang and in return he received a request for eight kilos of enriched uranium in exchange for half of the freshly arrived fur caps.

Infrastructure and energy . . . maybe that was the ticket. Just a few days ago, he and his deceased wife's cousin at the airport had been discussing the possibility of paving the road into and out of the city. Maybe even the runway, while they were at it.

"I don't know," said Aleko.

That wasn't the point. The point was that the Condors deserved the respect of the other African countries! An important position would enhance the country's international significance even as it created even more pride among the citizens. And in the long run it would mean that Aleko remained safely in his palace. It was all connected.

But his colleagues in the union's assembly waved off the president of the lilliputian nation when he came to them with his demands. So Aleko had changed tactics and launched a war of attrition: he obstructed everyone and everything. And he intended to keep it up until they gave in.

What's more, the union's special session was just a few weeks away. Günther was his chief strategist when it came to the ways they might put the rest of Africa in a bad mood; he would soon be drawing up some guidelines for the upcoming meeting in Addis Ababa.

Johan wanted to know if he'd understood his father correctly. For it wasn't unheard of for Johan to misunderstand things.

"You mean you're behaving as badly as you possibly can in front of the union until they start to like you?"

This question sounded almost like a trap. His son had grossly oversimplified the conflict. But did that necessarily make him wrong?

"More or less," Aleko said defensively.

"How's it working out so far?"

This fucking kid! It wasn't working out at all. Aleko felt he needed to explain himself. There was, in fact, an agreeable side effect to the fact that the union kept refusing to do what he wanted.

"A tasty little commissioner appointment would really hit the spot, that's true. But while I'm waiting for that: the angrier the African Union is with me, the more popular I get here at home. That's called *polarization*. The more outside enemies, the more a group will stick together. Even Idi Amin understood that in his day."

"Who?"

Explaining to his son who Idi Amin was would take too long. Johan was extremely lovable, but he seemed to be more master chef than he was genius. Aleko got right to the heart of the matter:

"He blamed everything on the Ugandan Indians. They were given a few days to pack their bags and leave."

"And that made everything better?"

It was a sincere question.

"Hardly. The Indians ran all the businesses. Everything ground to a halt. But Idi Amin was very popular until people figured out what had happened. And that took a while."

Johan nodded without actually knowing which country they were talking about; there were just so many countries all over the place. But he'd noticed how close he and Petra had become when they were working together against a common outside enemy.

Even so, it didn't mean he liked that nice Obrama going around considering his dad an asshole. Couldn't there maybe be some sort of middle way?

"What do you mean?"

"You know, that you act a bit *less* assholey to Obrama, Idomin, and everyone else."

"What good would that do me? And, it's *Idi Amin* by the way. And he's been dead for nearly ten years."

Aleko thought his son sounded kind of like Gorbachev back in the day. The man who tried to make his people decently happy and in doing so made enemies of everyone. He left his own advisory significance in the matter out of it.

Agnes approached father and son and asked to join them. She said she needed a break from Petra.

"I like her an awful lot, and I have so many reasons to thank her. But if I sit over there I'll have to hear all about the next time the world is ending, and I can't take it right now."

"What has she come up with?" Aleko wondered.

"She's working on it. Last I heard it was sometime between last spring and two hundred years from now. What are you two talking about?"

"Dad was just explaining to me how politics work. As president, you have to see to it that people don't have food on the table, and you should start fights with as many people from other countries as possible. That's how to get the best results."

Agnes recalled her conversation with Aleko about Condorian healthcare policy. With nonexistent healthcare, people kicked the bucket well before they had time to get old, which meant the president didn't have to foot the bill for any elderly care.

"Clever dad you've got there, Johan," she said tartly. "But I'm not so sure he'll be welcomed into heaven on Judgment Day."

Judgment Day was a concept Johan had recently become familiar with.

"Wasn't that yesterday?"

CHAPTER 45

Thursday, September 8, 2011

Aleko was feeling the pressure from all sides: that old Agnes, his son Johan—and, increasingly, himself. Up to now, everything had been so simple: it had all been about lining your own pockets as best you could, and then positioning yourself to line them some more. That was how it had been under Gorbachev. When that ship sank, he didn't follow it into the depths; he hopped over to Yeltsin's. And that, in turn, lasted until the mafia felt enough was enough. What followed was a meandering escape to a country that hardly anyone but Khrushchev knew existed. And he was as dead as Idi Amin by this point.

In his time as chief advisor with the Kremlin, Aleko had spent time browsing through old and secret archives, looking back to the nation's birth in the hunt for any mistakes made by former leaders from which he might draw wisdom. This was how he had come to understand the Supreme Soviet's reasoning around Africa, and it was also how he came to learn of the existence of the country he would, much later, come to rule.

Since the Soviet Union didn't exist before 1922, they had missed the boat when Belgium, Great Britain, France, the German Empire, Italy, Portugal, and Spain laid claim to the continent of Africa. They regained some footing during the Cold War by supporting independence campaigns in Angola, Mozambique, and Guinea-Bissau. Thousands of young Africans were also able to get a free education at Soviet universities, including a suitable amount of schooling in the tenets of blessed socialism. These youth then returned home to their respective countries. Some of them stood on the barricades and were shot to death. But the quickest learners among them had snapped up not only the correct ideology but also how best to navigate the corridors of communism. It was all about slipping a coin into the right pocket at the right moment, about piggybacking on the right person and holding off stabbing said back until the time was right.

Aleko had sometimes spent days in a row in the secret archive, especially in those periods when Yeltsin was in such a thorough state of drunkenness that he wouldn't notice the absence of his chief advisor or anyone else. Like the week after he returned from a visit to Washington, DC, and President Clinton, who elegantly hushed up the fact that the Russian president had roamed about the White House in only his underpants one night, on the hunt for pizza.

In the Kremlin files he found everything from individual agents' field reports to Khrushchev's expertly handled speeches in front of the Politburo. The latter were full of astonishingly detailed historical context.

Thanks to Khrushchev's various writings, Aleko learned that the Condors had never sparked the interest of the colonial powers during the previous century, for the simple reason that the island nation was so tiny and far-flung. Some of them had certainly been there in the early twentieth century, but only because there had been rumors of striking gold. After killing a few thousand local inhabitants, and completing the search for what wasn't there, the British left, followed by the French. At least the latter left a school behind. And some venereal diseases.

The very poorest of poor nations had several decades in which to mismanage itself before the first secretary of the

Soviet Communist Party saw the potential there. A completely moldable nation: a few hundred thousand citizens, no real leadership.

Over the centuries, the Condors' geographical location, with Africa to the west, the Arabian Peninsula to the north, and India far to the east, created a diverse population that mixed with itself as well. Some were the descendants of enslaved Africans, others of seafarers from afar who ended up staying for the monthslong stormy seasons, and who found other ways to make a living while they waited.

Khrushchev imagined it was just a matter of appointing the right person and helping him oppress anyone who put up any opposition. As well as building a socialist model society from the outside, a role model for all of Africa—and, for that matter, for Yemen on the Arabian Peninsula not far away.

According to the secret archives, he had handpicked the four most talented characters on the island upon whom to build the future of the nation and of communism. They were sent to Moscow to be educated in the proper ways. After two years, Khrushchev would personally select a winner.

But he never had to make that choice. One of the students stepped in front of a tram after only three weeks, and then there were three. Two of them discovered the healing power of vodka, emptied a bottle each, and launched into a knife fight together. Since both of them found equal success in their ambition of killing the other, that left just one for Khrushchev to choose.

The fourth one made it through both years of his schooling, partly the official drills in Marxist doctrine, partly the more unofficial matter of how to get ahead at the expense of others. Number four was sent back to the Condors to take over the country with Soviet aid and his own cunning. Khrushchev was pleased. What could go wrong?

Basically everything, as it happened.

Number four started a political party, put two scuffling clans in their place with Soviet support, and managed in under nine months to become the country's first democratically elected president. In point of fact, the way this happened was that he neglected to communicate that it was time for an election, or tell anyone where and how to vote. Thus voter participation was limited to a single person, number four himself.

The newly elected president's first act was to make French the official language alongside the ancient variety of Arabic almost everyone spoke. French had *style*, and he knew some of it himself after two years at the school the Frenchmen once left behind. His second act was to start a communist newspaper, *La Vérité Condorienne*. In a language few others understood, in a country where nearly everyone was illiterate, and with contents that did not live up to its name.

After that, he blew half the country's assets before he was deposed by his second-in-command in a coup. This successor continued down the same path. He felt he had earned it.

Khrushchev wondered what was wrong with the Condorians, but he wouldn't give up. More students were educated at Soviet universities. Soviet-financed schools were established on the island; trade agreements were drawn up between the sister countries (one of them a few thousand times larger than the other, but still).

He didn't take his dream of African communism any further than this. First the Cuban Missile Crisis landed on his plate. Then he had a falling-out with everything and everyone, and was placed under house arrest in Moscow, where he sat in his rocking chair, pondering the true meaning of life. Until he had a heart attack and died.

* * *

Aleko was different from Khrushchev in the sense that he'd never believed in communism. Or in anything besides himself. And Günther. And, much later, his wife.

And now, all of a sudden, he had a son! A kindhearted one, it seemed. And honest. Curious. Master chef. Apparently a genius as well, although that wasn't quite as apparent.

And then there was this old purple-haired woman who spoke to the president as though it was not clear that he was both in charge and in the right. And—just in case he should turn out to be in the wrong after all—he could decide at any given moment what was true or untrue, so that he would be right in the end no matter what.

And then there was the doomsday prophet who'd attacked Aleko with both fists and insolence. At which point the Supreme Court pardoned her! Which would have been a very upsetting decision indeed, if it weren't for the fact that Aleko knew perfectly well who sat on the Supreme Court.

All in all, the Condorian president was heading for an existential crisis. He could no longer simply exploit the country he ruled over until his rule was over, because if he did that then Johan could never take over. If he was being honest with himself, what did he, the fourteenth president of the Condors, have—honestly—that his thirteen predecessors hadn't?

Nothing?

No, that would be overdoing it. Aleko saw two distinguishing features. One was the bit about pride. No one could be prouder than a Condorian, and that was all thanks to Aleko!

The other was *Game of Thrones*. As soon as the new American TV series could be pirated from the internet, Aleko had made sure station manager Fariba broadcast one episode per week, during prime time. There had only been ten episodes so far, but when she ran out of episodes she would just start over from the beginning. Aleko knew that Marx considered religion to be the opium of the people, but according to the president of the Condors that honor went to *Game of Thrones*. In a good way, because a drugged population was a compliant population. No one in the Condors had ever seen more naked-ness outside their own bedrooms.

Food on the table? thought the president. No, he knew his people. If there was anything they hungered for, it was national pride and sex on TV. Every Wednesday at 8 p.m.

On the other hand: What kind of accomplishment was this to hitch a presidential wagon to? Would it be enough for Johan to take over one day *without* the constant whining about elec-tion fraud taking hold?

Probably not.

Ugh! The president was about to do his only son a monu-mental disservice. It seemed as though the son in question sus-pected as much. And that purple-haired lady was openly critical.

Shit.

In the midst of this mental muddle, the doomsday prophet butted in. She apologized for her miscalculations the day be-fore and promised to deliver a new answer shortly. In the meantime, she suggested that the president review his leader-ship with an eye to helping his son. For the risk was that the world would continue to exist for years longer. She would have loved to lend him a hand, but she felt she would be of greatest service to humanity if she focused on her sixty-four-step equa-tion, version 2.0.

"As soon as I finish that, I'll be happy to be at your disposal. If you'd like, I have a flowchart we can go through together for starters. For now, my best advice is for you to listen to Agnes. She may be a doomsday skeptic, but that aside there's a lot of cleverness in that head of hers."

The fact that Agnes had thus far been correct to be skeptical was not something Petra wished to acknowledge.

Aleko considered all of this. And decided to listen to the prophet who thought he should listen to the old lady who'd had all those repugnant ideas about healthcare, elderly care, and all that stuff.

During his first three years in power, the president handed out minister posts to a series of his wife's least ungifted relatives. But when she died, there went the last plausible reason not to fire them all. After all, everything went through him anyway.

During the mourning period after his wife's funeral, he gave speeches in honor of the deceased and went on to say that he had just dissolved his government, excepting himself. The timing for this notice was spot-on given that the whole family, and thus the government, was gathered there.

Uncles, aunts, nieces and nephews, cousins, second cousins, and third cousins were immediately assigned other jobs and given pay raises to keep them from grumbling. One became director of the airport, another director of tourism, a third director of the Condorian passport authority . . .

And this particular one (the president's wife's second cousin) was of good use to Aleko now that he intended to expand the government once again. Because you couldn't hire foreigners for ministerial positions, that would be a direct threat to the country's security.

The president's wife's second cousin sent an assistant to the palace to take photographs and obtain signatures. By dinner that same day, she personally delivered three diplomatic passports, fresh off the press.

Johan and Petra were still called what they had been called, while Agnes was given the surname Massode Mohadji.

"Where'd you get that from?" she asked.

Aleko said that anyone on the run from INTERPOL had best change names. But he did admit it had been a snap decision. His Russian origins also limited his creativity. He'd caught sight of the pool attendant and his apprentice and asked their names. One was called Massode; the other, Mohadji, and he just put those two answers together.

"Agnes Massode Mohadji," said the violet-haired Condorian, testing it out. "Oh, why not? Thank you very much for the new name and the new citizenship—this should mean I can move around in the world again without being arrested. But, a *diplomatic* passport—isn't that a bit much?"

"Not at all! You're the minister of healthcare now."

"I am?"

CHAPTER 46

September 8–14, 2011

Aleko had an interesting opinion of what constituted justice. It didn't matter if something was unjust, as long as everyone was equally mistreated. So he didn't fire just one or two of his relatives from his government when he was displeased. He sent them all packing at the same time. And now that he'd named Agnes minister of healthcare, it simply wouldn't be right, according to the president's worldview, to leave out Petra and Johan.

He began with the more difficult one to place. This was the group's leader, of course. And the one who had assaulted him, insulted him, and shown him the proper way. It would take a job interview to get this right.

He found Petra where he'd guessed she would be: beneath the umbrella by the pool, scribbling furiously at her equation.

"Would you like a job?" he asked.

"I've already got one," said Petra, pointing at the numbers on her paper.

Aleko didn't wish to detract from that work, but what he had in mind was a position in his government.

"What would you say to minister of information technology?"

"No thanks," said Petra.

"Minister of future planning?"

"No thanks."

Aleko was starting to feel annoyed. Who turned down a position as a government minister?

"Something outside of the government, then? General director of the Bureau of Meteorology and Hydrology?"

"Does that exist?"

"I can make it happen."

"No thanks."

"The Condorian Center for Space Research?"

"That doesn't exist either, does it?"

Aleko sighed and gave up.

"Fine, just sit here doing calculations all by yourself. But please feel free to give us a few months before you have the atmosphere come crashing down on top of us. Agnes has some healthcare reforms in the pipeline, and it would really be too bad if everyone died before she got them up and running."

Petra didn't dignify this with a response, just a question:

"Was there anything else on your mind before I go back to my calculations?"

It went much more smoothly with Johan.

"What do you say to becoming the Condors' new minister of foreign affairs?"

The best way to prepare his son to take over one day was to toss him in the deep end right away.

"I'd love to!" said Johan. "What does one of those do?"

Foreign countries were, of course, all the countries in the world except the one you currently found yourself in. Thus Minister of Foreign Affairs Löwenhult felt comfortable making his very first decision in the role: he ordered salmon from the foreign country of Norway and Västerbotten cheese and crayfish tails from the foreign country of Sweden.

Meanwhile, Minister of Healthcare Agnes Massode Mohadji traveled to Kenya and Nigeria to recruit some healthcare providers. The Condorian minister passed right under the watchful eye of INTERPOL no matter where she landed or took off. After all, her name was no longer her name.

The newly appointed minister returned after four days, with sixteen doctors and two hundred nurses in tow. They all spoke English—how else could the minister have communicated with them? She realized a little too late that the staff also needed to be able to talk to their patients. This was a mistake she owned up to over coffee with the president and minister of foreign affairs one morning.

"I'll just make another run to the continent and shop for a dozen interpreters," she said.

"I know what an interpreter does," said Johan.

It was thanks to one of those that breakfast, lunch, and dinner were edible nowadays.

* * *

The doomsday prophet was left to her own devices. Like Ferdinand the Bull, who sat under his cork tree smelling the flowers, she sat under her umbrella by the pool at the presidential palace, working on her equation. This time, she really could not make a mistake, that would be beyond humiliating.

But that didn't stop her from shooting the president a piece of advice now and then. Like how he ought to take advantage of the violet-haired minister's creativity and fresh zeal for life.

"Don't spare any expense. Give her free rein!"

Aleko had to fight his own inclinations. It certainly was not cheap to help his citizens live longer. But if Agnes succeeded, he could give Johan the credit. Just think what a proud father he would be if his son were to one day win a presidential election with hardly any funny business!

"Free rein, you say. Do you think that should go for Johan as well?"

Petra couldn't bring herself to lie. Or tell the truth.

"You'll have to excuse me, but I need to get back to my numbers."

The president slunk off while the prophet allowed herself a moment of reflection before turning back to her equation.

Because she should be dead now, transformed into a minus-459.67-degree lump of ice. All around the world there should be seven billion identical human lumps. All in a deep freeze, in the exact pose they'd been in when the atmosphere fell down on top of them.

Not a single person should have lived to tell about what they saw. Or have anyone to tell it to.

And then what happened happened. Suddenly there were seven billion very much alive witnesses. But, witnesses to what? After all, no one knew about Petra's mistake. She felt trapped between disappointment at having made a math error and enjoyment that she could now, for that very reason, continue her calculations for the actual end of the world.

A *bit* trapped, but not much. She had stopped wasting time on problematizing her own thoughts. As a lost young woman she had spent basically every minute brooding over the secrets of the universe and the transience of everything. That had got her nowhere but a spot behind a school lectern.

Instead of thinking too much, she thought of everyone who had done just that throughout history. Like Descartes. The guy who said, "I think, therefore I am." At which point he thought so poorly that he traveled to Stockholm and froze to death in Queen Christina's drafty castle. What if the French philosopher could have been one of the people she and Johan tracked down to set right? Petra smiled at the thought. How would that meeting have begun? Maybe like this:

"Look, René. I'm thinking about you, therefore I exist. But you're not thinking at all, so what do you think about that?"

* * *

Everyone had been assigned a role. The African Union's special session in Ethiopia was fast approaching, with the president of the United States and the secretary-general of the UN as guests of honor.

Before Aleko got himself a minister of foreign affairs, he had only his brother in spirit Günther to discuss arrangements with, given that the union's sessions were his best chance to infuriate the whole of the rest of the continent. Johan was still a bit green, best to let Günther be in charge of tactics this time as well.

"But you'll join us at the meeting, won't you, Johan? I'd really like to show you off."

His son nodded. Obrama without an *r* would be there, and he needed his Västerbotten cheese.

CHAPTER 47

September 15–25, 2011

Special Agent Sergio Conte was getting calls each day from the chairman of the fly-fishing club and at least two of the eight lawyers for the innocent billion-dollar firm. One from the Rome-based Bvlgari and one from the parent company in Paris. The Instagram-, Facebook-, and blog-based campaign against what was considered to be Bvlgari's "cynical plan to make even more money off the backs of ordinary hardworking people" was reaching new heights all the time. Inventing a fake role model for young people was beyond disgusting. Hundreds of thousands of teenage girls had considered Traveling Eklund their guiding star.

And she didn't even exist! And never had.

The global campaign to boycott all products made by the greedy company had already made it onto news and debate programs on TV. Newspaper columnists complained that bottomless greed had got so bad that billion-dollar companies had turned to sheer fraud. Sure, none of this had actually been proven yet, but where there was smoke there was fire.

Bvlgari and LVMH arranged a press conference at which the CEO and group president swore to the company's innocence. Both were booed off. One of them had had the poor taste to arrive in a limousine. Which ended up with Greek yogurt smeared on the windows. It didn't seem that this would end until the woman responsible was arrested so that she could confess and let Bvlgari off the hook on camera.

But first, they had to find her.

To the lawyers, Agent Conte told it like it was: Agnes Eklund had been located in the Condors, one of INTERPOL's 187 member countries, and the top police official in the country had assured him they were looking for her. But also—since the Condors (so to speak) were the Condors—measures had been taken to ensure the immediate arrest of Eklund the moment she set foot on the mainland again.

The excuse "the Condors were the Condors" did not cut it for the lawyers. Again and again, the harried Sergio Conte felt compelled to pick up the phone and drop a line to the Condorian chief of police.

"Why, hello there, Mr. Special Agent," said Günther. "It's been ages! Wait, scratch that, no it hasn't."

Conte was liking him less and less.

"Any news on Agnes Eklund?"

"It's a big island, Mr. Special Agent," said Aleko's best friend and the new uncle in spirit to the good friend of the wanted woman.

"It most certainly is not," said Agent Conte.

Günther was getting tired of INTERPOL's persistence. He went to the palace and sat down with the wanted woman.

"Wouldn't it just be easier to kill you?" he said.

"Which one of me? Agnes or Eklund?"

* * *

The terrible traffic accident between car and horse-drawn carriage was the top news item that evening on Condorian TV. There were only still images to be had, but they were plenty dramatic. It had taken Agnes hours to create them with her photo-editing software.

A wanted, foreign white woman with purple hair had crashed a stolen car head-on into a horse-drawn carriage. The horse was killed instantly; the woman bled to death at the scene. The driver of the carriage (Günther's Condorian wife's best friend's brother) painted a vivid picture of how he first tried to save the life of the horse, then the woman. But it was all in vain.

"We found her at last," said the chief of police to Special Agent Conte.

"There is no doubt as to the identity of the deceased?"

"We don't have all that many seventy-five-year-old white ladies with purple hair in this country. What was left of her appearance matched the passport she was carrying."

"Can we come over to inspect the body?"

Oh no! Time for some quick thinking.

"I'm sorry, that won't be possible. We don't have cold storage here. She's already been incinerated. But I could send you her blood-stained passport, if you'd like."

Conte would be satisfied with that. The damn lawyers wouldn't be happy, and his spot on the waiting list for the fly-fishing club was precarious. But dead was dead.

CHAPTER 48

September 15–25, 2011

Günther had found the daily phone calls from Rome entertaining. He told Agnes it was a pity the special agent would probably stop calling now that she was dead.

To console himself, the chief of police turned to his assignment as the one in charge of Aleko's strategy vis-à-vis the continued obstructionism of all the rest of the leaders on the continent of Africa. He had learned a lot in his years as deceitful Stasi collaborator, followed by his years in the Soviet Union and the young Russia, as one of the leading criminals in the field of fake ration cards. And on the theme of making trouble for others.

For instance, there was the time he had sixteen smallish air balloons sent over Belarus on behalf of Yeltsin's chief advisor, there to drop two hundred thousand food ration cards over Minsk in the hopes of infuriating Lukashenko. Unfortunately, the wind shifted at the last second and the ration cards landed in a Belarusian border city that suddenly had ten times as many ration cards as it did citizens, and a hundred times more ration cards than there was food. It ended in plenty of chaos, but Lukashenko, a hundred miles away, didn't even get his supper disturbed.

On the one hand, Günther was happy to dial up the bedlam when it came to the African Union. On the other, he wasn't sure how to handle the presence of the American president and the secretary-general of the UN. There was clearly a greater purpose to messing with the whole AU. But what would be the consequences of Aleko's making more of a fool of himself than he actually was in front of two of the most powerful men in the world? It was a bit fuzzy.

Still, needs must. Most recently, the chief of police had sold his best friend on the idea of playing half deaf. It had been a great success (thought Günther) when his brother in spirit misheard, or heard not at all, in turns:

"So: a special envoy dedicated to the potential unrest in Tunisia. Who aside from President Aleko is not in favor?" said the then-chairperson from Malawi, referring to the greengrocer in Sidi Bouzid who had just self-immolated to protest the fact that the police had seized his vegetable cart without reasonable cause.

"Amnesia?" said Aleko.

"Tunisia, for God's sake," said the chairman. "Are you for or against, Aleko?"

The Condorian president didn't respond.

"Aleko?"

"Yes, what is it?"

And so it went. For two days.

But this time? Günther felt it was important to think of something new and fresh, for the sake of their own pride if nothing else. He was drawn to the idea of the president mooning the assembly, but he hadn't yet found the way to make it happen. He couldn't just pull down his pants for no reason. Or could he?

While Günther waited for the right idea to come to him, he signed his president up at the last minute to speak at the session. What he would speak about remained to be seen. Unless the mooning thing came to fruition.

CHAPTER 49

Monday, September 26, 2011

Between the sixteenth and seventeenth ordinary sessions of the African Union assembly, a special session was convened in late September of 2011. On the agenda were Libya and the climate. As well as the ongoing global financial crisis.

Fifty-five state and government heads from Africa were in attendance, plus their paper-shufflers. As well as the secretary-general of the UN and the president of the United States, with their respective entourages.

The setting was Addis Ababa, Ethiopia.

The 327-foot-high main office was so newly built that it hadn't even been dedicated yet. The building had been erected with generous support from the Chinese government, and partially with a Chinese workforce. In their haste, someone had accidentally built in a sophisticated surveillance system. Or, more accurately, three of them: in the walls, in the Chinese furniture, and in the IT system itself. Everything that was said or typed was forwarded each night to an unknown server in Shanghai. This all came to light when the building's IT department identified a recurring and unreasonably high amount of data traffic between 2 and 4 a.m., so high that it couldn't be explained by the porn-surfing night watchman alone. Admittedly, he did watch porn constantly, but he only watched one video at a time, not 225 of them.

The discovery was published in the French newspaper *Le Monde*. The Chinese benefactors soon became suspects, and accordingly they became first upset and then offended when the Ethiopian government kindly but firmly declined a Chinese offer to rebuild the IT system for free.

Right next door to the main office is the African Union Grand Hotel, whose guest list is largely made up of potentates. When the secretary-general of the UN comes for a visit, it's the continental suite for him. When the president of the United States does the same, he gets a whole floor. Security is comprehensive, from the hotel's immediate surroundings to the entryway, lobby, restaurants, inward. None of the furniture is from China.

During the two days of the assembly's special session, only those with the proper accreditation, such as [insert African minister of foreign affairs of your choice here], could go all the way to the elevators, step inside, and give a measured nod to the attendant.

More was required of someone who responded "Sixteen, please" when the aforementioned attendant asked which floor was desired. When the elevator doors opened again, a man and a woman from the Secret Service were waiting.

"What is your business? Who are you looking for?"

"I'm looking for *Obrama*," said Johan. "He's the president in the US."

The Secret Service both knew who Obama was and could pronounce his name.

*   *   *

Following his meetings with Angela Merkel, Ban Ki-moon, and Donald Tusk earlier that month, the American president got to spend some time at home before returning to Europe and London for a session with the young prime minister David Cameron, who told Obama almost in a whisper that he was considering backing a referendum to address the country's continued membership of the EU. In so doing he intended to nip the populist UKIP in the bud.

"An ounce of prevention is worth a pound of cure," Cameron said with a smile.

Obama nodded. He agreed that this was a proactive measure that ought to silence the worst of the loudmouths. UKIP had scraped up 3 percent or so in the last election. Unreasonable that they should be allowed to set the agenda in any way.

Otherwise, the best thing about his meeting at Downing Street was that there was hardly any time difference between London and Addis Ababa. The American president would be spared further jet lag. For this reason, he was in a good mood ahead of that evening's opening of the special session. But how long this good mood might last was hard to say. He had discovered that the Condorian rabble-rouser of a president had put himself forward as one of the speakers the next day.

There was a knock on the door to the office of the suite where the president was preparing. The Secret Service had conferred with the president's chief of staff, who in turn came to find the president.

"Yes, Bill?" said Obama.

William Daley looked concerned.

"You have a visitor, Mr. President."

"I do? Who is it?"

"The Condorian minister of foreign affairs."

"No way in hell!" said Obama.

"He says his name is Johan Löwenhult and he's come to deliver thirty pounds of *Väster-bottens-ost*, I might not be pronouncing that correctly. In any case, the Secret Service has se-cured the cheese, you're not in any danger."

To the astonishment of his chief of staff, the president's face split into a huge smile.

"The cheese is probably safe as it is," he said. "Both it and Johan Löwenhult are more than welcome. But what was that about the Condorian minister of foreign affairs?"

"That's how Mr. Löwenhult introduced himself, sir."

Obama smiled again.

"He's messing with you, Bill. Bring him on in. And please find us a cheese knife."

* * *

"Oho, so you know what it is you do after all!" said Johan when he spotted the president.

"Nice to see you again, Johan, what a lovely surprise! But what do you mean?"

"Last time we met, you said you didn't know what you do, but obviously you're here to save the environment and the economy both. I've read and heard all about it."

Obama saw that his new friend from the Swedish embassy was the same as ever. Master chef and genius. Frank and straightforward.

"We'll see about that. But don't keep me waiting—I've got to taste that Västerbotten cheese of yours."

"It's not mine, it's yours. But we can't eat it straight up, we need something to go with it," Johan said, and pulled the proper ingredients from his freshly scanned backpack.

* * *

The assembly's Equatoguinean chairperson had a name that was even longer than the country he came from. Teodoro Obiang

Nguema Mbasogo was, like all the rest of the leaders from the continent, deeply annoyed with Condorian president Aleko, who thought he could *badger* his way into a position in the assembly. What's more, the asshole had signed up as a speaker during the special session. No matter how fervently the chairperson wished he could stop this, it was not possible—the assembly had its rules. It was easier back home, where Teodoro Obiang had done as little as he wished ever since deposing his crazy uncle in a coup thirty-two years earlier.

Each head of state had the right to spend twenty minutes at the speaker's podium. Not a minute more in Aleko's case, thought the chairperson, who had no intention of abiding by the twenty-minute rule in his own welcome address.

It took him forty-seven minutes to speak about bonds of friendship, common efforts, focus, and lights at the ends of tunnels. All he did not manage to touch upon was the climate, global economy, and corruption.

President Obama, meanwhile, was sitting in the front row and thinking of other things. Such as salmon canapés, crayfish tails, and Västerbotten cheese. Fourteen rows behind him the Condorian president, Aleko, sat dozing. He wouldn't be giving his speech and possibly mooning the assembly for another twenty hours. He didn't yet know quite what this year's performance would be like, but he trusted his best friend, brother in spirit, and chief of police.

Günther had promised to deliver the speech via email in plenty of time, and he always kept his promises.

CHAPTER 50

Monday, September 26, 2011

Agnes took her job as minister of healthcare seriously. She made improvements starting from day one, but that was no wonder. It would have been hard to achieve *worse* healthcare.

After the initial shake-up, everything began to move far too slowly for the woman who was born and raised in a village that existed at a standstill. At least she had a reasonable budget, since the president had agreed to refrain, temporarily, from taking portions of his self-assigned percent of the GDP. But the various construction projects were commencing slowly, to the extent they'd commenced at all (it had only been a few weeks, but still). The enterprising minister had eight medical tents set up next to the construction sites and got the healthcare system off the ground with the help of said tents plus some diesel-driven generators.

Life was extremely worth living, but Agnes missed her journeys with Traveling Eklund. In the evenings, she turned to her photo-editing software as a type of self-guided therapy. There she built the hospital she wanted to have, integrated with a dignified care home. Out of sheer momentum she placed schools in every valley and built a new airport and a stock exchange building. Then she added a shopping center and tore down the better part of the capital city's center and built it anew. The cost exceeded the nation's total assets many times over. No point in being stingy when it was all for pretend anyway.

Chief of Police Günther had reason to visit the presidential palace at least three times a week, along with his daughter. That was where Pocahontas the Pony lived, after all. While Angelika was busy with her pony and her riding instructor, her father was happy to sit down with Agnes. He was less happy to see the doomsday prophet, who spent day after day sitting under the same umbrella in the garden with her numbers. Judging by the grunting and the expression on her face, she was making progress.

"She seems to be getting closer to the doomsday solution," Günther said to Agnes.

"I hope Judgment Day beats her to it," said the minister of healthcare. "I can't handle another countdown."

"What's that?" said Günther, looking at the violet-haired creative's renderings of everything from hospitals to airports.

Agnes told him. They could probably make these images a reality in twenty or thirty years, if the president didn't cling too tightly to his cash. Which, of course, he did.

Aleko's friend suddenly saw the light!

In just a few hours he had to deliver the final draft of the president's speech before the assembly. Composing it had been slow going so far. He so wanted to make the mooning happen, but he couldn't figure out how. At some point the president would have to pull his pants back up, and if not done just right it might be interpreted as some sort of capitulation.

Enter: these fantastic fantasies from the minister of healthcare! Altogether it was probably too much, but they could use a careful selection of images. Günther suddenly knew how he and Aleko would cause chaos in the assembly—again!

He immediately called his brother-in-arms-slash-the-president to bring him up to speed. Aleko saw who was calling and answered the phone with a question.

"Did you figure it out?"

Günther asked a question back:

"What is the worst thing ever in the minds of at least ten of those pigs in the assembly?"

"AIDS?" Aleko speculated.

"No: free, democratic elections."

Günther was right, of course. The progression of AIDS could be slowed with medicine, but a presidential election without any fraud would mean the end for quite a few of the representatives who most deserved to be messed with. The question was, What was Günther after here? Weren't he and Aleko in complete agreement with those pigs, that democracy could not be allowed to go too far?

Sure they were. But what did the assembly know about that?

CHAPTER 51

Tuesday, September 27, 2011

The union chairperson had miscalculated when he scheduled Aleko as the last speaker on that day's agenda. His hope had been that most of the delegates would already be on their way home and that the asshole would be addressing empty seats. But no one left the special session ahead of time, partly because the two guests of honor were still there, and partly because there was a lot of curiosity about what shenanigans the asshole would get up to this time. Considering the presence of the secretary-general and the American president, all of Africa was likely to suffer humiliation that would go down in history.

A conference tech hooked up Aleko's laptop to the big screen. Evidently this time there would be *visual aids* to accompany his craziness.

"Honored members of the assembly," he began. "Honored guests of honor."

Ten seconds into his speech, and he hadn't made a fool of himself yet, but now it was definitely about to happen.

Aleko brought up his first image.

"This is our architects' vision of the Condors' future healthcare and senior living facilities. It's not finished yet, but it will have capacity to treat two thousand patients at once, with five hundred permanent elderly-care housing units right next door."

The complex was right on the water; it was impressive, to say the least. Agnes had used every ounce of her skill on the details.

"The organization, however, has already been in place for a long time. Doctors, nurses, naprapaths, psychologists—all in a scaled-back and effective organization. We've seen remarkable medical results in the past twelve months, even while waiting for the project to reach completion."

Aleko brought up a new image.

"And this is an example of one of our planned village schools. When the primary education system is fully implemented, there will be a school in every valley, eighteen in all. Education is everything! This is how we will build a strong Condors for the future."

Without the help of any images, Aleko rattled off a series of other projects that were in the pipeline: the new university, the new shopping center, the new purification plant . . .

". . . for what could be more important than good stewardship of our natural world?"

Aleko felt that he wasn't shaking up the assembly as much as he would like, that Günther's script relied too heavily on the future. Anyone could have a *vision*. So when the next two images showed up on screen he added some extra zhush.

"Our proud nation is also on the way to developing into an economic hub, despite our slightly out-of-the-way location in the middle of the Indian Ocean."

At which point he happened to suggest that the country's new stock market building was as good as finished.

"And this, honored members and guests of honor, is *Aéroport Aleko International*, the Condors' new airport. Just opened! After all, as a remote island nation, we must primarily welcome our guests from the air. And we want everyone to feel equally welcome, whoever they are."

That last bit really took hold. A stock market and the most modern airport on the continent—those couldn't simply be dismissed as dreams or fantasies! Aleko heard a murmur go through the crowd. After this digression, he returned to the script. Time for the finale:

"Honored members and guests of honor, I can see that you are surprised. How could the tiny Condors afford all this? The answer to the question I know you are asking yourselves is: anti-corruption."

Günther's very latest mayhem-inducing idea really hit the mark. Every jaw in the room dropped.

"That's right! What you've just seen and heard is the result of my genuine crusade against the practice of passing money under the table to gain access to community services that should be free; against the abuse of power; against inadvisable bonds of friendship between government officials and criminals; and against trade without taxation. In just one year, we in the Condors have tripled our GDP by practicing zero tolerance for corruption. In the same amount of time, our literacy rate has increased by 22 percent and the life expectancy by 18 percent. Child mortality has been cut in half."

A brief pause for effect from the lectern. Followed by:

"And this is only the beginning."

Teodoro Obiang Nguema Mbasogo looked at his watch. The asshole was giving a catastrophic speech and had fourteen minutes left of his allotted twenty. Was it possible to bribe someone to turn off the power?

"Corruption, honored members and guests of honor, is a cancer on the continent—and the world. The Democratic People's Republic of the Condors is ready to take the lead in the fight against what might be the worst sickness humanity knows. If the assembly wishes, that is. The assembly has not always shown excessive faith in us and our ambitions."

Seven of the members were now squirming uncomfortably. At least three more should have been. Here and there, someone nodded. Everyone understood the explosive potential of this former asshole's speech in front of two of the most powerful men in the world.

President Aleko extended his hand and invited Johan onto the stage.

"Let me present my minister of foreign affairs, Johan Löwenhult. It's no lie to say he is the brains behind the outstanding developments in the Condors."

Johan let his father hyperbolize. He was prepared, and had promised to play along, although that wasn't to say he fully understood this whole situation. But it wasn't an unfamiliar feeling.

The master chef liked what he saw in the first row of the audience—Obrama without an *r*, eyes aglow. Aleko, though, looked remarkably pale.

"What's wrong, Dad?" Johan whispered. "Don't you feel well?"

"I don't know," Aleko whispered back.

"What don't you know?"

"Why I said that about the airport."

Johan nodded and said he, too, was surprised. He didn't know how long it usually took to build a new airport, but considering the construction hadn't yet begun when he and Dad took off yesterday, it seemed reasonable to assume there was still some work left to do.

That gave Johan an idea: couldn't they borrow the workforce from the almost completely finished stock market building and get the airport done before anyone had time to notice a problem?

Dammit, that's right. The stock market! That didn't exist either.

* * *

It was an idea as simple as it was beautiful. Instead of riling up the assembly by being the worst at absolutely everything, Günther realized they could do the opposite with the help of Agnes's images.

Playing the democracy card before the very eyes of Obama and Ban Ki-moon, and painting the Condors as the model nation in front of everyone—it was sheer genius!

At least until the point where Aleko got off script and promised a tad more than he could deliver. Or a heck of a lot more.

The new hero of the continent didn't have time to process his own remorse for more than a few seconds. For as soon as Aleko and Johan were done whispering, the American president strode up to his Condorian colleague to shake his hand.

"Congratulations on everything," he said, before turning to Minister of Foreign Affairs Löwenhult.

"And aren't you a clever rascal. Master chef, genius, *and minister of foreign affairs*! Why didn't you mention it when we met in Rome?"

Johan continued to play along with his dad's exciting game.

"Well, we were so busy talking food there wasn't time for much else."

The president asked both Johan and Aleko to forgive him for the harsh words he'd spoken at the Swedish embassy. It was proof that one shouldn't listen to rumors. To think that Johan was a government official as well as an expert in salmon canapés, crayfish tails, and cheese!

The minister of foreign affairs said that he too was astonished at how quickly his career had taken off. He never would have predicted it, back when he was getting lost as a postal worker.

Obama laughed. His presidential colleague Aleko chuckled sympathetically by his side. For a brief moment, he forgot the knot in his stomach. Just imagine, there he stood, beaming onstage in front of all of Africa. And CNN.

And it only got better from there. Or worse, depending on your point of view. Ban Ki-moon joined the trio in order to heap praise upon the Condorian president.

"What you just expressed will bring a new hope to the whole world," said the secretary-general.

"Thanks," said Aleko. "We do our best."

Ban Ki-moon was not actually a very spontaneous fellow, but there was something about the mood in this group.

"Just between us, Mr. President: I've got some pretty advanced plans for bringing life into the UN's anti-corruption work. I can't help but think . . ."

He drew out the rest of his sentence a bit.

". . . that your minister of foreign affairs here is perfectly suited to head up the whole thing."

Johan stood nearby, wondering what his suit had to do with anything.

CHAPTER 52

Tuesday, September 27, 2011

The situation managed to get even a little bit worse before the president and his son were in the limousine on their way to the annoyingly sleek airport in Addis Ababa. For Johan suggested that the Condors' nearly finished stock exchange could serve as head office for the UN's new anti-corruption efforts. Ban Ki-moon nodded in appreciation and promised to send an assistant soon, to take a look at the premises.

"The building doesn't exist, dammit!" Aleko said to his son as they sat in the back of the limousine. "Didn't you think of that?"

Johan said that he rarely thought as much as he ought to. Or at least not as well as he ought to.

"So now what do we do?"

The president didn't want to cave. Not yet. The first item on their to-do list was *damage control*.

During their twenty-minute limousine journey, Aleko managed to make two quick phone calls. The first thing he tackled was the issue of the nearly finished yet completely nonexistent stock exchange building.

There were only two buildings in the whole country that weren't totally or partially dilapidated. One was the presidential palace. The other was the Tax Authority building in the city center. Aleko thought it might suffice to freshen up its entrance, replace the sign on the roof, and spiff up the interior. Plus all the Tax Authority staff would have to move elsewhere, of course. A few years previously, the tax manager had appeared before his president to argue that they needed new offices. Aleko had only listened with one ear; it was something about how complicated it was to sustain the public's willingness to pay their taxes and how much staff it took to do so. In any case, the president had given the green light when the tax manager promised that new office space would result in enough increased revenue to pay for itself within just a few months.

But that was then. This was now. Aleko called the tax manager from the limousine and told him to pack his bags and move to a tent in a field on the outskirts of the capital city. There he would stay for the time being, computing his taxes.

"What?" said the tax manager.

He sounded more upset than surprised. And he was still extremely surprised.

Aleko told him to calm down. The move wouldn't need to take place this very evening; the tax manager had until tomorrow afternoon. He could borrow a tent from the minister of healthcare; she had rigged up a whole camp next to the site of the ongoing hospital construction.

"They do operations and all sorts of things in those tents, so you should have no problem calculating taxes there either, should you?"

The tax manager protested. They would have to start reviewing a hundred and ten thousand tax returns at the start of the year—how did the president expect the ninety employees of the Tax Authority to deal with this in a tent in a field?

But Aleko didn't have time for a recalcitrant head of a state authority (who he wasn't even related to) and told him to stop his whining immediately. And anyway, what was this nonsense about citizens doing their own tax returns?

The tax manager explained in a tone that was a little too patronizing:

"All this tax and duty stuff—it's complicated. There's the number of people in a household to consider, or deferment, or the cost of running a business . . . It's important to make sure everything is correct."

"It most certainly is not," said Aleko, who knew perhaps better than anyone what complicated tax regulations could do to a country.

With just twelve minutes left of their journey to the airport in Addis, the president decided to implement a comprehensive tax reform, effective the next morning at nine o'clock. It was of a very different sort than the one he'd launched once upon a time in the blessedly long-dormant Soviet Union.

"From now on, tax everything you see at 50 percent."

The tax manager was astounded.

"But the corporate tax rate is only 7 percent. And the new child allowance is tax-free. And the nonprofits . . . and the high-income earners . . . this is far too complicated . . . we can't . . ."

"High-income earners? How many could there be in the Condors? Fifty percent, I said. Half. Do you know what half of something is? You just split it down the middle, no matter what it is. One side is half. The other is too, incidentally. Just do as I say! And fire the staff—you and your wife can administer the 50 percent rule on your own. But don't forget to take half of their final paycheck in tax when you fire them."

Aleko hung up without wasting his time on goodbyes.

There was more to figure out. Like how there should probably be some sort of activity visible at the stock exchange building when Ban Ki-moon's representative came to inspect it. Like stock trading, for instance. The president considered starting a handful of corporations that could buy and sell shares among themselves. If luck was on his side, the market would go up. Or however that kind of thing worked.

But that was all just details. The next call was to one of the president's deceased wife's cousins. He managed the Condors' miserable airport.

"I saw your talk on TV," said the airport manager.

"Good, then you know we have a problem to solve."

The airport manager was with him so far. But how?

"I haven't quite figured that out yet," Aleko confessed. "But you can start by closing your airport."

"I was afraid of that. What reason should I give?"

"Blame a nesting bird or whatever you like. The minister of foreign affairs and I will be landing there in an hour or two, and I want you to have the explanation ready by then."

Johan was sitting beside his father the president in the limo. He listened and tried to learn. He thought the plan for the Tax Authority building was a good one. But he didn't understand how they would be able to land if Aleko International was closed.

"But it's not closed for *us*," Aleko said patiently.

"What about the nesting bird, though?"

* * *

"I've got it!" said Petra.

While Aleko and Johan Löwenhult prepared to fly home from Addis Ababa, where they'd sent all of Africa into chaos, she had completed her new round of calculations.

"You've got what?" said Agnes. "The date of the next end of the world?"

"Yes!"

"Exciting. Do I have time to brush my teeth first?"

"With plenty of time to spare."

Petra had found a tiny error at a late stage of her sixty-four-step equation. That incorrect parameter had exerted a ripple effect on the remaining steps, contaminating all of them. Or, in Petra's words:

"The rate of change of the operating value is, of course, proportional to the operating value itself."

Loosely translated, this meant that the world was no longer going to end on September 7, 2011.

"I'd noticed," said Agnes. "But how long do I have to brush my teeth?"

Petra looked at her watch. She wanted to be as precise as possible.

"Five years, forty-two days, twelve hours, and twenty minutes. Give or take a minute or two."

* * *

There were so many ways Agnes could have messed with the failed doomsday prophet. But she refrained, for Petra had other talents.

How old was the earth again? Agnes searched on her tablet.

The information varied depending on the extent to which God was mixed up in the analysis, but the estimate Agnes had the most faith in said it was four and a half billion years old. That was a heck of a lot more than the seventy-five she'd made it through so far. The years she had left weren't even a blip in comparison. What Petra, in all her craziness, had managed to do was to remind Agnes that everything would be irreversibly over one day, no matter who went first: Agnes herself or all of humanity at once.

That meant she should live life while she had the chance. To be sure, she had never even considered that it might have been the wrong choice to get behind the wheel of the RV and set off for destinations unknown. Only now, though, did she understand just how perfectly right that choice had been. And she knew she wouldn't hesitate for even a split second when it came to new RVs or whatever might appear in her path as time went on.

Petra, for her part, was exhilarated by her new calculations. This was partly on account of the watertight nature of her scientific approach, and partly because it hadn't been so fun to live with constant reminders that all her fun would soon be over.

Because that's how life had turned out. It was *fun*—ever since she'd been shoved down a slope by the affable master chef. Now she was looking forward to his return from Addis Ababa so she could tell him that they all had a decent amount of future ahead of them.

Out of sheer exhilaration she wrote a flirty message to Malte on Facebook. Things were so much different now than they had been recently. Now they had over five years left to live. When Malte said she was his first secret something, they'd had less than two weeks.

Cheerful greetings from an island somewhere in the ocean. How're things going with Vickan? Is she still painting her nails? Tell her she should pick a different color, the one she has right now doesn't match her hair at all. Or don't bother, now that I think of it. Just writing to say I'm taking good care of your baseball bat. Hugs from your first secret one.

The part about the baseball bat wasn't true. It was still in the RV outside the airport in Rome. But he responded! He wrote that he was looking forward to getting it back one day. As long as it was handed over personally, otherwise forget it.

He ended the message with a heart!

Had he dumped Victoria?

Agnes interrupted the prophet's musings on love and said that the question was, what were they going to do with these five years and forty-two days? She suggested they start by splitting a bottle of wine. Petra thought this was a good idea, but it had the potential to be even better.

"We just got five bonus years. Doesn't that call for champagne, at the very least?"

Agnes was pleased that the new imaginary doomsday wasn't looming in their immediate future. This gave them all space to talk about other things. But first, champagne!

She spotted pool attendant Massode, or alternatively Mohadji.

"Waiter! Can we get a bottle of champagne, please? Or two, now that I think about it."

"At your service, Mrs. Massode Mohadji," said the man whose own name was one or the other.

"And some strawberries," said Petra.

CHAPTER 53

Tuesday, September 27, 2011

Aleko Airlines flight 884 from Addis Ababa was supposed to take off at 6:40 p.m., but it had to wait for two delayed passengers. This is only to be expected when one of the two latecomers shares a name with the whole airline and the other is his son.

Just as the check-in desk was meant to open, the airport screens showed that the flight was canceled. No particular reason was given.

Aleko was pleased with his wife's cousin; he sure hadn't dragged his feet. And not only that, he sent a text to say he'd arranged a private jet for the president and his son. This way, the only people who had to be bribed into silence were one captain, one first officer, and one flight attendant—way easier than a normal-service flight with eighty passengers and the accompanying crew. For anyone who landed at Aéroport Aleko International would notice that it was the same crappy airport it had always been: a dirt runway, a ramshackle arrivals hall, and a security checkpoint that wouldn't be any the wiser if someone tried to smuggle in an assault tank. The repercussions of Aleko's bluff would pile up until he was right back in the same pillory the rest of Africa had held him in until so recently.

There were still considerably more threats than there were chances of success. But Aleko repeated to himself that it wasn't time to give up. Not yet. He'd got a taste of not being an ass-hole, and he planned to cling to it as long as he could.

* * *

Günther and the airport manager met father and son at Aleko International.

"Welcome home," said Günther. "You are heroes through-out all of Africa and half the world! Everyone is talking about the Condors. But goodness, did you ever go overboard."

"I know," said Aleko.

The chief of police knew what had to be done. He'd brought a suitcase full of dollars for the flight crew, along with a prom-ise of eternal unhappiness for all three of them if they ever said a thing to anyone about anything when it came to the status of the airport.

"Understood? Good. Then you can go home again. But watch out for the potholes on the runway. It's easy to pop a tire."

Günther also informed them that all roads were blockaded in a radius of two miles around the airport, ensuring that from this day forward no Condorian would be able to see it and start any rumors. This seemed like a faster and simpler solu-tion than tracking down the fifty or sixty people who had phones and could theoretically call someone they shouldn't to share information they definitely shouldn't.

The manager of Aleko International circled back around with his president to inform him that the airport had been closed on account of the discovery of a habitat containing the rare bird *Cyanolanius condorensis*, located right at one end of the runway.

"No one may land or take off until this bird is finished nest-ing," he said authoritatively, as though the bird existed.

The president took a pragmatic view of man's relationship with nature. As soon as the national funds allowed, he had intended to blow up the country's third-highest mountaintop for coal. The plans had fizzled out when he sent people up to take measurements, at which point a village chief petitioned his president, saying he was speaking for the mountain goats. The goats, and their grazing pastures. It was something about grazing. Aleko didn't remember what.

And now this. No one in the Condors could care less about the small blue-and-white bird the airport manager had pulled out of thin air.

"Was a damn songbird the best you could think of?" he said, finding even as he said so that he sounded rather harsh, not least since the idea had been his own.

"An exceptionally unusual one," the airport manager clarified.

Ah well, pretending to care about animals might be its own sort of brand development. Aleko nodded. There was no reason to argue with his wife's cousin, who had done everything right so far.

"Well done. And good job with the bird. Is it an edible one, by the way?"

Then he gave orders to begin paving the runway as soon as possible, to be completed by the next week.

"Is that all?" the airport manager asked sarcastically.

"No—we need a new terminal building as well. I'll send a picture."

CHAPTER 54

Tuesday, September 27, 2011

President Aleko called an emergency meeting in the palace as soon as he and Johan got home. He needed all the help he could get from Günther, Johan, Agnes, and Petra. He hadn't expected the women to be all giggly from the champagne.

"Five years!" Petra cheered when she caught sight of Günther, Johan, and his father.

"Until the end of the world?" the president asked. Five minutes would have been his preference.

He explained the gravity of the situation. In the immediate term, they needed a new airport, terminal building included. In the short term, they needed to freshen up the capital city's tax offices and call it something else. In the slightly longer term, to maintain the president's reputation, Agnes needed to bring her hospital project to fruition, someone needed to build eight new schools, and someone else a whole university.

Agnes said she didn't want to rub salt in the wound, but they would also need things like teachers, textbooks, university lecturers, and a professor or two. This was all made more complicated by the fact that the majority of their intended university students couldn't read yet.

"Well, there are picture books," said Johan. "But I guess that's not quite the same thing?"

Aleko muttered about this foolish notion that people absolutely must learn to read.

"After all, there's nothing but trash in all the newspapers. Except for the ones I control. Which, when I think about it, is all of them."

* * *

A back-of-the-envelope calculation told them that the Condorian treasury needed a boost of at least four hundred million dollars. Which meant the situation was more or less hopeless. Hence Aleko's half-serious wish that doomsday would hurry up.

"Incidentally, couldn't we make money on that?"

"It would only be fair, considering how much time I've put into the equation," Petra said in a tone Agnes had never heard before.

Had she taken Aleko's question seriously?

* * *

Not only had the prophet taken Aleko's question seriously, she had actually posed it to herself a few times.

Nine years' unpaid labor. Without any thanks. Without the Royal Academy of Sciences even deigning to let her in so she could explain what was going to happen. Instead they sicced a doorman on her as though she were nothing but a charlatan.

Petra couldn't mask her dark thoughts, while Agnes was very careful not to point out that "charlatan" might be the right word after all. For the prophet had more to say.

"I've been thinking," she said.

"Not me," said Johan.

"Do tell," said Agnes.

Petra turned to Aleko.

"What would you say if I told you the world was going to end in three weeks' time?"

"Didn't you just say five years?"

"Forget about that, I'm trying to be pedagogical right now. Just answer my questions, please."

She repeated the first question. Aleko had no choice but to play along.

"Then I suppose I'd say I don't believe you."

"But what if I produced a complicated, sixty-four-step equation and claimed that the equation proved it?"

Aleko considered this for a second or two.

"Then I suppose I'd say I don't believe you and that there's no making sense of that equation."

The prophet nodded, pleased.

"Would you like to earn a hundred dollars?" she said.

A hundred dollars? Aleko needed more like four hundred million dollars, but he continued to play along.

"Yes, please."

"Good. Shall we make a bet? If you give me a hundred dollars, you'll get two hundred back in three weeks if the world hasn't ended."

"What was that again?"

Agnes was beginning to understand where Petra was going with this. She explained to the president that it was a win-win proposition all the way. Either he would double his money, or else the world really would end. And in that case, what use could he possibly have for a one-hundred-dollar bill?

Petra nodded. That violet-haired head was screwed on right. All they needed was a credible messenger for the equation, preferably someone other than Petra herself, since she didn't want to spend life in prison.

"For a hundred dollars?" said Aleko.

"Times a few million."

* * *

When the amount of money at play grew to a sum like that, Aleko was back in. But why should he trust this "credible" messenger? And who would collect all the money, only to make it vanish?

Petra had thought of that, too.

"Besides the messenger, we need an unscrupulous bank here in the Condors."

"Now that I've got," said Aleko.

"And who runs it? Someone's cousin?" said Agnes. "Half brother?"

"One of my wife's many second cousins. He does as I tell him. They all do."

"We also need a bank in Switzerland," said Petra. "For credibility reasons. Agnes has a boyfriend there."

The violet-haired lovebird blushed. Petra wasn't wrong. Agnes and the stylish, kind Herbert von Toll had been exchanging letters ever since the day they met in Zurich. Time to change the subject.

"If we're going to spread the word, we'll also need someone who's good at social media," she said. "And there's no need to look for her. I'm sitting right here."

"And we need a fall guy," said Petra.

"A fall guy?" said Johan.

The prophet didn't want to interrupt the tempo of their planning.

"I'll explain it all later, Johan."

* * *

Faced with the prospect of serious incoming revenue, Aleko rethought some things. Within a few days, his wife's most gifted cousin would have the runway-paving project at Aleko International in full swing.

That left the terminal. Aleko had decided that the best solution in this case was a tragic fire. Who could help it if the departure and arrival terminal burned to the ground before anyone even got to use it? From one day to the next, the asshole who had become Africa's greatest hope would transform into the president the whole world felt sorry for. All bolstered by footage from Condorian TV of a president near tears among the ashes of his glorious airport. With Agnes and Petra's promised millions in his pocket, he would have plenty of time to build the terminal again. Or rather for the first time.

To think that things were about to work out great, Aleko thought.

Without considering the unfortunate fact that his son had a half brother in Rome.

CHAPTER 55

A Third Secretary's Nightmare

While Agnes, Aleko, and Petra were forging plans for a bright future, Johan was battling Malik in the kitchen of the presidential palace. At least by this point the chef knew two words in Swedish. One for salmon. The other for Västerbotten cheese.

At the same time, Ambassador Ronny Guldén was calling Fredrik Löwenhult to a one-on-one meeting at the residence in Rome.

The third secretary thought things had been going well in the weeks following the disaster with Finland's second secretary, President Obama, his idiot brother Johan, and the social mixer at the embassy. Perhaps time healed all wounds after all.

And now, here was an opening. First Secretary Björkander was on her way to Beijing. It wasn't unreasonable to assume that Second Secretary Wester would be bumped a rung up the ladder and Fredrik would follow.

But Hanna Wester was no star employee. What's more, Fredrik had taken certain measures and steps to make sure she wouldn't shine brighter than him. Nothing big, just little stuff here and there. Like hiding her hole punch whenever he could get his hands on it, misplacing her pens, stuff like that. While everyone else was already tackling the day's work, Hanna Wester would be running around the corridors on the hunt for her missing belongings. She didn't want to ask if anyone had seen them, because that would make her seem careless. Instead she appeared just generally inadequate.

It was unusual, but every once in a while a third secretary might hopscotch over the next person in the hierarchy. He would have his answer in the next few minutes. Fredrik promised himself he wouldn't let his disappointment show in front of the ambassador if Hanna kept her spot in the pecking order after all.

"Thanks for coming."

"Of course, Ambassador."

"As you know, First Secretary Birgitta Björkander is on her way to a post in Beijing."

"So I heard."

"That means there's an open position here in Rome."

"I understand."

"I think I have the name of the man who will fill that empty space, but I want to hear your opinion."

A *man*! Sayonara, Hanna Wester.

"Do you think your brother Johan would accept a position as unglamorous as first secretary, if I asked him?"

Fredrik was experiencing the worst moment of his life. He had completely missed the news from Addis Ababa the day before.

"Johan?" he said.

The ambassador lowered his voice, spoke in closer confidence.

"I know what you're thinking. What am I going to do with Hanna? But between you and me, she's still almost as green as you are."

Almost as green? Fredrik was experiencing a moment even worse than the one he'd just identified as his worst ever.

"I . . . don't know what to say," he said.

But the ambassador did. CNN's report from the previous

evening had been an outright ode to Johan. Hadn't Fredrik heard about what his big brother had accomplished?

"Little brother," said Fredrik.

"Right, right. But to have the ear of Aleko, to lift up a whole nation . . . the *smallest* nation in Africa, to be sure, but still. There's no denying corruption is the scourge of the continent, of the whole world! Johan's contributions cannot be overestimated."

"I . . . don't know what to say," said Fredrik.

Hadn't he already said that once?

"Just answer me honestly. No one knows your brother better than you do. Do you think his loyalty to Sweden is strong enough that he might take a demotion?"

* * *

Fredrik survived his meeting with the ambassador. But one of the stupidest people in the whole world was about to destroy his career in diplomacy before it had even begun. Johan didn't know the difference between continents and incontinence, or between America and Africa; he couldn't point out Germany on a map of Central Europe—yet he had been their mother's favorite child when they were small! It had been that idiot's hand she reached for right before she died, not Fredrik's. And her last word was "Johan." Now her darling boy was about to become the diplomatic hero of the whole world. At Fredrik's expense.

Johan had to be revealed for what he was. And quick. For two reasons. Fredrik's career was one of them. The other was that Johan was about to drive him bonkers.

* * *

The third secretary concocted a story about how his wonderful father, the renowned ambassador, had fallen seriously ill. Was there any chance Fredrik could have a few days off to rush off to Montevideo to say his goodbyes?

By all means! Ambassador Guldén immediately gave his third secretary a week's vacation and sent his warmest greetings to Fredrik's father, if he was still conscious enough to receive them. By the way, would Fredrik be kind enough to ask Hanna to take over photocopier duty in the meantime, so that the ambassadorial works didn't get completely backed up in his absence?

* * *

Fredrik had no detailed plan; it was more like tunnel vision. Officially he was now on his way to Uruguay, where his allegedly dying father lived. In reality, he feverishly set off for the Condors. He was sure he would find something there. He didn't know what, but something. As soon as Johan was revealed to be what he was, everything could go back to normal.

On his flight to Mombasa, Johan's brother watched the TV clips from Addis Ababa over and over. The Condorian president's speech. Johan being invited up on stage. The obviously intimate conversations between little brother and two of the world's most powerful men. What had they said to one another? And why didn't the president and the secretary-general *get it*?

Something was wrong here, or possibly everywhere! The biggest idiot ever had joined forces with the most corrupt president from the worst shithole country. And now the idiot in question was going to lead the UN's anti-corruption efforts?

It was one thing that people refused to comprehend that Johan had the IQ of a freshwater perch. But, "the Condorian marvel"? Perch liked to swim around aimlessly, eating plankton, larvae, and smaller fish. They didn't have intelligent thoughts. And they didn't accomplish anything marvelous.

Fredrik's self-assigned task was to find the thing (or things) that was (or were) wrong. To do so, he needed to search on-site. Were they using slave labor for their construction projects? Were those pictures even real?

One last stop in Mombasa. But, what was this? The flight was canceled? And so was the previous one? And the next one? But he *had* to get to the Condors! What do you mean, "it's not possible"?

CHAPTER 56

A Concerned President

Aleko was well-versed in the art of communicating with Africa. All he had to do was plop the message he wanted to get out in the lap of TV manager and program host Fariba, who was also his deceased wife's twin sister. Unlike his wife, in her day, Fariba always did as Aleko said.

Today's biggest TV news story was the abruptly closed airport. Fariba told the viewers about the beautiful, endangered, rare bird that had been discovered nesting at the end of the runway, and declared that—as the president always said—nothing could be more important than being a good steward of Mother Nature. The noble state-run Conservation Agency was going to analyze the situation *Cyanolanius condorensis* had found itself in. For the time being all flights were canceled, and to be on the safe side the same went for all helicopter traffic.

"Anyone who hears the bird's characteristic *chrr-crrk-crrrrk-crk-crk* call is asked to call 122 237 immediately."

Right after this first news piece, Fariba dropped a line to her brother-in-law. She had presented the news in accordance with Günther's wording and illustrations. Now, out of pure consideration, she wanted to ask the president if he considered it a problem that the country didn't have a Conservation Agency.

"What would we do with one of those?" said Aleko.

* * *

The bird story flew rapidly around the globe. The secretary-general contacted President Aleko personally. He was sorry that they would have to postpone the visit to the stock exchange building but praised the president for showing such consideration toward the animal kingdom. The Condors' good stewardship of their island sent a message to the whole world.

Aleko thanked him for his understanding when it came to the importance of biodiversity. He said nothing about his plans for coal mining and that it was more important than ever before now that all the forests had been cut down. He definitely didn't quote the village-chief-slash-spokesman-for-the-Condorian-mountain-goats.

Ban Ki-moon had another matter to discuss. The thing was, famous Hollywood actor George Clooney was engaged in the global fight against corruption along with his delightful wife Amal. Mr. Clooney had just called the secretary-general with a request to help him get in touch with Aleko. Mr. Clooney wished to praise him and share some encouraging words. Would the president be comfortable with the secretary-general giving his phone number to the American?

Aleko knew that Clooney had played Batman in a Hollywood movie a few years before. The last thing they needed right now was a right-minded global conscience thrown into the mix.

"No, but I can take his number if you've got it handy? I promise to drop him a line before summertime."

But now Ban Ki-moon would have to excuse him; the president had other things to attend to.

It was a lot, with everything happening at once. Not least the money stuff. What if Agnes and Petra's betting project didn't work as planned? Making the airport presentable would cost Aleko more than all the unemployment reforms he'd never launched *together*. And that still left everything else.

How much was it reasonable to spend in order to save the president's newly won reputation? A lot, Aleko thought. He was tired of being an asshole, especially now that he'd got a taste of what the opposite was like and had reason to build a future for his son. But what if the national treasury simply ran out? Then what?

He could always have new money printed, of course. But something told him there was a downside to that kind of solution. Even Günther had warned him against it. In his experience, it wasn't enough to print lots of ration cards to get the people on your side. There had to be actual food available as well.

Günther didn't like seeing his brother in spirit so concerned.

"Can't we just decide that the old lady and the prophet will make it happen? After all, they've done it before."

CHAPTER 57

Friday, September 30, 2011

"Do you offer helicopter service?" Fredrik said to the man behind the desk at Mombasa Helicopter Service Ltd.

The owner, pilot, and sole employee nodded and said that was why the company was called what it was called.

"Where do you want to go?"

"The Condors."

The job vanished before it even appeared.

"That would have cost two thousand dollars. But we're not allowed to land there right now. They've found a bird they feel sorry for."

Fredrik sat down on a chair. He needed to think.

"I don't think you can sit here waiting for that bird to finish nesting, that sort of thing takes time."

It seemed far-fetched that a nesting bird could close a whole, entire, newly constructed international airport. Fredrik took this ground stop as an indication that he was on the right track. Something was *very* peculiar. As peculiar as Johan had been all his life.

"I'll give you seven thousand to land wherever I tell you to," said the third secretary.

The owner of the company needed the money. For it so happened he was married to the most exciting woman in all of Mombasa, a currency speculator who had doubled the family's fortune every three months until she got hung up on a filthy-rich dairy farmer in Madagascar and decided he was the one who would make the family financially independent forever-more. The dairy farmer had the gift of the gab; he promised the moon to both investors and citizens until one day he found himself the country's president. So far so good for the currency speculator and her husband.

But then the former dairy farmer kicked off his presidency by buying a private jet with state money while the people who'd voted for him were still earning the equivalent of not even one dollar per day. Turned out the moon was meant for the dairy farmer and no one else.

Immediate grumbling arose among the citizens. The former dairy farmer swiftly and less amusingly became a former pres-ident as well; he was chased out of the country and replaced by chaos. The value of the Madagascan currency, the ariary, sank like a stone. One ariary equaled five iraimbilanja, which in turn became equal to 0.005 American dollars once it had shrunk beyond recognition. The pilot's wife watched what had once been the equivalent of four hundred thousand American dollars become more useful as paper towels, even though the ariary had little absorbency to speak of. With that, the most exciting woman in Mombasa was ruined.

All she had left was her love for her husband, and her irre-sistible charm. She ran her long fingers through her husband's hair, smiled sadly, and said that the Madagascan milk had soured and that, from this day on, her husband had best keep himself aloft as much as possible. As long as he got paid for it. In a sensible currency.

This was all to say that seven thousand dollars was an awful lot. But the client across from him appeared to have great will-ingness to pay.

"I don't know," said the pilot. "It's taking on a big risk, to land where you're not allowed to. Then again, I'm well acquainted with the island, so maybe . . . but, seven thousand . . ."

"Eight," said the third secretary.

The pilot didn't dare draw out negotiations for too long.

"Give me ten thousand and we're on. For that I'll land smack on top of the nest if you want me to."

"Takeoff in five minutes," said Fredrik.

* * *

The Condors have no military border control. The pilot knew no one would be there to shoot them down. Still, it was important to land wisely. The island's police force was still decently functional.

This was an aspect that concerned Fredrik as well. He had absolutely no desire to become acquainted with a Condorian prison, even if it was, contrary to expectations, newly built. Up to this point, he'd been running on adrenaline. Now, as he and the pilot neared the island, everything suddenly became real. Was he just going to let himself be dropped off? Should he ask the pilot to wait? If so, for what? It might take time to track down all these cracks in the facade.

Ugh. This had all happened too fast. Fredrik felt like an idiot. No, not like an idiot, that was too strong. But he had been sloppy. Had hurried into this.

Or not!

"I knew it!" he exclaimed when the helicopter got close enough to Aleko International.

The airport was *exactly* as substandard as you'd imagine. The runway was made of red dirt; the terminal building looked like it was begging to be put out of its misery. Nothing—not a single thing—was reminiscent of the picture the president had shown the assembly in Addis Ababa.

The pilot wondered what it was his passenger knew, but didn't ask. He just did as he was told. More than happily, even, because now apparently there wasn't any reason for them to land.

Fredrik ordered him to take a few low passes over the airport. Once he'd got the pictures he needed, he needed no more, and they could turn back. Fredrik Löwenhult—genius, future ambassador—was now sitting on proof that President Aleko was a fraud. And at the fraud's side: Fredrik's damn brother.

"*Little brother!*" he said loudly to Ambassador Guldén, who was many hundreds of miles away.

CHAPTER 58

Hebbe and Sweetie Pie

The friends were blissfully unaware of the oncoming disaster. Fredrik Löwenhult was perhaps one of the top three people on earth who must *not* become aware of the actual state of Aéroport Aleko International.

But since the third secretary was officially in Montevideo, he couldn't ruin the lives of Aleko and his idiot brother at once. He had to wait until he was back at the embassy. "Why, take a look at this, Mr. Ambassador—see what someone has posted online?"—something like that. And then Guldén would no longer want to touch Johan with a ten-foot pole, while Asshole Aleko would be transformed into a bigger asshole than ever.

* * *

The pieces were falling into place. Agnes wasn't sure at first, but she thought that her delightful Herbert in Zurich would go along with everything. And how right she was! Apparently it was time at last for the seventy-six-year-old to cut the umbilical cord to his ninety-six-year-old father.

During the excessive and lengthy Skype conversations between Agnes and Herbert, they not only agreed on how to proceed but also gave each other lovey-dovey nicknames. His was "Hebbe," while hers was "Sweetie Pie." Hebbe was so inspired by the many ways in which Agnes embraced life, despite her mature age, that he decided to do the same. And that in spades. Sweetie Pie had told him about the sleepy village she grew up in. If you swapped "Dödersjö" for "Bank von Toll," her life story was eerily similar to his own. One important difference was that Agnes's husband had stepped on a nail and departed this life, while Herbert's father only seemed to grow younger and healthier as time went on. It was ridiculous to be nearly seventy-seven years old and still an errand boy for your own father.

Both Herbert and Agnes longed for the next time they would meet in real life, and it was only a few days away. For "Project Doomsday" called for certain measures and steps to be undertaken in Zurich.

CHAPTER 59

The Last Piece of the Puzzle

The unscrupulous bank in the Condors was taken care of, as was the credible guarantor in Switzerland. The website and the accounts on Instagram, Twitter, and Facebook had been created, but they still weren't sure who the group would use as a mouthpiece for the sensational betting opportunity where no one could lose a thing (except for their lives).

Where would they find him or her? Agnes had experience making up fake profiles, of course, but the problem with those was that they are in fact fake—just as people who really existed had no reason to volunteer as messenger.

They were about to lose heart when Günther came to the rescue. He listened to the old woman and the prophet and came to the correct conclusion: what they needed was (1) a real person with a credible background, who (2) was dead without anyone being the wiser. That is to say, had vanished off the face of the earth.

"We had quite a few people matching that description in Russia in my day," said Günther. "Give me some time to think about it."

* * *

Günther dug through his past and came up with an astrophysicist and professor at Moscow University who had become too indispensable for his own good. He was brilliant at calculating the safest way for Russian spacecraft to travel through the various layers of the atmosphere, out into space, and back again. This professor had spent a few years living on the edge, given the way he kept demanding better pay, a bigger dacha, and more willing prostitutes if he was going to keep delivering his mathematical figures. At one point, he'd sat on a crucial parameter until two days before liftoff, citing his need for a new car. Not that there was any lack of available salary, prostitutes, or cars, but to mix these things up with the Russian space program? That was extortion!

Günther knew that anyone with at least one foot in the Kremlin would have checked with the Vory to see if they were prepared to have this displeasing professor taken out if given the order, and the thieves rarely hesitated when the opportunity arose to do a favor for those at the top. Especially when it wasn't painful.

Nothing came of it that time; the professor's talents were too essential. But a few years later, Günther read that the Moscow University professor in question had disappeared without a trace. *The Guardian* in London speculated that he might have fled to the West. Günther's analysis, though, was that instead he'd been stupid enough to train a student so well that the state and the thieves, working together, could allow themselves to give him what they felt he deserved. Permanently.

The chief of police smiled when he realized he'd found the solution.

"Done pondering?" Agnes wondered.

She thought it looked that way.

"Smirnoff," said Günther.

"But it's the middle of the day . . . ?"

"*Professor* Smirnoff," he clarified.

"Our man?"

Günther nodded.

"I'm pretty sure he won't get in touch to protest."

With this last piece of the puzzle, Agnes could finish up the website on which Professor Smirnoff announced that he'd been staying out of the public eye for several years while he worked on his most important mathematical and astronomical equation to date. He didn't want to disclose his exact location, but suggested it might be a mountain village somewhere in Tibet or thereabouts. He took the opportunity to apologize to his family that things had turned out the way they did, but an astronomer was an astronomer and this was important. The *most* important thing, even. Because there could be no second-guessing his calculations.

The professor was prepared to go so far as to make a bet with the whole world that he was right. To be taken seriously, he had engaged a well-respected bank in Zurich as a guarantor. His message was that the atmosphere would collapse, and thus the world would end, on October 18, 2011, at 9:20 p.m. Central European Time. The details of the bet he invited people to take were as follows:

Double your money!

Bet one hundred dollars against me. If I'm wrong, you'll receive two hundred dollars back by 4 p.m. CET on October 19. If I'm right, however, you won't have any use for your one hundred dollars anymore, will you?

The professor published the detailed calculations on the website: his entire complicated equation, complete with numbers, lines, arrows, pedagogical explanations, and examples of traps he had *not* fallen into during his work. The sum of one hundred dollars, by the way, was only an example. Anyone was welcome to bet as much as they liked.

This all gave the impression of being extremely credible, with the Swiss Bank von Toll standing behind the money to guarantee it. What's more, the equation and its sixty-four steps was so complicated that it would take any Einstein at least two months to spot the bluff.

And by then it would be too late.

CHAPTER 60

The Art of Neutralizing a Witness

Just as Johan's half brother made his wonderful discovery from the helicopter above Aleko International, Agnes, Aleko, Johan, and Petra were sitting in the small reception room and enjoying tea and scones to celebrate the fact that all preparations were in place ahead of the great doomsday fraud. Any moment now, a foreboding phone call would come in.

* * *

The airport manager had a substantial job ahead of him. He had, at least, assembled a capable team of two hundred men. The work on the runway would commence the next morning at seven. The airport truly was a sad sight, although he had never really thought about it before.

But what was this? A helicopter? Mombasa Helicopter Service Ltd. The airport manager recognized the craft. But he hadn't received any word from the president that someone was inbound. That was how it worked in the Condors—everything went through Aleko.

The pilot made a few passes over the field and then flew back the way he'd come.

Strange.

Aleko's wife's cousin immediately reported this to his president, who right then was feeling very content among friends, tea, and scones.

"Are you expecting any visitors, Johan?" Aleko asked.

"I don't know anyone but those of us who are already here. And my brother. And someone called Preben. And President Obrama without an *r*. And Secretary-General Ban Ki-something. And I sort of know someone who's the Swedish ambassador in Rome, but I can't imagine why he'd come here."

Aleko thought that a simple "no" would have sufficed to answer his useless question.

"I know rather more people than that, but I don't have time to rattle them all off. I'm not expecting any visitors either. It's no good if someone saw the condition of the airport before we've had time to transform it. *No good at all.*"

Aleko asked Agnes how much more time she needed before Zurich. She pointed out that they were celebrating that everything was ready! All that was left was proofreading, and she would have plenty of time to finish that by the next morning, as planned.

"What if we change that to now?"

"You mean, *now* now?"

"Yes."

"I can always work on the way."

Johan, his father, Agnes, and Petra set off for the airport. Agnes was preoccupied with her work. Johan ended up behind the wheel and was surprised by how smoothly it went.

"I don't think I've ever ridden with someone who's a worse driver than you, my son," said the president.

"No one has," said Petra.

Aleko asked Johan to slow down, lest he be unable to dial his phone correctly. He called the helicopter company in

Mombasa, the one that had been booked to pick them up from the palace gardens the next morning.

"Hello? President Aleko here. How much did you get paid to fly over my airfield just now?"

"I'm sorry, I don't understand."

"Fifteen thousand?"

The pilot didn't have the energy to lie to the man who would never believe him anyway.

"Ten."

"Come back here immediately—and land this time. At the airport."

"Are you going to arrest me?"

"Not at all. But ten thousand wasn't much for illegally violating the airspace of a foreign territory."

"I know. And landing was even included. At least I bartered up from seven."

"Did you land?"

"No, he changed his mind."

"We'll have to discuss that further. Hurry. My friends and I are waiting."

"Okay, but let me fuel up first. I just dropped off the cheapskate."

One hour and ten minutes later, the EC155 helicopter came in for a landing. The red dust swirled. Every last endangered bird nesting alongside the runway would have flown off, if only any existed.

The pilot disembarked, stooped under the slowing rotors, and hurried into the dilapidated and deserted arrivals hall.

"Welcome," said President Aleko.

"What he said," said Johan.

"Thank you," said the pilot.

One older and one younger woman were sitting at a table

nearby. No one else in the building. The president seemed to
have kept his word. The pilot wasn't going to be arrested. Not
yet, anyway.

"I have a certain need to revise history, or rather, to revise
the present," said Aleko.

The only thing the pilot understood about this was that it
would be in his best interest to comply.

"Revisions of various types is one thing I'm good at. Tell
me, how can I be of service?"

The president answered with a question:

"Have you ever seen a finer arrivals hall?" he said, looking
around.

Dust from the runway had blown in through the gaps in the
wall. The rusty X-ray scanner at the security checkpoint had to
have been out of service for years. There were cracks in the
ceiling. Broken windows everywhere.

The helicopter pilot knew what he was supposed to say, but
not why.

"This must be the finest airport terminal in Africa," he
said.

Aleko nodded, pleased.

"And what do you have to say about our paved runway?"

"Smooth, straight, and with a lovely shine to it."

"Correct. So we have an understanding."

Johan opened a briefcase. He had his instructions.

"You were supposed to pick us up this morning for two
thousand dollars. Shall we make it thirty?"

The pilot smiled.

"For thirty thousand, I could almost see a second terminal."

"One will do," said Aleko. "We're a small country."

Then the pilot took a closer look at Johan, recognizing him
from the TV in his kitchen.

"Aren't you supposed to be the UN's new anti-corruption
marshal?"

"Anti-corruption marshal" was just as tricky, for Johan, as "extraordinary" or "imbecile." But his career path from failed mailman through duped housewife to master chef, genius, and celebrated minister of foreign affairs had provided him with a backbone. He knew now that he wasn't worthless at all. That he was capable of learning. He thought thoughts like *How could someone worthless have my good sense for flavor and aroma?* It was a rhetorical question, although Johan didn't know that word either.

During the many long conversations with his father the president, he had made an effort to at least partially understand the culture he now represented to the world. Not least the importance of knowing which situations called for greasing certain palms in the hopes of getting what you wanted.

Now it felt like he was facing a test, with his father as witness.

The pilot had been offered thirty thousand dollars to testify, if necessary, that he had seen an airport that did not yet exist. Johan understood this much. At first it seemed like their agreement was settled, but then came that tricky word. It sounded like a challenge. What had Dad said? That it was important to get a sense for each individual situation, and regain control before your opponent had time to realize that he had the upper hand.

"*Anti-corruption marshal*, that's me," Johan said, slapping a veneer of confidence on his delivery. "Random thought, I think we have an extra ten thousand here in the briefcase."

The pilot lit up.

"Another ten thousand would make my wife happy. Don't worry. Everyone in Mombasa knows I keep my bribed word. Just tell me what more you want from me."

Aleko was proud of his son, even though this had just turned out to be unnecessarily expensive.

"Give him the money," he said.

Then he turned to the pilot.

"Tell us everything you know."

The owner of the helicopter company told them, but he didn't have as much to say as the president would have liked. A white man, thirty-five to forty years old. Spoke English. Wanted to get to the Condors at any price. As previously mentioned, they were supposed to land as well, but the customer changed his mind when he saw the miserable airport.

"Excuse me, the *newly built* airport."

The unknown man ordered the pilot to make a few passes as he took pictures on his phone. Then he was satisfied and wanted to be flown back to Mombasa.

"And then what?"

"He vanished into a taxi. They turned *left* onto the highway. Toward the airport, not toward the center, anyway. That was about when you called."

With that, one of two known witnesses to the truth had been neutralized. That left the other. The unknown man. The one with the pictures. Who the hell was it?

"Let's all head out now," said the president.

"Where to?" said the pilot. "If you don't mind my asking, Mr. President. Considering that I'll be doing the driving."

"Zurich. But we'll drop you and your helicopter off in Mombasa."

CHAPTER 61

The Condorian Fraud

Fredrik was back in Rome several days before his allotted time off was over. He had the proof it would take to make Ambassador Guldén's zeal for Johan cool off. Freeze. Or flat-out die.

But it had all happened so fast. His thoughts had not held to the same rapid tempo. He knew that Ambassador Guldén couldn't appoint Johan any position solely on his own initiative. That sort of thing had to be formally decided in Stockholm. Unfortunately, Fredrik's boss was on his fourth ambassador assignment, and was held in high esteem at the Department of Foreign Affairs. If Guldén told those in charge that Johan was the solution, no one would contradict him. From Fredrik's perspective, the idea of being a subordinate to his prize ass of a younger brother would be intolerable.

A neutral observer would have said that Johan's intellectual talents were focused on something other than what the Swedish ambassador in Rome had come to believe, and that Ambassador Guldén—otherwise known for his sound judgment—had misjudged both the situation and the person this time. But Fredrik's actions went beyond that assessment. Because even if Johan had been the objective answer to the question of how humanity could best attain peace on earth, he had to go! Big brother nearly passed out at the thought that peace might arise anywhere and to any extent if Johan was involved. While he himself was not.

And yet:

If Fredrik were to barge in and place those pictures on the ambassador's desk, Guldén might start to wonder what he'd been doing in Africa. After all, he'd been given time off to go see his dying father in Montevideo, on a totally different continent.

He couldn't present the evidence directly to Guldén, and he also couldn't go back to work early; after all, there was a limit to how fast a person could move between continents, especially if you wanted to demonstrate emotional engagement in the face of an immediate family member's failing health. Flying to Uruguay, saying hello and goodbye to a dying father, and immediately flying back didn't exactly suggest an abundance of care.

The empathically challenged Fredrik Löwenhult was eager to protect his reputation as an empathetic person. All these ruminations ended with his spending a few days in his Rome apartment, blinds closed. Although that didn't mean he couldn't be productive. He started an Instagram account and called it "The Condorian Fraud."

In rapid succession he posted picture after picture from the miserable airport in Monrovi and compared them to the images the country's president had presented to the African Union, the secretary-general of the UN, and President of the United States Obama. It was extra fun to write captions for each picture:

Everyone in the Union has always considered President Aleko to be a joke. And it's only got worse since he got himself a new minister of foreign affairs, one Johan Löwenhult. According to credible sources, Johan is

*dumb as a bicycle rack. The president and the idiot have
assembled a team that is trying to con an entire
continent. No, the entire world!*

After four or five posts and an equal number of captions with
similar contents, the third secretary's anonymous account began to follow as many newspapers, TV channels, political com-
mentators, and regular old opinionated people as possible.
Hundreds of them followed back, for reasons of politeness,
curiosity, or plain habit. With that, Fredrik's message had made
it out. The truth about the Condors' not-at-all-glorious airport
spread on the wind.

* * *

Pleasant autumn sunlight shone over Zurich. Everything was
set to go.

Agnes, Aleko, Johan, Petra, and Herbert von Toll were sitting on a restaurant patio off Bahnhofstrasse. Agnes and
Herbert were glad to be reunited and felt life was so sweet they
should each order a glass of white wine, while the rest of the
group settled for coffee. Agnes had her tablet open.

"So I should press the button?" she said.

The others nodded.

In fact, she had to press a few buttons. Project Doomsday
was launched simultaneously on three social media platforms,
all with a link to a website that boasted a design that inspired
confidence. And all with an offer that would be hard to resist
for anyone who had at least a hundred dollars to spare. Or
preferably even more.

Once Agnes had taken a deep breath and got the ball rolling,
she raised her glass of wine toward Herbert.

"May the force be with us," she said.

"*Star Wars*," said Johan. "First movie in 1977, second in 1980, third in 1983. Except it was 'you,' not 'us.' But you're forgiven."

Agnes was astounded at how Johan's mind could be so detail- and fact-oriented when it came to food, drink, and American movies, and so up in the clouds when it came to everything else. But she didn't have time to explore that thought. She had her nose in her tablet, right next to Herbert, who in turn had a direct link to the bank.

"We've already got five hundred," he said.

"Five hundred dollars in one minute," President Aleko said, impressed.

"Five hundred bets. Ninety-five thousand dollars. Now a hundred and twenty thousand. A hundred and eighty."

While the money poured in, Johan was fiddling with his phone. He knew you could make news appear on it if you did the right thing. But what was that thing? Papa Aleko had asked him to keep an eye on news alerts. The very best thing that could happen to Project Doomsday was for it to make it onto *USA Today* and CNN.

Aleko knew there were bigger media outlets elsewhere in the world, in Japan and India for instance, but nowhere would you find more American dollars than in the United States of America. Surely there was no way the media had got wind of this doomsday news yet, but . . .

"Look," said Johan. "That's funny!"

He'd found something else, and showed everyone a breaking news article—with a picture!—in Johannesburg's *Daily Sun.*

"'The Condorian Fraud?'"

The picture had been taken at a low altitude over Aéroport Aleko International, through a gleaming helicopter window. The article had been written by the newspaper's foreign correspondent, who had been on the scene in Addis Ababa just a few days ago to personally witness what the president had to say about the new construction in his country and the pictures he had to show of Aleko International—in a *very* different condition than what this image suggested. Now the reporter raised the question of whether the Condorian president had once again been toying with the rest of the continent. Apropos of an anonymous revelation on Instagram.

Aleko reacted with horror, at more or less the same time their revenues passed two million dollars.

What had Johan just called it? Funny?

"Exactly what is so funny about all this?" said the man who was about to become an asshole again.

And there would be no turning back this time.

"Do you see that green reflection in the window?"

Johan had discovered something about the picture that the others hadn't noticed.

"Yes?"

If you looked closely, you could make out the photographer's hand and wrist. The emerald-green bit was the watchcase of a Rolex Oyster Perpetual.

"My brother Fredrik has a watch just like that."

"Bought with your money," said Petra.

* * *

The cozy wine and coffee break, including the launch of Project Doomsday, turned into an emergency meeting. The most popular theory among those attendees who could think straight was that Johan's brother Fredrik was out to get them. And that he was leading the game 1–0.

Agnes, of course, moved as comfortably through real life as she did on the socials. She said it wasn't a disaster at all. And it didn't have to turn into one either.

"How can it not?" said Aleko. "The airport looks terrible!"

"In Fredrik's pictures, sure. But not in ours."

"The difference is that his are real, is it not?"

Agnes laughed.

"What does that have to do with anything?"

Meanwhile, Herbert was up to something else. He was deep inside the financial systems of Bank von Toll.

"What are you doing?" Petra wondered.

"I was searching our client database. It rang a bell when you all said the name Fredrik Löwenhult. He became a client of ours last summer, and wanted sixty-four million Swedish kronor managed in the best possible way. It's already up to sixty-seven. Dad isn't just old and mean. He's clever too."

"Sixty-four million," Petra mused. "Then he got a little more for the apartment than we guessed."

"Have I correctly surmised from the general mood here that we've just found our fall guy?" said Herbert.

"Fall guy?" said Johan.

"Shush," said Agnes.

CHAPTER 62

The Whole World Takes the Bet

While all the pieces fell into place for the president who no longer wanted to be an asshole, money continued to pour into an account locked and controlled by Herbert von Toll at his father's esteemed bank in Zurich. The rate of increase was as impressive as it was logical. After all, the internet has the ability to multiply itself under certain conditions. Two readers become four, then eight, then sixteen. Twenty-three steps later, the number of readers of an optimized post are up to 134,217,728. Another six steps, and the post would have more views than there are people on God's green Earth, if only that were possible.

Each viral instance of fraud will crash and burn eventually. Except for this one, because Professor Smirnoff's entire message was based on the idea that the bettor was welcome to believe him or not. No one had anything to lose but their entire life, along with everyone else at the exact same time. But if they didn't die, the bettor would have doubled their money. The only way to stop the spread of the viral bet would be to find an objective reason to challenge the bank that backed the whole arrangement. Many tried; no one succeeded.

Bank von Toll. Founded in 1935. Immaculate.

Perhaps—and it was a big perhaps—something would

change if some global authority spoke up and expressed doubt. Like, for instance, Britney Spears. Whose boyfriend, Jason Trawick, soon made it known that he and Britney had just bet a hundred thousand dollars, in the hopes of doubling the sum ahead of the lavish engagement party the couple were planning.

Or Bill Gates. Who became curious about the latest in a long line of doomsday prophets, and said he'd just tossed in a million dollars with the intent to get it back twofold in a few weeks, at which point he would donate it to climate research.

Next came windbag businessman Donald Trump, who in a series of Tweets declared that doomsday was garbage, that there was no reason to research the thing any further, that there was too much research in general, that he intended to become president of the United States someday, and that the first thing he would do as president was ban doomsday prophets as well as all talk about climate change. But in the meantime he had just thrown one million, one hundred thousand dollars in Bank von Toll's direction. He wouldn't be donating the money to anyone, by the way, because he—unlike Bill Gates—was no communist.

* * *

How eight million dollars could turn into three hundred million overnight was more than Herbert could comprehend at first. This was before he understood that some of the world's most powerful men had turned it into a pissing match. Not to mention all the celebrities.

If Agnes had ever been worried that no money would come in, she now felt more and more like things were heading the other direction. If people knew how much was streaming in, anyone could draw the reasonable conclusion that Professor

Smirnoff wouldn't be able to afford to pay up. Because who, aside from possibly Bill Gates, had hundreds of millions of dollars just lying around?

So she updated all the social media sites with comments from the professor, saying that he was surprised hardly anyone had dared to take him up on his bet.

Petra wanted to understand the psychology behind what was going on, and turned to her violet-haired partner in crime to learn more.

Ten intense years on the internet had taught Agnes many things. Like each published truth would be met with resistance from some direction or another, since there was always someone who wanted something different. Also, on the internet fact and fiction blended together to such a degree that soon no one would be able to tell one from the other. Almost everything ended with people clinging tightly to whatever it was they wished was true, totally unmoored from what science or probability had to say. This led to intellectual exchanges of approximately this sort:

A: "Consequently, it is scientifically proven that—"
B: "Shut up, you dick."

Translated into their current reality, that meant that since hardly anyone wanted to die, there was also hardly anyone who believed Petra's fake truth.

The fact that they were right on that count had more to do with luck than with intelligence.

The most common reaction in the global debate that ensued was that the prophecy was a bunch of bunk and clearly nothing to worry about. But of course, everyone who said as much came under fire: "Then why don't you back up your ideas with everything you've got?"

The next most common reaction was endless arguments on social media about the accuracy of the equation that was said to prove the claim. Some maintained (untruthfully) that they'd ploughed their way through all sixty-four steps, but none of them arrived at the same result. Yes, the world was going to end, they agreed on that much. But when? One claimed it would happen in six thousand years; another, two thousand; a third, that the end of the world had actually happened back in 1882, but he thought he should do the math one more time and he would get back to them. The self-appointed authorities canceled each other out; no one listened any more to them than they did the professor.

Petra had feared that the doomsday fraud would unleash a global panic, or else spark various types of senseless behavior. But the closest thing she could find along those lines was a new Facebook group inviting people to an orgy in Hyde Park, starting immediately. A few hours later, the London police released a statement to say they had arrested a man and his wife in the act in that very park, and had shooed off a small group of on-lookers as well. The Facebook group had no greater reach than that.

The prophet accepted Agnes's reasoning about how the internet and humanity functioned, on their own and in combination. But she protested when the old woman called her equation a fake truth. She had quite purposefully changed one parameter pretty late in the equation from (the correct) 7.32 to 3.72. This way, anyone who took the time to work through all the steps could arrive at the same conclusion as the fictional Professor Smirnoff; namely, that everything would be over and done with on the evening of October 18 this very year. Or right after lunch for those in New York. Or early in the morning of the next day in Sydney. Petra's professional pride forbade her from publishing pure falsehoods.

"Speaking of," she said. "A miserable airport is still a miserable airport, even online, isn't it?"

"Oh, you," said Agnes, and smiled.

CHAPTER 63

Agnes Takes Command

The Doomsday Group was back in the Condors, now in the company of a seventy-six-year-old man who had just broken up with his father in favor of a seventy-five-year-old potential girlfriend.

Aleko was having a hard time maintaining a positive attitude after Fredrik Löwenhult's attack. He figured the only way to counter the article in the *Daily Sun* was to show off the new terminal to the paper's correspondent, on the theme of "Look here, that rando on Instagram is just telling lies."

The problem was, of course, that he wasn't.

But Agnes had no intention of giving up. She quickly drew up a three-step PR plan:

1. Have the helicopter pilot give an interview on the TV program *Our Condors*.
2. Create a temporary terminal solution.
3. Get their hands on a "useful idiot."

After these measures were taken, she promised, everything would be just fine again.

She was so close to right.

CHAPTER 64

Agnes's PR Plan

On the initiative of the violet-haired mastermind, the investigative journalism program *Our Condors* scored an exclusive interview with the helicopter pilot from Mombasa, to talk about the pictures of the shabby Condorian airport that were suddenly on the lips of half of Africa.

"I just don't understand," the pilot lied.

A man he didn't know had asked, a few days earlier, to be flown to the Condors and back.

"I told him it wasn't possible, that there was a ground stop on the island because of an endangered bird."

"What did this unknown man say to that?"

"That we weren't going to land, just fly to the border and back. He was willing to pay good money and I didn't see anything illegal about it, so I accepted the job."

President Aleko's wife's twin sister's day job was managing the station, of course, but she always jumped into the studio whenever it was important to get something just right. Like now. She put on a stern voice.

"But these pictures were taken from Condorian airspace, weren't they?"

The helicopter pilot pretended to be flustered.

"Yes," he said at last. "When we came to the border, the man told me he would give me an extra two thousand dollars if I went a few nautical miles farther. When I told him I would not land on the island without permission, he said we weren't going to land, just head in and circle a few times. I didn't think that could hurt the bird."

"You realize that you broke the law, don't you?"

The pilot squirmed.

"I'm sorry," he said.

"Don't apologize to me, apologize to the people of the Condors. Tell us what happened next."

"I broke the law, like you said. I made a quick pass over the airport and this unknown man took some pictures and said we could turn back. We were only in Condorian airspace for a few minutes. But I know it was wrong."

"What did you mean a moment ago, when you said you just don't understand?"

"I mean . . . the airport is gorgeous!"

"It doesn't look like in those pictures?"

"It doesn't make sense! He must have faked them, or been there to take pictures months ago. I don't get it . . ."

"Did you take pictures of our magnificent stock exchange building as well? Or the construction on our new hospital? All the schools that are being built?"

"No, no. I swear, it was just the airport."

CHAPTER 65

Agnes's PR Plan

The reddish-brown, uneven, dusty runway had become—in record time—black, gleaming, smooth, and beautiful.

"Well done," said Agnes, clapping the exhausted airport manager on the shoulder. "That just leaves the terminal."

"Are you kidding me?"

"You've got four days."

"You are kidding."

But Agnes wasn't. Aleko's brilliant idea about burning down the old terminal and pretending it was the new one that had gone up in flames had fallen flat as a result of Fredrik Löwenhult's stunt. No one would believe a tale like that now.

She took out some renderings to show what she meant. The airport manager would build a new facade, three hundred sixty feet wide and twenty-five feet high, and erect it in front of the side of the terminal building that faced the runway. It would be made of wood but painted pale gray to look like concrete. According to her drawings, it would be propped up by a whole bunch of poles on the back side. From the right angle and proper distance, the actual and increasingly miserable terminal building would be hidden entirely. From this same angle and distance, the airport would look just as Aleko had lied about a week earlier.

With this false front in place, the imaginary bird could finish nesting in peace and quiet, and the airport manager could begin the toilsome work of tearing down and hauling away all the old crap inside the building (Aleko wanted the rubble dumped in the mountain-goat-loving village chief's valley to give that guy something else to focus on for a while).

The airport manager wondered if Agnes wasn't worried that this fraud would be revealed as soon as the first traveler arrived and stepped through the main entrance of the facade. She told him he didn't need to worry about that.

"You've got four days. Did I mention that?"

CHAPTER 66

Agnes's PR Plan

PART 3 OF 3

The so carefully bribed helicopter pilot was a better actor than anyone could have predicted. His interview on *Our Condors* spread across the continent. Suddenly, news desks were bustling with activity. Was the asshole an asshole or not?

South Africa's *Daily Sun* had been first to call Aleko's motives into question after the pictures showed up on Instagram. Foreign correspondent Samuel Duma had, of course, been there in the room in Addis Ababa to hear the president talk about the Condorian miracle and he had seen with his own eyes the pictures Aleko presented.

Followed by that anonymous Instagram account.

Followed by a helicopter pilot who was nearly in tears as he testified that the Instagram photos weren't real.

The ugly duckling turned into a swan and then a duckling again, and then—well, what? Had Samuel Duma raked an innocent man through the coals?

The Condorian president's statement didn't help at all:

I ordered our international airport here in the Condors to close with the intent of helping an endangered bird survive here on our planet. Now, powerful forces want to drag all of Africa back into the eternal darkness of corruption. They are exploiting a poor defenseless bird

for their deplorable objectives, a little songbird who
wants nothing more than to spread its wings and fly. But
I would rather sacrifice my international reputation than
reopen our great airport before *Cyanolanius condorensis*
has finished nesting.

Samuel Duma felt that it was his responsibility, above anyone
else's, to get to the bottom of all this. The foreign correspondent
sent a proposal to the Condorian presidential palace requesting
permission to visit the island, even if it took a boat. Of course,
a reasonable alternative—thought the correspondent—might
be a helicopter. It could land wherever it liked, keeping a safe
distance from the endangered songbird. "In this manner, the
Daily Sun hopes to put an end to speculation once and for all,
and—we expect—restore the honor of the Condorian president."

With that, Samuel Duma had saved Agnes some time. She
didn't need to find a useful idiot—he'd come to her. He was
immediately offered a helicopter ride to the Condors from
Mombasa. However, the spokesperson for the presidential palace (the president himself, but of course Samuel Duma had no
way of knowing that) also included an apology: the helicopter
trip could not be arranged until four days later, for reasons
that were inchoate.

The violet-haired PR maven read Aleko's response to the
correspondent.

"That's good about the four days, but where did you get the
word 'inchoate' from?"

"That's a word I used to toss around back in Moscow when
I needed to put someone in their place. Language is power."

"Do you know what it means?"

"You have no idea how long I've been meaning to find out,
but I never got around to it."

"Incoherent."

"I thought I was being crystal clear!"

"'Inchoate' means incoherent."

"Oh! Well, there you go."

Like father, like son, Agnes thought, but she didn't say so. The word "inchoate" would make the palace's invitation somewhat inchoate, but it would probably serve its function anyhow.

CHAPTER 67

As Wrong as Anything Can Get

The only thing Aleko disliked more than all the African Union put together was journalists. As a freshly minted president he had been subjected to several of them during a session in Gambia. They posed disgustingly bold questions about all sorts of things, including Aleko's view on human rights, as though human rights were a human right.

He managed to shake them off that time, and ever since he had avoided them like the plague. No wonder he was hesitant about Agnes's suggestion of planning a "spontaneous" meeting with a journalist for the greater good. But she seemed to know what she was doing, and she argued her position well.

That was why he was now well hidden inside the helicopter pilot's office in Mombasa, biding his time as the pilot greeted foreign correspondent Samuel Duma in the waiting room just outside.

The correspondent believed he would get to land on the island and have the opportunity to interview the proud airport manager on-site. But the pilot had secret instructions to realize at a crucial moment that he didn't have enough fuel, meaning that they must turn back to base. At which point he would take the helicopter in a broad arc across the brand-new runway—putting the concrete-like wooden facade of the terminal building at the perfect angle for the correspondent's pictures.

Back in Mombasa, President Aleko would just happen to pop up after an important meeting in Cairo (or wherever) and, with a perfectly acted hint of reluctance, agree to an interview.

With that, the asshole would become the hero of the continent for the second time in under a month.

Was the plan.

How come things never go according to plan?

*   *   *

It seemed to be going so well for Dad. Johan tried not to interfere with the details, but some important person was going to be flown over the airport to take pictures that would prove that Aleko wasn't an asshole at all. Then Dad would meet with this important person in Mombasa and accept a whole load of praise before flying home, while the important guy told the world what a delight the Condorian president was.

Johan was so eager to find a way to contribute. Aleko talked a lot about the importance of taking the initiative, helping oneself, acting rather than being acted upon. This gave Johan an idea, and he saw to it that within a few hours of having it he was interviewed on Condorian TV.

In his role as minister of foreign affairs, he declared that in order to support the president's hard work he had just decided that from this day on, corruption was forbidden by law.

He felt very proud of himself.

*   *   *

The Condorian climate is characterized by a dry period from May to October and a rainy season full of storms, cyclones, and high humidity from November to April. But in the era of climate change, not even this pattern could be trusted. In 2011, the rainy season decided to start on the afternoon of October 10.

The helicopter pilot was surprised, to say the least, when drops of rain began hitting his windshield. Soon navigation became more difficult as well, as the winds picked up. The pilot had tens of thousands of hours' experience, though, so forty or fifty feet per second wouldn't scare him. Up to sixty-five, with gusts.

The journey continued as planned. And he was able to deliver the commentary he'd rehearsed over the headset just as the pilot and the South African crossed into Condorian airspace.

"Dammit!"

Samuel Duma wondered why the pilot was cursing.

"I forgot to refuel, I'm such an idiot!"

The correspondent perceived a threat to his scoop.

"But we're almost there! Can't you refuel in the Condors?"

The pilot was ready for this.

"No way in hell! The shit they sell there could bind up any engine. Or would you like to make an emergency landing in the Indian Ocean on the way home?"

Samuel Duma would not like that. He would like to make it home in time to celebrate his second anniversary with his wife, however. They were planning to stroll through the Walter Sisulu Botanical Gardens while holding hands.

"We're turning back," said the pilot, starting his arc just north of the airport. At a low altitude, so they would be at the correct angle in relation to the false front.

Duma didn't have time to consider that it ought to take more or less the same amount of fuel whether the pilot turned around right away or landed and took off again. He caught sight of the airport and began to take pictures. He went back and forth between still photos and video. And felt that his story was in the bag. This airport was clearly brand-new! He ended up with some great aerial shots of the gleaming, asphalted runway in the foreground and the grand concrete terminal just past it.

Even as the gusts grew stronger and the rain whipped the windows harder and harder.

It makes quite a racket when fourteen sturdy wooden poles break in quick succession. Still, it wasn't audible from the cabin of the helicopter. Besides, both pilot and passenger were wearing headsets.

It sure was visible, though. The still images and videos both recorded the razor-sharp evidence as what looked like an airport terminal gave way in the gale and revealed what was hidden behind.

CHAPTER 68

The Horrors of Journalism

The EC155 helicopter landed once more, back in Mombasa. The trip had been a bumpy one, in the increasing rain and wind. Even so, foreign correspondent Samuel Duma managed to compose an introduction while aloft.

> MONROVI-MOMBASA (*Daily Sun*). President Aleko of the Condors caused a sensation in Addis Ababa sixteen days ago when he declared that his country was launching a new battle against corruption.
>
> In a split second he gave an entire continent fresh hope. He was embraced by the UN and the president of the United States of America.
>
> But Aleko was conning them all. He has a reputation for being corrupt, cynical, and fraudulent.
>
> Today the *Daily Sun* can reveal that this reputation is deserved.

The rest would have to wait until he was checked in and ready for his flight back to Johannesburg. But preferably no longer; after all, he was sitting on a scoop, and you don't want to hold on to one of those. Then again, he ought to fire an email to the palace and give that fraudster of a president— the man who for good reason was known as the asshole—the chance to comment. Duma knew he wouldn't receive a reply, but he had journalistic ethics to consider. "President Aleko has not responded to the *Daily Sun*'s request for a comment," more or less.

The correspondent booked a taxi as soon as the helicopter touched down and jogged over to the taxi company's small enclosure to keep from waiting outside in the pouring rain.

To his surprise, the room wasn't empty. A man was standing in a corner, apparently waiting to be flown somewhere. In this weather? Wasn't there something familiar about him?

"Oh my goodness, isn't this a stroke of bad luck. I never give interviews."

Everything was going according to plan. He was in a terrific mood, despite the awful weather. Agnes was brilliant at crisis management.

"Why, I remember you—you're the news correspondent from back in Addis! Of course you may ask a question or two since we just happened to run into each other like this."

It took a second for Samuel Duma to realize who he was sharing the waiting room with. But he quickly recovered.

"That's great, Mr. President. Then my first question will be, Why are you trying to fool the whole world into believing something that's not true?"

This was not at all the introduction that Aleko had pictured.

"I don't understand," he said. "I assume you've just returned from your investigative journalism trip to the Condors, there and back? Am I missing something? Did you fly off course?"

"Mr. President, I have a series of photographs, and video as well, that show your pathetic false front blowing away and revealing one of Africa's most miserable airport terminals. You tried to fool me into being your errand boy. My question is, *Why?*"

Aleko saw his accolades vanish. Damn weather! Damn everything! Thoughts sailed through his mind at a hundred miles per hour. Might one option be to jump the correspondent here and now and beat him to death?

Duma could see that the president was shaken.

"Are you trying to cook up an explanation on the spot? Believe me, it won't work. I saw what I saw, I've got photographic evidence of it, and I've already composed the introduction to the article I'm going to write. The best thing you can do, Mr. President, is admit—"

This was as far as Samuel Duma got before he was cut off.

"Twenty-five thousand," said Aleko. "Dollars, of course."

"What for?" Samuel Duma said, astonished.

"Did I say twenty-five thousand? I meant fifty. That's three years' salary, more or less, right?"

Aleko felt that few men were as skilled at bribery as he was.

"I'd say more like five years' salary, Mr. President. Or fifty, if I were a farmer in the Condors."

"Only idiots are farmers in the Condors. And I don't think you're an idiot. I think this could be the best day of your life. I say we shake on a hundred thousand, even. I've got some things to attend to at home, and I'd like to get going before the weather deteriorates even more. I just want to make this unfortunate story disappear off the face of the earth first."

Samuel Duma said the same went for him. If the president would excuse him, he planned to finish writing his article first.

"And look at that—here comes my taxi. Thank you for the interview, Mr. President. And I wish you the best of luck. Farewell."

Said Samuel Duma, who then walked out into the rain, jumped into his taxi—and disappeared. A hundred thousand dollars was a ridiculous amount of money for any South African foreign correspondent. But no one could put a price on Samuel Duma's integrity.

* * *

The helicopter pilot had finished all the routines involved in turning off and shutting down his aircraft. He had checked off every item on the checklist and was now returning to his office. In the waiting area stood President Aleko.

"Hello, Mr. President," said the pilot. "All good?"

"Shut up," said Aleko. "How could you be so stupid as to let the correspondent return after he saw what he saw?"

The pilot had already had a suspicion that today would not end well. But what could he do?

"What could I do?" he said.

"For starters, you could have made sure to crash into the ocean," said Aleko. "Or at least shove your passenger out at an altitude of five thousand feet. Anything but this!"

The helicopter pilot had an internal barometer calibrated to measure different levels of bribery for different situations. He didn't think that what he'd been given so far was enough for him to kill himself, his helicopter, and his traveling companion. And leaving the controls even for a few seconds, in that gale, to try to shove his companion out—no, that would have ended poorly for all involved.

"Except for me," Aleko muttered. "Start up your damn machine now, and take me home."

"Not in this weather, Mr. President," said the pilot. "It's far too dangerous."

But Aleko had no intention of spending the night in a waiting area. The look he gave the pilot did the trick.

"Although perhaps it'll clear up, if luck is on our side," said the pilot. "Takeoff in three."

"Takeoff in two," said Aleko.

MONROVI-MOMBASA (*Daily Sun*). President Aleko of the Condors caused a sensation in Addis Ababa sixteen days ago when he declared that his country was launching a new battle against corruption.

In a split second he gave an entire continent fresh hope. He was embraced by the UN and the president of the United States of America.

But Aleko was conning them all. He has a reputation for being corrupt, cynical, and fraudulent.

Today the *Daily Sun* can reveal that this reputation is deserved.

The accompanying photographs say it all. Just under three weeks ago, President Aleko showed off a new, gleaming airport terminal during his much-discussed speech on anti-corruption. This presentation was made before all the leaders of Africa, as well as President Obama and UN Secretary-General Ban Ki-moon.

But the terminal was nothing more than a wooden facade. One that fell flat on its face when a stiff breeze blew up.

The *Daily Sun* confronted President Aleko in an exclusive interview. The president did not make any effort to explain. Instead, he made three attempts to bribe this correspondent. When we declared that the sums he had suggested were shockingly large and compared them to what an everyday, honest Condorian citizen might earn in the country Aleko rules over, he made fun of his citizens and called them idiots.

A full report is to follow in tomorrow morning's edition of the *Daily Sun*.
SAMUEL DUMA

The rainy season seemed to lose the thread, as if it couldn't decide what to do about its horribly early arrival. The helicopter pilot landed safely in the grounds of the presidential palace, where he dropped off the president and took off again with a definite sense that Aleko's days were numbered. It was probably time to start asking for payment in advance. And perhaps to put that money in the hands of his wife, along with a tip to speculate on a seriously weakened Condorian franc.

When Aleko stepped into the room where the inner circle typically gathered, Agnes, Günther, Herbert, Johan, and Petra were already there. They were watching TV. The American news channel CNN had purchased four stills and a video. They all showed a fake airport terminal collapsing. Alongside the images, they deployed direct quotes from the article in the South African newspaper, including the interview with the president himself—the part where he called his citizens idiots. This was followed by brief video interviews with three Condorians who had been stuck in Addis Ababa for weeks, after the flights that were meant to bring them home had been canceled at the last minute. All three said they no longer wished to be represented by someone who didn't respect them and who evidently only told lies and made things up. Cut to: the Condorian minister of foreign affairs' statement about a total ban on corruption on the island from this day on.

The president's hair was damp with rain. He said nothing as he watched the fateful CNN story. Not until the clip of Johan was over.

"But hasn't it always been forbidden to take bribes? How could my wife's nutty sister have let you say that on live TV?"

Johan couldn't lie to his father.

"I slipped her a hundred."

Aleko's day wrapped up with a call from Ban Ki-moon. The secretary-general advised that Johan Löwenhult had been relieved of his duties as anti-corruption marshal, and as for the president, he could take his stock exchange and stick it where the sun did not shine. This was an expression Ban Ki-moon had never before used in his decades of diplomatic service, but he had no choice given that diplomatic language did not have the words to convey how he felt.

Jonas Jonasson

The call from the secretary-general reminded Johan of the phone number he'd got from his father, the one to the American Hollywood actor.

"I feel like the mood around here is extremely gloomy," he said. "Shouldn't I call George Clooney? He had such nice things to say about us."

"Good idea," Petra said sarcastically.

Johan's face lit up.

"Really?"

It was not.

CHAPTER 69

Time to Let Go

The next day, there was a demonstration outside the presidential palace. There must have been two hundred Condorians there, chanting "Resign!" They could be heard through the gate and all the way into the reception room where Aleko sat with Agnes, Günther, Herbert, Johan, and Petra. If the weather hadn't been so dismal, there probably would have been ten times as many protestors.

Aleko had made his people ashamed of him. According to their signs, he was a liar who bribed his way through life and called his subjects idiots.

"Being called an idiot isn't the end of the world, is it?" said Johan.

Petra said that the lying and bribing was plenty bad and then some.

Agnes had taught the rest of the group that you could turn almost any situation to your advantage with the right photo-editing program combined with making a big splash on as many social media platforms as possible. If anyone could turn public opinion around yet again, it was her. So it was a big letdown for the group to hear her swear for the first time:

"No bloody way am I going to figure this one out."

"You're extra beautiful when you swear," said Herbert.

Günther poured a whole drinking glass full of vodka and drained half of it. East German that he was, he was immediately filled with Russian melancholy.

"It's all my fault," he said.

Unclear why.

But a long life had taught Aleko when the time had come.

Time, for instance, to abandon the sinking ship that was Gorbachev. Time to pack his bags full of all the money he'd squirrelled away and abandon Yeltsin and all of Russia. Time to let go of a seven-year career as president.

"It's time for us to shake this off and reposition ourselves."

CHAPTER 70

Operation Go-Up-in-Smoke

PART 1 OF 5

Aleko didn't have any ideas beyond that of pursuing a change of scenery. With as much money as possible in their luggage.

Petra turned what ought to happen next into a math problem. Her equation went like this:

Buy time + secure finances + emigrate = peace and quiet.

She delegated the buying time part to Aleko. His first, immediate task was to calm the general mood of unrest in the country. They absolutely did not have time for a coup in the middle of everything else.

The president appreciated the prophet's leadership qualities. She could have been an important asset in his government, if only she hadn't refused a position. He called TV manager Fariba and told her that he planned to address his people on the tube that evening at 8:15.

"But that's in the middle of *Game of Thrones*!" said Fariba.

"I know," said Aleko.

That was how you reached the masses.

* * *

The president spent that whole afternoon polishing his statement. He allowed Günther to weigh in. And Agnes. And then he let Petra make some decisions. Just before 8:15 he took a large gulp of his best Russian vodka to get in the right frame of mind. Then the studio lights came up. The countdown began. Three, two, one, go!

Straight into the camera, his gaze steady:

My dear, proud Condorians. For over seven years I have toiled day and night for your sake and our own. I stood up to those who tried to walk all over us. But I have also made mistakes, and I know that in the past week I have disappointed many of you. Not only do I want to apologize for this, I now declare that I accept the consequences of my actions and hereby give notice that there will be a new presidential election. An election I do not intend to run in. It will take place in one week, and by one week after that I will hand responsibility for our nation over to the democratically elected winner. Long live democracy! Long live the Condors! With these words, I give the floor back to *Game of Thrones*. Go Ned Stark!

The Ned Stark bit wasn't in the script. It just slipped out. Aleko thought he had done a good job. Perhaps he was a man of the people after all.

* * *

It turned out this was exactly the manner in which the bull's horns should be grabbed. The number of protestors outside the presidential palace had swelled to over three thousand by now, but all but seven of them had taken a time-out for this week's episode of the American TV series. None returned.

After Aleko's national address, the last few protestors dropped off one by one as word of what the president had just announced reached them.

Aleko had made his announcement from the special studio deep inside his palace. Now he stood in a window on the third floor of the west wing, watching the very last protestor through binoculars. A young woman who had been enraged until just seconds ago, it seemed. She trudged off, dragging an upside-down sign behind her:

LEAVE
THE COUNTRY,
ALEKO!

The outgoing president had to tilt his head to read it.

"I am, for Christ's sake," he said from his window.

CHAPTER 71

Operation Go-Up-in-Smoke

With just three days left before the second doomsday in a month, the endless stream of money flowing into Herbert's locked account at his father's bank slowed to a trickle. During the traditional afternoon gathering on the large terrace (where Johan always surprised them with something delicious), Agnes said she was sorry about this outcome. Presumably, they'd already reached everyone in the whole world who might consider betting. The market, so to speak, was saturated.

"But five hundred and fourteen million isn't nothing," she felt.

Aleko was utterly fascinated by the disappointment radiating from his violet-haired friend.

"How much had you been expecting?" he asked.

"It would have been fun to hit a billion."

Everyone else thought that amount was plenty. Petra decided it was time to empty the account in Switzerland, repackage the money in the Condors, and send it onward. This would require the assistance of Herbert von Toll, now more than ever. The prophet asked Aleko to give the banker all his digital keys to Banque Condorienne. He was already in possession of the same for Bank von Toll.

Aleko did as he was asked, but not before posing a serious question:

"Can we trust you, Herbert?"

"You certainly can," said Agnes.

Inspired by the violet-haired lovebird's new relationship, Petra took a moment's pause in her strategizing for the future. Or perhaps she was thinking of her own personal future; she wasn't sure. In any case, suddenly her chats with Malte up in Stockholm were really gathering speed. She wasn't brave enough to ask him about Victoria's current status as regarded his heart, after the incidents with the baseball bat and the golf club, but she felt he was turning out to be just as genuine and lovely as she'd sensed back in school. Perhaps a little too nice? And indecisive? And perhaps life was punishing him for those very traits? Malte wrote that he was considering purchasing a new baseball bat to replace the one he'd loaned Petra, and that if he did he was going to name it after her.

If that wasn't flirting, what was?

* * *

Herbert glanced up from his screen and notified the group that $514,226,000 had taken off from Zurich and landed safely at Banque Condorienne. Since the betting would be open for another seventy hours, there was a chance another few hundred dollars might arrive, but it would be a sum they'd miss out on.

Aleko said Herbert should try not to lose sleep over it. No reason to get greedy.

But Herbert had discovered something strange.

"I found another five hundred million in your bank here in the Condors, Aleko. Where'd that come from?"

"Dammit, that's right," said Aleko.

He'd totally forgotten about that money in all the chaos.

* * *

Two years earlier, a Russian businesswoman had requested an audience with the Condorian president. The pretext was that she was considering investing a billion dollars in the country.

You didn't say no to this sort of meeting. It was a bit alarming, given his history. But Aleko had changed both his name and his appearance, and many years had passed. The chances that this businesswoman would recognize him as Aleksandr Kovalchuk were of little importance compared to the money she appeared to represent.

The president elected to bring Günther with him to the meeting. Across the table from them sat the well-dressed woman and her loyal interpreter. It slowly dawned on Aleko that the Vory had dropped in for a visit. These days they hid behind suits and ties, or, in this case, a bespoke Prada suit and Louboutin stilettos. But this was a young woman; she couldn't have been more than a child when Aleko escaped with his suitcases full of dollars. That was a relief.

Still, the negotiations were conducted in French just to be on the safe side. Speaking Russian in front of the very mafia that was looking for Aleksandr Kovalchuk would be tantamount to poking a sleeping Russian bear.

After a sufficient amount of chitchat and cautious tiptoeing around the matter at hand, Aleko chose to move things forward.

"We live in an unjust world," he said. "Accidentally misplace the tiniest receipt, or simply try to make a business partner happy, and you might suddenly find yourself sitting on a pile of money that states and authorities call 'dirty' for no reason whatsoever. I'm proud to stand at the forefront among those who wish to fight this financial anomaly. Let us make progress together. If you don't find me to be too forward, that is?"

It started with ten million grubby dollars. The Condors' job was to launder it clean. Günther knew just what to do. He took over as soon as the Prada woman and her interpreter left the palace.

Many years earlier, he'd had a faithful business contact, a man from Hong Kong who printed fake Soviet food stamps that were of such high quality that people with real food stamps were suspected of fraud. This business contact had long since moved to Florida, where he ran a chain of beauty salons and also imported Russian caviar that was produced and packaged in Vietnam. Günther and this acquaintance reestablished contact and came up with a suitable arrangement.

The man from Hong Kong began to copy his clients' credit card numbers and forwarded them to the Condors, where genuine copies of the stolen cards were printed. From there they were sent by courier to the Dominican Republic, where the man from Hong Kong had traveled, ostensibly on vacation. In an apartment in Santo Domingo he packed up and stamped two hundred credit cards and mailed them out to just as many exiled Chinese friends around the world. Günther's business contact had a network like no other.

With the help of the credit cards, these exiled Chinese friends bought high-end TVs and other electronics and sent them to the Condors. In flowed packages from Malaysia, Norway, Romania, Sierra Leone, Mexico, Lithuania, Ireland, Morocco, the Philippines, and many other nations as well.

Aleko gathered all these electronics into one big shipment, which he sent to Moscow, where the goods were sold again by what appeared to be a legitimate chain of stores that both paid a reasonable amount of taxes and had its books in order.

Anyone who sells expensive TVs at market price without having paid a cent to obtain them will soon make a considerable profit. The owner of the chain (the Vory, right?) received the profits and had, with the creative assistance of Aleko and Günther, got their money laundered. Since modern electronics were in short supply in Russia at the time, the sales price was accordingly high. In the long term, this meant that ten million unwashed dollars turned into nine and a half million washed ones in the span of a few weeks. All while Aleko, the man from Hong Kong, all his couriers, and the Russian tax authority had got their share too.

Of course, it wasn't possible to dupe the man from Hong Kong's beauty salon customers too many times. But Günther was always coming up with fresh variations on the same theme. In the next round, the Russians sent twenty million dollars, with the same positive results. The next time, fifty million. Then a hundred. And as recently as the day before—five hundred million dollars. The Condorian president had proved himself. This was a man to be trusted.

"Since we're enemies with everyone else anyway, might as well piss off the mafia too," said Aleko, who was not a man to be trusted. "Toss our five hundred million in with the Russians, Herbert, might be good to have on hand."

Agnes wasn't satisfied, even though she now had her billion dollars. After all, the whole point of having millions in the first place was to build up Aleko's mismanaged country. Now it sounded more like the president intended to resign, drain the country's coffers, and simply leave. And abandon her unfinished hospital?

Aleko squirmed. He had to search for the right words, since the truth happened to be exactly as Agnes had just described. In that moment, Johan came in bearing a large silver platter.

"Would anyone like some breaded sea scallops with an emulsion of chives and browned butter?"

"Yes, please," said Aleko. "May I point out that silence is the mark of a good meal?"

*　*　*

Herbert was skilled in the art of moving money. With a few clicks of a button, a billion dollars vanished from the Condors to Curaçao. And from there to Singapore. Latvia. Israel. The British Virgin Islands. Final destination: Barbados.

After the very timely sea scallops, Aleko wanted to reassure himself that the police couldn't trace the money. Herbert said that INTERPOL had some truly clever analysts and sophisticated tools. They would definitely find the money, in time.

"How much time?" said Aleko.

"A few thousand years. If they work around the clock. And have a few strokes of good luck along the way."

"If they're planning to take more than five years and a couple of weeks, they might as well not bother," said Petra.

"How's my hospital coming?" said Agnes.

CHAPTER 72

Operation Go-Up-in-Smoke

Aleko was capable of holding a grudge when he wanted to. But with just one day left of the self-nomination period for the vacant presidential post, and two days left until the election (lead times were short in the Condors), he discovered that there was only one candidate. And it was none other than that damn goat-loving village chief.

"I refuse to hand power over to him," Aleko said to his friend Günther.

"You might not have to, if things go as I hope," said his friend.

Aleko had taken it for granted that Günther would come along when they all went up in smoke. It was with a heavy heart that he received the news that his brother in spirit planned to stay behind. After all, he had his wife and daughter to think of. Sure, he could bring them with, but the same hardly went for Angelika's beloved pony Pocahontas. It would break her heart.

"I'm going to miss you, dear brother. But what do you want to do instead?"

Well, Günther's reasoning was that the new president, who-ever it turned out to be, would surely want to appoint his own chief of police. Accordingly, Günther would have to leave his uniform behind—a very unappealing thought.

One practical solution would be for Günther to become president himself. Then he could appoint himself chief of police on the side and keep his uniform, preferably with a whole bunch of medals to boot.

Aleko lit up. That was a brilliant idea!

But they couldn't rule out the possibility that the goat-lover would enjoy a certain amount of support out in the valleys. With Günther's consent, the president began to pull a number of strings. Happily, the chairman of the election commission happened to be the uncle of Aleko's deceased wife. She had begged her husband to set the old man up with a sinecure, since he was not only old and lazy but also—to be frank—not the brightest bulb. The election commission was the perfect job for him; after all, Aleko had no intention of holding any elections.

But now the old man's plate was suddenly full. The president instructed him to add 40 percent to the actual amount of votes Günther received. Perhaps that was overdoing it a bit, but better safe than sorry. At the same time, he tasked Fariba with running as many pro-Günther ads as possible, to show off his strengths. In several of them, he spoke directly to the people.

I'm Günther. I'm the chief of police of the country that boasts the lowest crime rate in Africa. I am prepared to shoulder responsibility as your leader. At the top of my agenda is lower taxes, higher wages, more jobs, and better weather. Together we will see the Condors flourish like never before.

He said this in mediocre French. Fariba made sure to subtitle him in Arabic. It was just too bad that so few people in the country knew French. And that even fewer of them could read.

* * *

With the village chief preliminarily neutralized, there was only one more thorn in Aleko's side (aside from every other leader on the African continent). That was Johan's half brother.

Fredrik was the one who had pushed Johan around during their whole upbringing, had defrauded Aleko's son out of millions, had destroyed his international career. And not least: he was the one who'd made sure Aleko himself was forced to resign and would soon have to flee the country.

To be sure, this half brother would get what was coming to him, given that he was the fall guy lurking in the depths of the von Tollian bank system, the one who would be blamed for the five-hundred-million-dollar swindle. Although he would claim he was innocent, of course. Not least because, from a purely objective standpoint, he was. So it would be nice to have another trick up their sleeve.

Aleko figured it was reasonable to expect that someone who had just become half a billion dollars richer might treat themselves to something nice. Since Fredrik—in contrast to Aleko and his friends—had *not* just become a half a billion dollars richer, Aleko got the bright idea of doing the treating for him. Preferably with some new toy whose price tag far surpassed what one could afford on the salary of a third secretary.

He called the man from Hong Kong in Miami, the man with unscrupulous contacts all over the world. And he got the response he was hoping for. The man from Hong Kong had at least three loyal underlings in Rome, all equally eager to earn a thousand bucks or two.

Aleko selected one of them, had a credit card and ID printed up in Fredrik Löwenhult's name, and made sure that the documents arrived in the right hands in the Italian capital. Aiding him were the bribed helicopter pilot from Mombasa and an international courier firm, from there all the way to Rome. From idea to confirmed delivery it only took nineteen hours and thirty-six minutes.

And that is how a red Ferrari, purchased by and registered to one Fredrik Löwenhult, came to be parked on a pedestrian crossing at the junction of Via Clitunno and Via Serchio, a stone's throw from the Swedish embassy in Rome. This maneuver wasn't without its costs for Aleko, but it felt right. And over their morning coffee the next day he gave the group a brief rundown of his handiwork.

Perhaps the rundown was a little too brief. Petra felt that she understood most things worth understanding, but in this particular instance she had to confess that she didn't follow.

"Can you please explain one more time why you bought a Ferrari for one of the people you hate most in the world?"

"A *red* Ferrari," said Agnes, confirming, in so doing, that she approved of Petra's question.

"Didn't they have any Honda Civics?" said Johan. "I think that would have been cheaper."

Aleko said he was sure that a Honda Civic was a good car, but at the same time, it wasn't the kind of car you'd run out and buy to celebrate suddenly becoming half a billion dollars richer. The point of the Ferrari was that it was supposed to look like Fredrik Löwenhult had millions to spend.

"Which he does," said Petra. "Partially stolen from Johan."

"A middling move at best," said Agnes. "If you'll excuse the honesty, Mr. President."

She would much rather have liked to see that money go toward her ongoing hospital project.

By the time Aleko explained that the car had been parked on a pedestrian crossing so that it would almost certainly draw the attention of the Italian police, the others had already stopped listening.

CHAPTER 73

The Condorian Presidential Election

The elderly, lazy, and possibly not so bright chairman of the election commission took his job seriously. Perhaps he had rested his way to fitness given that he hadn't had to lift a finger since 2006.

In the twenty-four hours he had to work with, he managed to distribute ballots to every valley and corner of the country. As there were only two candidates, the ballot design was very simple indeed.

All they needed was a picture of each candidate, along with each one's name, a short description, and two boxes, so the voter could pick one.

Next to the first photograph (it was slightly larger than the other) the blurb read:

"Presidential candidate 1: Günther. Longtime beloved chief of police with vast experience and always with the Condors' best interest in mind."

Next to the other photograph:

"Presidential candidate 2: former village chief. Possibly literate. Wants to raise taxes."

As they waited for the ballots to be collected, the chairman of the election commission sat down with his six children and voted for Günther at lightning speed. He was supposed to have an extra 40 percent of the votes, but there was no way to know how much 40 percent of what would come in might be. Their safest bet was to check away, and let the exact percentage turn out as it may.

The polling stations (which in most cases was just a hut) closed at 6 p.m. At that point, the ballots were transported by moped or bicycle to the election commission's offices in central Monrovi. The turnout was not so high that the chairman of the election commission shouldn't be able to announce the results on live TV at ten o'clock that same night. He had hired two hundred former woodsmen to handle the ballot counting. They were available since there were no longer any woods to man.

But among many other things, mathematics was not the chairman's strong suit. He had two election results to handle. The official results, on the one hand, and the ones he cooked up in his own kitchen, on the other. So, how did it go again? Was he supposed to add all the results together and divide them by two, somehow? Or by three, to be safe?

The chairman enlisted the help of the sharpest mind in his family, nine-year-old Camille, who almost always won their Yahtzee games. Camille really ought to be asleep by now, given that it was a school night. Her mother reluctantly allowed her five extra minutes in the name of democracy.

"Look at this, Dad," said Camille.

And she wrote in large letters and numbers on a blank piece of paper, in order to be as instructive as possible.

A total of 101,202 Condorians had actually voted. Then, 44,665 fake Condorians had all voted for Günther. Out of the real votes, the village chief had won 99.6 percent, and out of the fake votes, Günther had won 100 percent.

"Why, that means Günther won!" said the chairman. "Wonderful!"

But it wasn't quite that simple. The fact was, there was a greater number of real votes. So if you put together all of the votes, the chieftain got 69.1 percent, while Günther got 30.9 percent.

This was as far as Camille got before her mother said enough was enough. Straight to bed!

Camille's father looked at the percentages before him and decided that the correct thing to do was put them together, in two different columns.

And so, when asked for the results on live TV, the chairman of the election commission was able to report that presidential candidate Günther had got all of 130.9 percent of the vote.

This, of course, was considerably more than Aleko had requested.

"Wow," said host Fariba. "That's a high percentage."

Way *too* high, but she couldn't say so on air. Instead, she said:

"It seems that election turnout reflects the Condorian people's zeal to exercise their democratic rights."

At which point she made a fateful mistake. She asked another question.

"What percent of the votes did the loser receive?"

It turned out that the village chief had made it all the way up to 168.7 percent, according to the commissioner's complicated method of tallying.

"But that's more . . ." Fariba said, taken aback.

"You could look at it that way," said the chairman of the election commission, suspecting that something was about to go wrong.

So he added that Günther's 130.9 percent was still a respectable finish.

This comment was of no help to Fariba. There was no scenario in which 168 was not a larger number than 130. She had no choice but to congratulate the village chief on his win. But she did refrain from thanking the chairman of the election commission for his participation before the program was over.

Was she about to lose her job?

In reality, then, hardly anyone had voted for Günther. He had a weird name, he didn't know the right language, and he had close connections to the outgoing president. What's more, the village chief had spent four days in a row going from village to village to campaign.

Aleko was deeply upset with the uncle of his deceased wife. In the heat of the moment, he called up the chairman of the election commission. How could he have presented results that showed a voter turnout of 299.6 percent?

The uncle tried to point out that Aleko had got a much higher percentage of votes than he'd asked for. To get any more, it would have taken double the number of family members around the kitchen table. He only had *one* wife and six children, and the youngest was only five. Even so, the five-year-old had paid his respects to democracy at least two hundred times before his mother made him go to bed.

Aleko didn't even bother to fire the chairman as punishment. He settled for wishing him a miserable future and hanging up.

* * *

The formal transfer of power would take place in less than a week. Minister of Healthcare Agnes was basically chasing the current president down the halls, not at all pleased to think that construction on her hospital might stall simply because they were going to leave the country.

Aleko's incentive to give the country a facelift was grounded in his son Johan's future. Once that future was ruined by his damn half brother, he could no longer see any reason to do all the stuff Agnes had mustered into being.

Well, maybe *one* reason.

He was so sick of her chasing after him all the time.

"Yeah, yeah. I promise that your damn hospital will get built. One way or another. But only if you stop pestering me."

Agnes nodded, pleased. The Aleko she knew seldom made any promises. But once he did, a promise was a promise.

* * *

Things were going down to the wire. With three days left until the inauguration, Aleko called a governmental summit, the first and last of its kind. Besides Aleko himself, the attendees were Minister of Foreign Affairs Löwenhult, Minister of Healthcare Massode Mohadji—and also the president-elect, who surely had some name or other as well.

"Welcome to this governmental summit," Aleko said importantly. "The first and only item on the agenda has to do with our Condorian mountain goats. I have just decided to eradicate them all."

Johan and Agnes were in on the game.

"Smart decision, Dad, I mean, Mr. President. Those mountain goats are a danger to us all."

"Very smart," said Agnes. "The mountain goats are a scourge on our nation."

In perfect accordance with their plan, the friend-of-the-mountain-goats-slash-president-elect was absolutely horrified.

"No, please . . . you can't just . . . there's no . . . how would you even have the time . . ."

He stumbled over his words.

"Have the time?" said Aleko. "No problem. I've still got a day and a half left as president. If worst comes to worst, I guess I'll use napalm."

"I'm sure you can find some online," Agnes weighed in.

The village chief had no time to recover and offer further objections before Aleko continued:

"The only one who could stop me is Chief of Police Günther. He just gave his daughter a pony. Seems he's a real friend to the animals. Unfortunately, he's resigning today at two o'clock, ahead of your inauguration, Mr. Village Chief."

That was all it took. Aleko had brought documents to be signed. Two signatures later, Günther was reappointed with a fifteen-year contract, signed by both the sitting and the incoming president.

Agnes had prepared a similar kind of extortion, but Aleko had so much else to see to that he chose a more direct route.

"Moving on: you will complete the construction of the hospital, or else I'll make sure you yourself have reason to be admitted there."

The village chief promised. And he asked meekly if he might add a veterinary clinic next door.

"No, but I'll be sending you ten million hospital dollars. God help you if you use it for anything else."

PART THREE

*The Time Following the
Second End of the World*

CHAPTER 74

A Bank Director's Last Day on the Job

There was so much going on that the friends had no time to reflect upon the fact that it was suddenly 9:20 p.m. on October 18, 2011 (and the world had once again failed to end); soon after that it was 4 p.m. the next day, and not a single bettor had received their money back.

However, there were vast (*vast!*) numbers of people all over the world who were keeping a close eye on the clock. Police reports naming a certain Professor Smirnoff were soon streaming in from all seven continents, including two from Antarctica.

INTERPOL in Lyon collected these reports and, as a matter of routine, contacted the local NCB—in this case, Fedpol in Bern, about the alleged multi-million-dollar fraud. It wasn't yet possible to say exactly how much money was involved, but in a short amount of time the number of police reports had passed twenty thousand and was approaching thirty.

Two Swiss special agents, a man and a woman, headed to Zurich to pay a visit to the bank that had been named as an accessory to the crime.

They knocked. They rang the bell. They knocked again.

After a while, a very elderly man popped up in the reinforced glass door. The old man shook his head to signal that he did not intend to let them in.

"Can you hear me?" one of the two special agents said loudly through the door.

"No," said Konrad von Toll.

The agent raised his voice a little more. He declared who he was and the authority he represented. He also introduced his female colleague.

The old man stood his ground. He did not open the door. Then the woman took a piece of paper from her inner pocket. Through the glass she showed him a warrant to search the premises.

When this still didn't help, the two agents raised their voices another notch and informed the man that the bank was on the verge of having its accreditation revoked.

That hit home. The old man cracked the door.

"Is something wrong?" he said.

"More like everything," said the man. "We are special agents from Fedpol in Bern. I don't suppose you could offer us a cup of coffee, sir? We've got quite a bit to discuss."

Konrad von Toll could not. The guy who ran the coffee maker had legged it.

"Will a whiskey do?"

The female agent was an IT specialist; she could bust through firewalls like no other. To Konrad von Toll's absolute horror, she was now sitting at a monitor and peering inside the inner sanctum of the bank. Konrad noted that the male agent hadn't touched his whiskey, while Konrad's own glass was long since empty. He hadn't served any to the agent's colleague; in Konrad von Toll's world, women didn't drink hard liquor.

"Don't you want your drink, Mr. Special Agent?" he said to the agent whose nose wasn't buried in a screen.

"No, thank you. Please, help yourself. We wouldn't want the whiskey to go to waste."

"You could have had mine too," said the female agent, without taking her eyes from the computer. "If I'd been offered any, that is."

Bank Director von Toll immediately tossed back the male agent's glass, apologized to the woman for strategic reasons, and poured one for her as well.

"Thanks," she said. "That was kind of you. I'm about to gain access to your deposit records. If you find that too upsetting, my glass is right there."

It was possible to see, in those records, that half a billion American dollars had come into a secure account at Bank von Toll in recent weeks. Also plain to see was the current balance: three hundred and twenty dollars.

"Would you be so kind as to access this account for me, Mr. von Toll?"

The ninety-six-year-old was desperate. Every nerve in his body was screaming that no one—*no one*—could break into his accounts like that. Not even von Toll himself, in this instance, since it was his vanished whippersnapper of a son who had both created and secured it.

"No!" he said. "I forbid it. That is to say, I can't. That is to say, I don't know. Please—tell me what's going on here."

"That's what we'd like to hear from you, Director von Toll," said the male agent. "An untrained eye might think you've been getting up to some third-degree fraud. But I'm sure you can explain, isn't that right?"

The ninety-six-year-old hadn't felt this much distress since the time back in the thirties when he found out the diversion he'd temporarily amused himself with was pregnant. He grabbed the woman's whiskey as well and drained it. Three quick nips in addition to that morning's usual two. It was starting to add up. But the last one allowed him to gather his courage.

"Here at Bank von Toll, nothing is more important than our clients' integrity," he said. "You'll have to excuse me, Mr. Special Agent and . . . the lady . . . but—"

He got no further before he was interrupted.

"It so happens that it's theoretically possible to be a special agent and a woman at the same time," said the IT expert. "And well versed in the law, believe it or not."

She knew more or less by heart the relevant statutes as legislated by a variety of countries, so she picked one at random in the hopes of giving the old man a good scare.

"'A person who, by deception, induces someone into an action or omission that involves gain for the perpetrator and loss for the person deceived or someone in whose place they are is guilty of fraud and is sentenced to imprisonment.' Suck on that, Director von Toll."

It's possible that Konrad von Toll did just what she said. Sucked on that. Or perhaps he didn't have time, before his heart, after ninety-six taxing years, decided to stop beating. His blood ceased to circulate; all his organs—his brain included—suffered an acute lack of oxygen. The ninety-six-year-old fell face-first onto his desk, hitting his head on the American calculating machine he hadn't used for years, but which stood there as a monument to days gone by. Konrad von Toll's entire body had already stopped working, so his forehead smashing into a calculating machine didn't make things any worse.

"For Christ's sake!" said the male special agent. "Is there a defibrillator around here anywhere?"

"Couldn't he have waited until he unlocked the account for us?" said the female agent, feeling as though a whiskey then and there wouldn't have been such a bad thing after all.

* * *

It took a whole hour to get a doctor to come and declare what everyone already knew even before they carried the body away. In the meantime, the female agent battled the computer system. She arrived at the solution just as she and her colleague were alone again. She got into the account. Five hundred and fourteen million dollars had been transferred to the Condors a few days earlier. This occurred after a dialogue between the owner of the account, one Fredrik Löwenhult in Rome, and a yet-unknown recipient.

"I'm calling Italy," said the IT expert's colleague.

*   *   *

Special Agent Sergio Conte had got to enjoy a weekend in Sicily once everything finally calmed down, some time after Agnes Eklund managed to get herself killed in an accident between car and horse-drawn carriage. Conte himself believed she was dead, and after a lot of hard work he won a certain amount of acceptance from the furious lawyers of Bvlgari and LVMH, while the displeasure of the chairman of the fly-fishing club persisted.

And that damn internet was apparently here to stay. Now he'd been saddled with a multi-million-dollar fraud case at a Swiss bank. In which the main suspect was a Swedish diplomat stationed in Rome. Who had apparently sent all the stolen money to . . .

Sergio Conte heaved a deep sigh.

"Why is it always the Condors?"

*   *   *

Just over a thousand miles south of Zurich, Herbert von Toll sat at his laptop, following the progress of the IT expert. He didn't know who it was, but they were good at their job.

"I think they've found our fall guy," he said, after a particularly important breakthrough. "I bet Dad's having a heart attack right about now."

During the first fifty of his sixty-one total years in his father's service, Herbert's main job had been to keep the office clean, the coffee maker brewing, the cigar box full, and the whiskey cabinet well stocked. As digitization took over more and more, Konrad von Toll had no choice but to increase his son's scope of duty a smidge. In the decade that followed, Herbert's talents increased far beyond the old man's understanding.

Now he had hidden Fredrik Löwenhult's name and identification number behind some very sophisticated encryption; it appeared impossible to crack. Still, Herbert was sure that this is what INTERPOL had just done before his very digital eyes. And with that, he received confirmation that a theory he'd long held was true.

"Diffie–Hellman," he said to himself with satisfaction.

"You're going to have to explain that," said Petra.

"Do you want the long or the short version?"

"I'm in no rush."

Both Herbert and his father Konrad fervently disliked the united front of European governments, the OECD, and most of all, the United States of America. Working together, these entities were making strides in using legislation to pry open the doors of banks with such success that tens of thousands of sophisticated tax evaders had reason to start sweating.

But Herbert realized that the confidentiality provided by Swiss banks was under threat from multiple directions. In recent times, a number of Swiss financial actors had got between four and fifteen years behind bars for things that any Swiss bank with flexible morals would do. Herbert spent a lot of time pondering why some survived unscathed and others did not.

After considering the question for several months, he had come to the conclusion that the US National Security Agency and INTERPOL knew something that the bankers didn't know they knew. What banks had in common was that they would put a lot of money on the belief that no outsider (including the OECD) could get into their systems. At the same time, there had to be ways in and out, because how else could shady party A do business with equally shady party B? The answer went by the name *key exchange*. Or sophisticated encryption. The banks employed different solutions for the same purpose. What trash-emptier and coffee-machine-caretaker Herbert eventually figured out before anyone else was that the people who'd already gone to prison had all used the same secure key exchange method.

Diffie–Hellman.

It seemed highly unlikely that the NSA and INTERPOL could have outwitted the Diffie–Hellman protocol. It would be equally likely that someone could come and go as he liked at Fort Knox, where the United States kept their gold reserves. But *if* they had outwitted Diffie–Hellman, all they'd have to do was slip into the system and read messages and agreements protected by passwords of twenty-five characters or more.

When Herbert was done investigating and pondering, he came to two conclusions, and he was equally sure of both.

1. The Diffie–Hellman method of key exchange was impossible to crack, and:
2. The NSA and INTERPOL had found a way to do the impossible.

Bank von Toll hadn't used Diffie–Hellman up to this point, but Herbert saw to it that they started immediately. Then he created fictional person X and placed him in a supposedly inaccessible place, in this case, Banque Condorienne. He didn't even have to make up person Y. Fredrik Löwenhult had moved from Sweden to Italy some time earlier—and he'd chosen Bank von Toll in Zurich to manage his millions of kronor. This was as clever of him as it eventually turned out to be stupid, given that Herbert allowed X to send a message to Y (that is, Fredrik), containing the code to the most protected of the supposedly unbreakable numbered accounts at Bank von Toll. If Diffie–Hellman used enough prime numbers, it would take eons to crack. But they had been sloppy on that point. And the NSA and INTERPOL had figured that much out.

CHAPTER 75

Conte, Guldén, and Big Brother Löwenhult

"My name is Special Agent Conte, and I'm here on behalf of INTERPOL."

"Nice to meet you," said Ambassador Guldén.

"Sort of," said Conte. "I'm calling about the diplomat Löwenhult."

"Fredrik? Has he done something wrong? Run a red light?"

"No, but you're on the right track—he parked his red Ferrari right in the middle of a pedestrian crossing over here."

"He doesn't have a Ferrari, does he?"

"It's possible he has several," said Conte. "He could certainly afford it."

"How's that?"

"He's under suspicion of fraud."

"That's terrible! Who is the victim of this fraud?"

"Not victim, *victims*."

"Well, who are they?"

The ambassador didn't want to believe what he was hearing. He sounded impatient. So impatient that the special agent was annoyed.

"Would you like all the names, Mr. Ambassador?"

"Yes, please."

"There are approximately five million of them. Would you

be willing to settle for the sixty-seven thousand who've reported him so far?"

* * *

Diplomatic immunity is more useful at certain times than others. Fredrik wasn't at risk of spending thirty-plus years in an Italian prison; instead he faced merely being shipped home and possibly charged for his crimes there. The third secretary maintained his innocence and voluntarily submitted to questioning. Since an interview couldn't be held until later that day, and because there's always some gossipy police officer around who'd be delighted to make a few bucks without putting in too much effort, the suspected diplomat was a news item around half the world even before he knew what he was under suspicion for.

"Voluntary interview with Swedish diplomat Fredrik Löwenhult," Special Agent Conte began. "I'd like to record this conversation, do I have your consent to do so?"

"I demand that you record it!" Fredrik said. "I told you, I'm innocent."

To be safe, he had brought along the ambassador as a witness.

"Then we'll begin with the question of what you were doing in a helicopter over the Condors one week ago."

Fredrik didn't say a word. The ambassador answered for him.

"Ha! You're in the weeds from the very start. My assistant was on a business trip to Uruguay one week ago."

Assistant? Fredrik thought. "Third secretary" sounded better. Not as good as first or second secretary, but still better.

"Not according to the helicopter pilot in Mombasa who got in touch with us a little bit ago. Plus a few other internet-related facts. In computer language, it's called an IP address."

"Mombasa is not in Uruguay," said the ambassador, who knew his geography.

Fredrik Löwenhult thought as fast as he possibly could. Sergio Conte continued to offer select parts of his evidence:

Aggravating circumstance number one: Löwenhult's name had been found behind the encryption of a numbered bank account in the Condors. Number two: where he had got the money for his new Ferrari.

"I don't have a fucking Ferrari," said Fredrik.

"Yes you do," said the special agent. "As well as a Condorian credit card."

"What are you talking about? I've never set foot in the Condors!"

"Oh, so you never landed?"

Conte sensed that he had Löwenhult right where he wanted him. Circumstance number three was the posts on Instagram, sent from Löwenhult's laptop, which had been lawfully seized a few hours ago.

"Posted during working hours?" the ambassador wondered.

"No," Fredrik said in a pitiful voice.

The ambassador, by this point, was getting red in the face.

"But it was while you were in South America and Africa at the same time? Taking care of your dying father's infected elbow? And leaving the copier duties to Hanna?"

The ambassador was peeved. Guilty or not, this was the end of Löwenhult's career as a diplomat. Ronny Guldén would see to that.

"Europe, too," said Conte. "Don't forget the car he purchased in Rome."

"For Christ's sake, check with the bank!" said the desperate third secretary.

"That'll be tricky," said Conte.

The man who had the answers was ninety-six years old, and that was bad enough. But it got worse: he was also dead.

CHAPTER 76

Operation Go-Up-in-Smoke

The doomsday fraud group sat by the pool house at the president's palace, drinking tea and discussing which of their names was the worst to have, considering that none of them were viable any longer. Aleko was sure he would win this round. What could beat being the most prominent asshole on an entire continent?

Herbert von Toll launched into a polemic. He had the same last name as a foundering bank that had conned five million clients out of half a billion dollars. And on top of that, the Swiss are notorious for never forgetting a wrong.

"Just like me," said Aleko.

And the Vory, he might have added.

Petra reminded her friends that she was the one who could be considered the mastermind behind the doomsday prophecy that had just duped the whole world. If any of them were ever to appear on the cover of *Time* magazine as cynicism personified, it would probably be her. Right?

Agnes was aware that she was pretty well protected, despite all her shortcomings. Johan returned from the kitchen with a platter of freshly baked scones and homemade marmalade made of blackberries imported from Norway (why not, since they were shipping over pounds of salmon every other week anyway). He didn't quite know where this conversation was going, but he was eager to join in. He said he wanted to meet Obrama without an *r* again, as long as they were all heading out on a journey anyway.

"Why don't we move to America? I could call him up and see about that, he's in charge there, after all."

Everyone advised against dropping the American president a line. But Johan felt that he'd learned all about how the world works from his father, and explained that Obrama without an *r* was such a big fan of Västerbotten cheese that it would probably only take a few pounds of it for him to welcome them with open arms.

"Forget it," said Petra.

"I understand your thought process here," said Johan's father. "But I have to side with Petra on this one. Forget it."

In other ways, this America idea wasn't such a bad one. Or the cheese idea, for that matter. People in the US spoke a language one could understand. It was far away from Africa, where Aleko could no longer show his face. And from Russia, where the mafia had been looking for him even before they discovered he'd taken five hundred million dollars of their money.

Accompanied by the scones and Johan's incredible blackberry marmalade, a plan slowly took shape. It took two refills on tea, but eventually everyone was on board with a shared vision for the near future.

"A bold but wholly reasonable plan," was Petra's summary.

"And I even understand most of it," said the master chef and genius.

* * *

There are countries on earth where you can wave a wad of cash and boom, you're a citizen. A number of countries in the Caribbean have such opportunities on offer. But citizenship in

Grenada or Saint Kitts and Nevis wasn't the most attractive option.

New Zealand can work as well, but it's so far away. Not to mention that the New Zealanders know to ask good money for their services.

Cyprus is cheaper. Or, even better, Malta. Anyone who donates money or buys property for over a million dollars while pulling the right strings will soon be a Cypriot or a Maltese, and thus member of an EU country with automatic access to 180 countries, visa-free.

The problem for Agnes, Aleko, Herbert, Johan, and Petra was that no one in Europe liked them, especially not INTERPOL. No matter their citizenship. Actually, that went for the whole world.

The solution was that Aleko still had another day as president in the country where he made all the decisions.

Forty minutes after they arrived to see Aleko's wife's second cousin at the passport office, they all had new passports with new names. The process was preceded by lively conversations about what each one wanted to be called instead. Johan had picked up "Winston Churchill" in some context he no longer remembered, and called dibs on that name. Agnes sighed and said that was almost as ridiculous as expecting to fly under the radar after changing your name to Genghis Khan. Johan didn't understand the problem and insisted.

"On Winston Churchill, that is. That Genghis-whatever almost sounds violent."

After some back and forth, they agreed on a compromise. Aleko and Johan would become father and son Kevin and Winston *Church*.

Agnes, Herbert, and Petra selected names that blended in easily, with no complications. Günther came along to the passport office as their chauffeur; he was going to stay in the

Condors and wasn't a suspect in anything, after all. But the fact that he had lost the election was eating at him, and he wanted to blame that weird letter U with two dots. Perhaps a new name would bring him luck in the future.

"What do you all think of Konrad Adenauer?"

"As compared to Winston Churchill or Genghis Khan?" said Petra.

"Great!" said Johan.

Günther explained that he was eager to keep a certain connection to his origins in his name, without having to feel like he was being painted with a communist brush. Konrad Adenauer had been the first chancellor of West Germany, so perhaps that was sufficiently dignified?

Petra delegated the name issue to Agnes, who said that if she had to she could agree to Konrad G. Adenauer, G as in Günther, with or without dots on the U.

Aleko, aka Kevin Church, was not sure the name Konrad would help Günther in any future presidential elections, but his brother in spirit waved off this concern. There was no historical evidence to suggest that a sitting president in the Condors would voluntarily call a new election.

"I did," said Kevin Church.

"Voluntarily?" said Konrad G. Adenauer.

"Maybe not exactly."

CHAPTER 77

Operation Go-Up-in-Smoke

Aleko and the others left the Condors behind fifteen minutes before the new president was sworn in. The helicopter pilot had one last job to do.

"Are you willing to pay in cash this time, Mr. President?"

"I am fundamentally not okay with anything when it comes to you. Just take us to Mombasa. If I'm in a good mood when we land, you'll get paid instead of beaten up."

From Mombasa, their journey continued by plane. After nearly twenty-four hours, and stopovers in Nairobi and Frankfurt, the friends landed at the airport in Valletta.

Tired but eager, they went straight to the Maltese migration authority, where they learned that their case would be handled within three months.

"Three months?" said Aleko.

The case manager smiled slyly enough for both the ex-president and his son to understand.

"Will you handle this, or should I, Johan?" said Aleko.

"My name isn't Johan anymore," said Johan. "Who's got my passport? There's a name there, right next to a photograph of me. Winston, wasn't it?"

"You or me?"

The son didn't want to disappoint his father. Once you were

a master chef, genius, and former minister of foreign affairs, that was that.

He turned to the civil servant at the migration authority and said he would appreciate if this matter could be processed as quickly as he himself intended to purchase and deliver a 2011 Honda Civic to the woman's residence, including a ceremonial handover of keys.

He'd got the idea for make and model from an incident involving a golf club that had taken place some time earlier in Stockholm.

"I'll see what I can do," said the woman. "Would an Audi 80 be an option?"

"Certainly," said Johan. "French cars are the best."

Papa Aleko was proud, despite Johan's difficulty in recalling his own name. And which brand of car came from which country.

It cost three million dollars in pointless property investments, plus one Audi 80. But the very next day, Malta had five proud new citizens. Until very recently they had been called Agnes, Aleko, Herbert, Johan, and Petra. Now they had different names. Four of the five of them had already begun to get used to the new ones.

The next step was for Former Aleko and Former Johan to travel to northern Sweden, where they had unfinished cheese business.

CHAPTER 78

The Vory Is On the Trail

The man who had been ruling Russia since the turn of the century had a lot in common with the recently departed Condorian president. Both had quickly taken control over their respective nations' TV broadcasts. Putin infiltrated Russia's opinion-polling institutes, while Aleko shut down the sole example in the Condors and gave its director a position as manager of parks and leisure instead (in a city with no parks). In the long run, these measures meant that citizens held the opinions their leaders thought they should hold. Or at least—in certain cases—it seemed that way.

Furthermore, the Condorian democracy had always been a joke, while Putin, in his ten-plus years in power, had to work hard to dismantle the partial democracy he'd inherited from his predecessor.

Aleko had been forced to flee Russia more or less around the same time Putin swooped in as Yeltsin's new prime minister. They practically passed each other in the hallway.

Yeltsin had had democratic ambitions. He tried to listen to economists schooled in capitalism with one ear while Putin was whispering in the other, sharing truths about Russia's lost greatness and what ought to be done instead. No wonder the nation's first democratically elected president hit the bottle. And the next bottle. Before leaving his post several months early.

Vladimir Putin took over. And immediately ordered "Halt!" when it came to the Russian democratic experiment, although the world didn't quite understand that this was happening. The Russians themselves didn't care what their political system was called, or should be called. Their main concern was good order, and it seemed like this new guy was the man for the job.

Aleko and Putin did differ on at least one point. While the former always made sure to line his own pockets and no one else's, the latter tossed billions at the Russian mafia and the country's oligarchs. In doing so he embraced two parallel systems. The official one, with Putin himself in the driver's seat; and the criminal one that kept the wheels turning. To be safe, he drew a line in the sand, one that no one was allowed to cross. The message was more or less:

"Do what you like out there, but don't challenge me for political power. That would mean war!"

Putin whipped his Russia into shape. The combination of sham democracy and corrupt capitalism worked very well. He reworked the constitution so he would never have to resign. There was no knowing what other plans he had in the works. The former KGB boss was a clever rascal.

* * *

It would have been wrong to call Ekaterina Bykova *"Capo di tutti capi"* even if she were Italian. The Russian mob, after all, was more loosely organized. But she was definitely one of the main authorities in the thieves' Russian realm, ever since her father had handed responsibility over to her nine months before. Sergei was old and tired, not to mention weakened by a stroke. She was young, strong, and smart. She'd walked alongside her father for years, and he was always clear about who would take over one day.

His daughter was given the role of money handler early on.

This included the increasingly exhaustive work of making the money appear legal, because only with legal money could the Vory partake in truly illegal maneuvers.

At a time when the UN, USA, EU, WTO, OECD, and basically every other combination of letters in existence were sharpening their knives against the world's many tax and bank havens, the minuscule nation called the Condors was going in the exact opposite direction. Ekaterina admired this brash philosophy and traveled there along with a faithful interpreter who knew Russian, French, English, Arabic, and Persian. One of these languages ought to work.

Their meeting with the top leadership of the Condors led to an initial "launder-the-money" deal, followed by a second and third.

Everything had been going just fine until the current transaction, involving five hundred million dollars. The money had hardly even made it to the island nation when the president announced his imminent departure. By this point, Ekaterina had taken over from her father; it would be unprofessional, as the top leader of a multi-billion-dollar organization, to travel around exposing oneself to the CIA and other troublesome entities out there. But she immediately sent two of her closest colleagues to the Condors to secure the money and, with any luck, be introduced to the presumably equally corrupt president who was poised to take over.

But they didn't get any farther than Mombasa. It was impossible to get to the island any other way but by boat. And what's more, the rainy season had just begun. A nesting bird? Ekaterina smelled a rat. And she was right.

Now she regretted not taking a closer look at Aleko when she had the chance. He had spoken French when they met. No Arab features. As far as Ekaterina knew, he didn't even have a first name.

The future boss of the Vory didn't know any French herself. And she recalled a vague sense that Aleko's French had hints of a Slavic intonation.

So who was he?

And one more thing—now that Ekaterina reexamined what had happened—next to Aleko, that time, sat a man in a police uniform who was never introduced by name. And who never said a word. Evidently he was the president's right-hand man.

Two years later, a man in a police uniform ran for president of the Condors. In outward appearance, he looked like Aleko's sidekick. His name was Günther. That name sounded more German than Condorian.

The mob boss's preliminary investigation team contacted the top law enforcement leadership of the Condors to learn more about this Günther, under the pretense of being something other than what they were. From Chief of Police Konrad G. Adenauer they learned that Günther had been his predecessor. Adenauer had nothing else of value to share, except to say that his predecessor had been a fine person. The chief of police had no idea where this Günther had gone after losing the presidential election.

Aleko and Günther had vanished. With five hundred million of Ekaterina's money.

"I wish you both good luck," she muttered, tacking a photograph of each on the wall.

There they would stay for as long as they lived. And that wouldn't be long at all.

Ekaterina's father rolled into the office in his wheelchair. He had come to ask if they would be having lunch together; it had been several days since the last time. His daughter kissed him on the forehead and said she would love to.

Sergei Bykov was, to be sure, old and tired and sick. But he knew his daughter, and he could tell that she was out of sorts.

"Something is weighing on you, Katyusha. Want to talk about it?"

"No, Dad, it's nothing," his daughter lied.

She didn't want to worry him.

But the old man spotted the photographs on the wall.

"Aleksandr Kovalchuk," he said. "Older and with no moustache, and he's wearing glasses and has a different haircut. But that's definitely him. We never did catch that bastard. And that other guy . . . the German with the ration cards. What was his name again?"

CHAPTER 79

A Special Agent Turns the Page

Sergio Conte had until 5 p.m. that day. That was when his unit supervisor wanted the agent's report on his desk.

"You're the one who started this, Conte, when you decided we should put everything else aside to chase down a purple-haired granny who happened to cheat her way into a few euros online. It's up to you to end it as well."

Above all, his supervisor demanded Conte produce an obvious link between the old woman and the half-billion-dollar Swiss bank fraud, because this was suddenly a matter of great urgency. His supervisor was careful to point out that this was no thanks to the agent.

Conte quickly linked Agnes Eklund to the two other Swedes who'd fled alongside her from Rome to Addis Ababa and on to the Condors, the country that brought absolutely no joy to anyone.

The special agent's colleagues at the NCB in Sweden had been impressively meticulous in gathering background information. None of the trio had a criminal record, but a police report had been filed a few months earlier against one *Petra Rocklund* after she harassed the Swedish Academy of Sciences with information about the approaching end of the world.

Agnes Eklund, for her part, had moved a minor fortune from Svenska Handelsbanken in Sweden to that same bank's branch in Zurich. Those bankers kept their lips tightly zipped until Conte sicced his Swiss NCB colleagues on them. After a number of threats, they broke their holy vow of confidentiality and reported that the money had immediately been transferred to Bank von Toll, a few roads away.

Bank von Toll was now in ruins after standing as guarantor in the world-famous global doomsday fraud in which the initial main suspects were a Swedish diplomat and a Russian professor. The Russian professor was quickly cleared of suspicion after a call to INTERPOL's Moscow arm. According to his Russian colleagues, Professor Smirnoff had fallen into general disgrace and was thus, in all likelihood, long dead.

Suspect number two, the Swedish diplomat, had a brother by the name of *Johan Löwenhult*, the third person in the trio that had first traveled all the way from Sweden to Rome in an RV, only to continue by air to the damn Condors.

According to his Swedish colleagues' file on little brother Löwenhult, the man hadn't made a single meaningful contribution to Swedish society in all his adult life. At which point he'd headed to the Condors and landed there on the afternoon of September 6. Three days later, he had been introduced on Condorian TV as the country's new minister of foreign affairs. Seventeen days later, he represented his new homeland during the African Union's special session in Ethiopia, where—according to footage on TV— he appeared to be a close personal friend of President Obama.

How the hell did that happen?

Here, Special Agent Conte was forced to pause his summary of all he knew. One day, as a rookie cop, he had plucked off the street what remained of a man who had drawn the ire of the branch of the mafia called the 'Ndrangheta. The man had been shot thirty-eight times—and survived. In twenty-two years, this was the most confounding thing Conte had ever experienced. Johan Löwenhult's career path trumped it.

Oh well, in the grand scheme of things, it was irrelevant. The same was not true of his discovery that Bank von Toll's deceased owner and director had a son who had first disappeared and then turned out to have flown, under his own name, to—where else—the Condors.

In summary, Conte could demonstrate beyond a reasonable doubt:

- That Professor Smirnoff's doomsday offer was actually the work of doomsday prophet Petra Rocklund . . .
- That Konrad von Toll's bank in Zurich had been exploited in the fraud through the agency of his son Herbert . . .
- That the criminals had been under the thorough protection of Condorian President Aleko . . .
- And that big brother Fredrik Löwenhult was for all intents and purposes an innocent fall guy.

There was also no longer reason to believe that the purple-haired woman had really died in the traffic accident as stated by the Condorian chief of police. When an enraged Conte called up that damn Günther to nail him to the wall, it turned out he had been replaced by a Konrad G-something after the presidential election. Incidentally, the new guy was just as impossible to talk reason to as the old one. Their voices even sounded the same.

Conte felt there was ample reason to allow INTERPOL to put out an alert for former president Aleko along with Agnes

Eklund, Johan Löwenhult, Petra Rocklund, and Herbert von Toll. All of them were suspects in a fraud case worth many millions of dollars. Condorian Chief of Police Konrad promised to aid in the search. Sergio Conte had his misgivings.

Even so, the alert was delayed. This was for a deeply human and rather sorrowful reason. Special Agent Conte had spent over two decades in service to law enforcement, the last eleven of them with the NCB in Rome. Always under the same insufferable unit supervisor, whose office was also across the hall from Conte's. As he worked on his final report, it so happened that around eleven that morning Conte needed to heed the call of nature. He got no further than one step outside his own office door before he heard, from the office across the hall:

"Where are you going this time?"

The same thing happened at two in the afternoon. Conte thought he deserved a cup of coffee.

"Where are you going this time?"

The special agent wished his boss nothing but ill. Add to this the fact that he lived alone in a dreary one-bedroom apartment in a high-rise in an equally dreary suburb of the Italian capital. His life's passion was fly-fishing, and how did you find a lady fly-fishing enthusiast in Rome? Perhaps it all would have worked out if only he had been accepted as a member of the leading fly-fishing club in the southern metropolitan region. He'd been third in line for membership until unfortunate circumstances and that bloody Agnes Eklund caused him to plummet fifty slots. This left his ongoing chat with a Norwegian lady called Sigrid. They'd met on a dating site a few years previously and stayed in touch, even though both of them knew how unrealistic a relationship would be.

Sigrid was from somewhere called Søndre Landsjøåsen, and no one could tie on a fly like her! They exchanged tips and advice; she taught him a few words in Norwegian and he offered just as many in Italian. She invited him to Norway, but he never made it. His job ate up all his time.

Plus, there was Caesar, Sergio Conte's six-year-old angora cat. He couldn't be left alone in the apartment, and if you had no friends, well, that was that.

But then, just a week ago, tragedy struck. After six years, Caesar suddenly got a wild desire to find out what was on the other side of the balcony railing. He jumped up—and fell fourteen stories, right onto the pavement.

Sergio Conte's only companion died instantly, of course, even though he was a cat. And with that, the agent was more alone than ever.

At quarter past three, the report was finished. Conte placed it in a neat stack on one side of his desk and logged into his laptop. Perhaps Sigrid had sent a message that might cheer him up.

But Conte's unit supervisor discovered what he was up to through the two glass doors. He stood up, came over to Conte's office, stuck his head in, and said:

"What are you doing? Aren't you finished with that report yet?"

It was right there before their very eyes, of course, but rules were rules.

"You said I had until five o'clock."

"Okay, but has it ever occurred to you to overperform?"

Before Conte could respond, his boss went back to his own office.

Enough was enough. The special agent crumpled up the brand-new final report on the multi-million-dollar fraud case and the old woman with the purple hair. He tossed it all in the wastebasket and set it aflame. Then he put on his coat and walked out. On his way, he passed his boss's office.

"Where are you going this time?" said his boss, for the third time that day.

For the first time, Sergio Conte responded.

"To Norway."

"But your report—"

"—can be found in the wastebasket in my office. You'll want to bring a bucket of water."

CHAPTER 80

Västerbotten, Sweden, 1871

Rumor had it that farmhand Anton was curious about the new dairymaid, the one who had the lovely name *Ulrika Eleonora* and an ample bosom besides.

Anton was not the only one casting glances in the dairymaid's direction, but most of them refrained from approaching her. The fact was, she was both independent and resolute, traits that made men of any era nervous.

Anton was not like everyone else. He felt secure in the notion that he was a farmhand for reasons of history, not simply because he couldn't have made it as anything better. He had a vision of starting a regular service line between Burträsk and Skellefteå, with stops in Åbyn, Järvtjärn, Skråmträsk, Djupgroven, and Klutmark. In contrast to the other farmhands, he didn't spend his weekly salary swigging brännvin; instead, he sewed whatever he could spare into the lining of his pants. In under seven years he would be able to buy himself a cart. That would just leave a horse to pull it.

As he waited for the future to arrive, he pried stones out of the fields of the manor, whenever he wasn't feeding the pigs, stacking hay—or running errands to the dairymaid's domain.

* * *

Ulrika Eleonora knew she was considered cold and dismissive. This suited her just fine. Partly because her demanding job took all her focus, and partly because her reputation drove nine out of ten of the drunkard farmhands to other hunting grounds on Saturday nights. What were they good for? And it wasn't just the farmhands, as it happened. The occasional foreman had come sniffing around as well. Even the lord of the manor himself had suggested, now and then, that he might be interested. Men seemed to think with one organ alone, and it wasn't located in their heads.

Of course, there was no rule without exception. Pig-feeder Anton . . . well, there was just something about him. He looked her in the eye when they spoke, not at her breasts. He posed inquisitive questions about recipes for cheese. He seemed to see that she was a human being, not just someone or something with which he could have a moment's fun atop a haystack.

He was poorer than just about anyone, but he was considerate, funny, and—it seemed—had honest intentions. Long story short, she liked him. When he suggested that they take an evening stroll together, she trusted that he actually meant an evening stroll. She said yes. The curdling vat could be left to its own devices for another forty-five minutes.

Exactly how it happened she couldn't say, but when she and Anton had been kissing on the big rock by the lake for long enough, she realized a lot more than forty-five minutes had passed. She hurried back to the dairy, with Anton in tow. He wanted to help her, save what could be saved, but the fact was that it was too late. The curds had hardened too soon and too much. Now the lord of the manor would be a pain to deal with.

And one misfortune never comes alone. Suddenly there he stood in the door.

"May I ask what you are doing, Miss Ulrika Eleonora? Shouldn't the curds be set to cool by now?"

The dairymaid was near tears. She didn't know what to say. Farmhand Anton came to her rescue.

"So interesting that the lord of the manor would wonder the same thing as I, a simple farmhand, just asked. Miss Ulrika has just rebuffed me, saying that for the sake of the lord of the manor she chose to give the curds an extra thirty-seven minutes, as she is certain that this will bring a new dimension to the end product."

"Thirty-seven minutes?" said the lord of the manor, who could think of nothing else to say on account of being shocked to find himself conversing with a *farmhand*. One who had the word "dimension" in his vocabulary.

Ulrika Eleonora quickly collected herself.

"Pay no mind to what the pig-feeder says, my lord. Thirty-six minutes is the correct amount. Of course, I can't guarantee the result, and I'm sure I have exceeded my authority, but we dairymaids can never stop thinking about attaining an ever more perfect end product."

At which point she took a wild shot in the dark:

"Now we will age the curds for twice as long and at no more than eight degrees. In the deepest reaches of the cellar. It's extra work, I know, but that's exactly why I summoned the pig-feeder. What's your name, you lout?"

"Anton," said Anton, and from that moment on he was profoundly in love with Ulrika Eleonora.

"Don't just stand there, pig-feeder," said the lord of the manor. "Do as your dairymaid says. The deepest reaches of the cellar it is."

Then he absorbed what she'd just said.

"Twice as long?"

"At least fourteen months, my lord. I can't guarantee the result, as I said, but there's nothing wrong with the analysis."

Ulrika Eleonora had bought herself time. Fourteen months

from now, the lord of the manor would have long since forgotten the events of this evening. The old man went on his way, and after the carrying was done, there was plenty of time for more kisses between Ulrika Eleonora and the pig-feeder. In the deepest reaches of the cellar.

CHAPTER 81

Västerbotten, Sweden, 1872

One year and two months after the mistake in the dairy, Anton and Ulrika Eleonora were blessed with a daughter. The dairymaid was so highly valued at the dairy that she was given three days off after the birth. No one could imagine how the lord of the manor remembered, but fourteen months to the day after the evening he almost caught Ulrika Eleonora and the pig-feeder red-handed, he tasted the cheese in the deepest reaches of the cellar.

"Oh god!" he said.

He could not conceive of a tastier cheese.

The Burträsk cheese à la Ulrika Eleonora was small-eyed, hard, and had a heavenly aroma. The lord of the manor was so taken by the result that he elected to give it a new name.

"Västerbotten," he said.

The dairymaid (with little Sara in her arms) was astonished. It was audacious enough to claim they had the best cheese in Burträsk. Now the lord of the manor wanted to claim an entire province.

"Taste it for yourself, dear dairymaid," he said.

Ulrika Eleonora did.

"Oh god," she said.

CHAPTER 82

Sweden, Monday, October 31, 2011

One hundred and thirty-nine years and three weeks later, Aleko and Johan arrived in Burträsk to talk business, after a sixty-mile taxi ride from the airport. From the foreman they learned that the main offices of Västerbotten cheese had long since been relocated to Umeå, where the gentlemen had perhaps landed a few hours earlier.

Johan felt like the idiot he had once been, but he managed to catch the taxi driver in time and ask for another ride.

"Where to?" said the driver.

"Umeå," said Johan.

"That's where we started."

"Great. Then you know the way."

CEO Granlund of the dairy company Norrmejerier happened to be both on-site and available when father and son requested a meeting.

"How can I be of service?" the CEO asked in Swedish.

Johan didn't know what to say, and Aleko didn't understand the question.

"My name is Kevin Church," he said in English. "This is my son *Winston* Church."

"Without 'ill,'" said Johan.

CEO Granlund wondered who his secretary had let in.

* * *

Ten minutes later, he was considerably wiser. Mr. Church, citizen of Malta, wanted to open a Västerbotten cheese factory in the United States, and wished to purchase a license to do so. CEO Granlund was deeply opposed to this proposal. The fact was, not only did Västerbotten cheese owe its unique taste to a secret recipe dating to the 1870s, it was also dependent on the soil where the cows grazed before giving their milk. No one knew exactly why the cheese tasted the way it did. One theory was that a meteorite strike twenty thousand years ago had given rise to a lake and, in the long run, the calcium-rich hay. All perfectly suited for the cold winters and months of midnight sun from June to August.

Aleko, aka Mr. Church, didn't know what midnight sun was. CEO Granlund explained that the concept wasn't entirely relevant as regards Burträsk. In high summer, the sun went down just before midnight and came up again an hour or so later, before people and cows even noticed it was gone. A little farther north in the country, it didn't bother to go down at all. Granlund's point was that the cows' pasture was subjected to daylight almost around the clock. In the summertime, that is. On top of everything else, there was a bacterial culture in the walls of Burträsk that couldn't simply be replicated elsewhere. Complicated stuff that Granlund didn't have the energy to explain further.

Might as well cut off these weird Maltese men who were merely wasting his valuable time.

"In short: the concept cannot be recreated in the United States."

"I was thinking maybe around a hundred million dollars for the license," said ex-president Aleko.

CEO Granlund had an MBA from Umeå University and was better at math than most.

"As I was saying: the concept can certainly be recreated in the United States or elsewhere, but it will demand attention to detail. How much did you say, for the license?"

CHAPTER 83

Sweden, Monday, October 31, 2011

While Aleko and Johan were in the midst of cheese negotiations in Västerbotten, re Västerbotten, the three other freshly minted Maltese citizens waited in Stockholm. Agnes and Herbert took autumn strolls hand in hand, until they got too chilly. Then they retreated to his room, or hers, at the Grand Hôtel, to warm each other up.

Petra got tired of sitting by herself on the hotel's glass-fronted veranda with its view of the water. Furthermore, the passion between Agnes and Herbert reminded her of everything she'd never got to experience herself.

But instead of sending another tentative message to Malte on Facebook, she walked out to the street and hailed a taxi.

* * *

She wasn't nearly as anxious as last time. Now she would find out once and for all if Malte had been flirting with her, or if it had only taken place in the prophet's imagination. It was early evening, pitch-black outside, lights on in the house. No Honda Civic in the driveway.

Petra rang the doorbell and listened carefully. No female voice shouting that she was doing her nails. No one shouting at all. So—no one was home, or just one of them was.

Then she heard footsteps. Someone unlocked the door.

Malte opened it.

"Is she still here?" Petra said.

Her first, greatest, and only love stared at her with wide eyes. But he quickly found his footing.

"Who? Oh, her. No, I told her to move out. And take the car."

They stood on either side of the threshold, looking at each other. Petra hadn't made any plans beyond her initial question.

"I've been traveling," she said. "I misplaced your baseball bat in Rome. I apologize for that."

Malte seldom spoke up for himself. He hardly ever used foul language. But he realized it was now or never.

"I don't give a damn about the baseball bat," he said. "And I'm really glad to see you. May I give you a hug?"

"By all means."

CHAPTER 84

November–December 2011

Malte and Petra turned out to be more made for each other than either of them could have guessed. They had come to the same conclusion about the future of the planet, if from two different directions.

Soon after they consummated their fifteen-years-postponed relationship in Malte's bedroom, Petra told him the truth. She couldn't bear to keep secrets from her beloved.

The bad news was, they had less than five years together before everything would end. The good news was that a simple miscalculation on Petra's part meant they could look at it as having been given five bonus years instead of no years at all, including the night they'd just spent together.

Malte was sure Petra's calculations were correct this time; she'd almost always been right back in school. Not that there had been all that much competition in their classroom, but right was right, while wrong was always wrong. However, he wasn't sure the world would have time to end before it ended after all.

Petra humbly asked what he meant by that.

The fact was that golfer and baseball player Malte was first and foremost an economist. He worked as one at a crappy company with crappy assignments and didn't enjoy a second of it. But since he spent no more time on work than was strictly

THE PROPHET AND THE IDIOT

necessary, and since it had finally occurred to him to kick Vickan out, he'd had time to think.

"Whether it happens within the next five years remains to be seen, but I'm certain that everything's going to go to shit."

According to Malte, the capitalism he'd always embraced and depended upon was about to kill the whole planet. The pay differential in the United States was at the same level as when Wall Street crashed in October of 1929. He didn't care much for communists Marx and Engels, but at least their vision had been based on the masses uniting in pursuit of a higher ideal. Now it had somehow become everyone against everyone else, with everyone blaming everyone else for everything.

"Who is blaming who for what?" Petra said, feeling anxious that the world might end Malte's way before she had the chance to be right once and for all.

Her brand-new boyfriend went down a winding path of psychological-economical reasoning that he couldn't quite elucidate. But apparently, a few decades earlier, the apartheid regime in South Africa had sown discord by handing out three lunch-time meatballs to Black prisoners and five to colored ones. In this way, the white superiors sowed discord among the majority of the population, which might otherwise unite against them.

"Meatballs?" said Petra.

She thought this sounded more Swedish than South African.

"Or potatoes. I don't quite remember."

Malte's point was that the reigning "it's someone else's fault" mentality was mutating at warp speed. Black against white, bourgeois against broke, native-born against immigrant, left against right, up against down, here against there, and the rich against all the rest. He assured her he appreciated the free market, but that it was about to get out of control given the reigning global everyone-against-everyone mindset.

"If no one throws a wet blanket over capitalism, it will soon be all over," he said.

Petra immediately felt better. Malte had just had a little too much time alone to think. Her scientific doomsday would absolutely have time to happen before his more emotional one. Besides, capitalism had always had the ability to recalibrate itself when necessary, unlike her collapsed atmosphere.

This left the more down-to-earth and concrete fear she felt when thinking of how Malte might react once she'd shared *all* of her story.

"May I ask a hypothetical question?"

"Of course, honey."

"Say we were, completely hypothetically of course, to con the Russian mafia out of, for instance, half a billion dollars . . ."

Her boyfriend giggled.

"That would probably make the Russian mafia pretty mad."

Petra squirmed. She didn't like being interrupted.

"It's completely hypothetical, like I said. Would you consider this an appalling act that will bring us all closer to destruction? Or something else?"

Malte truly loved his Petra. What an interesting question! To think that in all his years with Victoria he'd hardly had to use his brain even once! He wanted his response to reflect great moral clarity.

"Well, we must begin from the assumption that the mafia's money was stolen from regular people in the first place, right?" he mused. "So as long as we do something good for them . . . well, in that case I think we'd be helping the world more than hurting it."

Petra nodded. "Something good" sounded reasonable. But where to draw the line?

"A cheese factory in the United States. Really delicious cheese! Hundreds of jobs created. Good salary and benefits. What would you think of that?"

* * *

Petra stayed with Malte in the suburbs while Former Aleko and Former Johan conducted the final negotiations with CEO Granlund and half of Burträsk.

"No rush on my end," she assured them.

It also took some time before the final documents could be ceremoniously signed at the Grand Hôtel in Stockholm. The multi-million-dollar deal included a whole cargo ship's worth of the special Burträsk soil. To be safe, there were also two hundred cows—after all, it was crucial for the American Västerbotten cheese to be as close to the original as possible. Granlund also put into the contract that the American version should get rid of the two dots above the second letter in the brand name. This way it wasn't quite as painful to consider that the copy might not quite match the excellent quality of the original.

But above all, the parties had to take into account point 4.9, which stipulated that nothing would come of any of this if the United States didn't let the Maltese citizens, the soil, and the cows enter the country.

Agnes was working on this detail in the meantime. She applied to the United States Citizenship and Immigration Services (USCIS), saying that she was a representative for a progressive Maltese agricultural company that had well-developed plans to establish a branch in Randolph, Vermont, with an initial local budget of ninety million dollars. The plan was to hire 180 employees for a conservative start.

Since the corner of Randolph in question thus far only consisted of a field, a few buildings, a crossroads, a gas station, and a shuttered grocery store, the immigration office took a positive outlook on her application and promised to handle it swiftly. Included in the package were permanent residence permits for six proud citizens of the EU (five of whom had just changed their names. The sixth, Malte Magnusson, could continue to be called what he'd always been called).

"Are you sure you want to come with us, honey?" Petra said as the couple had breakfast together one morning. "We've got . . . I mean, it's only a few weeks . . . I mean, it's a big decision . . . I mean, INTERPOL, the mafia, and all that."

Malte replied that he'd never been sure about a single thing in his life. Until now.

* * *

The USCIS was not an entity you could bribe with dollars, cars, or anything else. For some time, they demanded one completed form every day. Each individual cow had to have a certificate from a veterinarian. The soil would have to be quarantined on American shores until enough samples had been taken and thoroughly analyzed. What's more, the USCIS needed guarantees and massive deposits. The concrete, all the cargo vehicles, and fourteen other prespecified products must be purchased regionally. A small oversight committee consisting of three people must be financed by the applicant.

Agnes agreed to all of this and a little more. "Perhaps an oversight committee of *five* people would make everyone feel more secure?"

After eight weeks, the decision was handed down.

"Welcome to the United States of America."

"If you'd just let me call Obrama without an *r*, it would have been taken care of in fifteen minutes," said Johan.

The man who could no longer be called what he'd been called after he could no longer be called the name he was born with was touched.

Aleksandr Kovalchuk was the son of a waste-collecting general in the southern part of the Soviet Union. Circumstances were such that as an adult he happened to get the whole gigantic country shut down. At which point he'd introduced so many conflicting tax laws into Boris Yeltsin's Russia that nearly every corrupt figure around him wanted his head on a platter.

Under the name Aleko he launched a new career on an island in the Indian Ocean. This went so well that it wasn't long before he took over the whole place. After shutting down the Soviet Union and making himself persona non grata in Russia, he drove all of Africa up the wall. Until it was no longer advisable. That left him no choice but to con the world's most feared mafia out of half a billion dollars, and five million bettors out of just as much.

Aleksandr Kovalchuk became President Aleko became Kevin Church. Now he was poised to take on his third continent in as many decades.

"America, here we come!" he said.

If Dad was happy, so was Johan.

"'This is America, babe, you gotta think big to be big!'"

"Huh?" said Aleko.

"Christopher Walken, in a film whose name I've forgotten. But I remember all the rest. Master chef and genius. And film aficionado. That's me!"

CHAPTER 85

January 2012

Johan was still barred from calling Obama, with or without an
r. This didn't stop Obama from deciding, one day, to call Johan.
He'd been following the drama surrounding the now both resigned and missing President Aleko from a distance. He'd also
revisited his conversations with the refreshing Swede and arrived at the realization that Johan was probably more master
chef and *child of nature* than genius. That would explain his
limited success both as postal worker and minister of foreign
affairs. And it boosted the American president's sympathy toward him. Now he wanted to know how Johan was doing.

"Hello, my friend. It's Barack."

"Who?" said Johan.

"Obama. The president. Perhaps you remember me?"

Johan lit up.

"Of course I do!"

Barack Obama thanked him for their last visit and said that
the Västerbotten cheese he'd received as a gift was nearly gone,
but that he was dropping a line mostly out of curiosity. Would
Johan be willing to tell him what had happened after that day
in Addis Ababa? After all, things hadn't turned out quite as
planned.

Johan replied that a lot had happened both before and after that. Nothing was the same now. Including his name; he was no longer Johan but something else, not Winston Churchill, but almost.

Barack Obama said he wasn't sure he wanted any more details on that particular topic. But Johan had no intention of sharing too little. He, his father Aleko, Agnes, Herbert, and Petra had got new passports, then traveled to another country where they got new passports again. After that they went to Sweden and bought the American rights to the cheese of cheeses. And scooped up a boyfriend for Petra.

Petra's boyfriend was nowhere near as interesting to the president as this cheese-rights bit. Were they going to start importing Västerbotten cheese to the United States? That would be fantastic.

"No, we're about to move there. We're going to open a factory in Ver . . . something. Versailles? No, something else."

"Vermont?"

"Maybe."

Barack Obama was back in the position of wanting to know, and yet not. It seemed likely to him that President Aleko had made off with the national treasury and created new identities for himself and his close friends. But what had Johan said? Was Aleko his father?

Yes, he sure was. But Johan hadn't known that back when the two of them met at the Swedish embassy some time ago. So Barack shouldn't feel bad that he'd called Dad an asshole. There was no way either of them could have known. Just as little as Johan could have known, a few months earlier, that he would become friends with a doomsday prophet, an old lady with violet hair who pretended to be nineteen, and an elderly banker from a country that either was or was not part of the EU.

"Moving on. Barack must have an *r* in the middle, right?"

Obama thought that the course of events from the day at the embassy onward rather substantiated Aleko's epithet, but since Johan appeared to like his newfound father he didn't bring it up. He confirmed the spelling of his first name, and stopped there.

"So, how are things?" said Johan.

"Oh, fine," said Obama. "Keeping busy."

* * *

Sometimes things are slow to sink in.

Barack Obama had been a silent witness to the circus during the much-discussed half-billion-dollar fraud case surrounding the prediction that doomsday would arrive on October 18 the previous year. The one that conned millions of people all over the world.

Many people were angry with Professor Smirnoff, the doomsday fraudster no one had seen since (or for quite some time before, for that matter). Angriest of all was American businessman Donald Trump. He tweeted angrily that Barack Obama ought to get his head out of the sand and start seriously investigating the allegations that an underground movement was behind it, one led by Hillary Clinton, Tom Hanks, and Pope Benedict XVI.

All while another of the defrauded, Bill Gates, took the fraud calmly.

"I wasn't expecting to be conned by a prestigious Swiss bank. But I promised two million dollars for climate research, and that's all there is to it," he said, tossing in the money even so.

"Idiot," said Trump.

* * *

Now the president was sitting in the Oval Office, absorbing what his friend from Sweden had told him. Johan had mentioned a doomsday prophet and a banker as examples of the type of people he hung out with. How many such combinations could there be? In times like these?

Businessman Trump's advice was that the president shouldn't stick his head in the sand. Barack Obama decided that for everyone's sake, this was exactly what he *should* do.

Way deep down in the sand.

PART FOUR

*The First Days Before the
Third End of the World*

CHAPTER 86

Almost a Year Later

With just ten days left before the American presidential election, things were looking bright for the sitting president. His challenger, Mitt Romney, kept traveling from state to undecided state. His message, initially so strictly conservative, was softening as the campaign wore on. Now his rhetoric sounded practically liberal.

Barack Obama had failed to rein in the out-of-control unemployment rate, and the budget shortfall was so great that numbers could hardly capture it. Still, he was the clear leader in opinion polls. If the nation were made up of white, middle-aged men alone he wouldn't have had a chance. But America was more than that.

Still, the election result wasn't a sure bet. So it was noteworthy that the president chose to head to Vermont in the final days of the campaign. If there was any state he was certain to win, it was that one. There was speculation that he was repaying some sort of debt to Bernie Sanders, the crazy liberal senator who had been voted into Congress by Vermont mandate again and again.

Things got even stranger when Barack and Michelle Obama and entourage headed to the countryside in order to . . . well, what? Visit a newly opened cheese factory!

CNN preferred to remain no more than a step or two behind

Obama. This trip was no different. The president wasn't available for comment, but the journalists could speak with the staff of the cheese factory. A certain CEO Church (in a hat and sunglasses) said he was proud of what he'd accomplished, and although he missed the Maltese mountains, rivers, and lakes he loved his cheese factory and his new homeland, the United States of America. Even more so in election times like this! What could be more beautiful than true democracy?

Happily, the CNN reporter was not well informed about Malta, which has neither rivers nor lakes and whose highest mountain reaches a height of 820 feet above sea level.

Out of the staff cafeteria came a man in sunglasses, a cap, and chef's garb. This was strange enough as it was, and even stranger when the cook wasn't blocked from striding up to Obama. Strangest of all: he gave the president a hug. And received one in return.

Some time later, the CNN reporter managed to approach the cap-wearing chef.

"Excuse me, but may I ask you a few questions?"

"Of course."

"Who are you, and what is your relationship with President Obama?"

Johan had learned his new name and grown used to it.

"I'm Winston Church without the 'ill,' and I'm in charge of the staff cafeteria. We were supposed to prepare something special for the president and First Lady this evening, but there was a bit of a mix-up so it'll have to be the leftovers from today's lunch."

The CNN reporter hadn't received an answer to the second part of her question, but she let that go in favor of what she'd just heard.

"Mr. Church, did I just hear you say that the president and First Lady will be dining in the staff cafeteria of this cheese factory this evening? And that you intend to serve leftovers?"

"Not exactly leftovers," said Johan. "I'm in charge of the kitchen, and we were supposed to have visitors, and . . . well, even though I have some help . . . that's a hundred and eighty bellies to fill. I didn't have time to think up something new for this evening. I'm sure what we had for lunch will do."

"You didn't have time to come up with anything but the leftovers from an industry staff lunch to feed the president of the United States and his wife?"

"As I said."

"May I ask what you'll be serving?"

"Sure."

"What will you be serving?"

"Let's see. There's a lightly grilled salmon with horseradish sauce, finely grated Västerbotten cheese, and salt-roasted pistachios. And Västerbotten cheese quiche, haricots verts sautéed with garlic, and pickled onion. And chanterelle risotto with Västerbotten cheese and crispy bacon. Then there will be butter-fried elk steak with Västerbotten cheese, lingonberries, and fried kale. And for dessert, baked apples in caramel sauce with a hint of rosemary, topped with Västerbotten cheese. I like Västerbotten cheese, with or without the dots over the *a*. You're welcome to join us too—there's plenty of room in the cafeteria."

The reporter had to end the interview when a member of the Secret Service slid up, made sure the camera was turned off, and informed her that CNN was *not* welcome at that evening's dinner even though it may have seemed that way. This was a private event.

Cheese CEO Church—that is, ex-president Aleko—ex-changed Johan for Petra as interviewee. He introduced her as director of sales. Petra was wearing neither hat nor cap, but she did have sunglasses on. She told CNN that the Västerbotten cheese factory was thinking in the long term, that they had a detailed development plan covering the next four years, and after that it wouldn't matter so much.

She refrained from getting bogged down in the impending end of the world. Malte stood nearby, trying to decide if he should approach Obama in order to discuss wage disparities. He, too, refrained.

The final edit of the CNN piece gave the impression that the new cheese factory was run by a collection of Maltese-immigrant bohemians more than anything else. The channel's political analysts were in agreement that Obama had just cleverly demonstrated that he, unlike Mitt Romney, was president of the *entire* United States. The story ended with a slow-motion shot of the American president and the staff cafeteria chef exchanging a hug. What better way to illustrate the sitting president's folksiness?

EPILOGUE

The Russian mafia branch called the Vory had developed over at least a few centuries. Thanks to the wild swings from Russian to Soviet to Russian society again, the criminal network refined its methods, letting them be partially integrated with the state. In the many decades since, of course, the occasional figure who'd grown too big or too stupid for their boots had attempted to thwart the organization. Only in exceptional cases would any such figure survive the rest of the week.

Then again, never before had someone fooled the Vory out of such a grotesque amount of money as five hundred million dollars. Only to be missing but presumed alive a whole year later.

The thief of thieves in Moscow, Ekaterina Bykova, immediately tasked twenty of her best spies and hit men with finding Aleksandr Kovalchuk, aka ex-president Aleko. These professionals were anything but cheap.

The boss thief's right-hand-man-slash-bookkeeper-for-the-organization raised the question on the one-year anniversary of the incident.

"Boss, we've been searching for a year now. Twenty men, scattered all over the world. They've turned over every stone there is. As the person responsible for our finances, I must ask: Should we call off the manhunt?"

The bookkeeper's boss stared at him with a vacant and inscrutable gaze.

"Twenty men?" she said.

"Yes."

"A whole year?"

"Yes."

"Make it forty. And get back to me in twelve months."

EPILOGUE

Fredrik Löwenhult was ruled out as a suspect in the half-billion-dollar fraud case at an early stage of the investigation. But he had traveled to Africa during working hours instead of saying farewell to his dying father (who, for what it's worth, was still alive and in good health). Ambassador Guldén was not one to tolerate lying and cheating. What's more, there was something fundamentally the matter with those brothers. Both of them were disqualified as representatives for Sweden.

Johan's big brother had no choice but to start over. Without any funds, as well, since someone had donated the entire contents of his account at Bank von Toll in Zurich to the Foundation for the Protection of European Hard Cheeses. Stupidly enough he had so fervently denied any knowledge of the brand-new Ferrari INTERPOL claimed was his that eventually they believed him and seized possession of it. And, of course, he had told the police to destroy the RV.

His months in the diplomatic corps, at least, had brought him a certain amount of familiarity with the use of photocopiers. Fredrik changed his last name to Olsson and applied for and got a job at the main offices of the postal service, where he was responsible for maintaining the office machinery. He lived in a studio apartment in Märsta, an hour north of Strandvägen in Stockholm. His only comfort in life was that he'd made sure things went to hell for his idiot little brother too, that damned

Johan. He had been missing for over a year now, along with President Aleko, whom Fredrik had single-handedly got deposed. Best-case scenario, they had been killed by some Condorian mob. Or perhaps they were hiding out in the Brazilian rainforest. In fact, he would prefer they were being tortured rather than resting in peace.

His job at the post office was laborious and not at all stimulating. After his long journey on the commuter train, followed by six stops on the bus, Fredrik would typically buy a pizza and sit down to half watch some TV before it was time to go to bed to be ready for the next day.

He zapped between channels and settled for CNN. The American presidential election was drawing near. To think that he'd been in the same room as the president of the United States not even a year ago. Now Obama was in the final spurt of his campaign; he dearly wanted four more years in office. The footage showed that Michelle was with him this time. It seemed they were visiting some factory in Vermont. The president looked like he was bursting with joy as he greeted one of the workers there. He even gave him a hug!

This worker was wearing a cap and sunglasses, and he was decked out in chef's clothing. He looked kind of ridiculous.

And yet, wasn't there something familiar about him?

Yes, really familiar.

Wasn't that . . . ? Surely it couldn't be . . .

The idiot?

AUTHOR'S THANKS

. . . my early beta readers Rixon and brothers Lars & Martin. Their encouragement gives me strength even when everything is hardly half finished. I'd also like to thank my wonderful Uncle Hans, who's never said anything nicer than "I've read worse crap." This time he was even more crabby than usual, which might mean this is my best book to date. Sending thanks also to Laxå and Stefan Järlström, whom I once made laugh so hard he broke his bed. He's done some close reading in his new bed and provided helpful and important comments.

Even more thanks to . . .
    . . . my publisher Jonas Axelsson and agent Erik Larsson for liking what I write and taking such good care of it.

Most thanks of all to . . .
    . . . Ludwig Tjörnemo, Sweden's 2020 Chef of the Year and ruling champion along with the Swedish national chef team. Without his help, my fictional chef Johan would have seemed like . . . well, like an idiot.

Stockholm, June 1, 2022

A NOTE FROM THE TRANSLATOR

Dear reader,

Thanks for picking up this latest Jonas Jonasson adventure. Here's a bit of a translation Easter egg for you!

Literary translation is often about doing creative work within given parameters; it's important that I hew closely to an author's word choice, style, tone, and so on as best I can, within the confines and rules of English. I really enjoy the challenges and puzzles of working within a framework this way; along with research rabbit holes, it's my favorite part of my job. But once in a while, the grammatical differences between English and Swedish offer a chance for some extra creativity on my part, and I got just such a chance while working on *The Prophet and the Idiot*.

In Swedish, it's often possible to use a definite article plus an adjective to refer to someone, no noun needed. But in English, we need to include a noun to do the same thing. So when Jonas Jonasson refers to the character Agnes as "den lilahåriga," as he frequently does, I need to call her "the violet-haired [something]." (As an aside for those of you who also know Swedish: yes, I had a whole debate with myself about whether I should use "violet" or "purple." I simply decided "violet" sounded lovelier.) At first I just used "the violet-haired woman" but given how often the phrase is used it became repetitive and unnatural in English. So I sent a query to Jonas Jonasson: Would it be okay if I change up the noun I use here, for some variety, and make each one refer to whatever Agnes and the gang are up to at the moment? And not only did he agree, he put his trust in me to really go for it.

Not only would the use of varied nouns make the English text flow better, this was also an opportunity, in my mind, to introduce an extra bit of classic Jonasson zaniness to the story as well. As you read, keep an eye (or ear, for audiobook listeners!) out for the various labels Agnes receives throughout the tale. As you can imagine, if you've read other books by Jonas Jonasson, the journey is sure to be a wild one.

Happy reading!
Rachel Willson-Broyles

Here ends Jonas Jonasson's
The Prophet and the Idiot.

The first edition of the book was printed
and bound at Lakeside Book Company
in Harrisonburg, Virginia, March 2024.

A NOTE ON THE TYPE

The text of this novel was set in Sabon, an old-style serif typeface commissioned in the early 1960s by the German Master Printer's Association. Charged with designing a font that could be identically printed across Linotype, Monotype, and Stempel machines, famed typographer Jan Tschichold devised the ever adaptable Sabon. Based on the elegant and highly legible designs of Claude Garamond, Sabon has long been touted for its quintessential smooth texture and clean look, remaining a popular typeface in book design since its initial conception.

HARPERVIA

An imprint dedicated to publishing international voices,
offering readers a chance to encounter other lives and other
points of view via the language of the imagination.